LOVERS REUNITED

At the knight's embrace, the world seemed to dissolve away, leaving Aurora soaring in the universe of Frayne's arms. She had never known love could be like this—two souls awakening to life after an eternity of emptiness. Or was it more the terrifying agony of death? For suddenly she was lost to an aching, endless yearning, which only Frayne aroused and only Frayne could appease.

"Aurora," he breathed at last and buried his face in her luxurious raven hair. "Gods, I believed you were dead."

Fiercely Aurora clung to the knight, afraid that if she let go, he would suddenly vanish. Surely it was all a part of the madness, the sickness that had infested the forest.

When at last he gazed long into her face, his eyes were dark with passion. And Aurora knew that with one glance, the flames of desire would ignite in his silvery falcon eyes, and she would cleave to his lean strength and thrill to the caress of his lips and hands. She was Aurora the Enchantress, and he was Frayne. She would always be at his command. . . .

Crystal Paradise

Johanna Hailey

ZEBRA BOOKS
KENSINGTON PUBLISHING CORP.

ZEBRA BOOKS

are published by

Kensington Publishing Corp.
475 Park Avenue South
New York, NY 10016

Copyright © 1986 by Johanna Hailey

First printing: September 1986

Printed in the United States of America

This book is dedicated to Elbert and Pauline, my second mom and dad.

And to Steven.

Special thanks to William Hurt, who drew such a great map.

Prologue

Aurora walked slowly across the meadow toward the softly lapping water of Grendylmere. With the coming of dawn she had kissed the yawning Minta and a sad-eyed Valesia good-bye. Taking up her pack, which held the dead warrior-woman's crimson cloak bearing the undeciphered symbols of power, she had left Truewood, Father-Oak, to perform one final task before leaving all that she had known as a child, growing up nameless with her foster folk—her dryad mother-pair and the elves of Hawthorn Glade. All that seemingly endless summer she had shunned the place of painful memories, but now the time of departure was upon her, and she had come at last to Willowvale, where it had all begun, so long ago it now seemed, that she might remember it as it had been and thus give free rein to the ache locked tightly up within her before she bade farewell to her beloved forest home.

Aurora's golden eyes were suspiciously bright as they strayed from one familiar landmark to another.

There was the thicket of waterwillow, which hid the small hollow where first she had stolen on a starlit night in search of the man-beast. How her blood had throbbed in her veins with the keen thrill of danger as she sighted Boltar, the warrior-steed, grazing on a picketline at the edge of the flickering circle of firelight. Her lips curved in an oddly wistful smile as she recalled wondering if this great creature could be the dread interloper before whom all the denizens of forest home fled in fear—the man-beast, who was of the same human seed as herself.

She passed by the blackened humps of round stones arranged in a circle within which the man-beast's campfire once had burned and entered the rift in the thicket where the trail led through the waterwillow to the lake. The dull ache, which was become a part of her, deepened to a poignant thrust of bittersweet memory as she made her way through the flowering waterwillow and came to the shores of Grendylmere. Here she had first beheld the man coming from the waters, the sun at his back forming a dazzling halo around him, so that at first she had been blinded to his face and form. Then a cloud had drifted before the sun and she had seen his glorious naked body, the vision of a god with golden skin and long, rippling muscles.

"Frayne!" she whispered and sank slowly to her knees on the cool, damp sand at the edge of the lake.

He had cast his spell over her with that first vision of unexpected splendor, luring her from her hiding place so that she had stood, a trembling, mindless thing, before him. He had spoken to her in the language of mankind, and she had not understood, but it had broken his hold on her and she had fled, only to be captured like some hapless wild thing in his arms.

"But I was not so easily made captive, my arrogant knight," she murmured, remembering how she had erupted into a punishing fury that had carried them both plunging into the cold waters of Grendylmere.

The chill water had calmed her panic so that she had ceased to struggle. Then, wonder of wonders, the man had touched his mouth to hers, breathing fire into her veins.

She had lain with him—Frayne, the Knight of Tor, who served the mysterious Sorceress. And it had been he who named her Aurora in token of the dawning of her new life.

It seemed a distant dream now, she thought, as she stared, unseeing, at the shimmering ripples on the lake's surface and remembered the candescent flame of power that had awakened within her at his touch—the power of an Enchantress with the hand of the god upon her—her birthright and her destiny, which had led to the forging of the Sword of Power from the crystal in the forbidden depths of the Crystal Room.

She drew forth the crystal from the pouch that hung at her belt and felt it throb like a living thing in the palm of her hand. It was Andruvien, the sliver of the Vendrenin left behind in the Treasure Trove of the gnomes after the final battle between Harmon, the Warrior-God, and Dred, the Prince of Somn, beneath the Black Mountain in the Land of Throm. When wielded by the Enchantress, it became a dazzling sword of awesome power.

Her fingers closed convulsively over the thing of

power, and she shivered though the morning sun was warm upon her.

Even though they had been separated after the discovery of the unicorn's horn and the battle against the giants, Frayne's spirit had been with her, his strength melding to hers, shielding her from the crystal's icy flames. His power had called forth hers, and as the song of the Enchantress came at last to her lips, the god whose vassal she was had willed her to take the crystal unto herself.

"He felt it all," she said aloud, her voice husky with the hurt of remembering. "My doubts. My fears. And finally the crystal's flame forged into a living likeness of my mother's sword. The sword that I envisioned in my dream of Somn and that I plunged into the Asgeroth. Frayne knew. And he rode away. Back to the Sorceress of Tor. Even as he said he would before ever we left the shores of Grendylmere to seek the horn of the unicorn."

Aurora's eyes squeezed shut as she threw back her head, her face convulsed with pain.

"Why?" she cried, the haunting echo of her voice drifting back to her from off the serene waters of Grendylmere to mock her. She opened her eyes to reveal a curiously blank expression within their golden depths. "Why?" she repeated in a whisper and bent her head against her clenched fists.

She had known almost from the very first that their paths would one day part, though she had never ceased to hope that in the end her love would prove stronger than the Sorceress's strange power over Frayne. But she could not change what the gods had written. Nor was it bitterness that the gods had seen

12

fit to bring Frayne into her life, forever altering the even flow of her existence in Endrith's Forest, and then to take him from her that tormented her. Nay. It was this endless aching emptiness inside her, which nothing could dull or alleviate, that tortured her soul and made her want to cry out in anger against the gods or fate or whatever had condemned her to this seeming eternity of incompleteness. She, who had always been one with her world despite the fact that she was nameless and ignorant of her parentage, she, who had been Anduan, elf-foundling, and tree-child to the dryads, she was Anduan no more, but Aurora, enchantress of the Glade, some strange creature, half-woman, half-child, part elf, part dryad, and human, with all the longings of a human who was yet ignorant of the world of men.

Yet Vandrel, the kindly scholar who had tutored Crane, the shape-changer, had promised to teach her the language of the books, and the young Enchantress had sworn to return to the cottage among the elderberry trees when first the poinsettia bloomed beside Grendylmere. Throughout the long days of summer she had clutched that thought to her as a buttress against the loneliness she had never known before Frayne had ridden out of her life. That and Vandrel's prophecy that one day she would again lie in the arms of her love.

She had crowded the endless days with all the pursuits that had formerly filled her life. And for a time the persistent pain had receded before the joy of being once again in Hawthorn Glade with Garwin and Gleb, her elfin foster fathers. Her heart had been full, as well, as she reclined among the branches of

Truewood, the Father-Oak, and basked in the loving attention of Minta and Valesia, her dryad mother-fair, who had sent Anduan, tree-child, on the quest to find her true-name and had welcomed back Aurora, the Enchantress with the Sword of Power. She had hunted again with the wolf pack and run with the wild elk, led by Tasha, the white Elk-Lord. She had let her thoughts soar with Agrypha, Sky-Dancer, as the falcon drifted high above the earth on invisible pillars of air, and she had kept lonely vigil with Stebba, Night-Owl, who first had spotted Frayne riding through Endrith's Forest in search of a unicorn.

But never had she ventured near Willowvale where nestled Grendylmere, for she had not been ready yet to remember. Not until today, when she had awakened to the first brisk morning touched with the feel of autumn and the honking of the sandhill cranes on their first migratory flights. She had felt her blood stir as she watched the long V of the cranes' patterned flight, here and there and back again, aimlessly shifting and turning, as if practicing maneuvers in unison. They would keep at it ceaselessly for days on end before finally the first heavy frosts would drive them south at last. South, to the Fertile Plains, where no doubt they would pass over Tor, the city of the scheming Sorceress and her mysterious minion Frayne. Then she had known with sudden, overwhelming relief that beside Grendylmere the poinsettia had at last begun to bloom.

Thus she had come again to Frayne's abandoned camp to relive the halcyon days during which she had felt the first bewildering awakening to love and mystery and power and had not known what was happen-

14

ing to her.

The valley seemed empty now, its hushed serenity a mockery that drove her to her feet. There was nothing left for her here except memories, but out there, beyond the forest, waited the answers to the secrets of the Crimson Cloak of Power and her true-name. There also abided the wicked Sorceress, who was Aurora's enemy, and Frayne, who was still a mystery to her. But one day she would know, she vowed, and then she would win him to her side one way or another.

For now, it was time to say farewell to the past, and she did so without regret. She would go now to Vandrel's secluded valley and there learn the language of the books, and when she had unlocked their secrets, she would at long last be ready to begin again the quest for her true-name and her love.

Slowly she straightened her back, her small head held proudly. Impatiently she brushed the tears from her cheeks. Then, with a firm, light step, she left the shores of Grendylmere to return to the meadow filled with the red and white poinsettia. And there, shining in the sunlight like a vision of hope sent from the One, was Tasha, Elk-Lord, the white elk of good omen, he who had carried her on the quest for the horn of the unicorn. He had come to carry her once more. This time to the cottage below Krim's Keep, the Castle of Illusions, where once she had fought the mage-lord possessed by the Vendrenin's immortal flames and defied Dred, the Thromgilad Prince of Somn.

Unconsciously her hand sought the pouch in which the crystal rested. No doubt the Immortal Prince yet sought her and this small piece of the Vendrenin, which could release the foul creatures of the depths across the land. She must learn the secrets of Vandrel's books quickly if she were to survive.

"Greetings, tree-child," said Tasha, Elk-Lord, on a thought sent outward.

"Greetings, my old friend," answered Aurora in the same manner, for she possessed the gift that enabled her to think the thoughts of animals. "The morning wastes quickly away. Let us be on our way."

She leaped lightly astride the tall elk then turned to look one last time upon the camp beside the shimmering waters of Grendylmere. Here Frayne had forever altered the course of her life, awakening her woman's heart and the mystic power of the Enchantress. She was Anduan, Elf-Foundling no more. So be it. She would dare the awesome powers of the scheming Sorceress of Tor or even Dred himself to find her truename and win the love of the man called Frayne. With a defiant toss of her head, she sent the elk bounding swiftly across the glen, westward away from Grendylmere and the innocence of childhood. She was Aurora, and she was not afraid.

Chapter One

Aurora rubbed her hand in a circle against the frosted windowpane and looked out on a world dressed in glistening white. Autumn had fled swiftly before the onslaught of winter in Vandrel's hidden valley, but Aurora had been too busy to care. The language of the books had come easily to her. Eagerly she had devoured the written knowledge of sages and scholars, learned the spells of binding, summoning, and divination, studied the symbols of power, the astrological charts of being, the histories of the Beginnings, the genealogy of the gods—both Thromgilad and Eilderood—and at last, *The Tome of Prophecy*. And one morning she had awakened to find the world enfolded in winter and herself oddly at variance with the new pattern of her life.

She had snapped peevishly at Crane over nothing at all, sending the boy into a pucker of wounded sensibilities. Grudgingly she had washed the dozens of crucibles and carafes used in the multitude of potions Vandrel instructed her to concoct, scrubbed the kitchen floor after spilling on it a particularly noxious concoction of bats' liver, toad dung, and dried spiders' legs that was supposed to ward off warts, and had ended up stalking from the cottage in a temper after being soundly reprimanded by her tutor for woolgathering during recitation of the "Morphology of Transmutations." She had spent the bilious fit in a hard race through the snow astride Tasha, Elk-Lord, and had returned at the end of the day weary, contrite, and decidedly feverish from having dared the elements without benefit of jacket or cloak. Vandrel, after one look at the girl's wet and bedraggled appearance, had dosed her with a bitter tisane and sent her off to bed. All in all, it had been an unenlightening day fraught with frustration.

She had slept badly, plagued the night through with strange, troubled dreams, and had awakened feeling miserable, with puffy eyes, a scratchy throat, and a stuffy nose. But the fever had abated, leaving her mind clear again. The girl sighed and lay back against her pillow, her hands clasped behind her head, and tried to pin down the cause of her sudden discontent. When had the black mood come upon her? she wondered fitfully.

A few days earlier she had been poring over the prophecies of the Third Age in which Dred, it was written, would rise again. For the most part she had found the cryptic passages, couched in the poetic language of riddles, hints, and seemingly vague references to future events, curious and intriguing, and she had read them with detached interest. Until she had come upon a short passage dealing with the Thromholan, a mortal offspring of Thromgilad and a mortal. A sudden, unnameable fear had knotted her stomach as she recalled the lines that had seemed to burn themselves into her brain.

> From dreadful Night and purest Light
> Is born a noble Prince of might.
> Fair of face, of godly grace,
> The scion of a fallen race,
> With him lies the destiny
> To lead the Throm to victory—
> The mortal son of Somn—
> The mighty Thromholan.

What did the lines mean? she pondered in a perplexity born of optimism. It had never occurred to her that when Dred rose up again to challenge the forces of the One, he might be victorious. And yet here, in the *Tome of Prophecy* in which all things which were to be had already been written down, the Thromgilad were promised victory. But how could this be? What of the Chosen One who was to be a savior to the children of the One? Was the foretold mortal son of Throm to be the mightier of the two? She shifted fitfully on her cot. Who *was* the Thromholan, this half-god, half-mortal? She had heard of Eilderood joining with mortals to produce mortal offspring with gifts of power. Harmon, the Warrior-God, who had banished Dred to the Land of Somn in the Second Thromgilad Uprising, had produced such a child. But she had never heard of a mortal son of Throm. And later, when she asked Vandrel about him, the old scholar had been maddeningly vague about the prophecy.

19

"It is as you have read it," she had said. "And as it has been foretold, so shall it be. That is the way of prophecy. To tell the truth which none can understand. In the end we can only do what it is given us to do within the context of the choices presented to us. It is of little worth getting into a pother over what is beyond our control."

"Then why have you given me the prophecies to read? Would I not be better served studying that which can be of some use to me?" Aurora had retorted, impatient with what seemed an evasion.

"How else can you hope to understand the schemes and intrigues of those who play for power? Are they not motivated by the prophecies? Do they not believe they can manipulate the present to create the future for themselves?" the old scholar queried, then paused to study the young woman over the rim of her spectacles.

"What troubles you, child?" she asked, her blue eyes shrewd in the strangely ageless face.

"Surely it is obvious!" Aurora cried in exasperation. "Are you not troubled by this prophecy of doom?"

"Have a care, Enchantress," Vandrel cautioned. "Are you not making the same error as your enemies? Those who think they know what the prophecies portend?"

"I do wish you would not always answer a question with a question," Aurora said bitterly and began to pace restlessly about the narrow confines of the kitchen.

Vandrel watched the sensuous grace of the lovely child-woman and marveled that the elves had kept her safely hidden for so long. She seemed to shimmer with the power that love had awakened and that sorrow had intensified until the sage old scholar thought surely the truth must shout itself to the world. Here was such a one as could alter the fabric of existence, if only she could be made ready in time. Already the forces of destiny were gathering themselves to begin the game anew, and even here, within the timeless flux of Vandrel's magic, this gifted mage-child sensed their urgency. She is like the young, caged falcon who has never flown but beats against the bars of her cage with yearning, thought Vandrel with a faint, knowing smile. But you must have patience, my fledgling Enchantress, for you are not yet ready.

The girl halted before the old woman, who calmly met the golden flash of Aurora's eyes and waited for her to speak.

"I am come to believe that the entirety of knowledge is built upon nothing but questions," the Enchantress said irritably, "the answers to which are merely more questions. What killed Lil but the final question with no answer?"

"Ah, *The Book of Lil.* I wondered when we should come to that. And yet, who is to say that Lil did not resolve the unsolvable riddle?"

"But the Gandorf could not be resolved," Aurora retorted in petulant bewilderment. "By definition the Gandorf is the final unsolvable riddle, the answer to which remains always out of reach. It is the unanswerable question."

"And yet I suggest to you that Lil resolved the riddle of the Gandorf in the only way which could bring her peace," Vandrel insisted quietly.

21

"I do not understand. Lil died."

"Exactly."

Aurora stared with dawning comprehension into the old scholar's twinkling eyes.

"Ah, you begin to see," Vandrell said with a small nod of satisfaction. "Lil resolved the riddle by denying the question, which is to admit defeat. And in the end, she herself became the Gandorf. For is not death the final riddle?"

The Enchantress could not suppress a grin at Vandrel's masterful logic, and yet she was not comforted by the lesson of Lil and the Gandorf. Life was a process of growth, and growth was a process of learning. If one knew all the answers, or if there were no questions, then life would surely cease. Thus in the final analysis the prophecies were not answers, but questions yet to be resolved, ad infinitum, or until the world should come to an end. Yet it was foretold that the Thromgilad would be led to victory. Would not that be the end of the world?

"Oh, gods," Aurora groaned. "My heart is filled with dread. Why do you lead me into the Gandorf's maze, where even Frayne's strength has been denied to me? The god has withdrawn from me, and I am left to grope for the truth in darkness."

The Enchantress tossed restlessly for a time, her troubled thoughts giving her no peace, until at last in vexation she flung off the heavy quilt and left her cot. The wooden floor of the loft she shared with Vandrel was icy cold against her bare feet, the air chilled. She wasted little time donning her woolen shirt and breeches and pulling on her boots. Hastily she drew a comb through her raven hair before hurrying down

22

the narrow winding stairs to the ground floor.

Vandrel was in the midst of frying acorn griddle cakes on the cookstove, and Crane sat on a bench at the table in sullen dejection, one thin shoulder hunched in Aurora's direction. The elderly scholar nodded briefly at her cheerful greeting, but the boy retained a studied indifference to her presence. Aurora paused in sudden uncertainty. It was obvious she had not been forgiven her petulance of the previous day, and who could blame either one of them?

She had behaved abominably to Crane, calling him a wart-faced toad who must always be underfoot. Well, how was she to know he would take the suggestion to heart and immediately assume the croaking demeanor of a particularly loathsome red-spotted toad? She was sure he had done it out of spite, but Vandrel had muttered something about self-fulfilling prophecies and insisted the toad be captured lest indeed someone inadvertently step on him. He had eluded their every attempt to corner him, displaying an agility and a cunning that soon had Vandrel collapsed upon the kitchen bench, her legs aspraddle before her, her ample bosom heaving from exertion. She mopped her sweat-dampened brow with the hem of her apron and swore she would douse the little miscreant with her anti-wart potion if he did not return to himself immediately.

This had proved to be an unlucky threat, for no sooner had the words left her mouth than Aurora, diving full-length across the floor in a last-ditch effort to lay her hands on the miserable toad, had sent toppling the table upon which that very noxious potion had sat. It was equally unfortunate that Aurora had been in the process of preparing the horrid stuff from a recipe in *The Preventive Potion Cook Book* when the catastrophic chain of circumstances had been precipitated. Consequently, she had not as yet added the key ingredient of pickled lizard's tongue, with the result that instead of preventing warts, the kitchen floor began to sprout great hairy specimens of the the very thing the potion had been meant to prevent.

Vandrel's uncharacteristic shriek of pure invective had frozen her errant pupil in an attitude of a condemned criminal awaiting the executioner's axe. Slowly the object of so much strenuous activity began to waver and elongate until a boy with red hair and freckles squatted sheepishly amidst the warty mounds proliferating across the wooden floor.

Aurora's punishment had been to remove the pla-guy warts from the afflicted fundament and then to scrub and polish the wood to a mirrorlike shine. Crane had been assigned the task of collecting the needed and now depleted supply of toad dung from the cellar in which were kept rats, bats, toads, snakes, grubs, cockroaches, centipedes, spiders, and other unspeak-able creatures necessary for Vandrel's magic potions.

Actually Aurora had much preferred her penance to Crane's, as she had never felt over-fond of the lesser order of creatures with whom, by choice, she had little more than a speaking acquaintance. Indeed, she had discovered early on in life that she was acutely sensi-tive to spider bites and exhibited an allergic reaction to rat fur. Moreover, she had never forgotten her rather terrifying encounter with the Valkar, a sort of man-bat, who had sought to grant her the dubious honor of providing him with her blood in exchange for the exquisite pleasure of his bite. She had not been convinced, either then or since, that such an arrangement, which he had admitted, would lead eventually to her death, though she might manage to hang on for a week or more if she remained calm in order to prevent her heart from pumping too diligently, would be all that much to her advantage. She had been forced to dispatch him, moreover, before she had proven or disproven the veracity of his assertion that the bite of the Valkar would bear her to delirious heights of rapture, but she had nevertheless been left with a decided abhorrence of bats.

Well, all of that was neither here nor there. It was her fault the previously cozy cottage suddenly exuded an atmosphere of hardly contained disgruntlement, and it was up to her to set everything to rights again. She coughed slightly to clear her throat, then, squaring her shoulders and assuming a somewhat crooked conciliatory smile, stepped bravely into the breach.

"Vandrel. Crane," she said firmly. "I do most humbly beg your pardon for my behavior yesterday. I do not know why I am like to fly into the boughs for no good reason. Garwin is fond of saying, 'I be like a bear what has an itch it kinna scratch.' Nor can I promise the mood will not hit me again. It does sometimes, you know. And then I must do something which often lands me in a terrible coil. Like the time of my fifth summer in Endrith's Forest when I determined to discover the lair of Xantu, the Bushy-tailed Fox, and became stuck half in and half out of the hollow log through which she fled. And all because Garwin had kept me at spinning spider-silk nets to catch moon-spawned gilden fish for ever so many hours, until I was near to burst with bottled-up mischief." She paused to appraise how her ingenuously uttered explanation and apology were being received and was relieved to see the glimmering of a twinkle in Vandrel's blue eyes. But, alas! Crane appeared unmoved by her candor. The Shape-Changer was overly sensitive to any animadversion on the profusion of freckles which covered his face and no doubt had seen her unlucky allusion to warts as a comment on his hated spots. Poor Crane. He was so easily hurt by her undisciplined tongue.

She crossed the rest of the way to the boy, who stared sullenly at the floor as if expecting one of the hideous warts of the day before to suddenly creep from the seams between the boards and claim his person as a more efficacious place of residence.

"Crane, I'm sorry for what I said," she murmured and lightly touched his arm. She felt the muscles tighten spasmodically but did not withdraw her hand. "You know I didn't mean it. Why you haven't a single wart anywhere on your face. And you could hardly be underfoot when you must be well over six feet tall, now could you."

"Ye gods, Aurora! I may be a bumbling shape-changer, but I'm not stupid," he retorted disgustedly, then, glancing up into her face, grinned reluctantly as he spied the imp of laughter in her enchanting eyes.

"You really were the most loathsome-looking toad," she said, her infectious gurgle of laughter bubbling forth so that instantly the room seemed bathed in golden sunshine. "And so obnoxious, too. How dared you leap behind the woodbox so that I must become

26

covered with dust and cobwebs from trying to get you out?"

"Well, don't think I enjoyed being drenched in boiled toads' dung and bat liver," he countered, much incensed at her misplaced sense of humor. "Van made me rub the finished brew all over myself to counteract the warts I got from that stuff."

"Ugh! A horrid fate," Aurora agreed, stifling her giggle in order to assume a sufficiently sympathetic expression. But then Crane's shoulders began to shake and a suspicious gleam appeared in his eyes, until at last he let go an explosive chortle and thwacked the tabletop with the flat of his hand.

"You should have seen yourself diving neck or nothing at me. Ye gods! I thought you meant to squash me."

"Aye. And 'twould have served you right, too," she retorted, her voice quivering with mirth.

"A-and Van, p-puffing and heaving like an old b-bellows!" Crane choked and struggled to regain his breath.

Aurora shrieked with the memory of the old scholar's dismay at the sight of the floor sprouting warts in unseemly profusion and collapsed, giggling, onto the bench beside the convulsed shape-changer.

"Well, I never!" exclaimed the heartlessly maligned scholar. "An old bellows, indeed. I should think I might command a little more respect in my own house." But the smile in her eyes robbed the reproof of any sting. For a moment she watched the two youngsters howling with glee, then, nodding her grey head in satisfaction, she turned back to her griddle cakes.

Thus the days were made full with hours of usually

fascinating study and often tedious tasks such as memorizing endless lists of names of gods, sages, or events, ingredients for potions and their applications, riddles and their solutions, prophecies, spells, protection against spells, properties of the elements, cycles of the moon, and on and on, till she thought she could not force one more name, date, or recipe into her head. And still Vandrel proclaimed her a novice in all things pertaining to the art and science of enchantment.

At any rate, she was kept too busy to fret over the Thromholan and the predicted victory of Throm. Nor was she allowed to pine for Frayne. At least, not during the day.

It was in the night as she lay at the edge of sleep that memories of her lost love came to haunt her. Then her sleep would be troubled and she would awaken in the morning hollow-eyed and listless. At last she took to studying late into the night long after the others had gone to bed, so that finally she might fall into an exhausted sleep undisturbed by dreams of Frayne. Yet even this practice took its toll on her, as Crane pointed out one day.

"Just look at yourself," he said, the thin boyish face earnest beneath the unkempt thatch of fiery hair. "You're all skin and bones, with the look of the wraith about you."

"How very flattering," retorted the Enchantress tartly. She had plodded the night through with an ancient tome written in a spidery hand by a wordy, unenlightened historian with the rare gift of reducing otherwise fascinating events to the consistency of dehydrated pap. She was in no mood for Crane's

28

vituperations, no matter how well-intentioned they might be.

"Well, it wasn't meant to be," he stated flatly. "And don't lift your eyebrow at me like I was some brat bent on pestering the high and mighty likes of you. You were up all night again. That's two nights in a row. And I can't remember the last time you went out for a little fresh air and exercise."

"But I do," she promptly answered. "It was the last time you drove me into a pother with your incessant nagging. You turned yourself into a toad that time. I wonder what you're in the mood for today. A rock or a doornail would not go amiss. Either one would allow for some peace and quiet around here."

"Well, I like that!" he said, the freckles standing out on his face so that Aurora regretted a little that she had lashed out at him in her uncertain state of mind. She did indeed feel on the brink of exhaustion, and she would have liked nothing better than to go off traipsing through the woods, but there was so much left to learn and winter was half over. And here was Crane spouting at her like an overprotective parent. It really was the last straw.

"Children. Children!" interjected Vandrel, placing herself, hands on hips, between the two bristling youngsters. "I've had enough of your never-ending bickering for one day. Crane, you back off. There's no sense ragging the girl. It's too bad some of her diligence doesn't rub off on you. Oh, you're ready enough to lose yourself in a book about heroic knights or roving gypsies. But when it comes to anything that might strain that hard head of yours, you simply vanish like a will-o'-the-wisp. How you ever hope to make anything of yourself is beyond me."

"Ah, Van," Crane grimaced, shrinking beneath her tongue-lashing. "That's not fair. I've studied with Aurora lots of times. You're beginning to sound like Grandfather. You never used to get on to me like that."

"Well, maybe I should have. If you think you're going to ride out with Aurora someday, you'd best be about becoming prepared for it. The girl's made some bad enemies, and she's going to need all the help she can get. What she doesn't need is a half-baked shape-changer who's likely to turn into a butterfly or a philodendron in a crisis. Believe me, you shan't be going if you don't mend your ways."

Aurora, who was feeling a little sorry for the be-leaguered Crane, nearly jumped as the kindly scholar, turned fire-breathing-dragon, wheeled to pierce her with a pointed glance. Inwardly Aurora groaned.

"And as for you, Mistress Know-it-all," observed the metamorphosed virago, "the boy has the right of it. I thought you'd more sense than to drive yourself to the brink of a decline. Of what good will all your work be if you ruin your health? There'll be no more burning the candle at both ends. And from now on you'll get yourself outside every day for an hour or two. It'll clear the cobwebs from your brain and put some color back in your face. No. I've said all I'm going to say. The matter's closed. Now take yourself upstairs and get some sleep. I don't want to see your face down here again till the shadows are gone from beneath your eyes. Now get. Both of you. I've better things to do than to stand here arguing with you."

Thus it was that the following morning Aurora

found herself tramping through the snow beside a sullen Crane. Vandrel had sent them off immediately after breakfast, saying that today would be a holiday, as she must have time to take care of some matters of her own. She had been very mysterious about the whole thing, shooing them out of the house after having admonished them not to return until dusk.

"What do you think she is about?" Aurora asked her taciturn companion

The boy shrugged indifferently. "There's no telling. When I was a kid, she was always sending me off on one pretext or another with never a why or a wherefore. Used to say she could only take so much tomfoolery. The gods know, I never stopped to question her. I was too glad to have a day off on my own." He colored a little at this admission, and hunching his shoulders, dug his hands deeper into the pockets of his cloak.

Aurora glanced up out of the corners of her eyes at the boy's glum face. 'Twas obvious he was still smarting from Vandrel's scolding. The heretofore endlessly patient tutor had been uncommonly rough on the shape-changer, she thought. In fact, Vandrel had been unlike herself all that day. She had seemed irritable and preoccupied, and during Aurora's daily recitations, she had been singularly inattentive, missing the Enchantress's less than perfect rendering of the Galesian Strictures of Summoning. With a sinking heart, Aurora wondered if the scholar was growing disenchanted with the task she had taken upon herself. Living with two obstreperous charges who must be constantly bickering and plaguing her with questions might indeed prove onerous to one used to solitude.

Guiltily Aurora acknowledged to herself that she had come to take Vandrel's good nature for granted and recalled with shame how only a few days before she had rebelled at practicing for the millionth time the proper manner of greeting and conducting a polite conversation with a stranger, an acquaintance, a shopkeeper, a wayfarer, a gentleman, a lady, or a lord. Then what must she do but parade about for hours in confining skirts that she might learn what it was to be a lady in the society of gentlemen and other ladies. She had been made to perform the most absurd posturings, assuming a vapid smile while shyly ducking her head and fluttering her eyelashes or slinking across the room rather as if her hips were out of joint. She had succeeded only in making a fool of herself and in sending Crane off into paroxysms of gleeful laughter, which had seen her flying from the room in a tearful rage.

Vandrel had seemed to take it all in stride, merely admonishing the girl that if she did not wish to seem a country bumpkin when she eventually took her place in the world of men, she must apply herself to learning the niceties of polite society. Well, she had learned, fumed the Enchantress. She would show her mentor that she could function quite well in the world of men without trying to be something she was not, and suddenly her eyes began to gleam in such a way that should have sent Crane fleeing back to the cottage if he had not been so sunk in gloom that he failed to see it. He had learned to know that look all too well in the past weeks.

"Crane? Have you ever been to a town or village?" she asked nonchalantly.

"Sure. Lots of times," he said a little too expansively. "Why?"

"Because I never have. I've never even seen one from a distance."

"Well, you'll be going to Tor one of these days, and that's a lot bigger than any village or town. And if Vandrel has her way, you'll be going by yourself," he added dourly.

"Oh, don't pay any attention to that. She'll change her mind. All you have to do is try a little harder."

"I do try. It's just that I can't stick to any one thing for very long. My mind just seems to drift off, and before I know it I'm a mouse or a squirrel or even a shrub somewhere out in the woods. I don't even know how I got there. No, Van's right. I'll never be of any use to you. You'll be better off without me."

"Fiddlesticks! What a faradiddle of nonsense. You're just feeling sorry for yourself, and you know I have no patience with you when you're like that. Where's your gumption? Look, I have a plan to show Vandrel she's wrong about us. What do you say? Are you game?"

Crane halted abruptly to look down into the bewitching countenance turned expectantly up to him. His heart gave a little lurch at the sight of her elfin loveliness, even as an alarm bell seemed to ring somewhere in his brain. Prompted by an instinct of self-preservation, he backed off a step from the Enchantress, one hand raised as if to ward her off.

"Uhn-uhn. No way," he said and shook his head. "You're not talking me into another of your henwitted schemes."

"Oh, you're just nervous because I suggested you

33

try to materialize the two-headed Grumpus from the picture in *The Book of Lil* and Vandrel was a little upset at having to listen to it grumble and whine for three solid days before you could find the right spell to send it back again. She's probably forgotten all about it by now. And, after all, you did manage to get rid of it. I should think you'd be grateful for the chance to do something no one else has done since Lil."

"No one else has been stupid enough," he muttered, remembering his horror at suddenly discovering the loathsome creature, the two heads sending a constant stream of obscenities at one another, in Vandrel's kitchen. Somehow he very much doubted that Vandrel would ever forget the unfortunate episode.

"Oh, very well then. Never mind that we could have a glorious adventure and at the same time convince Vandrel we are ready to face the world of men," Aurora said and began to walk away from Crane.

The boy stared after her, his expression of utter certainty beginning to waver.

"Wait!" he called on an explosive breath and started after her.

Aurora halted, her lips curving in the suggestion of a smile.

"Tell me your plan," the boy said resignedly. "Though I'm a fool to listen."

It was Aurora who decided Crane should take them only to the outskirts of the tiny settlement of Twickham. It had occurred to her that it might prove rather unsettling to the inhabitants of the village if suddenly the two of them should materialize in their midst.

Nay. They must seem two inconspicuous wayfarers just passing through. Well, one inconspicuous wayfarer at least, for the Enchantress had likewise devised the plan that Crane should become a prancing warrior-horse patterned rather along the lines of Boltar, Frayne's noble steed, that she might ride in proudly on her first foray into the world of men. It was consequently with a slight sense of disappointment that she at last entered the single street of the village astride a disreputable-looking, rawboned, sadly lopeared mule.

Aurora, determined to make the best of a bad bargain, perched atop her ignoble steed with her head held high and her back straight and wondered how she should go about instigating a conversation with one of the handful of persons who had materialized on the street to view her entrance. Indeed, they seemed an uncommonly timid lot, staring at her as if they had never seen her like before. No doubt they were merely taken aback by Crane's ludicrous appearance. She could not know that they beheld a vision steeped in mystery and surrounded by an aura of power, for she wore the flowing white cloak given her by Endrith himself, and the deep hood pulled low over her forehead to ward off the cold hid her face in shadows.

Then Crane balked, his head down, to eye with distrust the snarling aspect of a half-starved mongrel crouched in his path, hackles raised. Aurora hardly spared the poor creature a glance as she looked the villagers over trying to decide which one she should accost first. The hood hampered her view, and she slipped it to her shoulders to glance curiously about her, unaware that these few poor specimens of human-

35

ity drew back in fear and awe at sight of her bewitching beauty and strange golden eyes.

It did not appear to be a prosperous community. The dozen or so houses that lined either side of the rutted road were little better than thatched hovels with greasy deer-hides covering the doors and windows. She saw what was apparently a smithy at the end of the row of dwellings, a great-thewed giant of a man in a leathern apron peering out at her from the smoke-filled interior. The faces turned toward her were unprepossessing, the males bearded and soiled, the females coarse and furtive. The sprinkling of women amongst them stared at her with dull, hungry eyes, envious, had she but known it, of her sylphlike beauty and her luxurious cloak.

The Enchantress searched her memory for the proper manner of greeting them. Should she display a friendly front, incline her head graciously, or simply nod coolly and inquire after their health? Or mayhap she should ask their opinion of the weather. Yet that seemed singularly absurd, as the state of the weather was obvious. It was snowing and the bitter cold nipped at her nose and cheeks. She had decided on a simple "good morning" when suddenly one of the men, a loutish creature with black, rotting teeth bared in a lascivious grin, lurched toward her to place a grimy hand wrapped in rags on the mule's neck. His breath was sour, his small, close-set eyes bloodshot and slightly glazed. 'Twas obvious he had been partaking freely of the local brew, and Aurora began to wish she had thought to bring her elfin dagger with her.

"Welcome t' Twickham, me pretty little snow-maid," he said with a leer. "Was ye just passin' through or was ye thinkin' t' git down and chew the fat fer a spell?"

Aurora's eyes widened a bit at the man's peculiar inquiry. Obviously the villagers had some odd customs Vandrel had neglected to tell her about.

"Thank you, but I never eat flesh," she answered in her politest voice. " 'Twould be distasteful to devour a creature with whom you have had friendly discourse, you see."

"Eh?" grunted her would-be host and scratched his head beneath the moth-eaten and probably flea-infested fur cap. "Is ye tryin' t' bamboozle Tom Aiken, wench? Well, you might as well lay an egg as try t' make a goat out of me."

"I beg your pardon," Aurora rejoined in some alarm. She certainly had no intention of practicing her recently acquired spells on the hapless villager, and she hastened to relieve the poor man's obvious misapprehension.

"Oh, I doubt very seriously that I could lay an egg. Nor shall I change you into a goat. 'Twould seem a poor way to make friends, methinks. Mayhap there is some other like service I could perform which would be more to your liking?" she inquired with a brilliant smile.

The beady eyes narrowed speculatively on the lovely face, then slowly traveled the length of her curvaceous form so that Aurora began to feel distinctly uneasy.

"Does ye wish to make friends, does ye? In that case a quick roll in th' hay'd be more to me likin'," he sniggered and laid his hand suggestively on her thigh.

Aurora stared in some perplexity at the brutish face.

She had had no notion that making contact with the world of men would necessitate such bizarre behavior. Rolling about in hay seemed an odd rite of friendship at best, and at the very least a most uncomfortable practice. She had no very strong desire to soil her lovely cloak in such a manner, and yet she did not wish to offend. She swept the gathered villagers with a quick glance. They were eyeing her expectantly, she thought, their faces creased in unlovely grins that might change into open hostility at any moment.

She had just made up her mind to get this odd "hay" business over with as quickly as possible, then make her excuses and leave with as much dignity as she could muster, when suddenly utter chaos seemed to break loose.

"Take yer bloomin' 'ands off the hussy!" a woman shrieked, as she bounded from one of the hovels, a broom in her hands and her skirts flapping wildly about her legs.

Simultaneously, the mongrel, which had continued to make a snarling nuisance of itself, leaped with a ferocious howl and sank its fangs into Crane's unprotected nose. In a frenzy of pain and rage, the shape-changer lost the shape and became suddenly a rangy wolf with gleaming yellow eyes. The mangy cur fled in whimpering terror, but amidst the sudden alterations, Aurora was sent sprawling atop the luckless lout, who collapsed beneath her unexpected weight. The termagant who had precipitated the unhappy chain of events descended upon them both, screaming obscenities and beating them about their heads with the broom. The villagers, faced with what appeared to be a werewolf in their midst, began flinging rocks at the snarling fiend. In the resulting confusion of people pouring from their houses with every sort of crude weapon, Aurora escaped the clutches of the outraged housewife. Calling to Crane, she fled the village and bounded for the safety of the nearby woods. Suddenly the wolf vanished from the vortex of the melee, and a ruby-crowned kinglet shot into the air. It was not until the cursed village was far behind them that the two fugitives stopped to catch their breath and tend to their battle wounds, and it was very much the worse for wear but wiser pair of mages who dragged into Vandrel's cozy kitchen that evening.

Vandrel made no comment on Aurora's newfound interest in the previously detested lessons of deportment. Nor did she do more than briefly remark that Crane seemed to have turned over a new leaf. For weeks after returning to the cottage with a fiendishly sore and swollen nose, the cause of which he would not divulge no matter how hard the scholar pressed him, the boy applied himself with admirable dedication to improving the mastery of his peculiar gifts. For a time, the cottage was unwontedly tranquil, its inhabitants apparently content with one another and their various pursuits. But for many years after, the villagers of Twickham told a peculiar tale of a beautiful witch and a werewolf who had sought unsuccessfully to take them by surprise.

Gradually things returned to normal, with Aurora and Crane bickering as of old. They continued their daily outings at Vandrel's insistence, but never again did they venture from the elderberry glen.

Aurora regained her brightness of eye, her light, quick step, her glitter of humor that filled the cottage with golden laughter. And finally Crane, who had never ceased to worship the beautiful Enchantress within his secretmost heart of hearts, forgave her for embroiling him in another of her never-ending coils. She was Aurora, the Enchantress, who charmed everyone around her; and within her, unbeknownst to the world outside, the power steadily grew.

It seemed there was no end to Aurora's insatiable need to know. Never had she dreamt the world was so wide or so full of wonders as the books described. For ages the elves had sought the sea in the West over which they once had roamed in sailing ships driven before Thymfolthrall, the Wind-Wraith, which comes upon command. And yet men, who had no magic to aid them, had sailed the oceans to the ends of the earth. In awed fascination, Aurora read accounts of the Maurstom, the dark maw that swallows unsuspecting ships into the black void of the Vorbyss, where they are forever lost, the sailors finally driven mad with visions conjured up by the Tantelleth of lovely, mist-enshrouded lands that vanish when any ship approaches. 'Twas on these magical isles that the sea-nymphs lived, singing their marvellous songs that granted the hearer fantastical visions of things beyond imagination, and weaving their spell-webs of changing. Long ago, Crane had told her, they could travel through time and space and make people or things materialize wherever or in whatever time they wished. Such a one had Shellandra been, Crane's mother, who had given her son the powers of the shape-changers.

Onc night, the enchantress dreamed a wonderful dream in which she sailed in a magical ship that skimmed across a still, crystal sea to the mystic islands of the sea-nymphs. She awoke feeling it had been a true-dream sent from the One. Someday she would cross such a sea and behold endless marvels. Meantime, she lost herself in her studies, and soon the dream became only a distant memory.

Then one day the winter storms fled before a southwesterly wind, and sunshine filled the glen with the promise of approaching spring. The white mountain lily burrowed through the snow to unfurl to the meager warmth of the slowly lengthening days. The bourne that wound through the dell began to rise. The icicles hanging from the eaves began to plop a steady rhythm of water droplets into the melting snow, and Aurora's thoughts turned again to Frayne.

In a few weeks' time the snows would be gone, and she would be free to travel south to Tor. Her spirit lifted as though relieved of a burden of which she had not been previously aware, and she plunged all the more determinedly into her studies. Soon the waiting would be over and the great adventure just begun. She would go to Tor to seek her true-name and the elusive knight who had stolen her heart and then ridden off without even a farewell, and Crane would go with her.

Where was Frayne? she wondered. Had he forgotten the magic they had woven together, the candescent flame of power that had swept through them as they tasted the sweet elixir of the gods, the mystic heights of passion that had melded their spirits and intertwined their destinies? Indeed, had he forgotten her?

Chapter Two

The Glendaron River, after leaving Grendylmere, flowed south through Endrith's Forest to the Fertile Plains, there to be joined by Englebrook before curling lazily to the southwest. Cradled in the graceful arm of the river, a city brooded in the shadow of a craggy knoll that overlooked the rich prairie to the south and east and the arid wasteland to the west. So far as anyone knew, neither the crag nor the city named for it had ever been called anything but simply "Tor." Here the slave caravans stopped over to replenish their depleted supplies of water and foodstuffs before entering the desert on their way to the western seaports; then they stopped again on the return trek bearing exotic goods from across the sea to the cities of Fengard and Britshelm, which sprawled amidst the vast farmlands in the east. Thus gold flowed freely into the coffers of the wealthy merchants of Tor. But it was not for this that the city was renowned to the farthest reaches of the Known Lands. Nor even for the stalwart order of knights who made yearly pilgrimage to the Menhir at the center of the city, before which they renewed their vows of unswerving allegiance to the One. Nor for the Menhir, which according to legend, marks the grave of Tristholm, True-Heart, who died in the service of the One. Nay. Tor was infamous throughout the land for its innumerable pleasure palaces and dens of vice in which for a price one's wildest fantasies could be realized—for these and for its powerful Sorceress, whose stronghold perched atop the knoll.

The most lavish of the pleasure palaces were constructed of black marble transported at tremendous expense in both gold and human lives from the Marble Cliffs that marked the southern boundary of the Known Lands. Beneath their domed roofs adorned with hedonistic carvings of the phantasmagoric creatures of Somn, only the wealthy or powerful could afford to feast on the plumed peacocks stuffed with oysters, the dried octupus marinated in goats' milk and seasoned with the leaves of the satyricon, or lizards baked with mandragora and wine sauce, to wager fortunes on the outcome of the half-naked Chandorn aborigine women pitted in armed combat against the wild boar, or to experience the exquisite entertainments of the fabled Eropsychans, magical creatures capable of stealing into the dark recesses of the human mind to assume the shapes of one's fantasies.

But these were reserved for the elite. Across the city along the river were more sordid establishments, which catered to the seamier elements of the back streets or to citizens whose interests were less exalted than those of their fellows who sported beneath the pleasure domes. Perhaps the meanest of these, and one which enjoyed a vast popularity among the vulgar set, was The Red Dragon. Here, for the price of fourpence, one could fill one's belly with coarse black bread, tangy cheese, mutton stew, and pease pudding, and for a few coppers more have a pint of ale to wash it all down. Moreover, for equally modest sums other basic hungers or more quixotic interests could be readily met behind the closed doors of the numerous back rooms. For this reason the smoky interior never lacked a boisterous crowd of cutthroats, brigands, and thieves who preyed upon the rich caravans by day and spent their ill-gotten gains in riotous pleasure by night. Slink-hipped paphians freely displayed their wares for all to see. Nor was it any different on this night, which was the Eve of Thrang in the third cycle of Shin, the Moon Goddess, except, perhaps, that the grog flowed more freely and the rivalry among the gamesters seemed even more frenzied than usual as they crowded around two men who had been tossing the bones steadily throughout the evening and placed their money on one or the other.

One of the two was well known among the nefarious society that ruled the maze of dark, narrow streets of Tor. He was a ruffian and a bruiser who once, it was rumored, had been a slave in Fengard and had been trained to kill in the arena until he murdered his own master and escaped to the city of Tor, where he allegedly served the powerful Sorceress. He was tall and broad, with arms and legs that bulged with muscle. His face was a battleground of old scars, one of which ran the length of the left side of his face from cheek to jawbone, there to disappear in a bristling red beard. He wore his blade, a curved scimitar, at his right hip, for the stump of his right arm was severed at the wrist and ended in a deadly-looking hook. The left hand, too, was twisted, the hideous skin wrinkled with scar-tissue as if at some time he had plunged the disfigured member into a raging fire. He had been losing steadily, and a slow fever seemed to burn in the brutish eyes as he studied the shadowed face of his opponent.

"I wager my horse on the next throw," he growled and rattled the dice in his partially crippled hand, but a soft voice edged in steel froze him ere he tossed the bones.

"I have no need for your horse, Baldrac. You must offer better than that if you wish to throw against me."

An ugly scowl distorted the scarred face.

"You've won all my gold, curse you. I've nothing left but the horse and the slave-girl."

Baldrac's vicious eyes glittered suddenly with the cunning of the jackal as he ran his heated gaze over the high, immature breasts and smooth, slender hips and thighs of a shrinking girl-child who was like a lovely rosebud just beginning to blossom forth. Thick, black hair the color of ravens' wings formed a dirty, tangled mane down her back. Her skin, where it was not marred by welts and bruises, was white and would have glowed with translucent beauty if she were clean, silently mused the soft-spoken man who had refused the wager of Baldrac's horse. She was small, her wrists and face delicately boned, her cheekbones prominent in the thin face. But her eyes were wrong, he thought, for they were a startling blue, and they

46

lacked the defiant sparkle of an indomitable will. It pained him to look at her, nonetheless.

Disgusted with himself, he lifted the heavy flagon and drank deeply, then wiped the back of his hand slowly across his mouth as he waited for Baldrac to make another offer or back off. He cared little one way or the other.

He was more than a little drunk, had been for longer than he cared to remember, but his silvery-grey eyes were cold and steady as he watched Baldrac lick dry lips and rattle the bones in taut nervousness.

"Well? What is it to be, Baldrac?" he asked, suddenly weary of the stink of stale beer and the sweating bodies pressing too close for comfort "Do I take my winnings and go, or have you something else to wager?"

He leaned forward and made as if to gather up the untidy heap of gold sovereigns from off the table where Baldrac and his cohorts had tossed them.

"The girl!" Baldrac snarled suddenly, his horrid fist clenching around the dice. "I stake the girl against what you've already won off me. Winner take all."

The silver-grey eyes lifted to study the villain's scarred visage in cold amusement. Doubtless the brat was yet a virgin, he judged from the bitter gall with which Baldrac had pledged her. He had little use for another slave, especially a female of tender years. Yet it might prove entertaining to take her from the brute. He leaned back on the crude wooden bench and propped his powerful shoulders against the wall.

"You think she is worth so much?" he said indifferently and let his glance flicker briefly over the child, who was garishly dressed in a flimsy scarlet gown that was too big for her small frame. The blue eyes were huge and frightened in the perfect oval of her face. The trembling lips, painted red, parted slightly over small white teeth, as if in a silent plea.

"She's a daughter of Ahbin-ben-ami, Khan of the desert tribes. I stole her off a slaver who claimed he won her from the Khan himself. It seems the noble Khan has more daughters than camels and still looks for a son," Baldrac sniggered and leaned suddenly across the table to peer through a drunken haze at his fellow gamester. "She's not been touched, my fine lord. That I swear," he said in a low, harsh voice, his breath sour in the other's face.

The man seemed to consider the wager for a time, the handsome lips curved slightly in a cynical smile. There was a small fortune in the pile of gold before him. He doubted not that it would purchase a dozen like this pitiful creature, even if she were the daughter of the desert Khan.

Abruptly he shrugged.

"So be it," he said, but, as Baldrac shook the bones and made as if to throw the first cast, a slender hand shot out to grasp his wrist in a bone-crunching grip.

"Eh?" the rogue grunted painfully and tensed, the cruel hook swinging up as if to impale the fool who dared to touch Baldrac, the warrior who had slain a dozen men with his bare hands in the arenas of Fengard. Sudden silence swept the room. "What'd you do that for?" he growled.

"You lost the toss, remember?" he was reminded in the same soft, deadly voice, and suddenly he remembered whom he faced. Slowly he relaxed and let the dice drop to the table.

"Sure. Sure. The toss is yours," he agreed gruffly. A sigh went through the crowd as the rogue's wrist was released, and he sank heavily into his seat.

The slender hand gathered up the dice, then, with only a brief shake, flung them to the table. Baldrac grinned wolfishly as the dice settled with a five and a three uppermost.

"Eight by the perilous path," said the quiet voice. The crowd erupted into an excited babble. Baldrac's fleshy chin dropped slightly, the bloodshot eyes hard on the cold planes of the gamester's face. Slowly a smile spread across the brutish lips, and his glance flew greedily to the gold lying on the table. Only a fool would try for the double fours. The odds were ten to one against the winning toss.

The second toss produced a two and a four, and the third, a one and a three. Baldrac began to fidget nervously, the sweat breaking out in beads on his forehead. He could not restrain a reluctant feeling of awe as, time and again, the steady hand cast the bones. An eleven, a ten, two totals of six, snake-eyes. Where was the blasted seven? he wondered and cursed the man for a warlock. What was the blighter doing in the Red Dragon anyway? It was not the usual haunt for a Knight of Tor, especially this one.

Baldrac struggled to focus bleary eyes on the other man's impassive features as the knight gathered up the bones and tossed again. He well knew and detested that cursed face, but suddenly he had the uncomfortable feeling that he sat across from a stranger somehow even more dangerous than the man he knew. Squinting hard, he tried to gather his slow wits, dulled further by the Dragon's potent brew. Aye. The knight was somehow changed, though the lips were curled in the usual cynical smile, the small scar at the corner of the mouth adding a bitter cast, and the long, straight nose and high brow looked the same as always. Nor was it the eyes, those cursed grey eyes with black rings about the irises. Like the eyes of an eagle, he thought with an involuntary shiver, and just as soulless, rot him. No. It was something else. Maybe the two- or three-day growth of beard that bristled on the strong chin, or the tousled fair hair that had been allowed to grow longer than was usual. Aye. That was part of it. But it was more than that. There was a recklessness in the way he cast the bones, and a dangerous gleam in the blasted eyes. Shades of Somn! the knave thought bitterly. The fool don't even care if he wins or not.

A slow rage began to burn in his thick brain. It seemed to him suddenly that the knight had come for the sole purpose of baiting him. Then the bile rose to his throat as the strong shapely hand reached for the dice, shook them negligently, and gave them a careless toss. The ivory cubes seemed to topple endlessly, over and over, finally to teeter then settle on the tabletop. His mind was oddly blank as he saw the double fours leering back at him, nor did he move at first as the knight smiled a strangely mocking smile and began to scoop the gold sovereigns into a leathern pouch. In a daze of disbelief he watched the lean, powerful warrior rise leisurely and beckon curtly toward the girl. It was then, when the bitter truth hit him, that the madness to kill robbed him of all reason.

"Frayne!" he shouted stridently, and suddenly

people were scattering in a wild rush to get away from the two deadly warriors.

The tall knight halted, stood for a moment with head down, then swiveled to face the crouching Baldrac. The silvery eyes swept contemptuously over the rogue, and a small mirthless smile played about the stern lips.

"Well, Baldrac?" he said quietly, his gaze level and dangerous.

Baldrac swallowed, sobered slightly by the sudden realization of what he had done. He had set himself up to challenge Frayne, the Sorceress's own knight, and he had done it before a roomful of witnesses. Inwardly he cursed himself for a fool. He should have kept his head, waited to catch the knight alone in a dark street. Well, it was too late for that now. With a low growl he drew the scimitar from his belt.

"Leave the girl," he said boldly, "and I'll not kill you."

The knight's eyebrow arched arrogantly. "How very generous, considering I have won the chit. Perhaps you would like the gold as well."

"Curse the gold. And curse you!" Baldrac snarled and lunged at the knight.

Frayne's movement was too swift to follow. Where before he had lounged carelessly, his cape slung lightly over his arm much in the attitude of a courtier indulging in pleasant conversation, he suddenly became an indistinct blur. Stepping lithely out of the path of the deadly blade, he grasped Baldrac's arm at the wrist, and twirling him in a tight arc, wrapped him neatly in the rogue's own cloak and booted him smartly on the rump.

The hapless villain pumped his thick legs valiantly in an effort to remain on his feet, but this only added to his momentum. With a crescendoing wail, he crashed headlong into one of the numerous rough-hewn tables, which split and shattered with the impact. His body shuddered as a low groan passed his lips, then his muscles went lax, and he lay still.

Frayne spared the rogue hardly a glance as he turned and once more headed for the exit. Suddenly he stopped and looked back over his shoulder at the shrinking child in the scarlet dress.

He jerked his head sharply in the direction of the door. A silent message seemed to pass between them, and briefly the hard contours of his face softened, a fleeting shadow of pain flickering in the cold grey eyes at sight of her sudden, brilliant smile. Then the moment was gone, and he was striding swiftly out the door, the girl following at a halting run behind him.

As Frayne stepped into the dark street which ran the length of the waterfront, he paused to breathe deeply of the brisk night air in an effort to rid himself of the foul stench of the Red Dragon and to clear his head. The cheap wine with which he had plied himself since nightfall burned his innards, and he vaguely wondered when he had eaten last. Had it been breakfast or supper the night before? He could not remember, and he shook his head, wishing he had thought to purchase a bottle before making his exit from the tavern. Perhaps a quick tumble with one of the Dragon's innovative harlots would not have gone amiss either, he mused cynically, then recalled his latest acquisition. He turned to find her hovering in the shadows behind him and could almost taste her fear.

Blast! What was he to do with her? He little relished the thought of ensconcing her in the rooms he kept in the city when he was not needed to play the obedient servant to his powerful mistress. Despite the girl's nubile charms, he had not yet sunk so low as to rut after children. Besides, had not his ever-generous mistress already presented him with one raven-haired slave-girl with whom to satisfy his lust? Thoughts of the long-limbed, agile Glyndora caused his loins to stir. She had proven imaginative and adept at the art of satisfying a man's passions, and once he would have been more than content to have her to warm his bed at night. But that was before the Enchantress had woven her spell about him.

"Gods! What do you want of me?" he ground out suddenly between clenched teeth. "The Enchantress is dead! Can you not leave me alone to go my own way to perdition?"

Suddenly he lurched blindly down the street, his one thought to find some distraction from the memories that tormented him. And, standing alone and forgotten beneath the slowly swinging sign made in the likeness of a red dragon, the young slave-girl watched him go, a look of uncertainty on her face, which was absurdly childish beneath the painted mask of the cyprian. Her glance swept nervously up and down the waterfront to linger in mounting terror on the deep shadows before the seamy establishments that were still boisterous with revelers, though the night was well advanced towards dawn. Then, covering her raven hair with the flimsy shawl that had been draped over her shoulders, she fled after the tall knight's retreating figure.

Frayne struggled in the throes of the nightmare, his face breaking out in beads of sweat, his head turning restlessly from side to side on the soiled pillow.

"No," he muttered and licked dry lips. "No, she is not dead."

She *could* not be dead. Had he not felt the Enchantress call to him, had he not seemed to become as one with her even though he had stood among the ruins of the City of Shallandorwas and she had yet been somewhere within the dark bowels of the dead volcano? He had felt the searing torment of icy flames and had beheld within his mind—linked with that of the young Enchantress—the marvel of the thing of power transformed into the Blade of Light. She had held it in her hand, and he had felt the surge of power coursing through her and into her until it was become one with her. And then for a brief time he had known nothing but darkness. He had awakened to the raucous scolding of Kreekow, Flesh-Eater, the black crow who served as the Sorceress's familiar, and to a vast emptiness within his soul, which had ever been desolate with his dark secret, but which had briefly known the wonder of Aurora's sweet innocence. Aurora, the Enchantress, whom he himself had named.

No, she could not be dead, and yet the dream that had come to haunt him again and again, which was but an echo of the nightmare of reality he had lived, said that she was indeed passed from the world of the living.

In the dream he stood within the Sorceress's dark Chamber of Visions in which was kept the Seeing Eye, the looking glass that reflected the Realm of the One and revealed glimpses of past, present, and future, and he was waiting for the Sorceress to make known her presence. Then she had appeared in the midst of a cloud of smoke that bore the scent of Enchanter's nightshade, her cold eyes glittering in her bloodless face like black diamonds. Her raven hair, streaked at either temple with silver wings, floated about her head and shoulders like an inky veil. Beholding the perfect features, which bore such a strong resemblance to Aurora's, filled him with bitter loathing. She was but a mockery of the lovely child-woman who had beguiled him and granted him a vision of an enchanted paradise. This woman's terrible beauty froze his soul, and it was all he could do to assume the arrogant mask of indifference that was his sole protection against her.

She drew near, a cold smile etched upon her soulless lips, which once had seduced his will, and ran the curved points of her long fingernails like elegant claws lightly down his cheek.

"Ah, you are back, my faithful knight," she murmured, her throaty voice, like the black velvet furnishings of the room, meant to be seductive. "And you have brought the horn? But of course you have," she said, as though it little mattered. "You have never yet failed me. But then you cannot afford to, can you."

Her laughter rippled through the brooding stillness like her claws against his skin, and the hair at the nape of his neck began to rise with sudden wariness.

"You do not speak," she said archly. "Do you not wish to inquire at least about your mother's health? Or has some other taken her place in your heart?

Perhaps your mother's well-being no longer matters to you."

The knight's hand closed mercilessly about the Sorceress's slender wrist. Drawing her near, he bent to peer into the treacherous face.

"I have done as you commanded," he said evenly, his voice soft and deadly. "If you would have me to do your bidding, you will see that my mother remains in perfect health. Is that understood?"

"Oh, I have always understood you, my dearest Frayne," she answered in a voice like winter wind or death as he abruptly released her. "I know you as well as I know myself. Are you not the only son of Dred, and am I not his servant?"

"You have been his concubine. But you serve no one but yourself, Sorceress, and your own wicked schemes. Beware lest you overreach yourself and anger the dark Lord of Somn. Or me."

"You go too far with your insolence, Knight of Tor," she said coldly. "Beware lest you cease to amuse me."

"I am but your humble servant, madam," he rejoined with an ironic bow and straightened to stare stonily before him.

She gazed speculatively up into the knight's face before turning with a billowing swirl of her ebony robe through which could be seen the pale outline of her magnificent body, the full white breasts swelling above the deep V of her gown. When she looked again at his stern features, there was a craftiness in her eyes that should have set him on his guard, but her next words ripped at the hard core of his reserve.

"No doubt I owe this little rebellion to your sweet

little Enchantress," she said, and suddenly he knew why she had seemed so smug since entering the chamber. "She is dead, Knight of Tor. Dead because of you."

"It's a lie!" he shouted and bolted upright in his bed.

His heart was hammering inside his chest, and his mouth was bitter with gall. With a groan he collapsed once more against his sweat-soaked pillow and pressed the back of his hand across his eyes as if to block out the image of his torment, which seemed bent on haunting him even in wakefulness, for a slender, raven-haired girl stood over him, her face hidden in shadows.

"M'lord?" a sweet voice queried uncertainly, and suddenly the fierce pressure in his chest eased. It was not the voice of the Enchantress whom he had left to die at the hands of the giants. He opened his eyes to glare at the frightened face of a child dressed hideously in the raiment of a paphian. Ye gods! he thought in disgust. He was growing daily more worthy of Dred, who had raped a Valdoran virgin to father him.

"Who are you?" he asked hoarsely.

"I am Janine," she said tremulously. "Your slave." Then when he merely continued to stare at her blankly, she hastened to explain her presence in his bedchamber. "You won me from the other one. The evil one with the red beard."

A vague recollection returned of his latest debauchery.

"Baldrac!" he muttered darkly and ran his tongue over parched lips. Shades of Somn! He must have

57

outdone himself last night. A red haze blurred his vision, and it felt as if all the fiends of Somn were battling inside his head. He winced as the girl knelt to lay a cool, damp towel against his feverish brow.

"You have been ill, I think," she said in the pleasing accents of the desert clans. "You were crying out in your sleep, but I could not wake you."

He looked at her in sudden suspicion, which brought the color to her cheeks.

"I slept over there," she added shyly and pointed to a rumpled blanket on the floor near his bed. "It was your command, m'lord." Then, "Will you not drink of the water which I have brought you, m'lord? It will perhaps ease your fever."

"You will fetch me something more potent if you wish to ease what ails me," he said harshly, then groaned as he shoved himself abruptly off the bed to stand weaving and panting for breath. Ignoring the fact that he was naked as a newborn, he began to rummage through his scattered belongings in search of a bottle. He seemed to remember having brought a full one to his rooms the day before, or had it been the day before that? His head throbbed to the beat of his pulse, and the filthy chamber, which little resembled the living quarters of a Knight of Tor, began to tilt and turn in a nauseating manner.

He groaned and clutched his head between his hands. Then he seemed to be falling endlessly into a black pit.

He dreamt he was in the enchanted paradise that Aurora had created beside the waters of Grendylmere, but nothing was as it had been. It was as if all the magic in the world had died with the Enchantress, leaving behind a ghastly forest of skeletal trees whose bony fingers pointed at him accusingly. Oh, gods! He wandered once more in the great mines carved by the gnomes beneath the Black Mountain, and everywhere the floors were littered with the brittle bones of the giants' victims. Empty skulls leered at him half-buried in volcanic dust, and he knew that Aurora's lay among them.

"Curse the gods!" he cried and tried to leave his bed, but a sweet voice came from beyond his dark torment and ordered him to rest.

"You are ill, m'lord. You must not leave your bed," it said, and he fell back into the agony of his dreams.

Oh, gods! How could he have been so fooled by the vision sent from Somn that he could leave the sweet Aurora to die by the giants' hands? For so it had been—a false vision wrought by Dred, the Thromgilad Prince whose cursed spawn he was. He had believed that Aurora had found the crystal and mastered it. Yet again and again he saw the Enchantress die as he gazed helplessly into the Sorceress's magic mirror, the Seeing Eye stolen from Sheelar, the Serpent-Lord of Somn.

He awakened at last, gaunt and weakened from the fever, to lie listlessly staring at the bare white walls of his chamber bathed in the slanting sunlight of late afternoon. How long had he been out? he wondered and tried to remember how he had gotten to his room. The last thing he recalled very clearly was entering the Red Dragon. And something about a girl.

The scent of fresh linen sprinkled lightly with lavender water teased his senses, and suddenly he became aware that he lay between clean sheets and that the filthy pillow on which he had slept had been replaced with a new one covered with cool silk. He noted ironically that his body, too, had been cleansed, except for his matted hair and bristling beard.

"What the blazes!" he muttered and let his gaze drift aimlessly about the room. Someone had been there as he lay witless with fever. The soiled clothing that had lain scattered about the room was gone, and the table was empty of its litter. A crystal vase sat at its center filled with freshly gathered wildflowers, the first of spring. No doubt Glyndora had cleaned up the mess, he thought with no little surprise, for such domesticity and thoughtfulness seemed out of character. The wench was a marvel between the sheets, which had ever been as filthy as herself, but he had nearly been forced to beat her just to get her to fetch him food from the marketplace. That she had stayed after he had fallen ill was equally a marvel, for he had soon tired of her cyprian skills, which had left him vaguely dissatisfied, and he had not touched her for weeks as he wandered from one low pleasure den to another, lain with one raven-haired woman after another, searching for something he could never seem to find.

The sound of the latch being lifted brought his head sharply around. As the door swung open, he reached for the dagger he kept beneath the pillow and found it was gone. Then he stared in disbelief at the slight figure of a child dressed in a plain, shapeless gown, her black hair falling in two long braids over budding breasts. Shy blue eyes stared gravely at him as she slipped into the room and closed the door softly behind her. She set a large woven basket on the table beside the wildflowers and came slowly to the bedside, a small, nervous smile fluttering across her face.

"M'lord," she murmured, and dropping gracefully to her knees beside the bed, she touched her forehead with the fingers of one hand in respectful obeisance. "I am pleased to see you are returned into yourself. Forgive me for not being here when you awakened. I have brought you sustenance from the marketplace." She paused then, a flicker of fear darkening her brow. "Please, m'lord, to forgive me. I have taken the gold from your purse to buy these things for you. But I have also bought this dress for me. I will bring you the leather strap if you wish it. Only tell me where it is."

It was on his tongue to ask her what in blazes she was talking about. Then a grim smile curved his lips. She expected him to beat her. And perhaps he would for such impertinence. But not now. He had not the strength, and the tantalizing aroma of freshly baked bread filled the room.

"Never mind the strap," he growled and wondered what twist of fate had seen fit to saddle him with an infant.

The knight, blessed with a strong constitution and denied access to the cheap spirits that had been nearly his sole sustenance for too long, regained his strength rapidly. Janine, the desert slave-girl, had become a gentle tyrant who mothered and scolded him, but always with the air of respectful obedience with which she had first entered his life. Yet beneath the fragile childish exterior he had discovered an iron will, which, while it was camouflaged in a cloak of humility and was ever calm, nevertheless poignantly reminded him of another raven-haired girl who had been able to mold him to her wishes. The child was balm to his ravaged spirit. Though she did not fill the void left by that other, tempestuous child-woman, she did soothe the torment of guilt that punished him for having left the Enchantress to die. And at last he began once more to turn his thoughts from the past to the future and to the dangerous game he played with the forces of destiny.

It had been almost a se'ennight since he had left his sickbed when he took the slave-girl to the marketplace and bought her some pretty gowns suitable to her tender youth, ribbons and combs for her hair, and other dainties that he thought necessary for a young female beginning to blossom into womanhood. He experienced a melancholy contentment with her child-ish pleasure and was oppressed by the sobering thought that inevitably, with the arrival of spring, the Sorceress would summon him, and the game would begin again.

What was he to do with Janine? he wondered somberly as he watched the child going through her new treasures, her sweet face aglow with quiet delight. She was like some lovely rare flower quietly blossoming in a barren field. The artful Glyndora had indeed run off, and there was no one to look after the child when he was gone from Tor. Nor would he have trusted such innocence to the care of the devious slave-woman, who would have sold her for gold before he had ridden through the city gates. Yet he could not leave her alone and unprotected in the city of the Sorceress, where young maidens were daily abducted and sold into slavery. Inwardly he smiled wryly at himself, realizing he had long ceased to think of

Janine as a slave. Gods! he had grown soft of late, he thought, for if he felt anything for the girl, it was a fatherly affection.

"Janine," he said suddenly and beckoned the girl to his side. She moved with a quiet grace unusual in one of her age. Dropping to her knees before his chair, she made the gesture of obedience and gazed expectantly up into his face. He nearly groaned at sight of the warmth in her eyes for him. The cynical thought came to him that she was no different from others of her sex whose hearts were easily purchased with a few trinkets. Then he recalled how she had cared for him as he lay out of his mind with fever, and he felt an unwonted prick of conscience. Blast the fates for having laid her in his lap like some helpless puppy that would have been better off drowned at birth!

The girl's blue eyes darkened as she saw the black mood descend over her lord's handsome brow.

"M'lord?" she said uncertainly. "I have displeased you?"

"Your presence here displeases me," he answered brutally and ignored her small gasp and the wilting of the innocent joy that had been hers only moments before. "You must be returned where you belong. To the Khan, if indeed you are his daughter."

"No, m'lord. I beg you," she cried. "It was my father who gave me to the slaver. He will not welcome me back. Please. If I have done something wrong, beat me as I deserve. But do not choose so cruel a punishment as to send me away."

"I have no choice, Janine," he said harshly and looked away from the wide, pleading eyes. "Soon I will leave Tor, and where I go, I cannot take you with me."

"Then leave me here. I will keep your home in readiness for your return."

"Enough, Janine!" he nearly shouted, and shoving her none too gently from him, rose abruptly from the chair. She lay sprawled on her side, her face pressed against her hand on the floor to stifle her sobs.

For a moment the knight seemed to waver, his grey eyes haunted as he gazed upon the crumpled form of the girl. Then his face hardened into a cold mask. He had allowed another child to ride with him, and it had cost her her life. He would not make the same mistake twice.

Suddenly he could not stand the muffled sounds of her weeping. With a low curse he swung away from her and crossed to the door. Then he stopped, his hand on the latch, and looked back at Janine.

"I can't leave you here," he said wearily. "You would not survive ten minutes once it became known I was gone. I will find someplace for you to stay. A family outside the city who would look upon you as a daughter. I'll give them money. You'll be safe."

"Yes, m'lord," the girl sniffed and wiped the back of her hand across her nose. "I am your slave, and you will do with me as you see fit. I am wrong to complain after your very great generosity to me. I beg your forgiveness."

The knight's lips curled in a wry hint of a grin.

"Just how old are you, Janine?" he queried drily.

"I have seen fifteen passings of the seasons, m'lord," she said, her gaze innocent upon his face.

"I might have known," he muttered enigmatically and strode out of the room.

Frayne was not amiss in guessing that the Sorceress was soon to summon him, for no sooner had he stepped into the street that ran in front of the house in which he kept rooms than he was met with a fluttering of wings and the raucous cry of a large crow, which settled on a low wall beside him.

" 'Tis time. The time is come," it squawked in the language of men. "The Sorceress commands and we obey."

"And what does she command this time, carrion-crow?" the knight queried, his face set and cold as he looked with loathing on Kreekow, Flesh-Eater, the Sorceress's familiar.

"Our mistress would have you leave the pretty harlot. Yes. Yes. Leave the child-slave who plays with Frayne. To the castle come. When the moon rises and not before," chanted the crow. "These are her words. The words are hers. Come. To the castle come," drifted back to the stone-faced knight as Kreekow fluttered away.

Frayne watched the carrion-crow disappear across the rooftops of the city, then turned grimly and re-entered the house. He should have known *she* would know about the slave-girl Janine. She saw everything with the cursed Eye. Yet he had hoped she would overlook the child, for Janine was insignificant in the scheme of things. He cursed himself for a blind fool. He had waited too long to get the child to safety. Now he had little choice in the matter and as little time to implement the desperate plan that had taken root even as the crow had fled. "When the moon rises and not before," Kreekow had said. It was perhaps an hour before sunset and another till the rising of the moon.

And it would take less than half that long to reach the castle. There might just be time.

The Sorceress was waiting in the Chamber of Visions when the Knight sauntered into the room just as Shin, the Moon Goddess, leapt into the sky. She stood over the oval of the looking glass, peering into the surface rippling with visions that she alone, outside of Somn, knew how to summon. Her face was cold and hard, her black eyes glittering with cold fury—and hatred, thought the knight with keen interest. Who or what did she see to make her fingers clench like the talons of a hawk closing on its helpless prey? He felt the hair at the nape of his neck lift and thought that somewhere someone had just walked across his grave.

Then the Sorceress looked up and saw him watching her.

"You will fetch me the perfect crystal rose, which cannot be plucked," she said, without preamble. "You will find it in the valley of the hills that know no height, in the kingdom where none can tread, beneath the castle that is or was or yet shall be."

"And where am I to find this land of paradoxes?" he queried drily.

The Sorceress's smile was not reassuring.

"That is all I have been able to discover. It is your quest to find the kingdom of the crystals and fetch the rose. And remember. It must be without flaw."

"You've given me little enough to go on. Why don't you look in your Seeing Eye? Or do you enjoy some perverse pleasure in being deliberately obscure?"

"Don't be a fool!" she snapped and whirled away

from the magic mirror. "I have looked. But one cannot always be sure of what one sees. The visions of past, present, and future are distorted with the shadows of Somn, and it may be that one sees only Dred's desires. If he ever found out that—" She did not finish what she had been about to say, but seemed to recall herself, and the cold, impenetrable mask of the Sorceress hid her thoughts again.

"But enough talk. If you are to be on your way by morning, we have no time for dalliance. As much as I enjoy your company, I fear I must insist that you leave me now," she said dismissingly. Then as Frayne turned to go, "Do not fail me, Knight or Tor. Remember. Your loyalty belongs only to me, if you would have your beloved mother remain in the Flux of Timelessness."

Frayne's silvery glance hardened to a piercing glitter.

"I will not fail," he said softly, "as long as you do not fail to keep your word, Sorceress. Only as long as my mother lives do I serve you. Be certain that *you* remember that."

Perhaps the Sorceress would have been gratified to know that her loyal knight did not intend to wait for morning's light to begin his search for the kingdom of the crystals. Certainly she would have been interested to learn that he had acquired a squire to accompany him on his journeys, but she knew neither of these things, for she gazed entranced into the rippling surface of the stolen Eye of Somn like one possessed. Nor was it a vision of Frayne that drained the color from her face and caused her eyes to glitter with bitter hatred. Nay, but the image of a beautiful girl with golden eyes and raven hair who trod the misty paths of Endrith's Forest toward the south, and with her a tall young man with the look of a mage about him.

Chapter Three

Endrith's Forest, shaking off the icy grip of winter, donned the bright colors of burgeoning spring. The budding leaves of maples, elms, ash, and oak sparkled beneath a blue sky lightly touched by drifting puffs of white clouds, and along the forest floor the first profusion of wildflowers opened to the golden shafts of sunlight seeping through the tree limbs— blue cowslip and forget-me-nots, the white mayflower and fairy wand, fragrant yellow lady's slipper, red toadshade, and purple trillium. The rich black earth was wet and spongy, the legacy of the vanishing snowcover, and countless streams and rivulets filtered down the hillsides to feed the already swollen Glendaron River as it rolled southward toward the Fertile Plain.

Thirty miles within the southern fringe of the forest a tall woodsman left the Glendaron and headed westward toward the Plain of Shintari, there to follow the borders of the forest north toward the Land of the Mages. There was the look of the hunter about his lean face, and with him he bore the long bow that one of great strength and skill can wield with deadly effectiveness. Yet he did not tarry to pursue the fresh spoor of Sheema, the Panther, nor did he pause to send one of the slender arrows at Meerkahn, the White-tailed Doe, when he surprised her feeding with her twin sons in a meadow. Never once did he slacken his pace or stop, except to sleep when dusk gave way to night and the way was hidden in darkness. Then he would rise with the dawn and continue steadily on, eating strips of dried meat as he walked and drinking sparingly from a leather bladder slung across one broad shoulder.

Four days he pursued his relentless trek, until at last he came to the wooded foothills a day's march west of Krim's Mountain. At noon on the fifth day he stood atop a tall knoll overlooking a small, secluded valley from which a trail of smoke curled lazily into the sky. Still, he paused only long enough to fix his bearings before heading purposefully down the steep incline into the dale in which a cozy cottage was snugly nestled.

Aurora, sitting beneath an elderberry tree in Vandrel's hidden glen, stared vacantly into space, *Kern's Book of Dreams* lying opened and forgotten in her lap. At sight of the still figure of the girl, Crane, who had come in search of the Enchantress, paused uncertainly beside the gushing bourne, one corner of his mouth suddenly twisting wryly downward. Obviously she was lost again in one of her daydreams, he thought and could not, despite the knowledge that he was intruding, stop himself from drinking in her sweet loveliness.

A small, wistful smile played about her lips, and he doubted not that she was thinking of the time she had lain with the Knight of Tor beneath that very tree after imbibing rather too freely of Vandrel's potent elderberry wine. He had been guilty of spying on her that time, too, for he had come upon her asleep beneath the tree and could not resist worshiping at his secret shrine. A familiar ache awakened in the region of his heart, and silently he cursed the gods for dooming him to a love that could never be returned. Yet he sorrowed for the Enchantress, too, for had not Frayne won her heart and then abandoned her to an emptiness greater than Crane's? At least the young shape-changer could still feast his eyes on her entrancing beauty, but Aurora could only dream of her lost love. Not for the first time he wished he had the power to wipe the memory of the Knight of Tor from her mind. Then might he have had a chance with her.

Why must the gods be so unjust? He had loved her ere she had ever laid eyes on the mysterious knight, indeed, had been lost to her when Krim, his grandfather, had first conjured amidst the flickering flames of the mage-fire the image of the young Enchantress reclining among the thick boughs of an old oak tree and told him that he had chosen the girl to be Crane's wife. Nor had he been able patiently to await the day when Krim should summon her to him in reality, but had ventured forth to see her for himself. Only he had become lost in the forest and for days had wandered aimlessly in search of the old oak tree. That was when he had come unwittingly upon Cranith, the Imposter, and Baldrac, the knight, preparing to torture the hapless Gleb, and in the innocuous form of a field mouse had helped to set the elf free. It had been love that had prompted him to warn the Enchantress against his grandfather's unsavory plot to seduce the girl through his grandson once she reached Krim's Keep, and it had been love that drove him, despite his terror of Sheelar, to trick the evil Serpent-Lord of Somn into promising Aurora's release from his spell once she had been lured into his sylvan glen. And while he regretted none of what he had done in her service, he could not help the galling bitterness he felt at having lost her ere he had ever had a real opportunity to win her, for he had never stood a chance against the godlike Frayne, in whom even Crane, despite his jealousy, had seen the hero he, the young shape-changer, longed to be.

Indeed, if he himself must be denied her love, then he could wish for none better to have won her than the Knight of Tor, he told himself, and silently renewed his vow to help the Enchantress find Frayne and win him back again.

That thought recalled him to his purpose in seeking Aurora beneath the elderberry trees. Vandrel had sent him to find her and bring her home, for she had news.

"Aurora!" he called, as though he had just come into the clearing. He saw her head come up, and he crossed quickly to her side. The beautiful eyes the color of gold coins swept up his long gangly form to fasten questioningly on his freckled face.

"Vandrel wants you at the cottage," he said and watched her smooth brow pucker in a frown.

"But it cannot be time for recitations," she said

irritably. "I haven't finished reading yet."

"No, it's not that. Vandrel has a visitor. You'd better hurry. She wants you there right away."

"A visitor? But who? Not Garwin? There's nothing amiss at Hawthorn Glade?" she cried, suddenly alarmed. In the six months she had been with the old scholar, there had never once been a visitor.

"Hey. Take it easy. It's got nothing to do with the elves. Or at least, I don't think it does. He's from the south. Sedgewick, I think, on the Glendaron. That's all I know, except from the looks of him I'd say he's a woodsman. Vandrel sent me to find you before I could hear anything else." He paused, one hand going to his chin as he appeared to reflect. "You know. It's strange. But it was like Vandrel was expecting him. Called him by name when she first laid eyes on him. 'Elwindolf!' she said and hustled him inside before he could say a word. But I heard her ask about Sedgewick before she closed the door."

"What is Sedgewick?" queried the Enchantress, scrambling to her feet, all vestiges of her former languid state quite vanished. For days she had been experiencing an odd prickling of her nerve endings, a vague feeling of waiting for something to happen that would forever alter her tranquil existence in Vandrel's valley. And now that something was arrived at last. She knew it.

Crane knew it, too, as his eyes slid suddenly away from the girl's eager glance. But it was foreboding he felt. As long as they remained in the elderberry glen, he had had the Enchantress to himself. But that time was over, he acknowledged with a sigh. Moreover, if he knew anything about the tempestuous Aurora, it was that she would plunge headlong into danger and land them both in a jam before many days had passed. And this time there would be no one to help her out of her coils but himself. The old uncertainty swept over him, making him sick to his stomach. With a shudder he recalled their previous excursion into the world of men. They'd been lucky to escape Twickham with a whole skin, and now, if he was right, they would be heading into much worse predicaments. He wasn't sure he was up to it yet.

"Crane? What is it?" Aurora said then, breaking into his somber thoughts. "You look as if you've eaten something that didn't agree with you. You aren't going to be ill, are you? Not now, when what we've been preparing for may be ready to begin at last."

"Probably," he answered fatalistically. "But it doesn't matter. Nothing could stop me from going with you when you leave here."

He grinned a little crookedly as her face magically cleared and she awarded him a dazzling smile.

"Thank goodness. I was afraid for a moment that you'd changed your mind, and I shouldn't like going without you. Now do stop looking so sour and tell me about this Sedgewick," she scolded, and taking him by the arm, began to pull him along in the direction of the cottage. "Where in the south is it?"

"I'm not sure," he confessed a trifle reluctantly. He was uncomfortably aware that, more than a little daunted by the scintillating power of the Enchantress, he had in the past led her to believe he knew and had done a great deal more than was strictly the truth. Actually, he had never really been in a town before their disastrous jaunt to Twickham, except once as a sparrow and another time as a particularly scroungy-looking mutt. Nor had the latter experience given him a very efficacious outlook on his fellow men, for he had received little in the way of welcome but a hobnailed boot in the ribs and a string of expletives that had sent him scurrying for the safety of the surrounding woods. In short, he knew very little more about mankind than did Aurora.

"I've never been there, but I've seen it on Vandrel's map. It's just north of Tor a little ways into the forest. They're mostly lumbermen and hunters, I think. I used to hear my grandfather talk about Sedgewick lumber. They cut the trees, then float them down the river to Tor where they are made into lumber and sold or sent on down the river on barges."

They had arrived at the cottage as Crane finished speaking, and Aurora, still puzzling why anyone from the south should have come all the way to the Land of Mages in search of Vandrel, opened the door and went quickly in.

"Ah, here they are now," Vandrel said as the two young mages halted just across the threshold. "Come in. Come in and meet an old friend of mine."

The old scholar bustled across the room to pull Aurora and Crane forward toward a long, lean man standing in the shadows, his slender, powerful hands resting easily atop the curved end of a deadly-looking bow propped against the floor. He was dressed in buckskins and soft leather boots that reached above the knees. A long knife hung from a wide leather belt about his lean waist. Straight dark hair streaked with grey was bound by a leather thong at the nape of his neck and trailed down his back. Yet his face was curiously smooth and deeply tanned, giving no hint as to his probable age. A hawklike nose, firm lips, and a strong jaw bespoke strength, while uncanny eyes like still pools of water reflecting a pale sky studied the two from beneath sweeping black eyebrows without a flicker of emotion. There was about him a studied reserve, which Aurora knew instinctively would not be easily breached. He was like the forest, she thought, still, patient, and enduring. And yet no doubt like Beorn, Brown-Bear, too—slow to arouse, but deadly, if provoked too far.

"Aurora, Crane, this is Elwindolf, an old rogue wolf if there ever was one. He has come from the south at the behest of Sedgewick to seek our aid in a curious matter." She turned to look at the tall woodsman. "These are the two young mages I was telling you about. If they choose to accept the task, they will accompany you."

"These be only cubs, Hertha Vandrel," said the woodsman quietly. " 'Twas ye I was sent to fetch."

Aurora grew suddenly alert at the visitor's use of the Droonish word for "Earth Mother." And, too, he bore an elfin name, which meant "Wolf Friend of the Elves." 'Twas most odd. How came the man to bear such a name and to be conversant in the Old Tongue as well? she wondered. But then the old scholar's next words drove the thought from her mind.

"Nonsense," Vandrel chided. "I'm far too old to be traipsing off through the woods. They may be young, but they are not without the ability to handle whatever troubles Sedgewick. You shan't need me."

The enchantress experienced a sudden fluttering in the region of her stomach. Unbelievably, Vandrel had at last judged her and Crane ready to set out into the world of men, and apparently the old scholar had seized upon the troubles besetting the town of Sedgewick to launch them on their way. Doubtless they would travel under the guise of healers, or possibly as students of gramarye summoned either to break a spell or to invoke one. After all, the offices of shaman and spellbinder were honorable, and, as such, they would be readily welcomed anywhere without undue comment. It was a perfect opportunity for them unobtrusively to begin their true quest. Still, Aurora, who had been intently studying the stranger even as her mind whirled with such heady speculations, saw with dismay that Vandrel had failed to persuade him to accept these unknown and untried apprentices in her stead. On a sudden impulse she stepped boldly forward and spoke quietly in the language of elves and beasts.

"I am Aurora, elf-daughter and tree-child to the dryads. And you are Elwindolf, 'Lone-Wolf' and 'Elf-Friend.' Can there be mistrust between those who have lived among the Old Ones?"

She felt her nerves tingle as the stranger's piercing gaze swept over her, but she held his glance without flinching.

"Ye speak the tongue of the Beginnings, Brenna with the golden eyes," he answered in like manner. "Yet ye've not the look of elves. By what right claim ye the name 'Elf-Daughter'?"

"Once I was called 'Anduan, Elf-Foundling,' for the elves rescued me, an infant orphaned in Hawthorn Glade, and reared me till they gave me over to the dryads when I became too large for them to care for.

Yet still I was elf-daughter to Garwin the Wise and Gleb, the son of Flem. And in my twelfth summer Thegne the Elder initiated me into the Hraldoonish Rites and Mysteries that betoken an elf's coming of age."

"I am Elwindolf, and many seasons have I lived with the Old Ones. I have heard of the *anduan* of Hawthorn Glade. Yet what proof have ye that ye be that one? By what sign shall I know these words be true and not the cunning of Xantu, the Fox?"

Aurora stared in disbelief at the hunter's impassive features. Ye gods, she thought. It had been easier to convince the villainous gnomes of Black Mountain of her identity. If her knowledge of the Old Tongue was not enough to allay his suspicions, then what could she do? Then her eyes alighted on the man's long bow, and the hint of a grin touched her lips.

"The elves have a saying that he who can string the bow wrought of Glinden Wood shall send the arrow true. May I see your bow, Elwindolf?"

She saw him hesitate, the suggestion of suspicion darkening his brow, but at last he lifted the bow and proffered it.

" 'Tis Valarc, Strong-Bow," he said. "And 'tis indeed wrought of Glinden Wood. Still, the knowledge of the bow proves naught that ye be what ye say ye be."

"Nay," Aurora agreed with a reluctant laugh. "It proves only that you are very hard to please. Can I persuade you, I wonder, to come outside with me? There you shall have the proof you demand, else there be naught which can win your trust, methinks."

"What's going on?" whispered Crane as he followed Aurora out the door. The familiar gleam in the golden eyes made him distinctly uneasy. Not for the first time since he had met the Enchantress did he wish he could speak and understand elf tongue. But though Aurora had tried to teach it to him, he had made little progress, for his mind tended to wander, and before he knew what had happened, he would find himself suddenly somewhere else. But he knew that look, and thus he knew as well that the Enchantress was up to something.

"Nothing much," she said. "I have just promised to string our visitor's bow to prove we are worthy to take on his quest."

The shape-changer's jaw went suddenly slack.

"Ye gods, Aurora! Have you gone daft? I doubt that even the two of us together could do that." He glanced furtively at the stone-faced hunter. Elwindolf appeared hard and fit, with long, sinewy muscles that promised a wiry strength. Even so, the great bow looked better suited to a god or a godlike man than to a mere mortal. "I wonder even that he can do it," he muttered to himself.

"Sh-h!" Aurora whispered back. "You shall just have to wait and see."

She led them all into the clearing in front of the cottage and confidently tested the weight of the bow. It was as long as she was tall, but Glinden Wood, which could be found only with the help of elfin magic, was light, and she held the bow easily. Yet she knew, too, that the bow, carved from the heartwood of the Glinden, was deceptive, for the roots of the fabulous tree tapped the Anglaron, which was the heart and soul of the land, and thus the Glinden was possessed of the very strength of the living earth.

Slowly the Enchantress straightened to her full height and deliberately grasped the end of the bow with one slender hand. Crane glanced anxiously at Vandrel, but the old scholar was staring fixedly at the slight figure of the girl and paid him no heed. Then he heard the Enchantress murmur strange, elfin words, and the shape-changer's eyes flew back to the girl.

Glinden dur varlen Anglaron svandroon.
Hendrak valoren yn varrin Hraldoon.

Aurora's voice faded into the sudden quiet that cloaked the glade. Crane blinked, unable to believe his own eyes, as he saw the stout bow slowly begin to bend beneath the hand of the Enchantress. Quickly she strung the bow, and, knocking an arrow from Elwindolf's quiver to the bowstring, nodded in the direction of a weathered stump that was located across the bourne and perhaps two hundred feet from where she stood.

"That shall be my target," she said, and drawing the butt of the arrow to her ear, released the shaft. The arrow shot in a sure arc across the bourne. Crane's stentorian shout shattered the stillness as Aurora's dart sped truly to its mark.

Then the Enchantress turned to face Elwindolf. Slowly she held forth one slim hand, the thumb pointing upward toward the light of the One and the fingers extended outward toward the man's heart in token of friendship.

"Elwin yn Phelan, vondren vadhi?" she queried, looking the hunter straight in the eye, then, at Crane's

ungentle prod with a bony elbow, she translated, "Elf-Friend and Brave-Wolf, do we go with thee?"

The man's still face turned gravely toward her. The dark head bowed slightly in a gesture of respect.

"I ask the pardon of Anduan of the Hraldoons," he said quietly. "There be strange happenings in the forest and creatures afoot which bear the false likeness of friends. I had to make sure of ye." The uncanny eyes probed the face turned guilelessly up to his. "Aye," he said and solemnly touched his palm to hers. "Ye shall go with me, for in truth ye must be *Eadwinaldas.* 'Friend to the Ancient Ones.' "

"But how did you do it?" Crane demanded as he struggled once again to flex the hunter's long bow. The old scholar and her two students had retired to the kitchen with their guest to enjoy a fresh pot of Vandrel's vegetable stew.

Aurora grinned around a mouthful of hot bread and winked conspiratorially at the taciturn hunter. Almost she thought she discerned the answering hint of a smile in the pale blue eyes, but she could not be sure. Deliberately she finished chewing and swallowed before satisfying the shape-changer's perplexity.

" 'Tis merely a matter of knowing how," she said finally. "But I fear I cannot teach it to you. 'Tis naught, you see, but a matter of concentration and using the proper tongue."

"The proper tongue?" echoed Crane incredulously and turned to fix a suspicious eye on the girl.

"Aye. Indeed, the tongue is the key element, wouldn't you agree, Elwindolf?" she queried innocently of the hunter, but the woodsman merely grunted noncommitally and kept his attention point-edly on the contents of his wooden bowl. "It takes years of practice, actually, and then, too, one must have special instruction from the elves, who have developed archery to a fine art."

"You're roasting me!" Crane stated flatly.

"Not at all. Everything I've told you is strictly the truth, and that is why I said I could not teach it to you. You see, one cannot be forever drifting off to another place in the middle of a lesson. Which is exactly what you do. And that is why you have no notion of what I am talking about now," she ended with an exasperating smile.

"Oh, have mercy on the boy, Aurora," Vandrel broke in, shaking a finger at the girl. "Tell him how you were able to wield the bow and have done with it. We have more important matters to discuss at present," she ended brusquely, but the twinkle in her eyes robbed the words of their sting, and the Enchantress's golden laughter brightened the room so that Elwindolf's piercing gaze lifted to fix with curious intensity on Aurora.

"It's very simple," she said, "to one who under-stands the old ways. The Glinden Tree, you see, is not like other trees, for it is sustained by the Anglaron itself and thus partakes of the pristine powers of earth. It cannot be corrupted or forced. Neither the strongest man nor ten such men could flex the bow wrought of Glinden Wood lest first the Hraldoonish words of command are invoked. That is what I did, and had you attended to the language lessons I tried to give you, you would have understood all that occurred today."

82

"Quite so, I am sure," Vandrel agreed sagely. "And yet it occurs to me that it was not Crane who passed the morning daydreaming beneath an elderberry tree with his lessons unread upon his lap."

A becoming blush tinged Aurora's cheeks.

"Nay. It was not Crane," she said ruefully. "And you are right. 'Tis not my place to scold him. I do beg your pardon, Crane."

The shape-changer shifted in embarrassment as the girl's sweet smile shone conciliatorily upon him.

"Well, you can just go beg it somewhere else," he retorted with a lopsided grin. "I'd rather have you baiting me than trying to turn me up sweet. It's more in character, to my way of thinking."

"And mine," Aurora confessed and turned laughing eyes upon her aged mentor. "However shall we get along without you to keep us in line, dearest Van?" she said then. "You never miss a thing. You see all and know all. Is that why, I wonder, Elwindolf calls you Hertha Vandrel? For you must know that 'Earth Mother' suits you very well, methinks."

"Pshaw! And next thing you'll be calling me Eilderood or some such faradiddle of nonsense," disclaimed the old scholar, flinging up her hands.

"And would it be so far-fetched?" queried the Enchantress with a sudden glint in her eyes. "Even Frayne guessed once that you are more than you would seem to be."

The old woman chuckled merrily and rose from the bench to begin clearing off the table.

"You tell them, Elwindolf, why you call me Hertha, and set the child's mind to rest," she said. "She's not like to believe anything *I* tell her. Then we can get

83

to the business of Sedgewick and the bizarre tale you have related to me."

The girl glanced expectantly at the grave-faced hunter as he sat at ease, his broad back propped against the wall near the bench. She watched him draw contentedly on a long-stemmed pipe and slowly expel a cloud of smoke, and suddenly it struck her that he seemed oddly at home in the cozy cottage, as if he belonged there, and for the first time Aurora wondered how he had been able to find Vandrel's secluded valley. For she was aware that the glen was veiled amidst the sage old scholar's potent spells of concealment, and only one who knew the correct counterspells or one whom Vandrel had granted free access to the valley could find the way to her. But then the hunter was speaking and she was forced to put off such interesting questions until later.

"I was born Drude, son of Ned, the woodcutter," Elwindolf began, his gaze distant. " 'Twas in the winter of my fifth year my father died, leaving me to fend for myself, my mother having gone before him at my birthing. There be little doubt I had been doomed to a like fate had not Phelan of the wolf pack found me lost in the forest and mewling like the babe I was. He took me up on his back and carried me deep into the woods to a place that was a haven to creatures in need of healing. And there he left me with the woman whom the animals call Earth Mother and the elves Hertha. But I, who grew to manhood at her hearth, have ever named her 'Hertha Vandrel.' "

"But that is a marvelous tale!" breathed Aurora, her eyes glowing softly. "Why did you never tell us you had a foster-son, Vandrel?" she queried. "How many such tales could you tell us did you choose to, I wonder."

"More than we have time for today," the old woman said dampeningly as she went brusquely about the business of setting the kitchen to rights.

"But how came you to be a friend to the elves, Elwindolf?" Aurora persisted, for she had heard of none other of man-seed who knew the Old Tongue besides herself. " 'Twas in my mind that perchance you, too, were *anduan*, elf-foundling. But now I see that is not the case."

"Nay," he answered reflectively, "I be not elf-fostered. But nor was I fated to become learned in the art of gramarye. For I cared little for bookish ways and even as a lad would seek out the wolf pack to learn the business of the hunt. 'Twas in my fourteenth season that the wanderlust took me from Hertha Vandrel, and I roamed the forest with Phelan and his brethren.

"To the far northern reaches and the southern and finally to the east we followed the hunt, still one day fortune turned on Drude called 'Wolf.' For along Glanden Bourne, near the place called Glindenfel, he surprised Grimhard, Grizzly-Bear, at a kill." Aurora's sudden gasp sounded harshly in the stillness of the cottage. Her eyes were huge in a face gone suddenly white as she gaped in awe at the unemotional utterance of the hunter. Of all the creatures of woodland, the grizzly was the most dangerous to antagonize. Nor did the great bear require much to rouse his uncertain temper, for he seemed peculiarly possessed of a perverse nature.

"The elves of the Droonish clan found me," Elwindolf continued calmly. "My wounds they healed with elfin magic. Even so, I was long in recovering from the lesson taught me by the old bear, and Phelan and the pack perforce took leave of me. Yet I was not discontent, for elves are wise in the ways of the Forest, and there was much that I would learn." Aurora shivered as the hunter's numinous eyes sought her face. Yet steadily she held his gaze as he seemed to look into her very soul.

" 'Tis in ye as well, the knowledge of the Old Ones. I see it in the face of Brenna with the golden eyes," he said, and a quizzical smile curved the girl's lips, for that was the second time he had called her "Brenna," which in the tongue of mankind means "Maiden with the Raven Hair." Slowly he shook his dark head. "Nay, I was wrong when I said ye had not the look of elves," he added and fell suddenly silent.

"Indeed, it was an uncommonly hasty judgment on your part," Vandrel observed with a twinkle as she once more joined the three at the table. " 'The lad must be sorely beset with troubles,' I told myself. And, indeed, things are come to a sad pass when Elwindolf begins to doubt Vandrel's word. Think you I am become senile with the passing years that I should not know the true character of those I have taken into my home? If so, then you are become a sad rogue-wolf indeed, Elwindolf."

For the first time it seemed that the hunter's impenetrable reserve had at last been shaken, as a sudden shadow like grief or pain flickered briefly across the man's face.

" 'Twas not your word I doubted, Hertha," he answered somberly, "nor your judgment. But the times. For trust no longer comes easily to a wolf who has been driven from the Pack."

The old woman's gaze flickered, then narrowed on the closed countenance of her foster-son.

"Tell me," she said gravely.

At first it seemed as if he would not answer, but at last he spoke in a voice carefully devoid of feeling.

"Not less than a fortnight past, he who was of the Pack was stalked by wolves, and as the light of Shin fell across the land, Phelan, Father-Wolf, stole into Elwindolf's camp to slay his foster-cub as he lay sleeping. But Elwindolf awakened and saw murder in his father's eyes. 'Nay, Phelan!' he cried, stricken to the heart. 'I be Elwindolf and of the Brethren of the Hunt.' But the old wolf answered, 'Thou art of the pack no longer, man-spawn. For thou art of the seed of the man-beast, who hast brought the evil to the land. Thee and all of thy kind must be driven from the forest that all may be again as it once was.' And Elwindolf saw the madness in the eyes of the father-wolf and knew he must fight his old friend or die. The Old One gathered himself to spring at the throat of the man-cub, but Elwindolf threw down his weapons. 'Long ago Phelan saved the life of the man-cub,' he said to the father-wolf. 'By law that life be Phelan's. Take it now, if ye will, for it be the law of the pack.' And Elwindolf prepared to give up his spirit to the One. But Phelan did not attack, and he looked upon the man with confusion and the first sign of returning reason. 'Take up thine arms, rogue,' he cried. 'Wilt thou die the coward's death?' 'To slay the giver of life wouldst be to die a thousand times the coward's death, Father-Wolf. Elwindolf would choose the path of honor.' 'Then choose the path which leads most quickly from the forest, Elwindolf,' Phelan warned. 'For though I give thee back thy life this night, though art cast off from the pack. Henceforth no wolf shall call thee brother.'

"But Elwindolf did not leave the forest, Hertha Vandrel. Nay. He searched for the source of the evil that Phelan said was come to the land. And near Sedgewick, the village of the woodcutters, he found it."

"The blight that kills the woods and brings the madness upon the animals," Vandrel said gravely.

"Aye. And the village, too, be sore beset, for the madness infects the minds of Men, as well." The pale blue eyes grew cloudy with some dark memory. "I have felt this evil, Earth-Mother. It be like a poison in the air, which spawns fear in the minds of brave men and bloodlust in the hearts of the craven. I have seen brother fall upon brother and sons turned against fathers." Elwindolf appeared to shudder. "I, too, was beset with the darkness and would have lost the way had not the gods deemed it otherwise. For they guided me to the Sacred Grove where still stands inviolate the Shrine of the Holy Maiden."

"The Valdoran Sanctuary," breathed the old scholar with a curious glint in her eye.

"Aye. 'Twere sanctuary for Elwindolf, for there the evil entered not, and the light of reason was returned to him who wandered in darkness. I be Elwindolf," he said then with telling dignity. "And more wolf, me-thinks, than man. Long have I trod the paths of the forest and followed the ways of the pack. I have partaken of the secret teachings of the Old Ones and learned the language of the Beginnings. But of gramarye I know naught. Hence, to Hertha Vandrel I bring these tidings. The evil spreads through the forest and grows daily stronger. Think ye these mage-cubs have the wherewithal to stop it?"

That night Aurora lay awake in her cot, prey to sudden doubts in herself and to uncertainties about all that might await them in the days and weeks ahead. Yet Vandrel had not seemed to suffer from any qualms about her apparently unalterable decision to remain behind, as she bluffly informed Elwindolf that the two young mages were equal to the trials ahead. Indeed, she had assured him they would be ready to leave with the first light of morning and then had shooed the two out of the room that she and her foster-son might have time alone to catch up on all that had occurred since last they had been together. But Aurora suspected the old scholar had wished to discuss weightier matters than a mere exchange of reminiscences. Indeed, might not Vandrel have thought to hear word from Elwindolf about the doings of the Sorceress? For she had said her foster-son wandered far and wide and knew all that occurred within the Forest and much of what went on beyond its boundaries. Aurora would have liked to have questioned their intriguing visitor herself and she decided that she would do so ere they reached Sedgewick.

Nay, Vandrel had not seemed bothered by doubts, but what of Crane and herself? Were they indeed ready? Recalling to mind the shape-changer's face as he sought his pallet before the fire that evening, Aurora knew that Crane, too, was afraid, and she felt suddenly ashamed for having teased him about his tendency to drift away in the midst of his studies. Since she had first encountered him at Krim's Keep, so long ago it now seemed, she had been painfully aware of his deep-seated feelings of inadequacy. Indeed, she had been often impatient with him for what she had seen as his childish indecisiveness. But that had been before Frayne had taught her the agony of love. Then she had been a child newly awakened to the wonder of a woman's passion and the hand of the god upon her, and, borne upon the crest of burgeoning power, she had had little sympathy for the vulnerabilities of the boy who had confessed his hopeless love for her. But then Frayne had ridden out of her life without even a farewell, and suddenly she had been made to understand what it was to suffer heartache.

Poor, dear Crane. Even knowing she could never love him as he would wish her to do, and fearful lest he should fail her, still he would ride with her into danger. She felt shaken by such steadfast devotion, and humbled, too. And suddenly, for the first time, she was stricken by a sense of her own responsibility for Crane's fate. He depended on her to put to rights whatever evil threatened Endrith's Forest and, beyond that, to guide them safely through the perils that awaited them in Tor, the Sorceress's domain.

"Oh, gods," she whispered to the darkened room. "Frayne spoke truly, for indeed I am alone within the darkness and see naught but myself and an uncertain fate. Where is the power of the god now that Frayne has gone?"

Her hand stole up to finger the small pouch she wore on a leather thong about her neck. Instantly she felt the crystal throb at her touch, as if in response to her uneasy thoughts, and abruptly her hands closed tightly over it. Nay, she would not be afraid, for was she not Aurora and Andruvien and had she not faced Dred and fought the Asgeroth? And somewhere, on some other plane, was not her spirit bound with Frayne's?

Aye, she thought, a smile coming at last to her lips, and suddenly the darkness was dispelled by a silvery shaft of moonlight streaming through the window beside her cot. Imbued with a sense of wonder, she sat up to look out upon the elderberry wood bathed in moonlight and felt that the god had sent her a sign. For even so had the light found her in the darkness of Krim's Keep, revealing to her the truth of her own power to see through the illusions wrought by the mage-lord. And she knew at last that she was not alone, for the god was with her still.

Slowly she sank once more against her pillow and closed her eyes. She would sleep now, she thought drowsily, for on the morrow would begin the true test of her courage. And she would meet it with confidence and daring, for she was the Enchantress, and she was not afraid.

The glen was yet enveloped in darkness as the company gathered in Vandrel's kitchen, made cozy by a crackling fire and the aroma of acorn cakes cooking on the griddle. Elwindolf sat brooding in his shadowy corner, the embers of his pipe glowing red as he silently smoked and watched the others make ready for the coming trek. The old scholar hummed softly to herself as she went about the business of putting together a hurried breakfast, and Elwindolf smiled a little to himself each time he saw her pause, one hand coming to rest on a plump hip and the other waving a wooden spatula, to send a flurry of orders at the distraught Crane, who was preparing a pack to take along with them.

The old woman had not changed a whit since last he had seen her, over five years before. In truth, she had ever been as she was now, for as long as he had known her. For she was Hertha Vandrel, who had ever a generous heart and a discerning eye. Yet again he wondered if she saw truly in this instance, for the boy-mage appeared very young and vulnerable with his unkempt mat of red hair, his freckled face, and the long, lanky frame, which held only the promise of a manly strength yet to come. He watched the lad move distractedly from one task to another as if he were dazed or in a trance, and wondered that such a one had dared the perils of the giants' den and lived to tell of it. Yet such had been the tale Vandrel had had to tell of the shape-changer, and so he must believe there was more to the stripling than met the eye.

Of his feelings concerning the beautiful young Enchantress he was even less certain, for from the first he had sensed in her a power beyond his ken. She had appeared, as she had come eagerly forward to greet Vandrel's guest, a bewitching child, but even in the shadowy interior of the cottage she had seemed to scintillate with an otherness that had set him on his guard. Then she had spoken in the Old Tongue, which he had not expected to hear coming from her lips, and he had thought for a moment that the madness had returned to him; indeed, that the evil had penetrated even into Vandrel's magic glen. But she had uttered the secret words of command, and Valarc had submitted to her hand, sending the shaft straight and true. Then could he doubt no longer, for, gazing into her golden eyes, he had seen the look of the Elves about her, and something more. Something that had made him want to bow down before her, as one would kneel before Eilderood, whether in fear or reverence, he was not certain.

Drude, called Elwindolf, lifted his head then, as his pulse seemed suddenly to quicken. He had known before he looked that the Enchantress was come into the room.

She stood at the foot of the stairs, a slender wood sprite clothed in forest green. She wore a soft woollen tunic, belted at the waist with a wide leather belt, and breeches tucked snugly into tall, supple boots. An elf's dagger hung from the belt, her only weapon, and her raven hair was gathered in a single thick braid that fell down her back to her waist. The strange, golden eyes glittered with a hardly controlled excitement, and a smile trembled on the lovely lips.

"Vandrel," she called and swept across the room to embrace her mentor. "You have seen to everything. Look, Crane. Our dearest Van has fitted me with new clothing." She pulled away from the woman to pirouette before the young shape-changer. Magically, the boy had seemed to change at sight of the girl, thought the bemused Elwindolf. Crane stood suddenly straighter, and the dreamy-eyed look had given way before a slightly dazzled expression that he sought to hide behind a wry quirk of the lips.

"If you take time to look," he said drily, "you will

see that I'm as well decked-out as you are."

"So you are," Aurora laughed and looked him over appreciatively, from his finely woven woollen shirt to his soft leather boots. "Indeed, I hardly know you, you are become suddenly so fine a gentleman."

"Pshaw!" ejaculated Vandrel with a twinkle in her eye. "And would a gentleman deign to show himself with such a mop of hair as could not have known the touch of a comb for a se'ennight or longer?"

Thus, what was to be the last gathering for many a day of the small company of friends around Vandrel's breakfast table was a merry affair. And when at last the dishes had been cleared away and the packs strapped shut and hefted to the backs of the three who were departing into unknown peril, the dawn had just begun to break in the east.

Aurora, her slim figure enveloped in a flowing cloak of elfin green and her eyes suspiciously bright as she gazed into the old woman's plump face, paused for a final farewell.

"Shall we meet again, dearest Vandrel?" she queried softly.

The old scholar smiled mistily and drew the girl close.

"Once the child Anduan left the Hawthorn Glade in search of her destiny and returned Aurora, the Enchantress with the Blade of Power. So shall it be again. Today I bid farewell to Aurora, but Aurora shall not return again to Vandrel's cottage."

"I do not understand," said the Enchantress with a suddenly heavy heart. "Shall I never see you again?"

The woman chuckled and firmly disentangled herself from the girl's embrace.

"Did I say that?" she countered, lightly brushing a tear from Aurora's cheek. "It's time you were going now. Elwindolf has small patience for those who would tarry on the trail. Farewell, my child. My thoughts go with you."

"Good-bye, Hertha Vandrel," Aurora whispered, then abruptly wheeled to follow the others from the glade.

"Not good-bye," murmured the old scholar as she watched the girl pause and turn at the edge of the woods to lift her hand in a last farewell. With a smile, she saw the slim figure straighten to its full height, the small head held high, as the Enchantress strode at last with a firm step into the forest.

"Never good-bye."

Chapter Four

Two horsemen stole through the gates of Tor, and, following the Glendaron north, raced across the moon-drenched plain toward the southern border of the Great Forest. The eerie sheen of silver mail glinted like a pale aura about the larger of the two as he twisted in the saddle to look back the way they had come. Behind him he saw the slight figure of his companion lean forward to call encouragement to the long-limbed steed, and a mirthless smile touched his lips as the sound of the high-pitched voice reached his ear, a wild, haunting cry in the brooding quiet of the night. At least the child could ride. But then, it would be exceedingly odd if a spawn of the horse-loving desert tribes could not, he thought cynically. For the nomads of the wasteland valued their horses above their lives.

At last, apparently satisfied that they were not followed, the Knight of Tor eased to a slower, mile-eating pace and turned to grim contemplation of the ambush that had awaited them in the narrow streets of the city. The four brigands had been draped in black, their faces concealed behind vizards, and he had been able to recognize none of them. But there had been a fifth, their ringleader, no doubt, lurking in the shadows. Even as the Knight of Tor had hastily drawn his sword against the surprise attack, he had been aware of that other, had felt his burning hatred like a poisoned dart aimed between the knight's shoulder blades. Indeed, it was the lingering image of that shadowed form that worried at him now, for in that single, brief glimpse, he had sensed something disturbingly familiar about the indistinct form, something that he could not quite put his finger on.

They had come to kill the Sorceress's knight, he doubted not, but it suddenly struck him that they had meant to take the girl alive, for though they could have slain her easily, they had made no attempt to do so. Rather had they sought with treacherous cunning to separate her from her protector and then to steal away with her. And they had nearly succeeded, too, he thought grimly, for he had been hard-pressed by three of the burly rogues and sorely hampered by the close confines of the alleyway. He grimaced as the fiery ache of the shallow sword wound across his ribs reminded him that he had not escaped unscathed. But neither had they. Two had fallen to his sword and a third beneath the hooves of Boltar, the warrior-steed, when the girl's terrified scream had shattered the night. Wheeling to see Janine struggling in the grips of the remaining villain, the knight had sent Boltar lunging toward them. Thrimheld, Swift-Blade, lashed out and down, and the girl was freed. Then would Frayne have sought the one who hid in the shadows had not Janine clung tearfully to him, begging him not to leave her. And when at last the girl was calm again, the leader of the band had vanished into the night.

There had been nothing for it but to get the child safely out of Tor. But what now? mused Frayne bitterly. He had managed to remove the girl from her immediate danger, but the one who had plotted her abduction had gone free, perhaps to try again. Why? And who? he pondered, knowing himself to be on the horns of a dilemma, for what was he to do with the child? He could ill afford the time either to search out and dispatch her enemies or to find a safe haven in which to leave her. He had other pressing concerns to which he must attend.

A plague on the Sorceress and her blasted potion! he thought savagely. She had given him little enough to go on in his search for her precious, perfect rose. It might take weeks, months even, to discover so much as a clue to the whereabouts of the kingdom of the crystals, and he was determined that Janine should not go with him. Well, there was nothing for it but that he must take her with him at least as far as Sedgewick on the Glendaron, for in the small, isolated village, he had heard, resided a master craftsman in the art of lapidary, and he had a most particular reason for wishing to speak with him.

Thus preoccupied with his unrewarding thoughts, the Knight of Tor, with Janine, the slave-girl, trailing closely in his wake, made steadily for the dark silhouette of trees, oblivious to the crimson stain seeping through his woollen shirt beneath the broken links of the silver mail. Shin, the Moon Goddess, completed her stately journey across the realm of the night as Frayne and the slave-girl left the flatlands at last to vanish into the forest. And hours later, as the first pink rays of dawn streaked the sky, five black shadows issued forth from Tor, moving swiftly across the grassy plain in unwavering pursuit.

Janine, daughter of the desert Khan, clung in silent fear to the coarse mane of her weary mount as the forest closed around her. Never, except when Red-Beard, the Evil One, had stolen her from the slave-caravan and carried her into the city of the Sorceress, had she ventured forth from the sweeping vastness of the plains. She had not liked the city, with its narrow, twisting streets, the tall buildings carved of sandstone crowded together so that one could catch a glimpse of the open sky only from the rooftops. Indeed, she had been terrified by the gloomy waterfront and the furtive, crafty-eyed creatures who reigned there in filth and squalor, and she had thought to die before she should be made one of them. Then Frayne had cast the bones for her and won her from ignominy and death.

When first she saw the handsome knight, she had felt that here was one whom she would gladly serve, for his was the face of a god, and within the long, lithe form she sensed a godly power. Then he had looked upon her with the cold, grey eyes of the falcon, and she had felt pierced by a sense of his inner torment. Her pulse throbbed with a slow-burning rage at the one who had hurt her lord and master. "Aurora," he had called out again and again in his delirium. "Enchantress." The memory of that cursed named uttered with such rending love ripped at her heart so that she writhed in the saddle, tortured by a fierce, passionate jealousy. Who was this Aurora, this Enchantress, whose magic was so powerful that it enslaved the heart and soul of Frayne? Frayne, before whom even Baldrac had trembled, Frayne whose very name inspired awed respect among the people of Tor and elsewhere. For she had heard stories of the Knight of Tor even among her people, the Wendaren.

And now she knew the stories were all true. For had she not seen the powerful knight slay four dogs of Amaur, the God of Darkness?

The low hoot of an owl brought the girl's head up, her eyes wide and staring as she tried to pierce the darkness left by Shin's passing into the west. The steady plash of water nearby and the musky scent of rich, damp earth assailed her senses. She breathed deeply of the unfamiliar aroma, then her breath caught painfully in her throat at the sudden sound of something crashing through the brush. She bit her lip to keep from crying out and fought to still the dreadful pounding of her heart, for the forest seemed to press around her with ghastly, grasping fingers which, in her sordid fancy, sought to tear her from her mount. She sensed a malevolence in the restless trees and struggled against the stultifying feeling that unseen within the darkness a multitude of eyes watched her with silent loathing.

A harsh gasp was startled from her at the warm touch of a hand upon her leg.

"Softly, child," came Frayne's low voice, rendering her suddenly faint with relief. "We camp here till dawn lights the way again." She felt his hands close around her waist to lift her down and frowned as he uttered a low grunt and seemed to sag a little against her as he set her on her feet. Then he straightened and moved away to lead the horse through a narrow break in a thorny thicket, and, afraid to be alone, she followed.

"Wait here," he said then, and obediently she stood where he left her, her limbs trembling and her ears filled with the sound of the river rushing beside her. A spark leaped out of the darkness as the knight struck flint and steel, and it was not long before she huddled before a crackling fire. Halfheartedly she nibbled at the strips of dried meat he had given her to eat. She was not hungry. She was too tired. After a time she became aware that the knight was watching her. She met his glance across the campfire and started abruptly at sight of his ashen face.

"What is it, my lord?" she said in sudden dread and felt the blood drain from her cheeks.

One corner of his mouth curled in a rueful smile.

"I fear I must ask your help," he answered calmly, "if I am not to swoon from loss of blood." And he drew forth a bloody hand from where it had been pressed against his side.

"You are hurt, my lord!" she cried and stumbled around the campfire to fall to her knees beside him, her hands fluttering to her throat as she beheld his red-stained shirt of mail.

His fingers closed firmly about her wrist, and her eyes flew questioningly to his.

"The wound itself is not serious," he said quietly and held her with his hawklike eyes till her breathing had slowed and she seemed in control of herself again. "It must be cleansed and bound, the bleeding

102

stopped. And you must help me out of this blasted armor."

Wordlessly she nodded, but her eyes were huge in the pale oval of her face, and her lips trembled with the hint of barely suppressed tears.

"You're not afraid at the sight of blood, are you, Janine?" he queried gently. "I'm not likely to die from this, you know."

"N-no, my lord," she answered haltingly, and then, at the quizzical glint in his eyes, added fiercely, "I shall not let you die!"

"Good girl," he said with the hint of a smile, but she noted in alarm that his voice was growing weak. "Now help me get this armor off."

She thought he must swoon from the effort of removing the cumbersome shirt of mail, and indeed, his breath came in short, hard gasps and the sweat stood out in beads on his forehead before at last she had him free of it. Then must she leave him to fetch water from the river with which to soak the bloodied shirt from the wound. But at last it was done and the wicked, jagged gash revealed.

She saw with relief that indeed the wound was not mortal, but the skin had been laid bare to the bone along one rib, and she felt suddenly helpless as it came to her what must be done. She looked up to find him staring at her, his eyes glazed with pain but steady on her face.

"The knife," he said on a whisper of breath. "It will be ready now."

For a moment she stared blankly at him. Then slowly she turned to see the blade glowing among the embers of the fire.

Mercifully consciousness left him as at last she pulled the blade away from the wound, and retching violently, tossed it with loathing from her. Summoning what was left of her rapidly waning strength, she bound the wound as best she could, and sinking down beside him, covered them both with a pelt of soft fur. Weeping softly, she fell asleep.

The sun was high in the sky when she awakened to find Frayne propped on his uninjured side, watching her. She blushed and made as if to scramble from the bed of pelts.

"Softly, child," he said, a smile in his voice. "I shan't eat you."

Her eyes fell away from his in mounting confusion. Absently she shoved the heavy mass of her hair back from her face, then remained with her head down, her mouth suddenly dry.

"Forgive me, my lord," she murmured. "I had not meant to share your bed. I-I was too weary. . . ."

"No doubt," he interrupted her awkward explanation. "And are you rested now?"

"Oh, yes, my lord. I have slept well and would now see to your wound, if it is permitted. And to food with which to break the fast."

"My wound is on the way to recovery, thanks to you," he said, and the girl's heart lifted at the warmth in his voice. Shyly she looked up to find him staring at her, his brow furrowed in a thoughtful frown.

"My lord?" she questioned in swift concern. "The wound is paining you?"

His short bark of laughter was mirthless.

"Like a cursed firebrand stuck in my side. But that's neither here nor there. What matters is that we find ourselves in a damnable coil."

She smothered a sharp exclamation as he abruptly shoved himself upright, and thrusting aside her fluttering hand, climbed to his feet to stand with his eyes tightly shut and his chest heaving.

Instantly the girl was at his side, tugging at his arm.

"My lord! You will open the wound. Please to lie down again."

"Enough, Janine," he grated between clenched teeth and shoved her impatiently from him. "We cannot linger here like sitting ducks waiting for the hunters to come." His lips curled in a cynical smile. "And I fear I'm of little use to either one of us in my present state. Thus it behooves us to keep moving."

"And when your blood flows from you again and you fall from your horse? What then, my lord?" she said bitterly.

"Then we shall see," he answered coldly and turned away from her.

They followed the river north through thick brakes, until at last they came to a place to ford the swollen stream. The river parted around a tree-covered island that looked to be perhaps thirty feet across and fifty yards in length.

Frayne sat with shoulders bowed in weariness as he studied the swift flow. The river was deep and the horses would be forced to swim the two dozen feet or more to the holm, but once there, they would have a reasonably safe haven in which to stay and rest until his strength was returned. He turned to eye critically the long-limbed mare on which the girl sat. She was smaller than Boltar, his rangy warrior-steed, but her

105

head was up and she looked fit for a lengthy ride. If she were good in the water, the girl should be safe enough. At any rate, he had little choice but to put her to the test, he thought wryly. For his own strength was nearly spent, and he doubted that he could stay in the saddle much longer.

Gritting his teeth against the persistent pain of his wound, he forced his shoulders back and turned to beckon the girl to his side.

She came reluctantly, her face studiously averted from his probing glance, and a grim smile touched his lips as he took in her slender form rigid with disapproval of his apparent foolhardiness. But he had not the strength to make her understand, and out of necessity must bend her to his will, for her life as well as his depended on their making it to the island.

"Can you swim, Janine?" he asked, his voice harsh to hide his own uncertainties.

Her eyes flew to his face in sudden realization of his intent. Slowly, as if she could not believe he really meant to try the river, she shook her head.

"Then you must take care not to come unhorsed," he said and looked away from the fear in her childish face. Curse the fates for having landed him with yet another raven-haired beauty to wreak havoc on his peace of mind. And where the one had been cursed with an impetuosity that led her ever heedless into danger, the other must be as helpless as a babe.

He led her up the river to a jut of land some twenty yards or so above the northern point of the island and leaned down to grasp her reins. He was rewarded with a sharp stab of pain that left him cursing softly and reeling in the saddle. Ignoring the girl's gasp of

106

alarm, he righted himself and headed Boltar for the roiling water.

"Hold tight to her mane," he said between clenched teeth. "I'll try to keep her upriver from Boltar. If you lose your seat, don't panic. I'll be there to grab you."

"And who shall grab you, my lord, when you swoon from loss of blood?" she queried in a small, tight voice and pointed accusingly to a telltale crimson splotch seeping through the fabric of his shirt.

He made no answer but sent the restless warrior-steed straight away into the river. Burdened by the man's weight and the heavy pack, the stallion went under the chilling flow, to come up at last snorting an angry protest. The man held grimly to the mare's reins, dragging her screaming into the water, and chanced a hurried glance at the girl. Her face was stiff and white with fear, but she was hanging on gamely. Then the river had washed over him, and he had all he could do to remain astride as they were carried helplessly along in the floodtide.

Both horses were swimming gallantly, and the Knight almost believed they would make the island without mishap. Then the girl's scream of terror brought his head around in time to see a tree uprooted by the flood hurtling down at them. Cursing, he turned the stallion downstream, the girl's mount trailing in his wake. But it was soon evident he had not been quick enough. As the tree bore down upon the struggling mare, the girl turned terror-stricken eyes toward the knight. Helplessly he watched the jagged branches sweep her from the horse. Then she was under. Knowing the bitterness of despair, he released the mare's reins and lunged for the girl. His hand found her woollen tunic and desperately he dragged her to the surface. Then the tree was past, and the girl's mount, freed of its burden, swam for the holm. But again Frayne cursed as he felt the stallion heave and begin to falter beneath its master's weight. In moments they would be carried beyond reach of the island, unless he could relieve the valiant steed of its load.

Dropping the reins, Frayne slid from the saddle. For a single, agonizing moment the current threatened to pull him under. Then he was up and swimming, the child held hard against his side, until, even as his great strength seemed utterly spent, one frantic hand grasped and held Boltar's tail as it streamed out behind the stallion. Instantly he felt the great-hearted warrior-steed surge forward, and, sending a silent prayer to the One, he fought to keep the child's head above the water. Even so, he was tortured by the fear that she had been submerged too long, so limply did she lie within his clasp.

It seemed that they should never reach dry land as the Knight of Tor struggled to maintain his grip on the girl and the horse in the midst of the raging torrent. His limbs were grown appallingly numb with the cold, and he was plagued with an alarming light-headedness, until at last he hung on only by dint of an iron will.

Then suddenly the valiant warrior-steed struck bottom and, lunging with powerful haunches, dragged them all to safety. With the last of his strength the knight carried the girl's inert body from the water and fell heavily to his knees as he laid her down on a cushiony bed of grass. In an agony of suspense he struggled to loosen the neck of her tunic, and with hands that had lost all sense of feeling, searched for some sign of life. Curse the gods! There had to be a pulse! Swept by sudden, unreasoning anger, the knight shook the lifeless form.

"Breathe, damn you!" he swore. "Breathe!" But still the child lay lifeless in his grasp, and at last, in bitter defeat, he lowered her once more to the ground. Gods! he thought wearily as he gazed upon the still face. She was so lovely and appeared so very young. Then with a sudden groan, the Knight of Tor lowered his head against clenched fists and cursed his own futility, for even so had he failed the Enchantress.

"My lord?"

The whispered words seemed to pierce his soul. In stunned disbelief he raised his head to look once more upon the lovely face.

A smile trembled weakly upon her lips, and eyes the color of the desert sky at dusk stared back at him.

"Janine," he groaned and gathered the weeping child to him.

Janine wandered in a wonderland of rich, burgeoning life such as she had never seen before. Trees and flowers, tall, waving grass, butterflies fluttering through golden shafts of sunlight, birds calling from the treetops. Kneeling amidst a profusion of purple nightshade, she gazed enraptured at a spotted orange ladybug cradled in one of the delicate star-shaped flowers. How unlike her harsh homeland of drifting dunes and far-reaching horizons! The tiny island was abloom with flowers—buttercups, fairy wand, forget-me-nots, the strange, fuzzy pussy-willow. She could not remember all their names, though Frayne had tried to teach them to her.

The sudden thought of her master brought a sigh to her lips. His wound was nearly healed, and soon they would leave their tiny island paradise and again he would ride into peril. Already she sensed his restlessness, the dark brooding of his thoughts. He was thinking of that other one. Aurora, the Enchantress, she told herself; for since that one, tender embrace as she had awakened from the nightmare of the river's clutches, there had been in the silvery eyes that haunted look that she ever associated with the weaver of enchantments. What was she, this Aurora, that she could hold him even from the darkness of the grave?

Then she was up and staring beyond the rush of water at the dense, silent woods. Even in the light of day she had not lost the feeling that something, perhaps the forest itself, watched and waited for her to return into it. She shuddered and turned away, walking quickly toward their camp at the center of the island where she had left Frayne sleeping, and suddenly she was striding faster and faster until she had nearly broken into a run as she came into the clearing, her heart pounding within her chest.

The knight glanced up from where he sat working with a piece of soft leather. Then his hand went swiftly to the knife at his belt as he beheld the slave-girl's wild eyes and pale cheeks.

"Janine! What is it? What has happened?"

The girl halted, one small hand pressed over her throbbing heart, and in sudden confusion looked away from the hard planes of her master's face.

"Nothing, my lord," she said in a small voice and

drew in a deep breath to steady her nerves. "Forgive me. I did not mean to startle you."

The man's eyebrows snapped together. For a long moment he studied the child's carefully impassive features. He saw with a surge of impatience that despite her struggle to appear calm, her lips trembled and her hands were clutched tightly before her, the knuckles showing white through the soft, translucent skin. *Something* had frightened her, he speculated darkly. Why was the absurd child trying to conceal it from him? Now he supposed he must try to worm it out of her if he was to have any peace of mind.

"Janine," he said sternly. "Come here to me."

Reluctantly the girl complied to his demand, sinking gracefully to her knees before him, her fingers going to her forehead in the gesture of obedience.

"My lord?" she murmured, her gaze hidden beneath long, quivering eyelashes.

A wry smile curled the knight's lips. She presented a disarmingly meek image greatly enhanced by an unconscious aura of feminine vulnerability. Yet he was not deceived. He knew from experience that she was quite capable of resisting with a daunting stubbornness all attempts to uncover the cause of her disquiet. Almost he was tempted to let her play the martyr, but then she raised blue eyes shimmering with unshed tears, and inwardly he groaned. Ye gods! He would rather face a score of armed brigands than a single female's tears, he thought as he brushed one of the treacherous droplets from her cheek with his thumb.

Then a memory of another raven-haired girl rose up to haunt him. There had been tears in those lovely

111

eyes, too—eyes the color of gold coins—as she pleaded with him to let her ride at his side into danger. His lips thinned to a hard line.

"Enough, Janine," he said harshly. "I have neither the time nor the patience for childish games. You are my slave, and I your master. You will tell me why you came fleeing into the clearing as though a fiend were at your heels."

The girl shrank before her master's obvious displeasure.

"There was nothing, my lord," she said. "Nothing but the forest." Then, when he did not speak, "I am of the desert, my lord. You cannot know what it is to be Wendaren. We are like the drifting hills of sand, never still, forever changing and yet unchanged. We learn to find the way from oasis to oasis with only the sun or the stars to guide us. For of one thing we can be certain, and that is that from one moment to the next, the sands will shift, and nothing will be forever the same. What was once a mountain becomes a plain and then a hill again. Indeed, it is like the legend of the palace that one day rises from the desert only to sink again."

She saw him stiffen and look strangely at her and wondered what she had said to make him appear as does the hawk that suddenly spots its prey.

"A castle in the valley of hills which know no heights," he murmured, a sudden smile touching his stern lips. Then the strange look was gone, and he was urging her to tell him more about the Wendaren.

"There is little more to tell, my lord. Except that I cannot be easy in the forest. I sense strange things. Eyes watching me. An evil I cannot explain, but which I know wishes me ill. We must leave the forest, my lord. I feel it! It is madness to remain here."

Her voice had risen as she spoke, and her eyes were huge and pleading on his face.

For a moment he said nothing. His brow furrowed in a thoughtful frown, and the girl experienced a wild flurry of hope that perhaps he would be persuaded to heed her warning. Then he spoke, and it was as though he had not even heard her pleas.

"Make ready, Janine," he said. "We leave for Sedgewick on the morrow." She trembled as his hand lifted to touch her hair. "But first I think we must improve your disguise. A pity to cut such lovely tresses. But they will grow again, after all."

The river was yet swollen with the run-off from the melting snow, and Janine gazed with a deep, abiding terror upon its fury. During the days of recuperation, Frayne had prepared a small raft of fallen timber lashed together with strips of leather. In dread, the girl watched him secure their packs and his sword and armor to the rude craft that was to be dragged across behind the two steeds. Then, stripped down to his breeches, the Knight of Tor beckoned to the girl.

She obeyed reluctantly. Ashamed that he must see the fear with which she looked to the task awaiting them, she came to him with head bowed, her hands clasped tightly in front of her. Trembling in every limb, she stood before him, a frightened child who yet sought to be worthy of him. Thus she did not see the wry tenderness with which he looked upon her newly shorn head shining brightly in the sunlight.

She seemed even smaller and more vulnerably

113

childish in the boyish tunic, which was too large for her slight form. And the leather breeches tucked into deerskin boots served to accentuate her graceful slenderness. He had sought to conceal her budding femininity beneath a leather vest and a flowing cape and had streaked her face with dirt to camouflage her smooth, translucent skin. Even so, there was no way to mask her lovely eyes luxuriously fringed with thick dusky eyelashes or to cover up the fine, delicate bone structure of her face. Blast! At first glance she might appear a comely youth, though rather too frail, perhaps, to be a knight's squire, but on closer observation, there could be no mistaking that this shy, dreamy-eyed stripling was in truth a girl.

Ye gods! Why could not the chit show more spirit? A knight's squire would not stand before his master in the poise of a wilting flower. Deliberately he tilted her head back, one lean hand beneath her chin, that he might better see her face. The dark lashes briefly quivered against her cheeks, then suddenly she unveiled her lustrous eyes, and inwardly he groaned. Her blue gaze met his steely glance guilelessly, indeed, with trusting innocence. Bitterly the man cursed himself for a fool. Twice he had nearly led this absurd child into the maw of death, and still would she follow him. It galled him that he had won such loyalty, he, who was the mortal son of Dred and the servant of the scheming Sorceress. And just so had one other looked upon him. Gods! It passed all bounds of reason.

He had meant to chide her for her timorousness, but the words died unspoken upon his tongue.

"It is time, little one," he said instead. "Nor shall I tell you not to fear. Yet I swear I shall let no harm befall you, if the gods are willing."

Then he lifted her to the saddle and turned to mount the warrior-steed.

The knight's bare torso shone whitely in the sun, and the newly healed scar along his ribs was an angry red against his skin. Nor was it the only mark of the warrior etched upon his strong, lean body, for he bore the record of many a battle. Yet he appeared young in years. His hair was golden in the sunlight, his face smooth, save for the week-old beard along his lean jaw. Broad shoulders tapered to a narrow waist, and his powerful limbs were well-muscled and finely molded. In aspect he appeared to the slave-girl almost a god, yet the sudden grin that bared his strong white teeth was that of a man who rejoices in a challenge to his manly strength.

Boltar, the warrior-steed, seeming to sense his master's mood, pranced and pawed the riverbank with powerful forefeet. The mare beside him sidled nervously, the whites of her eyes showing in fear. Then Frayne sent the stallion lunging into the water, and the mare was forced by the man's iron grip on the reins to plunge in after him. They came up swimming, and Janine uttered a wild cry as the current caught and swept them away.

Almost Janine forgot to breathe as terror for her master and the loyal steeds gripped her. Again she relived the nightmare of the the river pulling her into the roiling depths as she clutched the mare's tangled mane with icy fingers. But at last it was over, and the warrior-steed, his black coat streaming water, was scrambling up the far bank, the mare straggling after him. In dazed relief, the girl saw the knight leap down from the stallion's back and drag the laden raft from the grips of the river. Then she was slipping weakly from her mount, her legs giving way beneath her as her feet touched solid ground. Silently she sent a prayer of gratitude to the One.

The Knight of Tor, accompanied by his unlikely squire, followed the Glendaron northward for several leagues before topping a rise overlooking a narrow valley cupped between two low, wooded hummocks. Sprawled the length of the valley on either side of the river were a score or more log dwellings with thatched roofs. Moored to a rough wooden dock, which extended several feet into the water on the west side of the river, was a large railed barge that no doubt served as a ferry.

Frayne experienced a sudden prickle of danger as he looked out over the quiet scene. 'Twas *too* quiet, he thought, just as the forest had seemed unnaturally still the past two days of their journey through it.

At first he had sought to ignore the desert girl's growing uneasiness as they penetrated deeper into the dense woods. No doubt she would grow used to the unfamiliar confines of the forest, given time. But then he, too, had begun to sense that all was not as it should be, for the peculiar absence of wildlife had become increasingly evident. He had often had the need in the past to live off the land and had grown used to keeping an eye out for game, but he had not, since leaving the safe haven of the river island, spotted so much as a deer or even a rabbit, nor did the trees reverberate with the familiar calls of birds. He felt his nerves grow taut with a sense of waiting and more

116

than once caught himself glancing back over his shoulder, his hand upon the hilt of his knife, as he searched the shadows for something he sensed lurking just out of sight.

It was thus with a sense of relief that he looked down on the village of Sedgewick basking in the afternoon sun. It would be good to be among men again, perchance to learn what blighted the serenity of the forest. But instantly he noted the singular absence of activity about the scattered hovels. The village appeared deserted, with not even a stray dog to sound the alarm at the approach of two strangers. He wondered uneasily if the place had been visited by the plague, yet there were neither the ominous signs of newly dug graves nor the more sinister sight of corpses lying untended about the grounds—as he had witnessed before in towns visited by the black death.

His instincts, the instincts of a warrior who had ridden often into danger, urged him to give the town a wide berth. Nor was he unaware that Janine watched him with fear in her eyes, willing him to flee the brooding vale. 'Twas that which troubled him the most, for the child, huddled atop the restive mare, her face pinched and pale, seemed on the verge of panic, which was unlike the girl who had gallantly tended to his wound and so gamely overcome her terror to meet the challenge of the raging river. Still, there was a fey look about her he little liked. Blast! He was the Knight of Tor, on the Sorceress's business. He had no choice but to ride into the cursed village. Grimly he lifted the reins and touched spurs to the stallion's sides, and behind him Janine, the slave-girl, reluctantly followed.

A stiff breeze leapt suddenly out of the north carrying with it the promise of a storm, and Frayne saw the girl shiver and glance nervously about as they approached the village at a slow walk. The horses, too, grew increasingly mettlesome the nearer they came to the cluster of rude dwellings, till at last Frayne was compelled to call sharply to Janine to hold the sidling mare in lest she bolt out from under the girl.

And no wonder, mused the knight. Sedgewick was even less prepossessing when viewed close at hand than it had appeared from a distance. The mean dwellings huddled close to the ground were mere dugouts, atop which wattled log walls had been erected. Few boasted as much as a single window, and these, as well as the narrow doors, were covered with greased deer hides to keep out the cold. The interiors would be dark and airless, without so much as a hearth for a fire, and those who inhabited them would sleep huddled together for warmth on vermin-infested straw. They would cook outside over open fires when game was plentiful and chew dried strips of meat or go hungry when it was not.

The settlement appeared little different from any number of such villages Frayne had seen, which vaguely surprised him. For Sedgewick boasted a thriving lumber trade, and he had thought to see greater evidence of prosperity. Indeed, there was little sign that any logging was being done at all or had been done for quite some time. The knight began to wonder if he had come on a fool's errand, for it seemed increasingly unlikely that the man he sought would have chosen to dwell amidst such squalor.

They had traveled nearly the length of the village without spotting a soul when abruptly a long, grey shape hurtled from out of nowhere at the knight. Frayne, instinctively clutching at the beast's throat, was borne heavily to the ground beneath the snarling fury of a timber wolf. Boltar shied violently and reared, even as the mare squealed and bolted madly up the river. The enraged stallion lashed out with deadly hooves, and, striking the beast a crushing blow to the ribs, sent it tumbling from his master.

Instantly Frayne rolled from beneath the hooves of the frenzied warrior-steed and leaped agilely to his feet, Thrimheld, Swift-Blade, flashing from the scabbard. In moments he had dispatched the mortally wounded wolf from its agony and whistled shrilly to the stallion. But the great Boltar seemed utterly possessed of madness as he rolled the whites of his eyes at the knight and tossed his noble head. Nostrils flaring, the stallion pranced and pawed at the earth. Cautiously Frayne sheathed his sword and called softly to the faithful steed whose loyalty he had never before questioned. For Boltar, son of Alderon of the breed of Zendar, warrior-steeds all, had carried him through many a battle. But Boltar looked upon his master as though he beheld an enemy, and behind him appeared the slinking forms of wolves gathering for the kill.

"Ho, Boltar. Steady!" called Frayne and edged closer to the sidling steed. The horse snorted and reared, sending forth the clarion cry of the stallion whose blood runs hot with battlelust. Frayne ducked beneath the flailing forefeet and leaped for the bridle. The steed screamed in rage as the man's powerful arm closed over the arching neck to grasp the mane. Boltar wheeled and reared again, carrying the man with him. Then, when the horse came down on all fours, the man sprang to the saddle. Filled with hatred for the man-beast clinging to his back, Boltar, the warrior-steed, erupted into fury. He bowed his back and leaped into the air to come down stiff-legged, then leaped again, kicking high with back feet extended. But the man held grimly on, clinging with powerful thighs and riding out each jarring lunge with graceful suppleness. Still the battle-steed fought on. Curvetting and buckjumping, he pitched about the clearing, scattering the grinning wolves and working himself into a frenzy, until at last he plunged stiffly to a halt, head down and sides heaving, a foaming froth dripping from his mouth.

"So. The evil is real," breathed the knight and leaned down to run one lean hand along the stallion's neck lathered with sweat. The horse nickered softly, its ears twitching back, listening to the soft, crooning voice of the man who had mastered him. "But together we have fought the madness and perhaps conquered it." Yet the sudden low growl of a great, rangy white wolf reminded him that the real battle was yet to come. The knight glanced up to behold the wolf-pack gathered in a snarling circle about him. With a curse he drew his sword and thought fleetingly of Janine alone and helpless somewhere in the forest. May the gods keep her safe, he muttered harshly and steeled himself for the coming battle.

They were lean and hungry with dull, shaggy pelts and eyes that gleamed palely in the fading sunlight with mindless hate. Except for the white rogue who stood slightly apart from them. The man's hair stood on end as the great beast looked him boldly in the eye. What manner of wolf was this, he marveled, not to fear the look of a man's eyes. Larger and fitter than the rest, the white rogue emitted a low whine and suddenly sniffed the air as if sensing something about the man and the horse that made him warier than the others. Nor had he the crazed look of the circling pack, but seemed fretful and uncertain.

Then Frayne forgot the rogue as one of the grey, slinking creatures leaped suddenly at the stallion's throat. Boltar wheeled sluggishly and stumbled, nearly falling to his knees, but the knight's sword slashed out and down, cleaving the beast's skull. As if heartened by the smell of fresh blood, the pack rushed to the attack. In grim despair, Frayne fended them off and called to the weary warrior-steed's fighting heart. The great stallion, in whose veins flowed the blood of Zendar, rallied at the warrior's battle-cry. As of old, Boltar fought bravely for his master, and many wolves died. Yet more came to take their place, and at last even the stallion's strength was spent. Frayne felt him falter and flung himself into the midst of the snarling pack as the war-horse shuddered and went down.

It seemed then the madness took the knight as he slashed and yelled, eager to kill. The wolves fell away from him to circle cautiously, and the knight followed, wielding the sword with deadly efficiency. Until at last the pack broke and slunk away into dusk's deepening shadows—all of them but the white rogue.

Frayne stood with heaving chest before the final brute. The knight was gory with the blood of the wolves he had slain and with his own blood flowing

121

unheeded from countless wounds. Half a score of the dead beasts littered the ground, yet still his veins throbbed with the lust to kill as deliberately he lifted the sword toward the grinning rogue.

The white wolf bared gleaming fangs at the knight's approach. Noiselessly he began to weave with a gliding stride back and forth, his uncanny stare unwinking on the man's eyes glittering silvery between slitted lids. It came to the man that he faced something other than a wolf. Then all thought fled as the rogue suddenly stilled. With a low menacing growl, it crouched ready to spring.

"Crane, no!"

The rending cry echoed through the falling night. The white rogue leaped for the man balanced easily on the balls of his feet. The knight raised his sword. Then Frayne was neatly thrust to one side by a hurtling weight, and another, slighter warrior met the rangy wolf's snarling attack.

Frayne, quickly catching himself, wheeled to see a slender girl falling backward, her knees bent beneath the beast. Her legs straightened and the wolf was thrown toppling over her head. Instantly she somersaulted to her feet, and launching herself at the stunned creature, leaped quickly astride his back.

"Crane! In the name of the One, I command you to return to yourself."

Fearing that he had succumbed to the madness that plagued the blighted village, Frayne saw the wolf's form begin to waver, until he beheld not a wolf at all, but a red-haired, freckle-faced boy. Then he groaned and slowly shook his head. For unless he had indeed gone mad, he saw his sweet Enchantress standing there before him.

Caught in the grips of an unreality, he watched the girl walk slowly up to him. Her eyes shone golden in the fading light, and tears shimmered in their depths. Her lovely lips parted over kitten teeth, as hesitantly she raised trembling fingers to touch his cheek.

"Frayne?" she whispered when he neither moved nor spoke. "Do you not know me? 'Tis I, Aurora."

"Gods!" he groaned. "What madness is this?"

Then she was in his arms and his lips had found hers. And suddenly he no longer cared if it was madness or not. For indeed Aurora, his sweet Enchantress, had returned to him.

Chapter Five

With the knight's embrace, the world seemed to dissolve away, leaving Aurora soaring in the universe of Frayne's arms. She had never known love could be like this—two souls awakening to life after an eternity of emptiness. Or was it more the terrifying agony of death? For suddenly she was lost to an aching, endless yearning, which only Frayne aroused and only Frayne could appease. She had suffered the torment of the crystal's piercing flames and known the ecstasy of Andruvien's pulsating power. But that was as nothing compared to this—the bewitching, bewildering rapture of Frayne's kiss.

"Aurora," he breathed at last and buried his face in her luxurious raven hair. "Gods, I believed you were dead."

Fiercely Aurora clung to the knight, afraid that if she let go he would suddenly vanish. Surely it was all a part of the madness, the sickness that infested the forest and the village and had at last even taken over Crane. Was it only five days before that they had fled the stalking wolves and seen the first signs of mania in Elwindolf? It seemed longer. Indeed, she could not remember when she had not felt the unknown terror lurking always at the fringes of her mind. She shuddered uncontrollably recalling how at last they had had to bind the tormented woodsman to keep him from flinging himself to the relentless pack. It had been hard enough to watch the impenetrable Elwindolf slowly stripped of his reason, but then, suddenly to behold Crane a wolf disappearing into the forest to join the pack had been almost enough to break her mind. Yet she had not succumbed to the madness. Nay. For she was Aurora and Andruvien, and she had had Elwindolf to care for and protect. In the end it was the crystal that had sustained her, and the crystal that had led her to the safety of the Sacred Grove.

Suddenly she became aware that Frayne had pulled away from her. She glanced up into the shadowed planes of his face and could not believe the One had so quickly answered her prayers. How she had longed to have Frayne with her as she had tracked Crane for seemingly endless days through the hostile forest. How she had needed his indomitable strength to bolster her own and his cool judgment to temper her impulsiveness. And, miraculously, he had come.

The moon had risen in the east to bathe the valley in its gentle glow, but the man's face was unreadable in the shadows. Even so, Aurora sensed a sudden urgency in him. Then she remembered Crane and Boltar as the knight wordlessly put her from him to go to the stallion.

The warrior-steed lay on his side, the noble head outstretched upon the ground, but he was alive, for when Frayne knelt to run gentle hands along his neck, the stallion whickered and struggled to rise.

"Easy, old friend," the knight murmured, his voice husky as the stricken horse fell back again, the breath blowing heavily through quivering nostrils.

"He does not appear to be greatly injured," Aurora ventured uncertainly, for though he was marked with numerous slashes, none appeared to be mortal wounds.

"It is the sickness," Crane said harshly, stepping out of the shadows to stand peering down at the man who knelt beside the stallion. "It eats at the will until there is nothing left but the desire for death."

An uneasy silence fell over the three as Frayne stared up at the youth's rigid form. The thin features looked pale and drawn in the moonlight, and there was a tautness about the sensitive mouth that had not been there six months before. Yet he was the same gawky, dreamy-eyed boy the man remembered, and it was clear he still nourished a hopeless infatuation for Aurora. For the shape-changer was here with her, and Frayne could feel him bristling with the old pent-up resentment. Then the Enchantress had come to kneel beside him, and for a moment he forgot Crane as his senses reeled with the wonder of her tantalizing nearness. He would have taken her then, the boy be damned. But Janine was alone in the forest and he should already have been in pursuit of her. A grim smile touched his lips. His sweet Aurora would never know what it cost him to leave her untouched after the months of bitter anguish.

Then his lovely tormentress was speaking and he was forced to concentrate on her words.

"If what Crane says is true, then perchance there is hope," she said quietly. "There is a place where the evil cannot go. I have been there and seen the sickness banished from one who was afflicted. I had meant to take Crane there to bring him back to himself, but now he shall take us."

The knight's look was quizzical on her face.

"Can the shape-changer now materialize where he has never been?" he asked.

Oh, gods, Aurora thought and caught her lip between her teeth in sudden consternation. Frayne had never known she had learned to commune with Crane even as she had always done with the animals of the forest. Nor would he like it very well, she doubted not, for once she had assured him she could not read the thoughts of men and he had seemed much relieved. Well, there was nothing for it now but that she must admit the truth and hope he did not look upon her with the old, maddening suspicion.

"Nay," she said in a low voice. Then her head lifted in that proud gesture of stubborn independence that had ever been her way, and Frayne was hard put not to crush her to him. "But I have learned to meld my thoughts with his so that he sees what I have seen. Together we can go where I alone have been."

"Can you then read a man's thoughts?" he asked, his glance hard upon her face. "Can you read mine?"

"Not if you do not wish it," she hurried to answer him. Then, reluctantly, "Mayhap. I—I know not, for I have never tried."

Helplessly she watched him turn away from her.

Had nothing changed, then? Had he still not learned to trust her? And hard upon that thought came the first stirrings of indignation. Surely, even if she could read his thoughts, he did not dare to think she would seek to invade his ever-precious privacy. She would not use him so! Besides, she did not think the way she had of communing with Crane was reading his mind exactly, for it was no different from the way in which she spoke with the animals of the forest. She simply sent her thoughts outward and they responded in like manner. Nay. She had done nothing for which to feel ashamed.

Almost she voiced her indignation out loud, but then he was looking at her again, and she was struck suddenly speechless by something odd in his manner towards her.

"So. The Enchantress begins to grow into her power," he murmured enigmatically, and Aurora had the strange feeling that he had not been at all surprised at her revelation, indeed, that he might even have expected it of her. What else did he know or suspect about her? she wondered, and, naughtily, what *would* happen if ever she were to try to penetrate his closely guarded thoughts? But such interesting musings had perforce to wait until a later time, for Frayne had risen and was looking speculatively at Crane's sullen front.

"I should be grateful if you will do what you can for Boltar," the man said evenly.

The boy shifted nervously beneath the knight's unwavering stare. He still felt battered and a little bewildered at being so abruptly wrenched from the grips of the madness that had transformed him into a killing beast. Then suddenly to awaken to Aurora in Frayne's embrace! He shuddered a little, remembering how he had experienced a sharp regret that the Enchantress had interfered. And whether he regretted the prevention of Frayne's death or his own was unclear even in his own mind. But the Knight of Tor awaited an answer, and Aurora's gaze was expectant. Reluctantly he ducked his head in grudging assent.

"I'll do whatever Aurora wants," he muttered ungraciously.

Frayne nodded, then appeared to hesitate. When at last he spoke again, it was with the candor of one man to another.

"Crane, I'd never have ridden away if I hadn't believed you had gotten Aurora safely out of that cursed mountain. I have my own way of knowing things. It wasn't until later, when the Sorceress tricked me into believing you were both dead, that I ever suffered any doubts. You can believe that or not. But I'd like to think we could be friends again someday."

Without waiting for the boy to answer, the knight turned then to the Enchantress.

"Take Boltar to this protected place, if you will, and I shall come for him there when I am able."

A small gasp escaped the girl's lips.

"But you are coming with us?" she cried in sudden alarm and scrambled quickly to her feet. One small hand gripped his sleeve, as if by this she would keep him with her.

A strange, unreadable smile touched his lips as he gazed into the lovely eyes raised beseechingly to his. Deliberately he cupped her face between his hands

130

and slowly shook his head.

"No, not this time. I have other business in the Forest, which cannot wait." A shadow flickered across his brow. "I only hope I am not too late. Now quickly. Tell me about this place. How shall I find it?"

"It isn't far from here," Aurora answered, disappointment keen in her voice. "Go north along the river to the falls. 'Tis no more than a mile. Then west till you come to the tamaracks. You will know when you are there. You will feel a strange peacefulness steal over you. As if the troubles you carry with you are suddenly insignificant. 'Tis the Sacred Grove, and at its center stands the Shrine of the Holy Maiden."

She felt him go suddenly quite still.

"Frayne? What is it?" she queried sharply.

The silvery eyes were curiously blank as he stared beyond Aurora at the spreading valley. In alarm she saw the muscle leap along his jawline and his lips thin to a grim line. She reached up to cover his hands with hers.

"Frayne?" she repeated softly.

As if suddenly released from some dark spell, he expelled a long, shuddering breath and laughed shortly, an oddly harsh sound in the taut quiet of the night.

"I should have guessed," he muttered as if to himself, and the old hard, cynical smile curled his lip in the way she remembered all too well. "But then it was all so long ago, and this was not Sedgewick then."

"I-I don't understand," Aurora said doubtfully, then suddenly she experienced a growing pique at this exasperating turn of events. Why must he ever be so infuriatingly mysterious? And why did he seem so anxious to be quit of her? While she had suffered the desolation of having lost him, he apparently had forgotten her. Bitterly she recalled Vandrel's promise that she would again lie in the arms of her love. But he would leave her, no doubt, to carry out the Sorceress's bidding. Oh, this was not at all the way she had dreamt it would be! He was indeed the man-beast, for he had no heart!

Frayne, who had observed with tender amusement the interesting display of emotions sweep across the Enchantress's face, recognized the signs of her tempestuous temper.

"No. How could you," he drawled placatingly, but Aurora saw the suspicious twitch at the corners of his mouth. Gods! He dared to laugh at her! "Never mind," he continued maddeningly. "It need not concern you."

Then, before she could deliver the stinging retort that trembled on her lips, he drew her close and pressed his mouth hungrily to hers.

Even as Aurora cursed her traitorous body for melting so obligingly to his, she knew herself to be lost. No matter how odiously he treated her, still would the flames of desire ignite at a glance from the silvery falcon eyes, still would she cleave to his lean strength and thrill to the caress of his lips and hands. She was Aurora, the Enchantress, and he was Frayne. She would always be his to command.

When at last he lifted his head to gaze long into her face, he was breathing heavily and his eyes were dark with passion. Ruefully he acknowledged to himself that she had yet the power to unman him. She was the Enchantress, and he felt the hand of the god upon

132

her.

"Wait for me in the Sacred Grove," he whispered huskily.

"Frayne," she murmured, her golden eyes guileless on his face. "Just tell me one thing."

"If I can," he promised, dropping a kiss on the tip of her nose.

The fingers of one slim hand trickled beguilingly down his cheek.

"Does this business in the forest concern the Sorceress? Is it another quest?"

"That's two things," he chided and nibbled tantalizingly at her earlobe so that she shuddered in helpless pleasure. "Look after Boltar and the boy. And wait for me."

Then he left her to stride swiftly away through the moonlight.

He had nearly vanished into the shadows when suddenly the Enchantress straightened to her full height and called ringingly after him, "I'll see to Boltar, Knight of Tor! But don't expect to find me waiting tamely for you in the grove. I'm Aurora! I have business of my own in the forest!"

He gave no sign that he had heard her as he disappeared from view into the woods.

"Blast!" she exploded and whipped around to find Crane watching her sulkily. "And you!" she added witheringly, having suddenly recalled *his* multiple transgressions. "Have you any idea the trouble you have caused me? If ever you run off like that again, I swear I shall call down all eleven hundred Droonish curses on your head."

"Aw, Aurora. You know that's not fair. I couldn't

133

help myself," he protested miserably. He had never seen the raven-haired beauty so incensed. Indeed, she hardly resembled the sweet, impetuous girl who had won his heart. Suddenly he had an inkling of what Baldrac and Cranith must have felt as they faced the wrath of the Enchantress fully roused. For so she appeared at that moment as she fairly scintillated with frustrated power.

"Then go back to Vandrel's valley until you can," she said flatly. "Next time I might not be around to save you from your folly."

Her anger suffered a check as she saw the boy wince at her harsh judgment. But she would not take back her words. Nay. For he had endangered his life as well as hers. And Frayne! She could not forget the helpless terror of seeing the bloodied knight on the point of skewering the young shape-changer. He had been awesome. A god aroused to a vengeful fury. Another second, and she would have been too late to avert the tragedy. Nay. She could not call back her words. Crane would stay in the Sacred Grove or he would return to Vandrel's cottage.

The grove of tamaracks was as peaceful as Aurora had described it, and already Boltar was up and grazing contentedly. Yet it had seemingly lost the power to soothe the Enchantress's troubled heart, Crane mused somberly as he watched the slender girl pace up and down before a solemn-faced Elwindolf. The boy found it difficult to believe that he had ever beheld the taciturn woodsman raving like a maniac, for he appeared as enduring as the forest itself. But then, he had never thought to stalk the Knight of Tor

134

with murder in his heart, he reflected in bitter shame.

Since coming to the grove, he had begun to see things more clearly. He knew now that the madness had not come from outside himself. It had always lurked within him, his resentment toward Frayne, his jealousy. The knight was everything he would wish to be and could never become, and, too, Frayne possessed Aurora's love. That had been the seed from which the madness had sprouted, and the evil had fed it till it had made him the rogue wolf, keen to kill.

Bitterly he recalled the Enchantress's enraged denunciation of him. Oh, gods! She had been right to accuse him, for he stood condemned in his own eyes. But he was purged of the madness. He knew it. For he had gazed upon the serene face of the Holy Maiden and seen the truth.

His glance strayed to the vine-covered statuary intricately carved from wood. The life-sized figure of the sylphlike maiden seated among various creatures of the forest had been rendered with such an aura of reality that Crane almost expected her to speak. The serene countenance was possessed of a haunting beauty, and the eyes, gazing steadily toward the sky, as though they beheld a vision of the One—to whom she had been dedicated—were expressive of an all-encompassing love and enduring faith. They inspired a feeling of awe in the young shape-changer, who had never been much given to metaphysical contemplation. Yet there was about the Shrine enveloped in wildflowers and moonseed a feeling of timelessness. Indeed, Elwindolf had said the Shrine of the gentle Maiden of the Tamarack Grove was very old, though the legends that surrounded the coming of the

Valdoran Virgin to Dalmurn were yet told among the descendants of those who inhabited the valley. Thus, compelled by the Enchantress, Elwindolf had related the tale of Ariana, the Holy Maiden.

Dalmurn, called Sedgewick because of the triumph of light over dark, had been cursed by Dred, the Prince of Throm, against whose legions the dwellers of the valley had fought in the Second Uprising. Few of the stalwart Sons of Vail had returned from the wars, but those who had survived came home to a land enshrouded in a cloud of never-ending fog and mist, summoned, unbeknownst to them, by Dred himself, that he might conceal himself from the pursuing vengeance of Harmon, the Warrior-God of the Eilderood. Believing they had in some way incurred the displeasure of the One, the villagers sent forth Lathrop, the young son of the village elder, to seek the Valdoran of Kathoradign, which lies in the Land of Irid, amidst the Mountains of Thunder, that the Holy Maidens who serve the One might intercede on their behalf.

Many days did Lathrop journey to the north and east and many adventures had he ere at last he came to the mountains. Yet no trace of Kathoradign or the Holy Maidens could he discover, until at last, weary and heartsick, Lathrop lay beneath a Tamarack. Offering up a prayer to the One, he fell into a deep slumber. In his sleep the lad was visited with a dream of dark portent, for in it a lovely hind was slain by the jackal. Lathrop awakened greatly troubled, and sitting near him was a beautiful young girl weaving her long flaxen hair into braids.

Seeing that he was afraid, the maiden said unto

him, "Have no fear. For I am Ariana, and I am come into the land of darkness to show the way to him who would vanquish the Prince of Throm." So saying, she smiled and beckoned for him to rise, and, lo and behold, he found himself in the valley that was his homeland.

"Return to the village and tell your people all that I have said. And know this. When the blood of the hind seeps into the soil, the darkness shall be banished. Then shall you come to the Grove of the Tamaracks and build there a shrine to house the Arlana."

Then she wept a single tear, and taking it from her cheek upon one finger, gave it to the village boy, who beheld it in speechless wonder. For in his hand was a perfect crystal, from which radiated all the colors of the rainbow.

"In the Tongue of the Beginnings this is Arlana, which is the pledge of the One that so long as the Virgin's Tear remains undefiled the Sons of Vail shall prosper. Go now and be of good cheer, for soon you shall know again the triumph of the light over darkness."

Then had Lathrop knelt to kiss the Valdoran's hand, for so he knew her to be, and gazing up in heartfelt gratitude, he beheld her weep a second tear, which rolled unheeded from her cheek to fall into the grass. This one he left where it lay, for he was an honest lad who had no thought of taking unto himself that which was not his own. And 'twas he who returned to build the Shrine when the darkness had passed, and he who with his own hands and loving heart carved the figures of Ariana and the animals about her feet.

Thus had Elwindolf's story ended, leaving the Enchantress filled with questions that had set her to pacing restlessly before the shrine.

"There can be no doubt that the Arlana has been stolen," she said and paused to study the faint scratches on the statue where the crystal had been removed. "That is the cause of the sickness. But why is the grove unaffected? And how can the evil be placated?"

"The second tear," Crane interjected. "It must still be here. That's why the grove is safe."

"Aye." The Enchantress nodded. "That could explain it. And mayhap it needs only the restoration of the stolen tear to make things right again, though the legend does not promise it. But where do we look? Who could have taken it?"

Crane retreated once more into contemplative silence. Indeed, who? he wondered. Then Elwindolf, who had been quietly watching the other two, spoke at length, which in itself was curious, for seldom did the woodsman vouchsafe more than a word or two.

"There came to Sedgewick a man who little fitted in the company of woodsmen. Small and slippery was he, with the eyes of Ommat, the Ferret. When first he walked amongst the Vailmen, he was all smiles and friendliness to any that might tell the old tales of the Holy Maiden and the Arlana. Then one day he went into the woods and for three days was not seen. And when he appeared again, changed he be. None did he welcome into his hut, nor of Arlana and the tear would he speak. He looked at everyone suspiciously and watched his back if ever he ventured forth. He be a lapidary by trade and more used to the city, methinks. I have sometimes wondered what brought Anders Groul to Sedgewick."

The woodsman's soft-spoken words had stilled Aurora's fitful perambulations, and now she stared into the impassive features of Elwindolf with a singular intensity.

"Mayhap I should seek out this mysterious lapidary. What think you?" she said. "Know you were he is to be found?"

Slowly Elwindolf shook his head, his pale blue eyes never leaving Aurora's face.

"Groul be the first taken by the madness. Screaming like the banshee, he fled into the woods, and none has since laid eyes on him. None but Phelan, Father-Wolf."

"How do you know this, Elwindolf?" Aurora asked.

"When Phelan came to kill the man-cub, he said to Drude, called 'Wolf,' that Ommat, the Ferret, had been bewitched and wandered the forest in the shape of a man. The stench of evil about the man-beast was strong. Nor would the Brethren of the Hunt go near him. He be holed up somewhere in the brakes, methinks. Where none can find him."

"Nay. I shall find him," vowed the Enchantress darkly, and Crane, watching her, shivered.

"But it won't happen again. I swear, Aurora," Crane pleaded as he watched the girl carefully fold into her pack the raiment given her by Vandrel. Swiftly Aurora strapped the light pack to her back and straightened.

The Enchantress had donned her dryad gown,

belted about the waist with a leather girdle, from which hung her elfin blade, Glaiveling, or "Little Sword" in the tongue of men. Her raven locks she had plaited into a single braid down her back. Her legs and feet were bare beneath the thigh-length gown of green gossamer. She looked the elusive wood-sprite raised by dryads to slip unseen through the thick foliage of the trees; and more, thought Crane, self-consciously averting his eyes from her tantalizing beauty. For the thin gown did little to conceal her lithe form, nor was she conscious of the unsettling effect she was having on her youthful comrade. Her thoughts were on Groul and the stolen Arlana she was sworn to recover. And to Frayne, who also had had pressing business in the Forest. Nor would it have occurred to her that she should conceal herself from the eyes of men, thought Crane distractedly, for the Enchantress was yet as innocent as the forest that had fostered her.

"Nay, Crane," Aurora said at last and turned to look earnestly into his thin, sulky face. " 'Tis sorry I am that I must leave you, for I do believe the Sacred Grove has cured you of any lingering madness. But I shall travel more quickly in the manner of the Dryads. And unseen. 'Tis better thus, for the darkness grows, and I feel that time is precious now."

The boy glanced uneasily at the afternoon sky in which great, tumid clouds were slowly gathering. There was an ominous calm about the forest. Not even the whisper of a breeze disturbed the quiet of the trees, and the air was thick and oppressive with the promise of a storm.

"It's only going to rain," he insisted stubbornly, but

he could not conceal the slight shiver that rippled down his back and caused the hair to stand up at the nape of his neck. It had not the feel of a mere evening shower. Indeed, the woods seemed charged with a sense of taut expectancy. The storm, when it broke, would burst forth with the fury of an unbridled tempest. And Aurora would be somewhere alone in it.

"Then see that you and Elwindolf find shelter. I am sorry, Crane. But I don't have time to argue."

Her smile was a little crooked as she reached up on tiptoe to kiss his cheek.

"Have a care for yourself, Crane," she whispered. "And don't worry. I can take care of myself."

She was gone then, vanished into the thick, leafy branches of a tree before he could recover from her sweet caress. His hand rose to touch his cheek as he stared after her. Then he swallowed hard and dashed the back of his hand across his eyes. Fleetingly he glanced at the stone-faced Elwindolf.

"I can't let her go alone," he said shortly, and suddenly his lanky form began to waver and collapse upon itself, till naught was left but a ruby-crowned kinglet winging from the grove in swift pursuit of the Enchantress.

Phelan, Father-Wolf, slipped stealthily through the underbrush, six shadows, slinking noiselessly in his wake, all that remained of the pack. Periodically he paused to test the air with his pointed snout. Then his hackles would rise and a low growl would grate deep in his throat. It was the hated man-scent that fed the hard glitter of his eyes and drew him inexorably deeper into the forest.

They had been following the faint spoor all that day, their bellies hollow with hunger and their senses raw with bloodlust. Yet they practiced the patience of the hunt, for they had been born to this game, and none could play it better. Nor did their unsuspecting quarry promise to be anything but easy prey, for the stench of fear clung to the man-beast, and it fled in mindless panic as one who knew not the secret ways of the forest.

Phelan froze at the sudden crash of underbrush close by. Behind him one of the younger wolves snarled and tensed, ready to spring.

"Nay, Little Brother," Phelan growled warningly. "It be the slave-beast. We have easier game."

With hungry eyes the wolves watched the frightened horse bolt out of sight through the trees. Then Phelan sniffed the air and padded noiselessly along its backtrail, his blood running hot with the scent of the kill close at hand.

The larger game had fled north with the coming of the evil to the valley, and even mice and rats had grown scarce. Thus the pack had not eaten well for several days, not since the last of the man-beasts had gone south on the river crafts, abandoning Sedgewick to the ravaging beasts. They had all gone, save for Ommat who hid in the cave above the river, and these new ones who had come bearing the long tooth and riding the slave-beasts with the killing feet. The big one with the shiny skin had slain many of the Brethren. But the small one, the frightened cub, was somewhere very near, for the scent had grown strong indeed.

Phelan's mouth drooled at the thought of the tender

prey. For he had been the first to break Taboo, the first to slay a man-beast, and now he hungered for the salty flesh. Forgotten in his madness to kill was Elwindolf, the man-cub he had taken into his own den, the one who had run at Phelan's side and called him Father. There was only the burning lust for the blood of the spawn of the man-seed, till none should dare to enter the wolf's domain again. Then would Phelan rule the forest. Phelan, the king of wolves.

The muffled sob of the frightened man-cub carried easily to the wolf's keen ears despite the rising howl of an uneasy wind. The woods were dark with the deepening shadows of false dusk as the gathering storm clouds swallowed the rays of the fading sun. Yet Phelan noticed none of these, except for the whimper of the helpless prey so near, so very near at last.

The child lay weeping in a crumpled heap on the forest floor as the seven gaunt shadows stole out of the thornhedge thicket, yellowed fangs gleaming in wolf-ish smiles. Alerted by some primeval instinct for survival, it suddenly stiffened and raised its head. One small fist rose to stifle a pitiful cry of terror at sight of the malevolent creatures slinking near. Helplessly it scrambled backward through the dirt and grass till it came up against a tall cottonwood tree and froze, paralyzed with fright, its eyes wide and mesmerized on the stalking beasts.

Phelan licked ghoulish lips.

"Ah, little man-spawn," he crooned deep in his throat. "Thou needst not fear. Thy death shall come quick and painless upon thee. That much will Phelan grant thee, for his belly clamors to be fed."

"Then shall it clamor yet, yellow dog of Amaur,"

reverberated a soundless voice within Phelan's thoughts, "for thou shalt not harm the child."

The lean wolf snarled and spun sharply around to face the suddenly cowering beasts behind him.

"Darest one of the Brethren to mock the mighty Phelan?" he growled.

" 'The mighty Phelan' is a traitor to his kind, unworthy to lead a pack of hounds, for he has broken Taboo and brought grief to the Brethren. Thus shall ill-luck pursue him to the death, even as it has thinned the ranks of the once-proud wolves. How many lie dead already to the long tooth of the man-beast? How many more shall fall dost thou slay the man-beast's cub?"

"Who art thou to accuse Phelan? Show thyself, Serpent's Tongue, that I may know thee."

"I am Aurora, tree-child to the dryads and Enchantress of the Glade," taunted the hateful voice, and suddenly a slender figure dropped lightly down from the cottonwood beneath which the child cowered. "Behold, Phelan, Worm-Wolf, I am here." And boldly she stepped forward to stand between the wolf and the wide-eyed child, the silvery elfin blade in her hand.

Phelan sidled sinuously before the fearless man-spawn who dared to shower upon his head insults couched in the Ancient Tongue. Deadly malice glittered in the wolfish eyes, for instantly he recognized the one who had snatched Elwindolf from the maw of death.

"Then thou shalt die as well, fool!" he snarled and leaped for the unprotected throat of the girl.

The twang of a bowstring and the muffled thud of

144

an arrow into flesh was lost in the howling fury of the wolves springing in for the kill. The Enchantress went down beneath Phelan's hurtling weight, but the arrow had already done its work. Phelan, who would be king of the forest, lay stunned and mortally wounded on top of her.

Frantically Aurora struggled to free herself of the dying wolf, while all around her utter chaos seemed to have broken loose. The din of the attacking wolves changed suddenly to fear as joined to their keening voices came the bloodcurdling yowl of a mountain lion. Then, with a final frenzy of strength, Aurora had slipped out from under Phelan's limp body. Rolling clear of him, she scrambled quickly to her feet and turned to see Phelan's intended victim cringing against the tree, and before the child, a great, tawny, green-eyed cat.

"Ye gods!" Aurora thought fleetingly. "Crane! And Elwindolf!"

The shape-changer, in the form of the mountain lion, crouched protectively between the child and the snapping wolves, its ears back and fangs bared, and beside him Elwindolf, stone-faced and deadly, deliberately nocked another arrow. Aurora shivered at the sight of the pale eyes so utterly devoid of emotion, and then she was running swiftly across the glade as two of the maddened beasts sprang at Crane and another leaped for the unprotected tendons of his back legs. In moments one or both might lie dead, and certainly more than one of the attacking wolves. She must stop the bloodshed ere it had gone so far. Then, to add to the confusion, the Knight of Tor astride a white-eyed mare rode furiously into the fray, Thrimheld flashing in the fading light of the sun.

In momentary surprise she saw the child straighten, a look of glad-eyed joy lighting the bloodless face, and suddenly she realized the boy must be the knight's servant as she heard him cry, "My Lord Frayne! Master!"

Then Aurora drew forth Andruvien.

"Stop it!" she cried ringingly, and white flames leaped from her hand.

Instantly the wolves fell back whimpering, while Elwindolf and Crane suddenly froze. Frayne fought to still his fear-crazed mount, and beyond him the child stared in stricken silence at the raven-haired Enchantress shimmering with power.

Then the silvery fire seemed suddenly quenched, and Aurora strode fearlessly to confront the wolves unarmed.

"Aurora! No!" Frayne shouted, but the Enchantress paid him no heed as she gazed with sorrow at the hate-filled, bristling beasts, for wolfkind had been fashioned by the Creator's own hand, and thus once had been noble denizens of the wild.

"Peace, wolf brothers," she said in the Tongue of the Old Ones. "We are not your enemies."

"You lie," whispered Phelan's voice of loathing in her mind, and she turned to see the father-wolf crouched feebly on his haunches, front feet stiffly braced. The noble head hung low and blood discolored the saliva dripping from his mouth, but the pain-glazed eyes watched her with venomous hate.

"Nay, Phelan," she denied, grieved that one of her kind had been the cause of so much havoc. "For I am Aurora and Andruvien and can speak not but the

146

truth. Your enemy and ours is he who took from the Sacred Grove the Arlana, which kept the evil at bay. You know him and where he is, for he is the wild man-beast, whom you call Ommat."

But the madness yet burned in Phelan's brain, and though his lifeblood flowed in an ever-widening pool from his body, yet would he take this man-beast with him into the dark realm of death. Steeling himself to make the final leap, he slowly lifted his snout and sounded the chilling cry of the blood-rite. It was the ancient call for the gathering of the pack, and the Brethren, true to their kind, took up the keening cry.

"Aurora, get back!" Frayne shouted and swung down from the saddle in readiness to spring to the Enchantress's defense. Elwindolf, too, lifted the great bow, Valarc, and Crane, still in the awesome form of the mountain lion, growled menacingly. The wind prowled restlessly through the trees, and the darkness deepened as the storm clouds thickened ominously overhead. Yet the slim girl heeded none of it. Her golden eyes were fixed and staring on the defiant Phelan, who even in the face of death would seek to kill his hated enemy.

As if entranced, she watched the beast gather himself for the attack. Behind her she could feel the others closing in for the kill—and the evil, like malicious laughter, carried on the breeze, taunting her to call forth the power of the crystal.

"Andruvien," whispered the insidious voice within her brain. "Andruvien." And the crystal throbbed within her clenched fist as if in answer, bidding her to set loose its killing flame.

Slowly her hand lifted as if possessed of a will of its

own.

"Kill, kill," moaned the wind.

And then another's voice echoed hauntingly through her mind—Endrith's, as she had heard it long ago telling her of the Vendrenin's ancient power. "It is never possessed by another, but may be wielded by one whose will is greater. Even so is the sliver of the Vendrenin. Either you command it, or it shall command you."

"Nay!" she cried ringingly and dropped her hand. Behind her Frayne cursed as the wolves moved between him and his love. The child screamed, seeing the valiant girl about to be set upon by the closing circle of wolves.

Then the voice of the Enchantress lifted in spellbinding song, and from her slender form radiated a silvery glow. The wind hushed, and the trees grew still, and even the storm-clouded dusk seemed suddenly less dark. Slowly Frayne lowered his sword as he saw Phelan's eyes go blank with death and the wolfpack's killing fury tamed by the song of power. And behind him the great tawny cat began to waver and blur until Crane's boyish form materialized in its stead. Slowly Frayne relaxed, for the hand of the god was upon them all.

Elwindolf knelt beside Phelan, Father-Wolf, and his face was harsh with grief. Bitterly he cursed the fate that had brought him in pursuit of the shapechanger to this place of death. He should have been the one to die, for twice over he owed the old wolf his life. Yet he, Drude called "Wolf," still lived, and 'twas Phelan whose blood stained the ground. Why? What was the evil that could turn brethren against brethren and father against son? He winced as someone draped a woollen blanket across his shoulders. In hurt perplexity, he glanced up into the golden eyes of the Enchantress.

"I be not young in the ways of the forest," he said slowly. "Many times have I seen death. I have hunted with the pack and shared in the killing. But there was never shame in it. Mayhap 'tis cruel that some must die that others might live. Yet it be necessary and the Law of the Land. For 'tis the cycle of being set into motion by the Creator long ago. But this." And he turned to look once more upon the wolf's lifeless body. "This be a thing outside the Law."

"Aye. The sickness is a part of Dred's lingering evil. Yet you must not blame yourself for Phelan's death. Indeed, 'twas not Phelan who fell to your arrow, for the father-wolf was death long ere the shaft struck his heart. This was a thing of Dred's, and it had to die."

Elwindolf made no answer, and at last Aurora left him to his grief and returned to the campfire beside which Frayne waited, staring into the flames. For a moment Aurora stood looking down at the clear-cut profile of her beloved as he reclined upon the bed she had fashioned from their cloaks spread over freshly gathered fronds, his long legs outstretched before him crossed carelessly at the ankles and his powerful shoulders propped against a log at his back.

How many times in the past had she seen him thus, his brow dark with brooding, the firelight flickering shadows across the planes of his face. Somewhere since leaving her in the empty village he had taken time to rid himself of the stains of battle, and he appeared less the awesome knight and more the man who set her pulse to racing. How she longed to trail her fingers through his hair and tease him from his dark thoughts, until at last he crushed her to him and bent her to his will. And once she would have done it. Yet now she felt unwontedly daunted by his strange mood, for he had been forbiddingly silent and maddeningly aloof since they had at last found themselves alone. Alone except for Elwindolf, who was lost in grief, for Frayne had ordered the young shapechanger to take his servant and the mare to the Sacred Grove. The child had been feverish and ill, the blue eyes huge and fey in the bloodless face. And Aurora had thought it exceedingly strange that Frayne should choose to take such a one into danger with him.

"He's an odd boy," Aurora said at last, coming to stand before the knight.

Frayne's eyes, silvery in the firelight, lifted quizzically to hers.

"Since he's Krim's grandson, he's bound to be," he observed sardonically.

"Krim's grandson? Whatever you are talking about?"

"Crane, of course. Who are you talking about?"

"Your servant. What is his name? You whisked him out of here before I'd even the chance to get a proper look at him. Yet he seems not the sort to attend a knight on a quest. He's much too timorous and frail. Why in the name of the One have you brought him along?"

For a moment he stared at her as if he had never seen her before, then abruptly his fair head went back as he erupted into hearty laughter. Aurora stared at the convulsed knight in open-mouthed astonishment. Yet he looked so young and handsome with his stern features softened in merriment that she was hard put not to fling her arms around him. Then suddenly he stilled, and her breath caught in her throat as he looked at her.

"Gods! I had forgotten what an innocent you are," he murmured softly, and her heart lurched at the tenderness in his voice. So long did he stare at her that she was suddenly filled with confusion.

"F-Frayne?" she faltered, her golden eyes huge in her face.

"May the gods forgive me," he muttered on an explosive breath and reached up to pull her down astraddle on his lap.

His mouth sought hers with an urgency she had never known in him before, and like a spark to tinder ignited her own ravenous desire built up over all the months of longing.

"Frayne," she moaned as his lips left hers to devour her eyes, her face, her throat, and all the while his hands explored the delicious intimacies of her flesh till she thought she would die with yearning for him. In an agony of crescendoing need she pulled the Dryad gown over her head and arched against him, her head flung back and her breath coming in explosive gasps as he molded his lips to the budding desire of her breasts, first one and then the other. In rapture, she felt herself transported into the scintillating realm of the god in which Frayne and she had ever transcended the bounds of mortal flesh to become as one with the puissance of the immortals. With a shuddering sigh, she entwined her slender arms about his neck and wriggled more urgently against him.

Again he found her lips, and slowly, his mouth pressed to hers in a lingering kiss, he eased her down on the makeshift bed beside him. Feverish with desire, she writhed against him, murmuring his name over and over, until at last, filled with the need to rid himself of the confining clothes, he pulled away from her and rolled to his knees, only to have her transfix him with her eyes shimmering golden in the firelight. He saw, then, that she was possessed with the power of the god. Thus, spellbound, he waited in an ecstasy of suspense as, rising, she unlaced his woollen shirt and slipped it slowly, sensuously off his powerful shoulders and trailed it down his arms. His flesh quivered as she ran her hands lingeringly down his muscled chest to the lean waist.

Then, kneeling before him, she unloosed the bindings of his leather breeches and released the thrusting glory of his manhood. A groan was torn from deep within him as in renewed wonder she caressed the swollen length of him and tasted of its sweet mystery, until finally, engulfed in the rising tide of passion, Frayne fell back against the bed, and spreading wide her thighs, pulled the Enchantress down upon him.

The glory of their pulsating love carried them into the mystic heights where their spirits had ever been joined, their destinies entwined, and there they were made truly as one again, a single, numinous entity within their cresting passion. And when, an eternity later, they were returned to the less sublime reality of earth, they were yet sustained by the exalted vision that had been granted them by the gods. They were Frayne and Aurora, but they were inextricably bound.

Chapter Six

Aurora jerked awake to the jarring crack of thunder and the darkness sizzling with lightning bolts. Beside her, Frayne slung off the cloak under which they lay and bounded to his feet, his lean body shimmering whitely in the coruscating fury of the lightning storm. Shouting at her to hurry, he threw on his clothes and went in search of Elwindolf.

The Enchantress quickly followed suit, donning from her pack her woollen shirt and breeches and tugging on her boots. Then swiftly she placed her Dryad gown with the crimson cloak of power into the pack and strapped it to her back. By the time she had slung about her shoulders the elfin cloak given her by her father-pair, Frayne had returned alone, his face forbiddingly stern in the brief flashes of lightning.

"He's gone," said the knight, shouting to be heard above the storm. "And he left these behind."

Aurora's stomach clenched with terrible foreboding as she beheld the bundle of clothes and the great Glinden Bow Frayne held out to her. Wordlessly she swiveled and strode firmly to the place where she had left the hunter brooding over Phelan's body. The wolf, too, was gone, the only sign remaining of either, the telltale stain of blood upon the still-flattened grass where Phelan had lain in death. Deliberately Aurora knelt and sniffed at the ground as the wolves of the Glade had taught her long years before when they had instructed her in the secret ways of the hunt. Then, rising, she wandered in gradually widening circles about the spot where Elwindolf had mourned beside his fallen father-wolf, till at last she stood, her gaze fixed and staring into the darkness to the east.

Frayne, slinging the great bow over his shoulder, watched and waited patiently for her to fix the spoor clearly in her mind. Once before he had seen the Enchantress create such a mind-link. Only then it had been with the dying unicorn who had led them to the Black Mountain in search of the unicorns' burial ground. He had never fully understood this gift of hers that allowed her to become as one with another creature, and with grave misgivings he recalled how she had nearly succumbed to the unicorn's despair as they camped a two-days' journey from Krim's Keep and the unicorn had come so near to dying at the mage's hands. It had taken nearly all of Frayne's iron will to call Aurora back from the brink of death, and she had been only a fledgling Enchantress then, unsure as yet of her latent powers. She was much more than that now, for since that time she had mastered the Andruvien, and through Vandrel's tutoring, achieved a greater command of the scintillating power, which, if she were granted the time to grow into it, he knew would be greater than that of the Sorceress, indeed, would even rival his own. She was very nearly his equal now, in all but knowledge and experience. Uneasily, he wondered if he could sever her from Elwindolf's madness, if indeed the hunter had fallen prey once more to the evil that plagued Dalmurn. Thus far the Enchantress had not seemed much affected by the sickness that hung like a pall over the woods, but once she was mind-linked to one so afflicted, it could be a different story.

The knight was brought back to the present by the Enchantress's murmuring strange words that he knew to be of the Old Tongue, though he understood them not. For he was the mortal son of Dred, and the innocence that enabled Aurora to comprehend the language of the Ancient Ones had been denied him from birth. Even as his birth made impossible his love for this exquisite creature whom he himself had named Aurora and Enchantress, he was bitterly reminded.

"He has gone to perform the death rites for the father-wolf," she said then, in the language of Men. "He is not as he was with Hertha Vandrel, but neither is he filled with the madness that compelled him to seek his own death. Yet there is vengeance in his heart. And hatred for Ommat." A jagged burst of lightning filled the night, revealing to Frayne the Enchantress's troubled expression.

"We must stop him," she declared, reaching out to grasp the knight's arm in a strong grip. "If the lapidary dies before revealing what he has done with the Arlana, all may indeed be lost."

"Groul has taken the Virgin's Tear?" Frayne queried sharply, and hard upon this utterance came the realization that he had been a fool. Of course, the Arlana must be missing, for what could better explain the evil that plagued the valley and that had the stench of Dred about it. And why else would Anders Groul, who had been well touted in Tor for his artistry and craftsmanship, suddenly leave the city for the obscure poverty of Sedgewick? No doubt greed had brought him, for he had dared to come even to Frayne with questions about the legendary Arlana, but the knight had quashed the creature's obsequious presumption with the cold hauteur for which he was noted and had then forgotten the incident. It was only later that he had heard it rumored the master lapidary had mysteriously gone to Sedgewick, and even then he had not connected the lumber town to Dalmurn and Ariana, the Holy Maiden.

"Aye. Or so it would seem," Aurora said, startled by his tone and surprised that Frayne should know anything about the lapidary. "How do you know Anders Groul?"

"My business in Sedgewick is with him," he answered shortly and glanced at the sky as the first spattering of raindrops warned that the storm was beginning in earnest. "Can you hold the spoor in this storm?" he asked.

"Aye. I think so," she nodded, eyeing him askance. Obviously he was determined to tell her nothing further of his purpose in coming to the valley, and she had been able to learn little from Boltar, for the warrior-steed had been able to tell her only that the knight had been attacked and wounded as they prepared to leave the city.

The Enchantress frowned in the darkness. 'Twas

clear nothing had changed. Danger was yet the knight's constant companion, and he meant to ride away as he had done before rather than let her share his peril. Yet this time she was determined he would not have his way. She knew what it was to live without him. Now that she had found him, he would not find it so easy to be rid of her again, she vowed. After all, did he not owe her? For she had led him to the horn of the unicorn, even as she had promised. But he had yet to fulfill his part of the bargain, for he had given his word to help her to discover her true-name, and he had not done so.

"Then let us not tarry here," Frayne said and turned to stalk away in the direction in which Aurora had indicated Elwindolf had gone. "He will no doubt be forced to seek shelter in the worst of the storm, but then, so shall we," he added as the sprinkle quickened to what promised to be a deluge.

They were soon soaked to the skin, despite their hooded cloaks, and Aurora began to wish she had not changed out of the Dryad gown as she shivered in her sodden clothes. As Anduan, the tree-child, growing up with Minta and Valesia, her dryad mother-pair, she had run naked through the rain and rejoiced in such freedom. But now she was neither Anduan nor dryad but Aurora of the man-beasts, and she told herself she must learn the customs of her own kind. Yet it remained incomprehensible to her why humans could not follow the simpler ways of the Old Ones. Indeed, this insistence on keeping the body always confined and covered seemed absurd in the extreme. Then, dismissing such musings as fruitless, she hugged her cloak more tightly about her and struggled to stay up with the knight's long stride.

Frayne kept doggedly to the pace, his thoughts grim as he considered the difficulties ahead. If the storm continued unabated, they would find it hard going, indeed. Aside from the wet and the cold and the already ankle-deep mud that dragged at their feet and sapped their strength, they labored against the fury of the wind-driven rain that stung their faces and blinded their vision. He reached out to steady the Enchantress as she slipped and nearly went down. She was shivering, and he saw her grit her teeth to stop their chattering as she regained her balance and continued on, her eyes agleam with determination.

He had seen that look before. The girl would drop before she uttered a word of complaint or gave a thought to giving up the struggle. Yet he knew he must get her to shelter soon. It would avail them nothing if she were to exhaust herself and fall ill. Yet there seemed little hope of escaping the storm's unabated fury as they forced weary limbs to drag them ever onward through the malevolent, wailing night of blustery wind and chilling rain. It was the reawakened evil of Dred, whose spawn he was, and the knight bitterly cursed the Immortal Prince whose vile misdeed could yet corrupt all within its sphere after seven hundred mortal years.

It seemed to Aurora that ages had passed since they had awakened to the first burst of lightning and begun the endless march through the pelting storm, when suddenly she felt her skin crawl with the feel of danger. One hand went instinctively to the knife at her belt as she reached out with the other to grasp Frayne's cloak with fingers rendered numb by the cold.

"What is it?" Frayne shouted, stooping to peer into her face.

Wordlessly she shook her head and sniffed the air. Her nose wrinkled in distaste as, even amidst the deluge of wind and rain, she caught the stench of death close by. Deliberately she unsheathed Glaiveling and edged past the knight, who had also armed himself upon seeing the elfin dagger in her hand. He would have stopped her, but with the agility of the woodsprite, she eluded his grasp and vanished into a dwarf oak thicket. Cursing, he lunged after her to discover a narrow trail winding through the brakes, and ahead of him, revealed in the dazzling fulgurations like leaping dragon's flames, the Enchantress standing rigid and staring fixedly before her.

Swiftly Frayne came up behind the girl, his hand going out to grasp her shoulder. With a strangled cry she turned and threw herself against the knight's hard chest. Instinctively he closed one strong arm protectively about her and held her near. Then his mouth thinned to a grim line as he looked over his head at the clearing beyond.

The rotting, half-eaten corpses appeared to have been lying for several days where they had fallen. Three, two young boys and a man, had been taken by surprise, probably as they left the cabin to tend the livestock that must have been kept in the poled enclosures, now empty. Inside had been the gruesome remains of a woman and a young girl who had apparently taken their own lives.

"Who did this?" Aurora said in a low voice. At the

159

knight's insistence, she had removed her wet clothing
and now sat huddled in a woven woollen blanket
before a fire crackling in a stone fireplace. The cabin
itself was small but comfortable and gave evidence
that its former inhabitants had been rather more
industrious and certainly more prosperous than those
who had fled Sedgewick. Despite the hard-packed
earthen floor, the interior was clean and cheerful, with
simple but well-crafted furnishings—a table with
wooden benches roomy enough to seat six people, a
slat-backed rocking chair having a wicker seat, and a
wooden cupboard containing the few cooking and
eating utensils for the family of five. A bed hugged
one corner of the room, and a ladder led to a loft snug
beneath the high-sloped roof. There Aurora discovered three tidy pallets, a few items of clothing hanging
on wooden pegs in the walls, and a rag doll whose
faded, grinning face and patched body brought tears
of sorrow and rage to her eyes.

The knight, leaning with one arm propped along
the carved oak mantlepiece, glanced up from his
silent contemplation of the fire.

"Men on horseback," he answered curtly, taking in
with a measuring look the girl's haunted eyes under-
lined with dark shadows. His lips thinned to a grim
line as he saw a shudder shake her slender frame. The
absurd child fairly drooped from exhaustion, nor
would she eat. Cursing the obstinacy that kept her
from yielding to the oblivion of sleep, he settled beside
her on the pallet she had prepared for them on the
floor after she had flatly refused even to contemplate
sleeping in the bed. It would be a desecration, she had
insisted, her eyes huge in her white face, and he had

relented. Gratefully she cuddled close as he wrapped his arm securely around her.

"I couldn't tell how many there were," he added reflectively, the gleam in his silvery eyes decidedly unpleasant. "Most of the sign was washed out by the rain." That he had few doubts as to their identities, though he could not have called them by name, he did not mention. For he had seen the band of heavily armed men ride past the holm on which he and the slave-girl had taken refuge, and he knew that they came from Tor and had been searching for him and probably for Janine.

"But the bodies were partially e-eaten," she faltered, and swallowed convulsively. "I-I thought the wolves . . ."

"Scavengers," he said shortly. "No doubt they came after the cutthroats had finished with the poor bastards. The three in the yard were slain by swords."

"And the woman and the girl-child?" Aurora pursued in a constricted voice, the golden eyes huge and tortured on his face. The knight turned his gaze from her to stare broodingly into the red glow of the embers. Gods, why must she torment herself with it? he thought savagely. He could not bear to look at her, so closely did she resemble a brutalized child, her face pinched and white, and those eyes, those blasted eyes bleeding with her wounded innocence. Well, she *would* leave the protected glade to gain knowledge of the man-beasts, he mused darkly. And now she would learn her first bitter lesson.

"It seems likely the woman killed the child," he said deliberately. His lip curled cynically as he turned to pierce her with steely eyes. "And then herself. No doubt she was a woman with a practical outlook on life. She knew a quick death at her own hands would be more merciful than what the butchers would mete out."

He watched her flinch at his callousness and marveled despite himself as he saw her recover from his calculated assault on her pristine ignorance. She was no weakling, his stubborn Enchantress. Suddenly unutterably weary, he waited for her to ask the inevitable.

"But why? How do you know this?"

The knight's short, brutal laugh chilled Aurora's soul.

"Because they were comely wenches and had not been touched. And because they appeared to have been in good health when they died. 'Tis more than likely they would have been taken as slaves rather than killed," he said coldly, and Aurora shuddered at the hard gleam in his eyes. "After the brutes had had their way with them."

"I-I do not understand. Had their way with them?"

His arm tightened about her shoulders.

"That is one of the reasons you should not be allowed to wander around unprotected, my foolish little innocent," he said with a flinty laugh. "You know nothing of the human heart or the evil of which it is capable."

She was silent for a moment, but he watched her eyes grow dark with inner musing and knew she would not let it go at that. Warily he waited to hear her response. She had a way of thrusting to the heart of things, catching him off guard and putting him on the defensive.

"I know I have much to learn of mankind," she murmured after a time. "And there is much which seems incomprehensible to me. Yet I do know that some men have hearts black with evil, for I have faced Cranith and Baldrac. And some men are burdened with dark secrets, which teach them the bitter lessons of grief and loneliness, for I have not forgotten Shamar of the Shintari, who fathered a child on his Queen Mother and who was punished with forbidden love for Freyga, his sister-daughter. And I know, too, that there are some men who seek to guard their hearts behind impenetrable barriers of secrecy, for I have known you, Frayne, Knight of Tor and the Sorceress's minion."

The knight felt shaken to the core as she looked up at him with eyes shining golden in the firelight. Gods, he groaned inwardly. Her cursed sweet innocence and unwavering faith unmanned him. She, who was the favored one of the gods, had seen through the master magician's illusions and discerned the true nature of the Asgeroth. She, who had been born to command the secret symbols of power, had penetrated the black veils of Somn and beheld the Immortal Prince himself. Why could she not also see what he was?

"I know you are not like Cranith the Imposter, though you would have me believe your soul is blackened with some terrible iniquity," she went on, and a crease furrowed her lovely brow. "I know not what you are, even as I do not yet know what I am. But I do know that if you are evil, then so must I be. For we are one and the same, you and I. And nothing you can do or say can alter that."

The muscle along the knight's lean jaw leaped as her words ripped at his heart. Innocent little fool! he thought in bitter anguish. You know nothing of me. And were I to tell you I am Frayne, Prince of Throm, and Thromholan of Prophecy, would you still say it changes nothing? You who are come as the Savior of your people, and I who am meant to lead Thromgilad to victory, can we be one and the same?

He was unutterably wearied of the deceit and hypocrisy that circumstances had always seemed to deem necessary. Grimly he determined that she should know the truth at last, even though in telling her, he must inevitably destroy her faith in him just as he had foreseen he would in those enchanted weeks beside Grendylmere when first he had fallen to her spell. His lips parted to tell her the truth, but the sound of her gentle breathing and the weight of her head against his shoulder silenced him, for the Enchantress had succumbed to her weariness at last.

No doubt the Sorceress of Tor would have been vastly intrigued and not a little taken aback had she but witnessed her maddeningly impervious knight at that moment, for the jaded mask of the courtier was vanished, and it was the man Frayne who looked upon the lovely countenance of the sleeping girl with such passionate tenderness and disconsolate longing. His powerful frame shuddered as with an anguished groan he buried his face in her silken hair.

"Aurora," he whispered. "Where shall I ever find the strength to leave you? And when the time comes to betray your foolish trust, how shall I bear to see the contempt in those lovely eyes? The gods have mercy. I love you!"

Passionately he pressed his lips against her hair. Then, carefully, he eased her down on the pallet she had prepared for them earlier, and flinging off his clothes, stretched out beside her. One arm reached out to hug her slender warmth snugly to him, as gradually his tensed muscles relaxed. Yet it was late into the night ere sleep came to ease his troubled soul.

With morning came a let-up of the storm, though the sky was yet leaden and the woods dreary with fog. Aurora awakened to find Frayne still asleep beside her, his bearded face stern in the dim light of the cabin. Carefully she sat up that she might better behold her beloved knight. Gods! He was so beautiful, she thought poignantly and felt she could not bear the sweeping surge of tenderness that his nearness aroused in her. Compelled by the love she had borne for him since first she had beheld him emerging, godlike, from the shimmering waters of Grendylmere, she lowered her head to brush her lips against his cheek in a feather-light kiss.

He stirred at her touch, her name a sighing whisper on his lips, as she ran her nails lightly through the golden mat of hair tapering to a V above his navel. A frown touched her brow as her questing fingers found the pucker of the new scar along his ribs. Slowly she eased the blanket down till she could see the recently healed wound, an angry red welt against the ivory skin. A fierce flame ignited in the golden eyes as she realized how near he had come to death. She could not bear the thought that she had not been at his side when the villains fell upon him with murder in their black hearts. Had she been with him, he would not have had to fight alone, with only a frightened child to aid him in his peril.

Suddenly the Enchantress was overcome with dread that he would somehow slip away as before, perhaps this time to die at the hands of his scheming enemies so that she might never again know the delicious madness of his touch. Oh, gods, how she loved him! Death would be sweeter by far than ever to be parted from him. If only he could love her in return and keep her always at his side! Yet she knew such dreams were hopeless, for had he not sworn she should never have his heart?

Then a dangerous light glittered in her lovely eyes, and her raven head lifted in defiant pride. He was Frayne, and he served the scheming Sorceress, but was she not Aurora and Andruvien? Had she not felt the hand of the god return to her?

With a smile, she bent to taste his lips and felt her pulse quicken as, awakening to her, his mouth moved beneath hers. Her lips parted to the questing thrust of his tongue, and delicious waves of pleasure rippled over her. Then his arms had closed about her as he rolled to his side, dragging her down next to him, murmuring her name, kissing her passionately, hungrily, like a man possessed.

"Aurora. Aurora. My sweet love."

"Frayne," she gasped in frenzied rapture and willed him to enter her quickly, for already her body was aflame with overwhelming need.

He thrust deeply into her, again and again, and she met him with a passion as fierce as his own. Never had it been like this. The cresting waves of molten flame engulfed them, carried them to a scintillating burst of discovery. And when at last he lay once more beside her, his chest still heaving with each belabored breath, she felt dazed by the violence of their joining.

This had not been the passion of the gods, but the desperate desire of man and woman. In bewilderment she gazed into the silvery eyes and saw reflected there her own dawning wonder. Together they had breached the carefully constructed walls that kept them separate on this plane of existence and had briefly touched the essence of their shared passion. For the first time she began to wonder if, indeed, he might truly love her.

"Frayne?" she murmured tremulously, but he silenced her with a kiss, and pulling her almost convulsively to him, held her tightly for an endless moment. A nameless dread filled her as she felt his heart hammering against her breast. Then, just as abruptly, he released her and rose wordlessly to gather up his clothing hastily discarded the night before.

"It's late," he said, his tunic in his hand and his back turned to her as he stared out at the grey shroud of mist and fog. "Elwindolf will be on the move again."

"Aye," she agreed tonelessly, and her gaze on the long, lean back and powerful shoulders was troubled. She watched the muscles tense and ripple beneath the smooth skin and did not have to see his face to know that he had withdrawn again into his shell. Why? she agonized and wished that honor did not bind her from stealing into his mind to read his hidden thoughts. What terrible secret kept her from him? One day she would know, she vowed. But until that time she would hold to her the memory that this day she had experienced the marvel of his unfettered passion, had been granted a brief glimpse of the human vulnerability that he kept hidden behind the flinty facade of the warrior, and for the first time had had a glimmering of the nature of the power that was hers to command and that had broken through his formidable defenses at last.

Yet the vision had been too brief, the glory of their shared passion too furious for her to grasp it fully. She was left feeling shaken and bewildered by what had happened to them, and filled with the need to understand it. Not so Frayne, who was well-versed in the art of love. He understood all too well the awesome power of the Enchantress.

It was the mystique of Woman magnified a hundredfold, he thought. The power of the female to attract the male, and coupled with this, the feminine compulsion to create harmony out of chaos, permanence and stability out of the ever-changing flux, and continuity amidst the inevitableness of mortality. Then, too, the Enchantress was a beguiling composite of those paradoxes that were so bewildering to the male psyche. She could be both impetuous and sensible, unforgiving and generous, willful and yielding, tempestuous and calm. In her sublime innocence she was yet possessed of an extraordinary wisdom that never failed to astonish him, and while her fearlessness both appalled and infuriated him, her courage inspired his admiration and his love. She called forth the male urge to succor and protect and instilled in him the desire for home and family. All of which were anathema to what he perceived as his ultimate destiny, for he was a warrior and Thromholan, and the game he played was both deep and deadly.

Thus had he found himself in a constant state of ambivalence since first the fates had brought him into Aurora's sphere. He could not help loving her as he had never loved anyone before, other than his mother, for whom he had pledged himself to the path he now trod. Because of that brave and noble woman, he was a Knight of Tor dedicated to the One and yet, too, the son of Dred and the Sorceress's minion. Was that not perplexing enough without the additional dilemma of loving the Enchantress of Prophecy as well?

Frayne and Aurora ate a meager breakfast and set out once more in pursuit of Elwindolf. The Enchantress was not sorry to leave the cabin that had witnessed such violent death. The night before, they had laid the bodies in a shallow depression at the base of a low hill and covered them as best they could with mud and rocks. But she seemed to feel their restless spirits still. Nor did the terrible, silent fog trailing wraithlike through the trees relieve her somber mood. It dulled her senses and wore at her nerves till she thought she must go mad with longing to see the sun again, to hear birdsong and feel the woods quickening with life. It was as if the forest itself were haunted by the lingering memory of some dreadful deed, and suddenly Aurora wondered why the Arlana had been a tear shed by the Virgin.

Frayne's deep voice breaking abruptly into her thoughts startled her out of her reverie. She glanced up to find his dark-rimmed falcon's eyes fixed intently on her face and unaccountably blushed.

"Wha-at did you say?" she queried in unwonted confusion.

His amused smile softened the piercing quality of his gaze, and suddenly the day did not seem nearly so bleak. After all, so long as they were together, could she not face any obstacle, overcome any evil?

"You never told me how you came to be in the forest with my servant," he drawled meaningfully, and suddenly she braced herself against what she knew must come next. "Had we not agreed that I should come to you at the Sacred Grove?"

"Had we?" she returned lightly, but the glitter of battle leaped suddenly to her golden eyes. "I do not recall agreeing to any such thing. Nor am I here subservient to your whims. I am come at the behest of Sedgewick to put right the wrong that prevails here. I could hardly do that by dallying in the grove in the hopes that you might see fit to honor us with your presence. After all, you have not proven so very reliable in that respect. One never knows when you shall simply choose to vanish. Although," she added provocatively, the tip of one slender finger pressed to pursed lips as twin imps gazed up at him out of the corners of her eyes, "I suppose there is little doubt that you would have come eventually for Boltar."

"Indeed," he answered, hard put not to burst into laughter. The little fiend to tease him so! "I should never have left without Boltar."

She could not completely stifle a small gasp at his apparently heartless admission. Oh, the beast to use her so! But then, she had quickly recovered herself and assumed a nonchalance belied somewhat by the

170

dangerous glitter in her marvelous eyes.

"And 'twas a good thing I did not wait, methinks. For your servant was hard-pressed when I happened on to him."

"As were you when I came on the scene," he reminded her acerbically.

"Oh!" she cried, bristling up at him. "I could have slain Phelan had I wanted to. But I did not come to spill the blood of those afflicted by the madness. There has been enough blood shed."

"Unfortunately, Phelan was not of the same mind. But all that aside, why were you so conveniently on hand to save my squire's life?"

"I was trailing the wolf-pack, of course."

"Now why did I not think of that?" he retorted, much struck at the thought.

"No doubt because *you* did not know that Phelan had revealed to Elwindolf that he knew where Anders Groul was to be found. Or that Groul had gone into the forest after seeking information about the Arlana and returned some time later much altered in manner. For he was the first to fall to the madness, and not even the wolves would go near him. Does it not follow that 'twas he who stole the Virgin's Tear?"

"I feel quite certain of it," he said tonelessly. "Find him, and you will no doubt have found the root of the evil."

He spoke the last so strangely that she looked hard into his face. Yet though she could read nothing in the heavy-lidded eyes, she had the eerie feeling that he had not been referring solely to the theft of the Arlana, but to something much darker.

"Do you know the legend of Ariana?" she asked

suddenly, and his answering bark of laughter sounded harsh in the unnatural silence of the fog-enshrouded forest. Aurora winced and wondered at it, but his reply was couched in the slightly bored tones of one whom nothing could touch.

"And how not?" he quipped. "It is a lovely tale of sacrifice and rape. Just the sort to beguile the time away."

"Do not mock me, I beg you," she retorted stiffly. "I do not ask out of idle curiosity, but because I must know what happened then if I am to understand what is going on now."

They had been walking steadily as they talked, but suddenly he halted and stood staring into the distance as if his thoughts were very far away indeed. He remained thus for so long that Aurora nearly jumped when abruptly he turned to look at her, the hooded eyes glittering strangely in the gloom.

"I was not mocking you, Enchantress," he said quietly, but the slight, hard curl of his lips sent a shiver down her back. "Never you."

"Tell me how Ariana triumphed over Dred. I must know."

"By sacrificing herself," he answered, his falcon's eyes glinting icy sparks. "You see, she was the hind whose blood seeped into the earth. The sacrificial lamb staked out to lure Dred out of hiding. And it worked. Harmon was summoned by the Vandoran's cry for help, just as she knew he would be. Unfortunately, he arrived a trifle late to save the Virgin. Dred had already had his way with her. But the warrior-god did manage to ferret out the Prince. Indeed, the intrepid Eilderood pursued him clear to his evil den

172

beneath the Black Mountain and there banished him once again to Somn. Poor Dred. He has ever been fated to come out second best to Harmon, it would seem."

"You mean Dred killed Ariana?" Aurora gasped, too filled with sorrow for the courageous Valdoran to pay heed to the knight's final, cynical remark uttered in tones of sardonic amusement.

"Not quite, though perhaps it would have been better so. He merely took by force that which was most precious to her. Her virginity," he answered coldly, and stalked away.

The spoor led ever east toward the Glendaron, and it was not long ere they heard the rush of the river in the distance. The mist had given way to a steady drizzle as they topped a craggy knoll and looked out over a heavily wooded valley steeped in fog. Coming faintly to their ears was the keening cry of a wolf hot on the scent.

"He is here," Aurora said in a hushed voice. "But he is changed. I-I know him not, for he is no longer Elwindolf." Suddenly she shuddered convulsively. "His mind is dark. Savage. He is the beast."

Frayne's gaze narrowed on the Enchantress's face as the golden eyes grew glazed and distant. She appeared to have receded far into herself, and she spoke as one who was lost within some strange, tenebrous vision.

"Aurora!" he shouted, grasping her by the shoulders and shaking her. "Break the mind-link!"

A low gasp escaped her lips. Frayne stilled and waited as her gaze focused painfully on his face.

"He is Drude, the man-wolf," she whispered

hoarsely. "And he seeks the purification of the blood-letting. Quickly! We must stop him ere he catches up to Ommat!" And before he could stop her, she had wrenched out of his grasp and darted wildly down the slope.

"Aurora!" Frayne called and started after her, but the Enchantress had vanished into the fog.

The lithe form of the hunter gliding through the veils of mist seemed as insubstantial as the Eidola, the shadow-phantoms of Somn who steal forth at the bidding of Prince Dred to work mischief in the night. In his hand he carried the long-knife, as noiselessly he traveled, and swiftly, his still face fixed with single-minded purpose, his pale eyes cold as they scanned the murky depths of the woods before him. Little did he resemble the man called Elwindolf, for his long hair, worn free, flew wildly in the wind, and the lean, sinewy body was naked to the elements.

In truth, he was no longer Elwindolf, wolf-friend of the elves, but something primitive and wild, for as he had mourned beside Phelan's lifeless body, he had sensed the rising of the full moon above the pall of mist and cloud, and his blood had leaped with the instinct of the wolf to stalk the unsuspecting prey. It was the blood-rite of the hunt, the mystical time of the moon-madness when the wolves became as one, be-came the pack before whom all the lesser creatures fled in terror, and the despair of the rogue-wolf banished from the throng was bitter gall to him. Even as the Enchantress had left him to grieve alone, he sensed them gathering in the hills, the wolves, who had not fled the evil as had the other wild creatures, but who had stayed because they were hunters and would hold to their territories. Then had he yearned to be one with them again. But he had slain Phelan, the father-wolf, and was wolf no longer, but man-beast and outcast.

Once, long ago, he had been Drude, called Wolf, and then the elves had taken him in and taught him the old ways. Thus had he become Elwindolf, something more than wolf and less than elf, and yet more wolf and elf than man. Then had he abandoned the ways of the pack and wandered far and wide across the land, drifting in and out of the world of men, but always returning to the forest and Phelan and the wolves. And he had always been welcome and one with them. But no more, for one of his kind had brought evil to the forest and the old ways had fallen to the corruption of the one called Dred.

Thus had his troubled thoughts dwelt upon what had been and what could never be again, and all the time he had felt the gathering of the wolves and the full-bodied moon climbing toward the apex and the wronged spirit of Phelan bitterly accusing him, for the father-wolf had been slain by a traitor to the pack and could not rest until the wrong was made right again. Nor should Elwindolf ever know peace so long as he bore the taint of the renegade. This he knew in his heart. This, and that only through the blood-rite could he be cleansed. Ommat, the harbinger of the evil, must be slain, and he, Drude, must be the one to do the blood-letting. Yet to do so was to disavow his manhood. For Anders Groul was mad. And weak. The little man stood not a chance against Drude, called Wolf.

Almost he won the battle for his soul, for he was Elwindolf, and he had lived with elves. But then the clouds briefly parted, and a silvery shaft of moonlight fell upon Phelan's lifeless body. Elwindolf cried out in anguish as the sightless eyes, gleaming with the fleeting illusion of life, mercilessly accused him. And the wind, too, moaning through the trees, seemed suddenly to sigh his name.

"Elwindolf. Elwindolf." And in his tormented fancy, it was Phelan's restless spirit calling out to him.

Then the clouds closed again, and Elwindolf had risen to his feet as one who is compelled. Lifting his beardless face to the moon hidden from his eyes by the gloomy mantle of Dred's reawakened evil, but not hidden from his heart, Drude, called Wolf sounded the lament of the Brethren for the passing of Phelan, Hlafard of the Bredan, and out of the far reaches of the night had come the faint, answering wail, carried on the quickening wind, which fled before the impending storm.

As the distant cry of the wolf died away, the hunter shed the raiment of the man-beast and laid the garments beside the still body of the father-wolf. Then he released his hair from the braid that had been his pledge to the elves to honor the ways of his own kind, until at last he stood shorn of all that bore the taint of the man-beast, save only for the leather girdle and sheath that bore Dolfang, the long-knife. Finally, reverently, he laid the elfin bow of Glinden Wood upon the ground, then knelt to lift Phelan, father-wolf, into his arms and passed silently into the night.

He remembered little of the journey to the Hilgemot, where the wolf-clans gathered. They had known he was coming long before he surmounted the Crag, for they were waiting for him—Arthane, Saureth, Engar, Stahn, and the others. Their numbers had dwindled, and they had not the look of the fearless, proud breed of hunters who had ever freely roamed the forest. They crouched in the Circle of Bredan around the Fehald, the place of the Hlafard, which was unoccupied, for Phelan was dead, slain by the man-wolf's arrow. They looked upon him with hatred and distrust, as if he had never been one with them in the fellowship of the hunt. Even so, they parted before him, allowing him to come into the center of the Bredan, for he had brought Phelan once more among them. Solemnly he laid the corpse at the base of the Fehald and stepped back.

Stahn, who had once called the man-wolf brother and who was the last of Phelan's male cubs, the others having fallen to the man-beast's sword at the battle of Sedgewick, was the first to come forward. Hackles raised, he sniffed at the thing that had been Phelan and growled.

"This be not Phelan, Hlafard of the Bredan," he said in the tongue of beasts.

"Nay, Stahn. For Phelan has passed on, and the time has come to choose a new leader. Whom among the Bredan shall stand forth as Hlafard? Who shall take and hold the Fehald?"

The grey wolf sidled uneasily away from the man.

"Thou hast no voice here," he whined. "For thou art outcast and renegade. 'Twas thine arrow that slayed the Hlafard. Thou has come amongst the Bredan under the sign of truce. When thou hast departed, thou shall be hunted."

"Hunted and outcast I may be," answered Elwindolf fiercely. "But renegade I be nót. The Hlafard broke Taboo. 'Twas Phelan who betrayed the Bredan and Phelan who led the pack to grief. For Phelan was taken with the sickness of the mind. The ancient evil that Ommat released upon Dalmurn when he stole the Maiden's Tear. 'Tis Ommat who must suffer the vengeance of Bredan. And 'tis Drude who shall hunt him down."

"Enough!" snarled Engar of the Broken Tooth, leaping forth to confront the man. "Thou art tainted with the spilt blood of Hlafard and Bredan. Go forth from Hilgemot, Drude, foul spawn of the man-beast. Thou art unclean."

"Aye. Drude shall go forth," he who once was Elwindolf said in a steely voice, his pale eyes gleaming uncannily in the gloom. "But beware, Brethren of the Hunt! For he will come again. And then he shall be outcast no longer, but Hlafard of the Bredan!"

"The blood-rite!" Stahn growled. "The man-cub chooses the purification of blood!"

And the sizzling leap of a lightning bolt split asunder the firmament of darkness and storm, revealing the pale form of the man-wolf atop the Crag, his unfettered hair flying wildly in the wind and his arms uplifted as though to challenge the forces of darkness scintillating all about him.

Thus did Drude, called Wolf relinquish all to the savage instincts fostered in the years he had lived as one with the Bredan, and the madness of grief and bitter hatred ruled his heart. Like Phelan, he would seek the man-beast whose blood-letting would purge the man-wolf of the taint of renegade. Then would he be Bredan again and know the peace of oneness with his brethren the wolves.

Aurora, the Enchantress of the Glade, wove swiftly through the phantom trees, the stench of evil suffocating in the stillness, and within the pouch beneath her tunic the Andruvien throbbed against her breast with every pulsating beat of her heart. But its flames within her mind were like leaping tongues of darkness, and the cold fire of Vendrenin was like to freeze her soul, for she wandered the lightless maze of the man-wolf's savage madness, and forgotten were the god and Frayne and the glorious blaze of passion from whence her power sprang. She was Drude and wolf, and she thirsted for the living blood of the fleeing prey—Ommat, the fear-crazed man-beast.

With the cunning of the wolf, she found the hidden den tucked away in a narrow ravine choked with blackthorn and gorse. She had circled around to cut off Ommat's retreat and had scented the rotting remains of a carcass and the telltale signs of the man-beast that had led her to the mouth of the narrow cave. Ommat would come here to the place where he had known safety and seclusion, and she would be waiting for him, she thought with a cold glimmer of a smile as she concealed herself within the gorse growing thickly at the mouth of the ravine. Swiftly she scanned the meadow, thick with tall waving grass into which the ravine opened and through which flowed the Glendaron, leafy, green willow thickets hugging its banks. The river curled lazily around the rocky thrust of a low but sheer ridge to her back, effectively cutting off Ommat's retreat in that direction and to her left. He would come out of the woods in front of her, and he would be looking fearfully over his shoulder, never once suspecting that he fled straight into the arms of fate.

She had not long to wait before the crash of a body tearing through the underbrush came clearly to her ears. She tensed, the elfin dagger clutched in her hand and her glance sweeping the brakes. There! she thought, her blood leaping in her veins as she saw the branches of dwarf oak shiver and part before the scrambling flight of a shaggy, wild-eyed creature having the shape of a man. And not far behind him came Drude, his bare skin pale in the murky light and his lips stretched in a cold, mirthless grin as he flung back the hand in which gleamed Dolfang, the long-knife.

Chapter Seven

Crane, the shape-changer, perched on a fallen log, his elbows propped on bony knees and his hands dangling between his legs. The thin shoulders were hunched in dejection and a gloomy scowl darkened his brow as he thought of Aurora and Frayne in pursuit of the lapidary without him. And all because of the troublesome little whelp Frayne had ordered him to bring to the Sacred Grove and guard.

He bristled all over again as he recalled how the knight had coldly cut him short when he tried to protest such a gross injustice.

"You will do as I ask," Frayne had commanded in a flinty voice, and the boy had flinched beneath the hard gleam of those blasted falcon eyes. Then, even harder to bear, the hint of a smile had relieved the knight's features, harsh with lines of weariness, and the man's powerful hand had come to rest confidently on Crane's shoulder.

"You did well this day, shape-changer," the knight had said, and did not know that he battered the boy's tenuous defenses, for he was Frayne, Crane's ideal, and consequently a constant reminder of the young mage's own despised shortcomings. "I should be always proud to have you at my side when danger threatens. But the child is ill and requires the healing power of the Sacred Grove. A man knows when duty is of greater import than the pursuit of adventure. And oft times," he added, and it had seemed to Crane that a deucedly odd twinkle had seemed suddenly to glitter in the marvelous eyes, "the unexpected rewards are far greater." Then the brief warmth had inexplicably altered to a chilling gleam. "Just see that you do not take undue advantage of whatever might come your way. Return to the grove. Keep my servant there under your protection. And fear not for the Enchantress. She has her own protection."

"Oh, indeed," the boy muttered darkly, and reaching down to pick up a pebble, tossed it angrily from him. "She has you to protect her. The Knight of Tor, who can slay giants and face the Asgeroth without a quiver of fear."

"Do you hate him so much, my lord?" queried a shy voice at his back.

Crane started and whipped around, his expression fierce with dislike.

"Don't *do* that! Never sneak up on me like that!" he fairly shouted, then froze, his mouth slightly agape as he looked directly into huge eyes the color of the blue enchanted sea that appeared to him sometimes in dreams, for there his mother's people, the seanymphs, lived.

Immediately long, thick lashes veiled the startling orbs from Crane's astonished view, but not before he had glimpsed a flash of hurt resentment in their depths and experienced a disturbing pang somewhere in the vicinity of his breastbone.

"I beg my lord's forgiveness," murmured the Knight of Tor's servant in a low, melodic voice, and as the child's gaze dropped to fix woodenly on the ground between them, Crane had the odd notion that this unlikely squire had been about to kneel before him.

"I am not 'your lord,'" Crane grumbled peevishly, caught more than a little off-balance by this first actual encounter with his new charge. He had not had the opportunity to really observe the lad before as, grudgingly, he had thought them back to the grove and laid the swooning child beneath the scanty cover offered by the vine-covered shrine. It had been dark by then as well, and, with the storm threatening he had been hard put to make their humble refuge more habitable with tree boughs and the fur pelts from the pack Boltar had carried. Then he had had to struggle to remember the proper binding spell to keep all snug and in place in any sort of weather. And afterward, he had slept the sleep of the dead, not moving until he had finally awakened to the gloomy morning and the humiliating recollection that he had been left behind to serve as nursemaid to the knight's infant squire.

"Forgive me," rejoined the persistent whelp in a small, colorless voice. Even in his distraction Crane vaguely noted the unusual accent, but he paid it scant heed as he wished the boy a thousand leagues from him. "In what manner would my lord have me to address him, please?"

"I'd as lief not have you to address me at all,"

Crane retorted ill-humoredly. "But it looks like I'm stuck with you."

He had spoken heedlessly because he was worried about Aurora and childishly hurt at being ordered from her side. As if he were no longer needed now that she had Frayne with her, he thought resentfully. And, no doubt, they were right. They didn't need him. Nobody did. But someday he'd show them. Someday he would . . . oh, what was the use in fooling himself? His grandfather had been right about him all along. He'd likely never come to anything. In disgust he bent to pick up another pebble, but instead of flinging it from him, he tossed it carelessly into the air and caught it again, his thoughts far away from the Grove of Tamaracks and the small, slender figure standing before him. Thus he did not realize that the stone he absently joggled in his hand was not a pebble at all, but a small, tear-shaped crystal.

Nor did he see the shadow of pain flicker in the blue eyes as they fluttered uncertainly up to study the tall youth's gloomy profile. The lips parted as though to speak, then closed again. Reluctantly the stripling turned and moved away, only to come to a determined halt once more, the small frame straightening to its full height and the slender throat working convulsively as the child swallowed hard.

"I beg you will forgive my unwelcome intrusion," came the grave little voice, distracting the shape-changer once more from his dour musings. Without thinking, Crane closed his fingers around the pebble-stone and thrust his hand into his pocket.

"Well? What is it?" he asked impatiently. "Speak up, lad."

184

"I-I wished only to express the gratitude in my heart that you have saved me from those beasts of Amaur. You are the great mage-lord, and I am only a lowly sl . . . s-servant," the child stammered, and blushed painfully. "Please do not concern yourself further with my unworthy self, my lord. You will wish to join my lord Frayne and the golden-eyed daughter of the House of Doane, and I shall be safe enough now."

The child, wheeling with a barely stifled sob, stumbled blindly. Instinctively Crane's hand shot out to grasp the stripling's shoulder.

"Hey, wait a minute," he said impatiently, then quickly withdrew his hand as he felt the youngster shrink with a low gasp from beneath his touch.

"What's the matter? Are you hurt or something?" he queried sharply, and easing the child around to face him, stooped, trying to get a look at the stubbornly averted face. "Hey, stand still!" he finally ordered in exasperation as the boy continued to twist his head away from the shape-changer's probing glance.

Instantly the child ceased to struggle and straightened to rigid attention before him, the remarkable eyes stubbornly averted. Crane grimaced as he saw the sensitive lips tremble and the small hands clench tightly at the lad's sides. Now what had he done to hurt the nipper's feelings? he wondered irritably. Egad. He looked ready to cry.

"What's your name, boy?" he asked gruffly and wondered irritably if the whelp was this troublesome with Frayne.

"I am called Jan—" the child began, then abruptly

faltered, and Crane was dazzled anew by a brief glimpse of the incredibly blue eyes as they darted to his face, then swiftly down again. "Jan," the youngster repeated in a low voice, then stood with head bowed, the full underlip caught between even, white teeth and the oval face, beneath the streaks of dirt, oddly pale.

The shape-changer's irritation suddenly gave way to an uncomfortable twinge of guilt as he stared at the small, forlorn figure before him. The boy seemed hardly old enough to be away from his mama, let alone apprenticed as squire to the Knight of Tor, he thought. And why had Frayne seen fit to garb his servant in such an odd manner? The stripling's cloak and tunic, soiled and tattered from his recent harrowing experiences, were finely made and of rich texture, but they were sizes too large for the lad and hung incongruously on the slight frame. And even worse, the miserable little whelp was filthy. The unsightly mop of black hair, which appeared to have been hastily trimmed with a dull knife, clustered about the lowered head, bits of twigs and grass entangled in its thick mass, and what Crane could see of the lad's skin was streaked with dirt. Yet properly dressed and cleaned up, he no doubt would be a comely youth, and though he seemed rather too frail for a knight's squire—the bones of his face too fine and delicate, the wrists and hands well-molded but small and soft—he appeared a well-knit youngster and might yet be toughened into a hardier specimen of manhood, mused the shape-changer a trifle dubiously.

"Jan, eh?" he said bluffly. "Well, I'm Crane. And I'm no great mage-lord. So you don't need to look as if I might eat you."

"But I saw you one minute a great cat and the next as you are now!" the child exclaimed in awe. "And when you lifted me in your arms, it was if you had summoned the wind of the desert, the Khamsin, to flow through my body. And when the wind ceased, I opened my eyes to this holy place and knew that here I was safe at last."

Crane's face flushed a dusky red as the stripling fell suddenly to his knees before him in an attitude of reverence.

"I cannot be mistaken in this, my lord," the child murmured, mesmerizing him with a worshipful glance from the marvelous eyes. "You are what my people would call Mogush. One possessed of the power to command the elements. And I am in your debt for my life. Tell me how I may serve thee, my lord."

"Hey, cut it out, will you?" the shape-changer sputtered in an agony of embarrassment. "Get up, I say." But the child only stared up at him with those soul-shattering blue orbs, until at last Crane reached down in exasperation to drag the troublesome brat up by the scruff of the neck.

A short gasp was torn from the child's lips, and the face went alarmingly pale as, with a groan, the slight form suddenly slumped against the shape-changer.

"What the . . .?" Crane muttered in alarm, his long arm wrapping round the slender shoulders to keep the child from falling. The small head lolled back, the lips parting over a shuddering sigh, and the would-be squire had fainted dead away.

Bitterly chastising himself for a bumbling oaf,

Crane eased the child down on the cushiony grass and fumbled with shaking fingers to loosen the tunic at the slender throat.

"Blast!" he muttered, as the tightly knotted lacing refused to budge. "No wonder the little mite fainted. Probably couldn't breathe in this confounded thing."

Then the knot had come loose, and in a fit of impatience he yanked the shirt open to the waist.

"Good gods!" he choked and convulsively jerked his eyes away from the lovely swell of milk-white breasts. "A girl!"

For a moment he sat muttering distractedly to himself, his eyes squeezed tightly shut.

"Easy, lad. You're probably still just a little addled from the madness. You didn't see . . . what you thought you saw at all," he gulped. "It was only a trick of the light. A hallucination. When you open your eyes, they . . . *it* will be gone."

Cautiously he lifted one eyelid and peaked at the still form of the knight's squire.

"Aargh!" he groaned and popped it down again, his fists coming up to rub fiercely at the deluded eyeballs. "I am going mad again. I must be. One simply does not take a female to be one's squire. I mean, why would he? Frayne's no fool. He'd not be likely to make such an error."

Then abruptly his mutterings ceased, and his lanky frame stiffened with the birth of a sudden, insidious suspicion. Slowly he opened both eyes and stared down at what was undeniably a girl, and a very young and beautiful one at that, and suddenly the dirt-streaked face, the crudely shorn hair, the bulky, oversized clothing—everything made almost perfect sense. The Knight of Tor had sought to disguise his bogus squire's true sex, but why? Why such an outlandish charade? Who was this lovely child, and why had Frayne dragged her along with him on one of his blasted quests? Had his lusty appetites become so great that he must have his concubine with him? Crane wondered with slowly mounting rage. And when, conveniently, he had come across the Enchantress, had he thought to conceal this beauteous morsel from her?

With contemptuous eyes he scanned the delicate face with its finely arched sable eyebrows, short straight nose, and rosebud lips. The thick dusky eyelashes quivered against her cheeks, and despite himself he could not suppress a small sigh at the thought of the bewitching eyes hidden beneath the closed lids. There was a deceptive aura of childish innocence about the fragile, finely molded bones of her face. The small pointed chin would seem to promise a gentle stubbornness, which he had already witnessed, and the high, wide brow, smooth beneath the dirt, a quick intelligence. He frowned, then, as he made out an ugly purplish swelling amidst the smudges on the side of her head near the temple.

"Whew!" he breathed. "No wonder she keeled over." And, gazing down at the alarmingly pale face, the young mage experienced an odd sort of pressure in his chest. Swiftly he bent to examine her more closely for further injuries.

She was covered on one side with numerous small cuts and abrasions, as if she had had a nasty fall into a bramble bush, he thought, and his lips thinned to a grim line as he bared one shoulder to discover the milky smoothness marred by an angry bruise. He drew away from her with a growing feeling of perplexity.

Obviously the foolish chit had been in great discomfort, yet she had never once uttered a word. She might indeed be the Knight of Tor's plaything, and consequently one deserving of his scorn. Even so, there was no denying that she possessed an overabundance of both a remarkable courage and a fiercely stubborn pride, neither of which he would have thought to find in one of her kind. A dangerous gleam hardened the youth's usually gentle eyes. Who was she, this waif who did the bidding of the Knight of Tor? Despite her budding womanhood, she was little more than a child. Had Frayne indeed sunk so low as to dishonor innocent young maidens? he pondered, feeling betrayed somehow.

The girl moaned softly and stirred, bringing the young shape-changer abruptly to his senses. Swiftly he drew the front of her tunic together, and cursing beneath his breath at his suddenly unwieldy fingers, tied the lacing as best he could. Then he lurched to his feet and fled to the spring bubbling out of the earth near the Shrine. Kneeling, he removed his neckerchief and dipped it into the cool water, then hurried back to the girl.

Panting a little from his exertions, he bathed her face and with shaking hands smoothed the tousled hair from her brow. She really was a taking little thing, he thought as he beheld the translucent ivory skin free of dirt for the first time. What a dunce he had been not to recognize her for what she was from the very first. He must indeed have been mad. Then he saw her eyelids quiver and flutter open, and his breath caught painfully in his throat, for he stared entranced into the blue depths of her eyes and felt suddenly shaken to the core as slowly she awakened to him.

For a seemingly endless moment she gazed up at him, her brow creased in bewilderment as if she could not recall who he was. Then slowly her expression cleared.

"My lord Crane?" she whispered uncertainly and tried to sit up, only to sink back again with a low moan, one hand rising weakly to her bruised temple and her eyes closing tightly against the sudden dizziness.

"Easy," Crane muttered. "You have a nasty lump on your head. Just lie still for a while. Don't move now. I'm going to get you some water to drink."

She swallowed painfully and carefully nodded her head.

"*Julab*," she murmured faintly. "Water."

Her eyes were open when he returned from the spring, and as he lifted her against his shoulder and held the cup to her lips that she might drink of the Virgin's water, he noticed for the first time that the dazzling blue orbs were delicately slanted upward, giving her an exotic cast, and, recalling as well her unfamiliar accent, he wondered just who her people were. Then she had drunk her fill, and suddenly he became uncomfortably aware that he still held her to him and that a becoming tinge of color had relieved the alarming pallor of her cheeks as he continued to stare at her abstractedly. His gaze was drawn to her enticing lips, and her slender warmth awakened in

191

him unexpected longings previously reserved for Aurora, the goddess of his secret shrine.

With a jolt he realized that he had been about to kiss Frayne's concubine and was both revolted and ashamed that he could be so tempted.

His thoughts must have shown in his face, for suddenly the girl went white as a sheet and shrank pitifully away from him.

"What is it, my lord?" she whispered. "How have I displeased you?"

"Never mind," he muttered harshly, bewildered by the turmoil of conflicting emotions she evoked in him. He cleared his throat self-consciously and wondered what he should do next, when he felt her shiver convulsively against him and realized she must be miserably cold. For while they had been talking the mist had changed unnoticed to a steady drizzle, and the woods were dank and chill. Egad, what a dunce he was not to have carried her immediately to cover. The shelter he had rigged up the night before might be crude, but at least it was dry. No doubt she was half-starved, too, since they had not eaten the night before. As usual he had bungled things, he castigated himself. No matter who or what she might be, the chit had been given into his keeping, and he owed her better than this. A plague on the Knight of Tor! he thought bitterly as he considered the probable complications of being alone with a helpless female for any length of time. And suddenly the shelter beneath the Valdoran Shrine seemed very small, indeed.

Thus irritated with himself for not having better seen to the girl's needs, and furious with Frayne for having saddled him with his unwanted castoff, Crane fairly glared at his hapless charge.

"You're wet! And nearly frozen," he blurted churlishly. "And you've got no business wandering around with a lump the size of a goose egg on your head. I suppose you expect me to look out for you if you catch an inflammation of the lungs. But you'll be sadly disappointed. I don't plan to cool my heels here just because you don't have sense enough to take care of yourself, my lad."

"N-no, my lord," she murmured doubtfully, her eyes huge and questioning on his face.

"Crane!" he peevishly corrected. "I'm not anyone's lord. I am simply Crane. Is that understood?"

"I-I will try t-to remember, my lord," she stammered, then bit her lip and blushed hotly as he glowered down at her.

"See that you do." Then he shoved himself impatiently to his feet and bent to scoop her in his arms. Straightening, he was surprised anew at her feather-lightness and acutely conscious of her heaving breast pressed against his bony chest. At first she was rigid in the cradle of his arms, but as he stalked wordlessly toward their hidden bower, a fierce frown black upon his brow, he was surprised to feel her gradually relax, her hands stealing slowly up to grasp him tentatively behind the neck. He could not stop himself from sneaking a look at her from out of the corner of his eye and then wished he had not, as he beheld her deceptively sweet face, the soft cheek cuddled cozily against his shoulder, and the blue eyes like deep, mysterious pools fastened dreamily on his downy chin.

Egad! he groaned to himself, his stomach queasy

193

with new and only vaguely understood sensibilities. You've landed yourself in a proper bumblebroth now, you poor dunderhead.

Gratefully he came at last to the shelter beneath the Shrine and laid his burden down on the soft bed of pelts. But his relief at having successfully rid himself of the girl's disturbing encumbrance was short-lived, for as he made as if to leave her, she clung to him, her eyes huge and pleading on his face.

"Please do not go from me," she whispered huskily. "I cannot be easy in the forest. It frightens me. For I am Wendaren, and I know only the unfettered vastness of the desert and the infinitude of sky. To be in the forest is to be blind and surrounded by unknown enemies. Please stay, Crane. I beg you. When you are near, I feel nothing would dare harm me."

For an endless moment he felt as if he had been struck a paralyzing blow as he stared helplessly into her upturned face, and for the life of him he could not free himself from her twining arms. She was so very lovely, and her beguiling lips trembled so very near his own. Almost he lowered his head to taste of their sweetness when suddenly he remembered that she was supposed to be a boy and that she belonged to Frayne.

Blushing hotly, he none too gently disentangled himself from her hold and backed hastily away from her.

"You don't have anything to fear in the Sacred Grove," he managed in a somewhat muffled voice. "And I'm only going to fetch some food from Frayne's pack. I won't be gone long. You try to rest. I'll be back directly."

Then he turned and fled the suddenly stultifying

confines of the shadowy bower. Once safely outside, he paused to breathe in deeply, small beads of sweat breaking out on his forehead despite the cool spray of mist against his face.

Ye gods! What was happening to him? If he was mad, it was a kind of madness he had never felt before, not even when first he had beheld his beautiful Aurora in the mage-fire and had begun to worship her from afar. Then he had dreamt of touching her silken loveliness, even gone so far as to imagine her in his arms and felt the humiliating stirring of his groin. But his love for the Enchantress had always been a forbidden love, for she was favored by the gods and he—well, he was only Crane, the bumbling grandson of the great Mage-Lord Krim. She was his empress, his queen, and he had learned to content himself with simply being allowed to be near her, perhaps to serve her in some small way. But this dainty, black-haired girl-child who clung so helplessly to him and looked at him with worshipful awe affected him differently. In her eyes he was everything he longed to be—fearless, masterful, a great mage-lord and hero—Frayne.

"Egad! I am bewitched," he mumbled distraughtly and lurched away toward the pack lying beneath the tamaracks.

Janine, the desert slave-girl, sat cross-legged on the bed of pelts, her sweet lips curved in a wistful smile and her gaze distant and dreamy as she ran a comb through her poor, ragged locks. Driven by a strange compulsion she could not explain, she had disregarded her master's orders and had cleansed as best

195

she could using a cloth dipped in an earthen bowl filled with water, washing the detested filth from her face, neck and hands. Then, still buoyed by the unfamiliar thrill her small rebelliousness had occasioned, she had determined to free her hair of its tangles.

Tears blurred her eyes as she tugged the comb through the sadly shortened hair and remembered her lovely waist-length tresses, which for the women of her tribe were a symbol of virtue. She blushed to think what her gentle-hearted mother would have thought could she but see her now, for among the Wendaren a woman's hair was shorn only when she had been dishonored. But the gods had smiled upon the daughter of the desert Khan, for she had been saved from such degradation by a man who was finer by far than her own father, who had heartlessly wagered and lost her at the toss of *al zahr*, the hated dice. Ahbin-ben-ami had not even looked at her as the obscenely fat and malodorous slave-master had dragged her from her mother's arms and carried her off to a life of slavery. But then, she had never enjoyed the dubious distinction of being one of her father's favorites, for while she was one of seventeen daughters born to the desert Khan, she was her mother's only offspring, and her mother's failure to produce the desired male heir had been doubly damning to them both. She had served as a constant reminder to her esteemed father of her mother's unforgivable infertility. Well, he would never again be troubled with her disagreeable presence, she reflected bitterly.

The girl stifled a small sob as the comb snagged painfully on a particularly stubborn tangle. Impatiently she yanked the comb through the knot, then sniffed and brushed the back of her hand fleetingly across her eyes, her small bosom swelling with mutinous resentment for all the fear and humiliations she had been made to suffer before the gods had delivered her into the safekeeping of her beloved master. And thus did she manifest the subtle process of change that had been at work in her since she had been taken from the protected environment of the harem. For she had been reared to a life of unquestioning obedience. Yet, since awakening from the nightmare of the stalking wolves to the serenity of the glade, strange and unfamiliar forces had suddenly begun to stir in her. For she had beheld the Enchantress, and for the first time had seen what it was for a woman to be strong and free. And for the first time, too, she had met a man who did not treat her either as a child or an inferior.

Unaccountably she blushed as a vivid image came to her of the tall youth with the flaming hair and the gentle hands that could yet command the forces of wind and fire.

"Crane," she whispered, her lips curving in a mysterious smile.

He was like Shaheen, the Desert Hawk, she thought whimsically. Soaring unfettered with the winds and yet molding them to his will. Or like the drifting clouds of the *Mausim*, the time of the rains, forever altering his form to suit his mood. She had seen him vanish before her very eyes, to leave fluttering behind a fragile butterfly, which had perched on her shoulder. And when she had sought to capture the lovely creature, it, too, had evaporated into thin air, to be replaced by a delicately perfumed flower. Thus had the kindhearted Mogush transformed her melancholia into *kaif*, the feeling of well-being that bubbles forth in delighted laughter. Whereupon he had appeared again in his true-form, his brown eyes warm with shared enjoyment of her happiness, his smile endearingly askew and self-conscious. And suddenly she had longed to fling her arms about his neck, to have him see her as a woman rather than as the boy with whom he had come to share an easy camaraderie.

A long sigh escaped her lips, and the hand that held the comb stilled among her raven locks as she became momentarily lost in a lovely daydream in which she was again Bgim Janine, a princess of the desert tribes. Then would Crane learn to love her as she had loved him almost from the very first moment she had seen him emerging from the shape of the great cat that had fought in her defense. He would ask her beloved master for her freedom and her hand in marriage, and Sayyid Frayne would gladly grant it, for he had his beautiful Enchantress with him again and would wish for all around him to share in his great happiness.

At the thought of the golden-eyed Aurora, Janine's fantasy suddenly faded into bleak reality, for in the few hours she had shared with Crane in the Sacred Grove, she had learned that no man could resist the Enchantress's fatal charms. Crane, too, loved her, even as did the Knight of Tor. And if the Enchantress could hold the godlike knight within her spell even when he had believed her to be dead, then she, Janine, had little hope of winning Crane from such a one, she mused with a heavy sigh.

The rustle of the tree boughs that formed one wall of her cozy haven broke the slave-girl's reverie. Her heart quickened as she glanced up to find the young mage peering in at her through the leafy branches.

"I thought you were going to try to sleep," he said with a censorious quirk of one sandy eyebrow. His red hair clustered damply to his forehead, and the girl could see raindrops like tiny crystals clinging to his neck.

"Why do you not come in out of the rain?" she queried in quick concern. One small hand lifted gracefully to indicate the statue of the Valdoran at whose feet she reclined. "There is room for both of us beneath this beautiful lady's roof. Come in. I beg you." But still the youth hesitated, and gradually the girl's sweet smile drooped and faded altogether.

"Or mayhap it is I who keep you from seeking a dry haven," she murmured with bowed head. "If so, then I shall walk among the trees for a time that you may rest untroubled by my presence."

The youth's lips twisted in a wry grimace. Egad, the girl had hit the mark. He had supped with her on the dried foodstuffs from Frayne's pack, and, troubled because she had been so quiet and because he had seen a shadow of sorrow in her eyes, he had sought to win a smile from her with a few simple tricks. But when at last he had returned to himself and beheld her lovely features alight with laughter and a warm glow that had seemed meant for him, he had turned craven and fled, mumbling some inane excuse for absenting himself from her disturbing presence, and then had huddled miserably beneath a tamarack.

Where the blazes were Frayne and Aurora? he wondered, not for the first time. By the gods, they had best show up soon, for he could not keep up this ridiculous charade much longer. It must soon come out that he had discovered her secret, and then the fat would be in the fire for certain.

He would have left her again, preferring the discomfort of the bone-chilling drizzle to the confounded torment of being near her and having to pretend she was not the most wonderfully enticing creature he had ever encountered, indeed, to behave toward her as if she were the bantling she was made up to be. But she looked so hurt and bewildered by his aloofness that at last he shrugged fatalistically and pushed through the leafy barrier into the close confines of the shelter. Shrugging off his wet cloak and draping it over the carved antlers of the figure of a hart, he settled gingerly beside the girl.

For a long moment they sat in uncomfortable silence listening to the splatter of raindrops dripping from the trees. In vain the youth sought for something to say, but his mind was seemingly paralyzed by the girl's throbbing presence in the shadowy confines of the bower. The sweet scent of honeysuckle trailing thickly over the Shrine cloyed in the air, and he thought that forever afterward when the fragrance of that flower assailed his senses, he would be reminded of this day and of the girl.

"Tell me about the Enchantress," the girl said at last, her voice subdued in the quiet. "How did she and my master, the Knight of Tor, meet?"

"He was on a quest that led him into Endrith's Forest near Hawthorn Glade where Aurora lived with the elves and the dryads," Crane answered abstractedly, his mind occupied with trying to maintain a few inches of empty space between them in their cramped quarters. "Afterward, she went with him until the quest was completed and he rode away. Back to Tor."

"She is very beautiful. And brave. No wonder he loves her," Janine murmured, and the wistfulness in her voice tore at Crane's heart. Egad, he had never considered that the girl might be in love with her master. Somehow, as he had succumbed more and more to her air of gentle innocence, he had come to think of her as an unwitting pawn in whatever deadly game Frayne was playing on behalf of his scheming mistress. Yet he might have known the child would not be immune to the knight's potent magnetism, that aura of leashed power that made him seem something irresistibly more than mere mortal. It was something that Aurora possessed, too, and something that she and Frayne both unconsciously wielded over others. He should know. He had succumbed often enough to it, he reflected wryly, then became aware that the girl was watching him curiously in the dim light of the bower, waiting for him to answer.

"You can't help loving Aurora," he said dismissively and wondered if he had been cursed by a vindictive god to fall victim to females whose hearts had already been won by the blasted Knight of Tor.

"It is true, then. She is blessed of the gods," sighed the girl. "It is said among my people that those of the House of Doane are *al-marmann*, the god-favored, for they have the eyes of *zarcun-nar*, golden like the fire, and wear the *mandilbaraka*, the mantle of power."

Crane's head came up sharply.

"You said something about the House of Doane before," he observed, trying to keep from his voice the sudden surge of excitement he was experiencing. After all, he did not really know this strange girl, and she might be hand-in-glove with the Sorceress who had tried to have Aurora killed. "Why? What do you know about Aurora?"

"Nothing," the girl replied in wonder. What had she said to spark such interest in the young Mogush? "It is only that she has the golden eyes, like Al-Murabit, the sage of Seraisharaqa, the Palace of the Rising Sun."

"Seraisharaqa," breathed the shape-changer. "Tell me about this sage and his palace. Everything that you can remember. It's important."

"I will tell you what I have heard. But these are legends only. I myself have never seen this place," she said dubiously. The young Mogush was behaving very oddly, she thought, and was uneasy that he might be disappointed with what little she knew about the House of Doane. "Strange tales are told of Al-Murabit and the palace of the dunes. He was not Wendaren, but came out of the east ages past. None knew his name, but he said unto the desert tribes, 'Henceforth, I shall be called Doane,' and so saying, he built his palace among the dunes. The legends tell us that he brought with him two infant daughters. The elder was called Leilah, for she had eyes black as the moonless night and a temper to match. But the younger was Almira, the exalted one with the golden eyes like those of her father. It is said that the two girl-children were close to the heart of Al-Murabit and that when the elder was stolen from him by desert raiders, he never more came forth from Seraisharaqa. It is a very sad story, I think," the girl sighed, thinking how her own father had been only too glad to see his daughter carried off.

"Where is this palace? Does it still stand?" Crane pursued eagerly.

"But of course. Seraisharaqa is *al-barakadar*, possessed of the power of magic. Much of the time it is hidden beneath the desert sands. But then it will rise again for a time to shimmer in the light of the sun or the moon before returning once more to its dark kingdom beneath the dunes."

"And the desert sage. What became of him?"

"Mata," she said simply. "He is dead. For Almira, the younger daughter with the heart of the warrior, left him against his wishes to fight the forces of Amaur, the one your people call Dred. When the wars ended and still she did not return, the old one lost the will to live. He sealed himself within the palace walls and placed a spell of protection over Seraisharaqa, which could be broken only by one possessed of the secrets of Doane."

"And didn't Almira ever come back? Don't the legends tell what happened to her?"

The desert slave-girl shrugged.

"There is a tale told by one who claimed to be *mamluk*, a slave, to the House of Doane. He was found wandering in the desert, half-dead and speaking with the madness of Amaur. He said he had been to Seraisharaqa and seen *al-manarat*—the light of a lamp shining from a turret of the palace. And in the light, the silhouette of a woman gazing out over the desert. 'Almira,' he cried out. *'Banat-ur-zarcun-nar—*

Daughter of the Golden Fire—has returned.' Whereupon he fell silent, for the breath of life had left him. Twice only since that time has anyone of my clan seen the palace of the shifting dunes, and then they saw no signs of life. Nor could they gain entrance, for the spell of Al-Murabit yet protected the palace."

The girl paused in her narrative, her head lifting as she tried to see the young mage-lord's face in the deepening shadows of the bower.

"I cannot say if the old one's tale is the truth. Or if he saw the golden-eyed warrior-woman. The *fellahin*, how do you say—the people of the land . . ."

"The peasants?" Crane interjected.

"Yes the peasants believe the spirit of Almira inhabits Seraisharaqa and that any who would seek entrance shall be struck dead by *Al-nar-baraka*—the flames of power. They will not go near when the palace rises from the sands. But there was one called Sakhira, because he ridiculed the old tales told by *fellahin*, and he wore *Shest*, the girdle of Gawr, who are fire-worshipers. Sakhira went alone into the desert, for he wished to see for himself *Al-nar-baraka*, and no one was so foolish as to go with him. For many days he was not seen and was thought to be dead. Whereupon a caravan traveling east found him, like the old one, lost in the desert and mad. He appeared untouched, without injury or mark. Yet was he without sight, for he had summoned the fire of the Gawr and beheld the way into the palace and a door that led beneath the palace. But as he opened the door, a thousand piercing flames leapt out at him from the dark. And thus was Sakhira, who made fun of the old tales, stricken blind by *Al-nar-baraka*," she ended on a haunting note.

For a long moment Crane sat in silence, his nerves tingling and his muscles taut with a sense of foreboding. He almost wished he had not urged the girl to tell the tales of Al-Murabit and his cursed palace amidst the dunes. Maybe it was just coincidence that this Almira had had golden eyes like Aurora and coincidence that she had been a warrior-woman, he told himself, but he did not believe it for a second. And when he told Aurora, as tell her he was honorbound to do, she would undoubtedly dash off half-cocked to see this Seri-whatchamaduzit herself. And then where would they be? Struck blind, no doubt, by a thousand piercing flames. Or dead, more like.

Suddenly he jumped as a small hand gripped his arm.

"Something troubles you?" queried the girl softly. "You are anxious about my lord Frayne and your Enchantress, perhaps?"

"I guess I am," he admitted. Though not in the way you mean, he added to himself. "It's been two days since we separated. They should have returned by now. Unless they've run into trouble." And, knowing Aurora, he little doubted that they had landed themselves in a coil of some sort. But she had Frayne to protect her, and Elwindolf and the Andruvien. It seemed unlikely anything could seriously threaten a combination of such formidable strength. No. He seriously doubted that he had anything to worry about at this point. But when the Enchantress had returned and he told her what he had discovered, then he would have ample to concern him, for the Enchantress would be determined to seek out this possible new clue to her true-name and then, too, she would see Jan clearly for the first time and realize she had been duped by her beloved Knight of Tor. A curiously twisted grin touched his lips at the thought of the possible repercussions of that inevitable discovery. And for the first time he was glad he was not in Frayne's shoes. No, Aurora was not likely to be tolerant of her knight's latest peccadillo.

Boltar's sudden piercing challenge split the air. For an instant Crane froze, startled, his stomach lurching sickeningly. The stallion's clarion cry had not been the sound of the loyal steed who welcomes his master's return, but rather the ringing defiance of the warhorse who scents an enemy. Then the muffled thud of hooves and the distant answering whinny of a horse came clearly to the shape-changer's ears, and he was suddenly scrambling to his feet.

"Wait here!" he said to the girl, who was staring at him with wide, frightened eyes, one hand lifted unconsciously to her mouth as though to stifle a scream.

Crane slipped stealthily from beneath the shelter into the clearing, his senses strained for the smallest sign of danger. The girl's grey mare and the rangy black stallion were restless shadows amidst the tamaracks as the boy peered tautly into the gloom. Suddenly the hoarse shout of a man filtered through the darkness, and Crane stiffened.

"It came from over there!" he heard, and an answering cry from further away followed by the crash of underbrush and the pound of hooves sent him racing across the glade toward Boltar and the mare.

"Shoo! Get out of here!" he whispered harshly and waved his lanky arms at the already spooked animals so that they bolted out of the clearing away from the sounds of shouting. Then swiftly he gathered up Frayne's pack and carried it to the crude shelter where the girl crouched in silent terror.

"It is the evil ones who pursue my lord Frayne," she breathed tremulously. "They have followed us here."

"Don't worry," Crane said, his thin, boyish face suddenly hard in the dim light of dusk. "They won't find you. Just promise not to move or call out whatever happens, and everything'll be all right."

"I shall do as you command," she answered in a small, determined voice, but her eyes were huge in the oval of her face gleaming palely in the shadows. "Have a care for yourself, my lord Crane."

"Don't worry. They'll never see a sign of me or the Shrine," he whispered back and vanished once more into the gloom.

For an instant longer he stood just outside the shelter. Then suddenly his tall, spare frame began to waver and elongate. Woody shoots sprang out from a spreading growth of impenetrable thorny hedge, which swallowed the shelter and the shrine just as five dark-clad horsemen broke into the clearing on heaving mounts.

The leader, a burly, broad-set knight, pulled his horse to a sliding stop before the thicket and raised a grotesque hooked limb into the air to signal the others to a precipitous halt behind him. The rangy beast he rode sidled nervously, chomping the bit as the knight peered about the deserted clearing. The red-bearded face marred by a cruel scar shone hideously in the fading light of day.

"There's nothing here," he rumbled. "They must

be further on."

"Wait!" rasped a breathy voice like a dry wind slithering through dead leaves.

The brawny knight's mount backed stiffly and tossed its head as its rider cursed softly and jerked at the reins. Then a pale horse sidled from the close-packed horsemen, bearing to the fore a fleshless apparition of a man draped in shadows.

The falling night moaned with a malevolent blast of wintry wind as the ghostly horseman rode in a slow circle about the glade, probing with a chilling patience every bush and every shrinking shadow, until at last he paused before the thornhedge shivering in the breeze.

"As you see," blustered the knight, "there is nothing here. Groul, the miserable little backsnipe, has brought us on a wild goose chase."

"Perhaps," the specter whispered throatily. "And yet I sense someone or something I have sensed before. All may not be as it seems." The creature appeared to shiver. "The crystal was here. I can feel its cursed presence yet."

"If it was, it's gone now," snarled the knight maliciously. "I say let's backtrack to Sedgewick and pick up the trail where we lost it. I'll be damned if I let the Sorceress's precious knight slip away with my property just because you *think* you sense something. We've lost enough time following your blasted hunches."

"Indeed?" rasped the wraithlike creature chillingly. "And yet was it not I who guessed the knight's squire was in truth the object of your thwarted lust? The virgin daughter of the desert Khan whom Frayne won

208

from you with a toss of the bones? But enough. I little care whether you retrieve your lost property or not. I am come in search of a greater prize, and it suits my purpose at present to return to Sedgewick."

"Then let's be off ere the storm breaks. I little like the looks of those plaguy clouds." And with that, the burly rogue wheeled his mount, and sinking home the spurs, plunged from the glade into the deepening darkness, the others following at a slower pace in his wake.

When at last all sounds of the retreating intruders had died away, the thornhedge suddenly shook and shrank in upon itself, until at last Crane, the shape-changer, stood staring into the inky blackness into which they had vanished.

"May the gods have mercy," he muttered in a strained voice. "Baldrac! And Cranith, that black-hearted fiend of Tor!"

He turned slowly then, at the soft rustle of tree boughs and the timid touch of a hand upon his arm.

"Are they gone?" whispered the girl fearfully.

"Yes," he answered harshly, still shaken at having faced and survived untouched the malevolent shape-changer of Tor. "And now you will explain to me what a girl is doing masquerading as Frayne's squire!"

Chapter Eight

A slow smile touched the stern lips as the Knight of Tor slipped Valarc, Elwindolf's long-bow, off his shoulder and knelt to examine the faint outline of a bootprint in the forest floor. There was little doubt that Aurora's small foot had left the imprint and that he had found her trail at last after nearly half an hour of fruitless search. The Enchantress had seemed to vanish into the vapor-filled air just moments after she had bolted from him on top of the ridge. Then, when he had failed to discover any sign of her flight after Elwindolf, he had been afraid she had taken to the trees as her dryad mother-pair had taught her to do. Thus he was doubly grateful to have found her trail at last, for otherwise he would have had to resort to other means of detecting her in this plaguy soup created out of the lurking evil of Somn, something that he had preferred for his own reasons not to do.

With the lithe grace of a woodsman, he rose, the great bow balanced easily in one hand, and followed the lingering signs of the Enchantress's stealthy flight through the trees, until he came to another set of footprints. His glance narrowed as he made out the imprint of bare feet in the mud.

"Elwindolf!" he muttered and frowned.

The hunter's trail led in nearly a straight line north, roughly paralleling the course of the river, but Aurora's tracks cut sharply west. What was the headstrong Enchantress up to now? he wondered and worked his way a few yards further along the girl's trail, then back again to follow Elwindolf's along the Glendaron.

A hard glint came to the silvery eyes as he found the third set of tracks, a pair of boots larger than Aurora's and badly worn down on the inside of the left heel, as if the one fleeing before the hunter had been lame in that leg.

His lean hand came up to thoughtfully pull at his chin. The signs did not look at all auspicious for the little man from Tor, he thought with a cynical curl of the lip. That the tracks belonged to Groul he did not doubt, for the man who had come to him for information about the legend of the Arlana had had a decided limp. And it appeared, too, that Aurora had joined Elwindolf in hunting down the luckless lapidary. It was, after all, an old ploy of a pair of tracking wolves to separate, one circling ahead of the unsuspecting prey to wait for the other to drive the quarry into the trap. He had seen dogs bring down rabbits in the same way. But while the strategy of the girl who had run with the wolf pack was obvious, her motivation was not.

Had she indeed become one with the renegade woodsman, a cunning wolf out for the kill? Or was she

212

yet the Enchantress hoping to snatch Groul from the jaws of death? He could not be sure, but one thing was certain, and that was that he must find her or Anders Groul before the trap was sprung. Pausing only the briefest of moments to fix his bearings, he set out at a mile-eating lope in the direction that Elwindolf and Groul had taken, for he knew from experience that in the woods the Enchantress could be as elusive as the mist itself when she took the notion not to be found. He would have a better chance of overtaking the other two.

The tall knight ran noiselessly, weaving lithely through the trees looming ghostlike out of the grey sworl of mist and fog. He could feel Dred's growing presence amidst the thickening pall, as if the shapeless flux of Somn itself were bleeding across the land from the open wound left by the stolen Arlana. And sighing through the ghastly branches, the disembodied voices of his father's fallen race called to that in him which was akin to them—"Son of Somn. Prince of Throm. Mighty Thromholan"—until at last he groped blindly through a dense, murky blackness created out of his own ambivalence. For he was ever Frayne of Tor, a knight dedicated to the One, yet mortal son of Throm.

The knight stumbled on a gnarled root to plunge head over heels down a steep incline, the long-bow flying from his hand. With a grunt he came up hard against a tree trunk scant feet from the turgid waters of the Glendaron. For a long moment he lay still, his forehead pressed against the sodden ground as he sucked in great gulps of air. Slowly, convulsively, his long fingers dug into the black earth, the powerful muscles bulging across his shoulders.

"Leave me be!" he rasped. But still the voices clamored in his ear, calling to him, claiming the son of Dred as their own.

"A plague on my father and all his ill-gotten race!" he finally cursed and dragged himself to his feet to stand swaying slightly, the silvery eyes glittering with bitter hatred. Blood flowed freely from an angry gash on his forehead, blinding him. Impatiently he dashed a hand across his eyes to clear them. Then, drawing in a deep, whistling breath, the Knight of Tor straightened to his full height. Thrimheld, Swift-Blade, flashed in his hand.

"You have no claim on me!" he thundered into the sworling mist. "I swear it on the sword pledged to the service of the One. Be gone, fiends of darkness. I, Frayne, command you!"

And suddenly Thrimheld shimmered with a silvery sheen that seemed to burn through the mist. The pall thinned to a soggy grey gauze, and the insidious, soughing voices were silent before the thundering roar of the Glendaron.

Sheathing the sword, Frayne made his way back up the slope. There he paused just long enough to bind about his forehead a strip of cloth torn from his undertunic. Then, after retrieving the long-bow, he searched the forest floor once more for the lost trail. A sudden crash and rustle of underbrush off to the left away from the river brought him up short. The silvery eyes narrowed on the pale gleam of bare skin against the green foliage as a lithe form stole phantomlike through the woods only a few yards from where the knight stood.

Frayne scarcely recognized in this savagely naked creature the dispassionate woodsman who had coolly faced ravaging wolves and slain the father-wolf to preserve Aurora's life. Even as the knight bitterly cursed the potency of Dred's malevolence, which could strip such a man of all rationale and leave him with the cunning of the stalking beast, he had already leaped in swift pursuit. He might still be in time to save the lapidary from his probably deserved fate, for the silently stalking Man-Wolf had certainly not made the noise that had attracted the knight's attention. That had to be Groul fleeing with mindless panic through the dense copse of dwarf oak ahead of Elwindolf.

Briefly Frayne lost sight of his quarry as the man-wolf slipped into the thicket in a crouching run, the silvery gleam of the long-knife glinting with deadly promise in his hand. Then the knight, too, was weaving through the underbrush, his skin crawling with the feel of danger and the bitter certainty that he must come undetected upon the hunter if he were to take him without seriously injuring him. This he knew was imperative, for the knight had not forgotten the nearly disastrous binding of the Enchantress with the despairing unicorn. He had not yet spotted Aurora, but he sensed her hidden presence somewhere near, and if she were indeed one with Elwindolf, to slay or wound him would surely be to do the same to her.

Then he had broken free of the blasted copse into a broad meadow. Yet he must have veered too far west as he struggled through the dense thicket, for as he emerged to behold Groul lurching in terror across the swale, he spotted Elwindolf off at an angle and several yards from where the knight stood. The man called Elwindolf and Drude was posed with deadly intent, one arm lifting to send Dolfang, the long-knife, into Groul's exposed back.

At once the knight saw he could not reach the man-wolf in time to stop his throw. As swift as thought, he drew an arrow from the quiver on his back and fitted it to the elfin-bow, Valarc. But the bow was of Glinden Wood, and Frayne felt the indomitable will of the long-bow resisting even his great strength. Suddenly, off to his left, Aurora bounded out of nowhere into Groul's path. Startled by her sudden appearance, the lapidary stumbled and fell just as Elwindolf's arm flashed down, and the silver gleam of the knife streaked across the glade straight for the Enchantress's heart.

Simultaneously the knight's aim shifted, the corded muscles of his back bulged beneath his shirt, and the silvery eyes glowed with inner power as he uttered a prayer to the One. Then the bow had given way to his greater will, the will of Throm, and with a harsh twang the arrow was sent winging to the mark. Borne with the sure swiftness of the Thromholan's guiding thought, the arrow struck the knife to deflect it from its deadly arc.

Then Groul was up and running, and Elwindolf, uttering the wolf's blood-chilling wail, had leaped in swift pursuit. But Aurora stood as if entranced, her golden eyes fixed on the Knight of Tor. One hand rose convulsively to the pouch that hung on a thong about her neck.

"Aurora—Groul!" Frayne shouted, slinging the

bow over his shoulder and starting across the mead at a run. "Stop Elwindolf!"

As if awakening from a dream, the Enchantress turned to see the lapidary coming toward her, and behind him, Drude, his teeth bared and the long hair streaming wildly in the wind. She made no effort to halt Groul as he fled past her, his face grotesque with fear and loathing. 'Twas the hunter's madness she must somehow breach.

"Hold, Drude!" she cried, flinging herself into the man-wolf's path. "Leave be the man-beast. For ye be not wolf, but man."

But he who had once been Elwindolf knew her not. The pale, glittering eyes flew past her to the lumbering form of the one he had sworn to kill. Roughly he shoved the slender girl aside, for he was mad for the blood-letting.

"I be Drude!" he exulted as he lunged past her. "And Hlafard of the Bredan!"

"Nay, Drude!" the Enchantress shouted after him. "I cannot let you kill the man-beast."

"Little fool. You cannot stop me! Nothing can."

Then he had reached the man whom the wolves called Ommat. A terrible scream rent the air as the long, lithe form leaped to the kill, the powerful fingers closing savagely about the lapidary's fleshy throat. In moments Anders Groul would be dead and the secret of the Arlana forever lost.

Aurora shot a hopeless glance at Frayne, but the Knight was still too far away to be of any help. Only she could keep Elwindolf from slaying Ommat. Only she could thwart Dred's evil. Without further thought, the Enchantress bounded for the two men

217

enjoined in mortal combat.

"Drude! Stop, I beg you!" she cried, vainly struggling to break the man-wolf's death-hold. In dismay she saw the smaller man's face turn grey, the bulging eyes rolling back in his head, and Drude grinning wolfishly, the muscles leaping across his back as he choked the life from the one whose greed had plunged them all into Dred's endless nightmare.

In desperation she drew forth Glaiveling and raised high her arm above Drude's unprotected back. The knife quivered, and the sky darkened. A chill wind leaped out of nowhere to whip fiendishly about the three figures enmeshed in the madness wrought by Dred's ancient evil.

A chorus of mournful wails moaned with the wind, and Aurora looked up to see the slinking shadows of the Bredan closing in around her.

At sight of the lean, wild beasts gathering in answer to the blood-call of the Hlafard, something snapped inside the Enchantress. Suddenly she saw that if she slayed the man who had been her friend, she would be like them, like Drude, mindless and savage, a slave to the primitive lust to kill. Then would the victory in truth be Dred's. With a cry she flung the knife from her. Not even if it meant the Arlana must be lost forever could she bring herself willingly to slay the man who had been Elwindolf.

Yet there had to be a way to put an end to it. Bending down, she grasped a large flat rock between her hands and straightened.

"May the One forgive me," she prayed and brought the crude weapon down hard against the back of Drude's head.

With a groan the man slumped into a lifeless heap atop the limp form of the lapidary.

"Elwindolf!" Aurora cried and heaved the bloodied rock from her. Then, fearful lest she had struck him too hard, the Enchantress knelt, sobbing bitterly, beside the man-wolf. In vain did she try to roll him off the other man. But at last Frayne was beside her, and she glanced gratefully up into the strong countenance.

"I-I beg you," she choked, her golden eyes streaming tears. "Say he yet lives."

For a seemingly endless moment their glances locked, then, grave-faced, the knight knelt beside the fallen Elwindolf. Clasping his hands beneath the man-wolf's chest, Frayne eased the hunter's body off the softly moaning Anders Groul and laid him gently on his back amidst the waving grass. The long, sensitive fingers felt for a pulse while Aurora looked on, crouched on folded knees, the side of her clenched fist pressed to her mouth.

"Let him be alive," she prayed. "Oh, gods! Do not let him die!"

But the knight's gaze was grim when at last he lifted his head to look the Enchantress straight in the eye, for he had detected no sign of life in the felled hunter.

"Nay!" Aurora cried as she read death in Frayne's eyes, and covering her face with her hands, she began to rock to and fro, her slender frame bowed with grief.

"Gods have mercy," she groaned. "I have slain him!"

Frayne's arms folded protectively around her and pulled her to him.

"You did not slay the man-wolf," he said in a hard

voice, and the cold eyes glittered silvery in the gloom. "This was Dred's work."

Then Stahn of the Bredan stole near to sniff the inert form of the man-cub, whom he had called brother. A low growl grated in the wolf's throat.

"Take the one called Ommat and leave us," he commanded in the language of beasts and elves.

Slowly Aurora straightened and, heedless of the tears still streaming down her cheeks, sent an answering thought outward to the wolf.

"But he is our kind," she said, in silent communion with Stahn, Phelan's last living son.

"Nay. The man-cub was of the Circle of Bredan. Leave him with us. And mourn not for him. For now he is at peace with the spirit of Phelan, Father-Wolf. Fear not. He shall rest easy. But ye must go whilst ye can," warned Stahn, who henceforth would be Hlafard in his father's stead.

As the grief-stricken Enchantress looked down at the hunter's still face, it was in her mind to take up Stahn's challenge, for it seemed she beheld once more the Elwindolf of old, he who had been wolf-friend of the elves. The sternly chiseled features appeared calm and peaceful, as if, freed at last from Dred's tormenting madness, he merely slept. Indeed, for a moment she thought that the eyelids fluttered ever so slightly and the faintest tinge of returning color touched his cheeks. But then Frayne had laid the great Glinden Wood bow next to the flaccid body and was solemnly holding out a hand to her.

"There's nothing more we can do here," he said softly. "And there's still the Arlana to recover. Come. Elwindolf is at rest among the brethren."

She started to protest, her glance returning again to Elwindolf, and suddenly she was no longer sure of what she had seen, for the hunter lay so still. Nay. She must have imagined it. With a shuddering sigh, she let Frayne pull her to her feet and watched with a vague sense of unreality as the knight lifted Groul and slung him easily across one broad shoulder. Whereupon Frayne strode firmly away from the circling pack.

For a long moment Aurora gazed after the knight's tall, retreating form. Then suddenly her slender shoulders sagged and she, too, turned, pausing only to retrieve Glaiveling, as she followed after the Knight of Tor, never once looking back. And unseen behind her, a plump figure in billowing, full-length skirts appeared out of the wisps of fog to enter the circle of wolves surrounding Elwindolf. The woman knelt heavily beside the still form of the hunter and deliberately bent her grey head to whisper in the man-wolf's ear while the silent circle of Bredan looked on with knowing eyes.

With a heavy heart, Aurora led Frayne into the ravine in which the lapidary's secret burrow lay concealed behind the thickly growing blackthorn and gorse. Unerringly she found the narrow aperture and halted before it.

"This is his den," she said hollowly. "I have not searched it for the Virgin's Tear."

The knight's falcon gaze flicked to Aurora's bloodless face and lingered on the huge golden eyes, shadowed and haunted with thoughts of death. The inner fire that had ever radiated from the young Enchantress with a glowing vibrancy, a seemingly inexhaustible vitality, now appeared woefully quenched. So, she thought to wallow in self-pity, did she? Now, when Dred's evil was growing more potent with every passing hour? The man's stern lips curled in a mirthless grin.

"Well, what are you waiting for?" he drawled insinuatingly. "Think you the crystal tear will suddenly appear to us as we stand here?"

The slender frame flinched at his icy sarcasm. Briefly the golden eyes flickered toward the mouth of the cave and back again, as if just awakening to a dreadful reality, he thought with an odd pang.

"Must we go in just now?" she queried in fading tones. "There is the stench of death about this place that I cannot like." One hand fluttered uncertainly up to whisk a stray lock of hair from her face. "And I feel so strangely empty, as if all the dreams I had ever dreamt had been suddenly just swept away. If only I could sleep for a while. Forget for a time. . . ."

"What's the matter, Enchantress?" Frayne mocked. "Are things outside your protected glade a bit rougher, a little uglier perhaps, than you had fancied in your childish innocence? Well, we must all grow up sometime, it seems. If you've not the stomach for it, perhaps you should return to the Sacred Grove. Or better yet, to Hawthorne Glade, where you belong."

"How dare you?" she cried, stung at last to a bitter retort. "Are you in truth so cold? Does it mean nothing to you that I have slain a man who was my friend?"

"At one time or another we are all forced to do

things that are painful," he said, one side of his mouth curling self-derisively, and shrugged. "Nobody ever said it was easy to take one's place in the world of men. But you did what you had to do. The question is, what are you going to do now? Do you just walk away, or do you see the thing through? It doesn't matter all that much to me one way or the other. I have pressing business elsewhere."

"Oh, no doubt," she retorted witheringly, her lovely eyes flaring with resentment. "After all, you serve an exacting mistress do you not? 'Tis likely she would be displeased to learn her precious knight has been delayed in fulfilling her demands. Whatever they might be."

"Exactly so," coolly rejoined the knight. "So if you will kindly come to a decision, I would happily be relieved of this rather irksome burden, one way or the other."

"Oh!" she gasped, just coming to the realization that the plaguy man still held Groul's limp body across his shoulder and that she blocked him from entering the loathsome burrow in which he wished to deposit his malodorous charge. "By all means, enter Groul's humble abode," she invited and moved magnanimously aside, her raven head held high in proud disdain. "I pray you will forgive my oversight."

"Quite," he generously agreed, hard put to conceal a grin at her suddenly revived spirit. She was all aglitter with anger, was his lovely Enchantress, just as he had meant for her to be.

"And perhaps a torch of some sort might be in order," he added as he edged past her into the narrow cleft. "If you can overcome your delicate sensibilities long enough to summon the mage's fire."

Ere the outraged Enchantress could deign to answer him, the knight had vanished into the dark interior of the cave. For a moment she stood with her hands clenched at her sides, the golden eyes sparkling dangerously. Then the chill wind of Dred's malevolence touched her with icy fingers, and she shivered.

Frayne was right, she realized as she glanced up at the swirling ceiling of black, roiling clouds fulgurating lightning bolts. There was no time now to mourn for the dead. The desecration of the Virgin's Tear had created a rift in the barrier between their world and Somn, the Land of Limbo, where dwelt the First Immortals in hated exile. Hourly the schism was growing larger, the dark influence of Somn over the land greater. Time was precious now, for instinctively she knew that they approached the point of no return. The rift must soon be sealed or even the Arlana would not be sufficient to turn back the tides of Dred's malevolence.

Bitterly she castigated herself for having failed to uphold her mentor's faith in her, for Elwindolf had come to the hidden valley seeking Vandrel's help in putting things right again, and the old scholar had entrusted the task to the untried young Enchantress. It had been obvious from the first that the woodsman had been reluctant to accept her as a substitute for the more experienced Vandrel, and thus far, Aurora bitterly reflected, she had only managed to bring about the death of the man she had come to help. She simply could not fail him in the final task. The Arlana must be restored to its rightful place in the Sacred Grove. She owed Elwindolf and Vandrel that much, at the very least, she told herself, and with an effort put aside her grief till a later time.

Thus, swallowing her pride, the Enchantress went about the task of providing the knight with his requested torch. Gathering a few sticks of wood, she bound them together with moonseed vines, which clung tenaciously to the rocky cliffs. Then, with a word, she called forth the cold flames that burn without consuming, and, unable to suppress a shudder of revulsion, entered Groul's unsavory den.

The knight had laid his unconscious burden on the cavern floor amidst the awful remains of the beastly little man's grisly meals. Aurora covered her mouth and nose at the stench of rotting flesh and gingerly stepped over and around the scattered debris of bones and other less certain remnants of the jeweler's questionable diet. The steady plop of water dripping into a still pool echoed eerily beyond the spray of torchlight, and her skin crawled with the utter certainty that Groul shared his cave with a menagerie of bats. Reluctantly the Enchantress came up behind Frayne, who was bent over the black mound of Groul's slowly reviving body. The little man twitched and groaned, his head moving feebly from side to side.

"He's starting to come around," observed the knight dispassionately and slapped the bristly jowls lightly a few times with the flat of his hand. "Come on, you," he muttered ill-humoredly. "We've no desire for a lengthy sampling of your less than enticing hospitality."

"Could he have it on him?" Aurora queried hopefully. "Have you searched his pockets?"

"It's hardly likely we could be so fortunate," he

rejoined with a shrug. "But I suppose it's worth a try. Shall the honor be yours or mine?"

"You do it," she shuddered, recalling the creature's clothing, which at one time must have been rich and fine but now was ragged and torn and reeked with unmentionable filth.

Obligingly the knight turned the rogue's pockets inside out, but other than a handful of slithery grubs and the horrid remains of a dead rat, which must have been intended as the main course in Groul's exotic cuisine, he discovered nothing to indicate the wretched man had ever possessed the fabled Arlana.

"Well, that's that," Frayne observed, settling back on his heels and sweeping the unprepossessing interior of the cave with a speculative glance.

The chamber in which they found themselves measured perhaps ten feet in diameter, with a roughly domed roof of just sufficient height to allow the Knight to stand. The first cave gave way at the back to a minuscule tunnel little larger than a rabbit's burrow. The man might have the mean nature of a weasel, the knight reflected sardonically, and 'twas obvious he had shed a great deal of the corpulence that had covered the squat frame of the prosperous merchant of precious gems in Tor, yet not even this much-reduced Groul could have squeezed into the cramped recesses of the tunnel to secrete the crystal. No. If he had chosen to keep it near him in his foul den, then it had to be somewhere in the larger chamber. But where?

A low groan from the lapidary brought the knight's attention back to the prostrate Groul. The small, sunken eyes blinked open amidst the loose folds of skin that once had been fleshy cheeks and jowls and

226

squinted against the painful glare of Aurora's torch. Moaning, Groul turned his face from the light and feebly lifted an arm to shade his eyes. The filthy, badly bruised neck worked convulsively as Groul swallowed then ran his tongue tentatively over dry lips.

"Water," he croaked pitifully.

At Frayne's nod, the Enchantress grimaced. Reluctantly she wedged the end of the flaring torch securely in a jumble of small rocks that had at some time been dislodged from the cavern wall and groped her way to the shadowy depths of Groul's lair where water seeping from the domed roof had formed a shallow pool. As she knelt to fill a crudely wrought wooden bowl she discovered among the scattered debris, she shuddered at the sudden squeak of a bat somewhere in the black recesses of the tunnel. Feeling foolish, yet unable to quell her unreasonable revulsion for the winged creatures who stalked the night, she quickly climbed to her feet and hurried back to the others. She knelt a trifle breathlessly, sloshing water from the bowl, and blushed as Frayne raised one quizzical eyebrow.

"Bats!" she exclaimed, making a face. "Since the time that miserable Valkar thought to drain the blood from me, I have not been able to stomach the creatures."

"Understandable," Frayne grinned, amused to discover that the appallingly dauntless Enchantress should fear anything so innocuous.

"You may laugh if you wish," she retorted, delightfully tilting her chin at him. "But you did not have the thing breathing on your bared neck."

"Oh, I should never laugh," he rejoined, properly

227

grave and thankful the little innocent had not witnessed the surviving man-bat feeding on his dying comrades, as he had.

"Pooh! You are laughing now," she rejoined and suddenly giggled at her own absurdity. Immediately the cavern seemed somehow less gloomy, their hearts lighter, as her golden laughter echoed through the cavern.

Aurora caught her breath as she looked up, her face yet aglow with lingering humor, to encounter the knight's silvery eyes intent upon her and a strange gleam in their depths.

"I had forgotten the sweet enchantment of your laughter," he murmured as if to himself, and suddenly a delicious warmth pervaded her body, dispelling for a time the damp chill of Groul's unlovely lair. A tentative smile curved her lips. Then the sweet spell was broken by a harsh whisper.

"Who in the name of Somn are you?"

The Enchantress's startled glance discovered the lapidary squinting suspiciously up at her, his fleshy lip screwed into a sneer beneath grisled clumps of whiskers.

"I am Aurora," she said forthrightly and thought the beastly little man did not seem at all mad, but crafty rather, and shrewd, as his ferretlike eyes appeared coolly to appraise her, then strayed to wander askance about his unprepossessing surroundings. "And that is Frayne of Tor."

"Him I know," Groul muttered disagreeably, though his cunning glance paused speculatively on the knight's cold, impassive features before sliding away again. "But where am I? How did I get here? And

228

what am I doing in this disgusting place, with the Knight of Tor and a creature whom I must presume to be one of his many wenches—though in that outlandish garb it is somewhat questionable?"

Aurora stifled a small gasp at the man's outrageous arrogance. One of Frayne's many wenches, indeed! The golden eyes glinted dangerously. The insufferable wretch would learn soon enough to mind his tongue with her, she mused darkly. Nor was her uncertain temper made easier by the flicker of sardonic amusement on Frayne's handsome face as he all too accurately read her thoughts.

"You, sir, were attacked by a less fortunate victim of Dred's madness," replied the Enchantress coldly. "And if you must be told, we saved your miserable skin and returned you to this wretched cave where you have apparently just been managing to survive by rather dubious means."

"C-cave? But that's preposterous. One does not find Anders Groul living in such vile squalor. He who has consorted with potentates and princes." The beady eyes narrowed to suspicious slits. "If you have abducted me and brought me to this pestilent covert to coerce me, you are sadly mistaken in your man. I have dealt with rogues intent on parting me from my money before. You will find I am not easily intimidated."

"Silence, you sniveling worm!" Aurora hissed and impaled the loathsome creature with a piercing glance. Egad! she reflected bitterly. Had Elwindolf died that such a one as this might live? "We care nothing for you or your money. We want only that which you have taken from the Sacred Grove. Tell us where you have hidden it, or you will experience the torment you have made others suffer. This I swear in Elwindolf's name."

After a single look at the barely suppressed fury of the golden-eyed Enchantress, the horrid little man suddenly groaned and clutched between his hands his nearly bald pate from which wispy strands of grey hair appeared to sprout through his grimy fingers. "Oh, my head. Everything's fuzzy. I-I can't seem to remember anything."

"Truly?" queried the Enchantress acidly, her lovely face expressive of utter contempt for the puling wretch. "I am sure I must be sorry for you. But you really must try, you know. Else I would not give a whit for your continued well-being."

"Quit stalling, Groul," interposed the Knight of Tor in deadly bored tones, and casually drawing the dagger from the sheath at his belt, he began to clean his fingernails with the gleaming point. "We know you stole the crystal. All you have to do is tell us where it is and you can go back to whatever it is you've been doing here. Though I shouldn't have thought running wild through the woods and dining on grubs and rats when you can catch them is exactly your accustomed style."

With an effort the lapidary wrenched his fascinated gaze from the blade's menacing sheen, his horrified glance fluttering to Aurora whom he mistakenly considered less of a threat.

"G-rubs and r-rats?" he choked, looking distinctly ill. "You must be mad. Apparently you have no idea who I am." Drawing himself up on one elbow, the master lapidary of Tor assumed a haughty expression, ludicrous in view of his tattered and utterly disreputable appearance. "I'll have you know I am considered a man of no little consequence in the world," he informed them in a grand manner. "I have extremely powerful connections in Tor and elsewhere. You can't talk to me as if I were some sort of peasant. A-a common thief."

"Indeed, I should never consider you a *common* thief," observed the Enchantress obligingly. "A common thief surely would never dream of stealing the Arlana. 'Tis a most *un*common crystal after all."

"I don't know what you're talking about," the creature whined and licked his lips. "I know nothing of any crystal."

"But of course you do," Aurora insisted in a voice so soft and yet so deadly that it sent a shiver down Groul's spine. "You must. It's because of you that we are in this terrible fix. If we do not restore the crystal to its proper place, Prince Dred will have won a foothold in the Realm of the One. Then who knows what evil he will do. Do you truly wish to bear for the rest of your days—and who knows how many they might be if we fail to learn the whereabouts of the crystal—the shame of having invited chaos into the land?"

"But I tell you I don't *know* anything about a crystal," Groul whimpered, beginning to squirm. "I swear it. I'm a wealthy man. I haven't any need to steal."

"Then how do you explain your present state?" queried Frayne, leaning deliberately forward, the knife balanced easily in one powerful hand, so that the point glowing redly in the torchlight was scant inches from Groul's twitching face.

The little man swallowed drily and strained back away from the knife so casually poised at his throat.

"Aye. Just look at yourself," Aurora added and waved a disparaging hand at the lapidary. "I know little of the world of men. Yet even I cannot think this is the aspect of a man of substance."

Compelled by the Enchantress's withering contempt, Groul's reluctant gaze traveled slowly down his length, his eyes beginning to bulge as he beheld the disreputable state of his once fine clothes.

"No," he moaned, and like one forced to look upon an horrendous sight, held up trembling hands before his face. "No!" he groaned again as he stared in horrified fascination at the torn and broken nails, black with grime, the tortured fingers curled like hideous claws, fingers that had ever been soft and supple, the skilled and sensitive instruments of a master lapidary. The arrogance of the wealthy merchant crumpled as Groul's stunned gaze flitted piteously from one to the other of his two sternly waiting judges, and beads of sweat began to thread their way through the filth encrusted on his flabby cheeks to disappear into the matted weeks-old beard.

"I-I can't explain it," he gulped and fell back with a whimper, his eyes squeezed shut as if to blot out the truth of his hideous degradation. "The last thing I remember I was called to attend a powerful client," he mumbled after a time. "There might have been some mention of a crystal." He shuddered. "It was a black and terrible place. A nightmare. I don't remember much about what was said."

Aurora leaned forward eagerly. Her lips parted to

speak, but Frayne silenced her with a furtive gesture. Puzzled, she settled back to see what he was up to.

"What client?" the knight said softly, testing the edge of the knife with his finger. The dark-rimmed falcon eyes were expressionless as he watched one side of Groul's face begin to twitch. Swallowing, the lapidary swiped a filthy hand across his mouth.

"I can't tell you that." A feeble grin etched its way through the loose folds of flesh as the knife suddenly stilled in Frayne's hand. "I-It would be breaking a professional confidence. I do a lot of private business for customers who for one reason or another want such transactions kept quiet. It would ruin me if it got out that I broke that confidence."

"A pity. But at least that way you'll be alive," observed the knight dispassionately and bent suddenly forward. His lean hand reached out to grasp one side of Groul's scraggly moustache. The knife flashed down, and Groul screamed as Frayne neatly severed the whiskers with a single slash.

The little man's eyes bulged, the quivering fingers of one hand going up to touch the bristles where the moustache had been cut. As Frayne casually let the wisps of hair flutter to the floor, his chilling gaze lifted to impale the terrified lapidary, the point of the knife coming to rest a fraction of an inch from the lapidary's throat.

"Who was it, Groul?"

"Cranith!" he screamed. "The one called the Imposter. But he was only an emissary for someone else. I-I don't know who. I swear it!"

"And the crystal?"

"It's there. At the bottom of the pool. Cranith was

coming for it. He said he wanted to make sure I destroyed it. Wanted it crushed, ground into powder. B-But when I saw it, I couldn't do it." The ferret eyes glittered with a sort of awe. "It is beautiful. Without a single flaw. The finest of its kind I've ever seen. It would be sacrilege to destroy it. And so I hid here and kept it with me, knowing that if he ever found me, he would grant me a slow, miserable death. But I was mad, I think. I didn't care what he might do to me as long as the crystal was safe from him."

Slowly his gaze refocused on the knight's impassive features. "I am a master of my trade, you see," he said with an oddly touching dignity previously lacking in his demeanor. "An artist. A crystal is a delicate thing. A single wrong move and it is shattered forever. One must know exactly where to cut—with the plane, never against it. And one must have a steady hand. The finest crystals can only be cleaved with another crystal. These are the secrets of the lapidary. The highly developed skills which that barbarian would have had me use to destroy so rare a treasure."

"But why did not Cranith come for the crystal himself?" Aurora queried, still a little shaken at the discovery that her old enemy had had a part in all that had happened.

"He did not dare to enter the Sacred Grove," Frayne answered and sheathed the knife. "Not so long as the Arlana guarded it. The crystal is anathema to Dred's minions."

"Dred? 'Twas Dred who sent the Imposter to Groul?" the Enchantress gasped. "But I thought he was the Sorceress's tool."

"And so he is," observed the Knight of Tor indiffer-

234

ently. "When it suits Dred's purpose."

Then he had risen to his feet. One hand went out to grasp the torch.

"Are you coming?" he queried, pausing to fix the Enchantress with a penetrating glance.

Aurora looked up into the hooded falcon-eyes, her brow puckered in troubled thought. How did the blasted man know so much about the subtle workings of Somn and the Immortal Prince of Throm? And what could he reveal to her of her true identity, so enshrouded in mystery, if he chose to? she wondered with an old, familiar feeling of frustration. Curse the knight's obstinacy! What was the dark secret he so painstakingly kept from her? And suddenly, unbidden, a memory of her confrontation with Krim in the dungeons of the mage's castle of illusions came to her mind. She shuddered remembering the anguish of having discovered Frayne's maimed body strapped to the magician's torture rack, his spirit departed to Dred's nightmarish realm.

"I merely gave him what he wanted," Krim had said when she asked him how he had managed to lure the Knight of Tor into his trap. "An interview with my former master, Prince Dred."

Why had she never before questioned the magician's assertion? she marveled. Indeed, why had she not wondered ere this why the Knight of Tor should seek an interview with Dred?

And then the darkness of Somn seemed to pervade her very soul as the agonizing suspicion that Frayne was in league with the Immortal Prince staggered her like a knife thrust through her heart. Suddenly the cavern seemed to lurch and spin sickeningly about her.

"Oh, gods," she groaned and sank weakly to her knees, her hands pressed over her breast as though she had indeed been mortally wounded.

Instantly Frayne was beside her, his strong hands reaching out to grasp her arms.

"Aurora! What is it?" he cried, his voice harsh in the stricken silence. With a low moan she averted her face, afraid to look at him, afraid to read deceit and perfidy in the beloved countenance. After all, had he not warned her that he would one day destroy her faith in him through just such a betrayal?

"Aurora, look at me!" he ordered, and with one hand beneath her chin firmly forced her head back.

Even amidst the torment of doubt, she vibrated to his touch, for was he not the wellspring of her desire, the touchstone of her existence? Were they not one? And as her eyes fluttered open, the godlike face loomed in her vision, untouched by her sordid fancy, unchanged. He was Frayne as she had always known him—an enigma, a strange compilation of opposing forces that she had ever sensed and never quite understood. But he was her love, and with all the intensity of her young heart, she knew she could never belong to another. Nay! Nor could she doubt him. Not now. Not ever. For she was the Enchantress, touched by the hand of the god. She could not be deceived in Frayne. She would have known if he were false.

With a stifled cry she threw her arms around his neck and hugged him almost desperately close.

She felt him stiffen in surprise, then slowly he enclosed her in a warm embrace, one hand endlessly stroking her hair as he waited for her trembling to cease. And at last she was comforted.

With a sigh, she stirred and pulled a little away from him that she might gaze into his eyes. She read a question in their depths, and the old wariness she had learned to dread.

"Forgive me," she whispered huskily, one slim hand rising to caress his lean jaw. "For a moment I felt Dred's hand upon me. But it is gone now. You have banished it."

For a long moment he stared at her, his face unreadable in the flickering shadows. Then, slowly, he nodded.

"The malevolence of the Prince grows stronger with each passing moment," he said, and she could see that he was not wholly satisfied with her answer.

"Then let us find the crystal," she answered steadily. "And put an end to the sickness."

Chapter Nine

Janine, the desert slave-girl, shrank with a small gasp from the young mage-lord who had spoken with such harshness.

"W-what do you mean?" she stammered. "A girl?"

"Enough, Jan, or whatever your name is," he retorted belligerantly lest he give in to the tremor in her soft, husky voice and fall to comforting her. "You're going to tell me why you're dressed up like a boy and why Baldrac and Cranith have gone to so much trouble to hunt you down. And you'll tell me now or-or I'll simply vanish and leave you to face those two vipers alone."

The girl's small hand rose convulsively to her mouth as she sought to stifle a frightened sob. *Marha-kim!* The young *Mogush* clearly despised her for the deceit that had been thrust upon her. He was so cold and forbidding where before he had been all kindness and gentleness. Alas, she had lost her kind protector, her *sajad-pava*, and could no longer feel safe amidst the terrifying uncertainties of the forest, which seemed to lurk with *ghuwalin*, demons of the woods. Yet the abrupt dissolution of the fragile fantasies she had woven about the unsuspecting Crane was far more devastating to the slave-girl than the discovery that she must again face an indeterminate fate alone. She was, after all, Wendaren; indeed, the despised and dispossessed daughter of the desert Khan. She knew well how cruel could be the laughing gods, for had she not twice been made to suffer the judgment of *al zahr*, the cast of the dice?

Yet despite her worldly wisdom, unusual in one so very young, Janine had no way of knowing that the boy's heart had begun to race with sudden hope. Indeed, he had heard Cranith, the Imposter, call her the virgin daughter of the desert Khan, whereupon it had suddenly occurred to him that Frayne might have instigated the whole charade in order to preserve the child from harm. And if so, then perhaps the girl was not his concubine at all. Abruptly the boy recalled the odd gleam in the knight's eyes as he had seemed to promise Crane a greater reward for freely forsaking his part in the larger adventure to look after Jan. And the dire warning, as well, not to take "undue advantage" of whatever came his way. Obviously Frayne had known all along that the girl's true identity could not remain hidden from him. In fact, it now seemed probable that he had never intended to keep it a secret either from the young shape-changer or from the Enchantress. And suddenly he needed to make certain beyond a doubt just what the girl's relationship was to Frayne, though why it was of such paramount importance, he could not have explained even to himself.

He felt the girl tremble next to him and abruptly captured her hand in his to drag her precipitously into the bower.

"Wrap yourself up in one of the pelts," he ordered gruffly and left her to gather a small bundle of sticks for a fire. Then, pausing before the entrance to the bower, he bethought himself to invoke a more potent spell of binding and concealment than he had previously employed. It was a curious rhyme based upon the riddle of the Gandorf, which Aurora had discovered one day recorded in vanishing ink in *The Book of Lil*. Vandrel, coming upon them, their heads bent conspiratorially over the musty tome, had paused to inquire into their suspicious behavior, for she had become well-versed in their propensity for dabbling in mischief. Whereupon she had become greatly agitated, snatching up the yellowed parchments bound between hard leather and admonishing them upon threat of life and limb to erase the incident forever from their addlepated brains.

The freckled face screwed into a speculative frown. Common sense, which he heeded only rarely, told him in no uncertain terms that only trouble could come from disregarding Vandrel's well-meaning advice. Yet he had ever been possessed of a lively curiosity, which had never ceased to get the better of him. And since he was responsible for the young girl's well-being, did it not behoove him to utilize whatever means lay at his command to ensure her safety? Especially now that he knew the source of her peril? And anyway, he would sleep better knowing they were so well protected. He was uncommonly tired after having spent the major portion of his stay at the grove roaming

241

about in the rain as he kept a lookout for intruders and at the same time removed himself from the girl's unsettling proximity. He simply had to get some sleep soon or he would literally drop into a swoon of exhaustion. Nor was he keen about assuming a shape better suited for inclement weather, for he little knew what to expect from such a move amidst the nimbus of Dred's wicked influence. He might be trapped forever as a fly-eating frog or a mud-turtle or even a towering tamarack tree. And then what would become of the poor, unprotected girl should Cranith and Baldrac return?

Or so did he reason as he sought to convince himself there could be very little real harm and a great deal of good to be gotten from employing Lil's forbidden spell. And, after all, it would only be for the night, since naturally he would dis-spell it first thing in the morning after having gotten a good night's sleep. Without another troublesome qualm, the young shape-changer dismissed the voice of conscience and repeated the curious words of concealment and binding. Then, gathering up his bundle of firewood, he re-entered the bower.

The girl uttered not a word when at last he returned, yet he was acutely aware of her disturbing nearness as he knelt to lay the wood in a hollow he had prepared earlier before the opening to the shelter. He was careful to keep his face averted from her as he summoned the mage-fire and then settled back on his heels to stare into the leaping flames. Finally, when he could no longer stand the taut silence that lay between them, he sank to a seat on the soft bed of pelts and turned to gaze at the girl expectantly.

"Well?" he queried uncompromisingly. "Are you ready to talk?"

"What would you know, *sayyid*?" she returned in accents carefully devoid of expression. She was Janine, the slave-girl, and before that, *banat ur haram*, a daughter of the Khan's protected household, in which survival oft depended on having the wiles of Shaghal, the fox. Early on she had learned the art of concealing her thoughts behind the impassive facade of humility and obedience.

"Everything," Crane flatly demanded. "Your name, for a start. And how you came to be with the Knight of Tor."

The boy's heart constricted as the hushed sound of her shuddering sigh whispered through the shadows. Yet her voice was calm when at last she spoke. Calm with hopeless resignation, for she was *mamluk*, "possessed by another," a slave, and *wazara-ur-fatwa*, cursed to bear the burden of judgment. And in her youthful despair, Crane loomed as *al-gadi*, her judge.

"My name is Janine, and I am a daughter of the desert Khan, Ahbin-ben-ami, who sold me into slavery because my Mother failed to bear him *al-walad*, the son of his loins who would insure his immortality," she began, and slowly the sordid tale of her capture by the red-bearded brigand and her eventual rescue by the Knight of Tor unfolded.

"My lord Frayne has been nothing but kindness," she finished, her huge, sorrowful eyes lifting at last to Crane's boyish face. "He told me he had many enemies who wished to see him dead and that there are evil men who would kill to possess a beautiful young girl. And so I must hide myself in the clothes of

243

a boy and seem to be his squire until he can find for me a place of safety. Then he will go on alone. But I do not wish for him to leave me. *Al-hajr*, the separation, would fill me with sadness, for I have come to love Sayyid Frayne as a daughter loves a good and generous father. And I would seek to comfort him when the black spell darkens his heart with despair. He is very alone and so full of secret pain. And though he loves this Enchantress who torments his soul, I do not think even she can win the secret from his heart."

Crane coughed to clear his throat as her sweet voice died away. Her tale had both appalled and humbled him, for though she had spoken with such poised detachment, he had had no difficulty in imagining the grief and despair she had been made to suffer. Then, as she had described Frayne's illness, his secret torment, the kindness with which he had treated the little slave-girl, Crane had been made suddenly to see the forbidding knight in a new light. No doubt Aurora, like Janine, had beheld this softer, more vulnerable side of the enigmatic Frayne, had experienced the man behind the stern facade of the world-weary warrior. Indeed, he was uncomfortably aware that he himself had denied the evidence of Frayne's magnanimity out of jealousy, for the knight had ever treated him with an understanding and tolerance that both his own father, who had despised him, and his grandfather, who had held him in utter contempt, had denied him. Henceforth, he told himself, he would see more clearly.

Then he became aware that the girl was watching him, her lovely eyes strangely wistful on his face, and suddenly all thoughts of Aurora and Frayne fled his mind. Egad, he groaned inwardly. What now? For night was in earnest upon them, and outside the rain had become a steady downpour. He little relished the thought of spending another night huddled in his cloak beneath a tree, yet if he had not been able to bring himself to remain in the shelter when the girl had thought herself safe in her disguise, then how much less could he do so now?

"Er—I guess you must be tired," he muttered a trifle hoarsely, and wished she would stop staring at him out of those enormous, sorrowful orbs. "I'll be going now so you can get some sleep."

"Must you go?" she said quietly. "I-I know you do not—like me very well. But I promise not to bother you. I will be as silent as the night before the dawn. You will not know I am even here. But, I beg you, do not leave me alone. I am afraid."

"Not *like* you!" he repeated in no little astonishment. "What a piece of nonsense. Didn't I do my best just to win a smile from you? Haven't I just risked my life to save you from those two fiends from Tor? Not like you. I'd just like to know what gave you such a hare-brained notion."

"B-but I deceived you," she whispered, her sweet lips parted in dawning wonder. "A-and you spoke with such harshness that I knew you could not like me as a g-girl. And a slave," she added, her head drooping in shame. "How could the great *Mogush* have a fondness for such a one as I?"

"There's no understanding it, I know," he said, his eyes rolling ceilingward. "But I do, even though you are a silly kid of a girl. And as for your being a slave, you could hardly help that, could you? And no doubt

Frayne will be only too glad to give you your freedom once he finds a place for you. And come to think of it, I know just the place."

"But I told you I have no wish to be parted from my lord Frayne," she said a trifle petulantly. After all, the young *sayyid* had called her a silly kid of a girl when she was easily of an age to be married. Indeed, had she remained among her own people, she no doubt should have had a husband chosen for her by now, might even have already borne her lord and master a child.

"Well, maybe *you* don't want Frayne to leave you behind, but it's a cinch he will, just as soon as he finds someone to take you in," Crane said, mercifully oblivious to the darkling glance in the veiled eyes. "He's always in some kind of danger, and you can bet he won't want a helpless girl tagging along getting into all sorts of trouble."

"I am not helpless," she began indignantly.

"Oh, yes you are," the young mage interrupted with the air of one possessed of vast worldly experience. "All girls are, except for Aurora. And believe me, Frayne did his best to discourage *her* from going with him on the quest for the unicorn horn. If he balked at taking *her* just because she was a female, *you* don't stand a chance. But like I said, I know just the place for you. You'll love it with my old tutor, Vandrel. She's a scholar, you know, and can teach you all sorts of things if you're of a mind. And if you're not," he added with a wry grin, "well, she's a brick anyway. They don't come better than her."

"You are very fond of this Vandrel," observed the slave-girl in a subdued voice, for the young *Mogush* had spoken with the assurance of great knowledge, and no doubt he was right. Her master had seemed most determined to find a family with whom to leave her. And no wonder. She had indeed been a great deal of trouble to him already, and she still cringed with shame when she remembered the helpless fright she had felt upon finding herself suddenly alone in the terrifying forest. She had even allowed herself to be thrown from one of the little mares whom her people called *banatin-ur-rih*, daughters of the wind, because they carried the *sipahin*, the horse-soldiers, with sure-footed swiftness. She, Janine of the desert clans, had been thrown! She did not deserve the joy of being allowed to accompany her master into danger. But the knowledge that Crane spoke only the truth did not lessen the hurt his words had caused, for he had compared her to the Enchantress and found her sadly wanting.

"Well, yes. I suppose I am," Crane admitted. "And you will be too." Then he seemed to become aware that the girl had grown markedly quiet, for suddenly he shifted nervously and glanced uneasily about him. "But you'd better get some sleep now," he suggested, unaware of the condescension in his manner toward her as reluctantly he unfolded his long legs and made as if to rise. "I'll see you in the morning."

But the sudden brilliant flare of lightning followed by a deafening crash of thunder sent Janine flying into his arms. Caught off-balance, he toppled over backward, the girl sprawled on top of him, her sweet lips scant inches from his face. The young mage's breath whistled in his throat as he looked up into her huge eyes and glimpsed the mystery of a woman's soul reflected in their depths.

"Do you find me beautiful, Sayyid Crane?" she whispered softly.

"Ye gods," he groaned and kissed her.

Aurora staggered amidst the renewed fury of Dred's malice as the sky burst asunder with a deluge of wind-driven rain. Her very soul seemed battered by the persistent sizzle and crack of thunderbolts crashing in endless fulminations overhead. Curse Dred! she thought miserably as she forced her leaden limbs to carry her another step into the face of the storm. And curse Groul for having been his unwitting pawn! She was heartily weary of the trouble they had caused and wished only for an end to it. It was that thought and the knowledge that they were not far now from the Sacred Grove that kept her doggedly to the pace. Soon now the Arlana would be restored to its rightful place.

As if in need of reassurance, the Enchantress slipped her hand beneath her cloak and closed slender fingers about the pouch slung on a thong about her neck. There resided the Virgin's Tear, along with the Andruvien. Though they were both crystals possessed of mysterious powers, they were as different from each other as a splendorous flashing star is different from a dewdrop sparkling in the early morning sun. She marveled, remembering how she had held them, side by side, up to the light of the torch in Groul's horrid cave. For the sliver of the Vendrenin, created by the gods as an awesome instrument of destruction, had pulsated icy fulgurations of brilliant flame, while the tear-shaped Arlana had seemed to glisten a soft iridescence from a shimmering heart of purest crystal.

No wonder Groul had prized it enough to dare Cranith's fury, she thought, then frowned, for she had not liked to turn loose the crafty old reprobate.

She had exchanged heated words with Frayne over that very subject, but the knight had remained unmoved by her fear that the scheming lapidary would betray them to Cranith at the first opportunity.

"Just what do you propose we do?" he had queried, the cynical curl of his lips mocking her. "The storm clouds are even now gathering without. Ere we have covered half the ground back to the grove, we shall be visited with a tempest such as try men's souls. Shall we be further encumbered with this puling coxcomb, who will of a certainty have either to be dragged or driven through quagmire and storm?"

The Enchantress had not been able to conceal her dismay at such a notion. Having once more to suffer unencumbered the vicissitudes of one of Dred's upheavals was bad enough. To be further saddled with an unwilling Groul at such a time was not to be thought of.

"The idea does not appeal to you?" the knight had commented ironically, and she seethed impotently even yet as she recalled his arrogant self-assurance. The insufferable wretch! He knew her all too well, as had been infuriatingly evident in his next derisive speech. "Of course, we could leave him here securely bound. Perhaps he shall even manage to free himself ere he starves to death. But the uncertainty of his fate would belike prey upon your mind. No. 'Twould be kinder and far less worrisome to simply knock the miscreant alongside the head and put a quick period to his existence. Who shall have that dubious honor, I wonder? I rather doubt that Groul would so oblige us as to perish on his own."

There had seemed little use in attempting to gainsay him after that. It had been obvious that they had little choice but to leave Groul to his own questionable devices, and she had stormed from the beastly lair, grateful at least that in all likelihood she should never again encounter the loathsome creature. But Frayne had remained at some length within, conversing in low tones with the master lapidary of Tor.

About what? she wondered as she lifted her head to behold the Knight of Tor as he loomed against the brilliant flare of lightning bolts ripping through the firmament, his cloak billowing about the tall, powerful frame as he leaned into the gale. She knew he had come to the forest in search of the lapidary, for he had admitted his business was with Groul. But his ventures were ever connected in some way to the Sorceress of Tor. What had *she* to do with the lapidary? Aurora wondered. Indeed, what had she to do with a mysterious Kingdom of Crystals and a castle that appeared and vanished amidst the dunes? For she had heard that much of the murmured conversation ere Frayne had spotted her eavesdropping at the cavern mouth and taken greater care that she heard nothing more. No doubt it all had something to do with the potion for which the Sorceress had required the horn of a unicorn, and, now that Frayne had what he wanted from Groul, he would be like to steal away anon. But he would not go without her, she vowed. Never again would she be parted from her enigmatic love.

The frenzy of the storm continued unabated as the Enchantress and the Knight of Tor groped endlessly through the thick slough generated by the evil set loose upon Dalmurn by the theft of the Arlana. Until at last Aurora plodded mindlessly, carried only by a will that would not admit defeat. And then suddenly she was gripped in arms of steel and borne down into the ooze of mud, a hand held tightly over her mouth.

For a moment she was too stunned by surprise to resist. But at last, as she felt the hard grip relax ever so slightly, she erupted into fury, twisting and kicking at her assailant.

A low curse sounded in her ear, and she stiffened as she recognized Frayne's voice.

"Softly, little spitfire," he growled. "Someone's coming."

Instantly she stilled, her eyes wide with sudden understanding on the obscure shadow of the knight bent over her. Slowly she nodded her head, and the lean hand was withdrawn from her mouth. The knight eased off her slender form to settle beside her, the dark head lifted to peer into the storm-ridden night. The pale gleam of a knife blade flashed in his hand, and swiftly Aurora drew her own elfin dagger, Glaiveling. Then the muffled thud of horses' hooves and the crash of underbrush brought her tautly to her knees. Her stomach clenched with the premonition of danger as she realized a band of horsemen was issuing in haste from the direction of the Sacred Grove.

They swept past in a close-packed group, black-cloaked and heavily armed, a formidable company of rogues and up to no good, she doubted not. Then Frayne's hand darted out to drag her roughly down as she started violently, a low hiss whistling through her teeth. For the one in the lead had been Baldrac. She could never mistake that cruelly scarred face. And trailing behind the others, a thin, wraithlike creature, the grotesque, bloodless death's skull seeming to leer at her from beneath a black hood as a brilliant flash of lightning illuminated the night. Oh, gods! 'Twas Cranith. He, who had sworn a terrible vengeance on the young Enchantress and her loyal friend, Crane, the shape-changer. Fear was a sudden knife thrust through her vitals. Did the young mage-lord even now lie brutally murdered in the Grove of Tamaracks? She fretted as she waited for the sounds of the villains' retreat to fade into the distance.

Then Frayne had released her, and she was scrambling to her feet to stand trembling in every limb, shaken by a terrible loathing for Dred's evil minions.

"Did you see those fiends of Tor?" she rasped, her voice taut with bitter accusation.

The knight's falcon eyes fastened quizzically on her face, gleaming whitely in the leaping fulgurations.

"How not?" He shrugged indifferently and sheathed his knife.

"Well?" she said, her hands propped on her hips as she waited for an explanation. "Did you know they were in pursuit of you again?"

One arrogant eyebrow arched sardonically upward as, coolly, he met her fulminating glance. The slim shoulders had lost their weary droop, he noticed with interest, and she fairly bristled with suppressed indignation at his apparent dispassionate reaction to having encountered her two old enemies once more in the forest. Yet had the fiery young Enchantress been able to see past the practiced mask of cynical detachment, she might have glimpsed the weariness of his soul, for he was well aware that sometime, somehow, something had occurred to tarnish the pure and innocent faith that she had ever nourished for her Knight in shining armor. Well, it had always been inevitable, and no doubt it was best that her foolish attachment for him should die a natural death. And the sooner the better, he thought brutally as he looked upon the beautiful child-woman scintillating with fiery passion. For she was the Enchantress, fully roused and magnificent in her fury, and she wounded him to the heart.

But she was waiting for his answer, and for once he must not fail her, he told himself with a bitter curl of his lips.

"I knew someone was after me," he answered smoothly. "I should, perhaps, have guessed it was Cranith and his lapdog. But what would you? One is not, alas, infallible."

She stared at him doubtfully, her regal head cocked slightly to one side as she studied the coldly impassive features of her beloved. Why must he be so closed to her? Why could he not trust her? Had they not been forged by the gods' passion into one? Had she not proved time and again her indestructible love for him? Blast his arrogance, his cursed pride or cynicism or whatever it was that kept her in the dark. Why must he ever seek to drive her from him? Because he is not what he seems, whispered an insidious voice inside her teeming brain.

But, nay! She would not listen. She was Aurora and he was Frayne. If he were false, then even so must be she.

Then her brow furrowed suddenly with a new puzzle. He had known he was pursued. How? The ambush in the streets of Tor! she thought. They had sought to kill him then, but why? Once, beside Grendylmere, he had said Cranith and Baldrac were no threat to him. What had changed all that? Who had sent them to slay the Knight of Tor? Dred? The Sorceress? Who?

It made no sense to her. None of it. Yet who could think, with Dred's malice a waking nightmare all around? And, too, she was bone-weary, her mind dulled by all that had happened to her. At present she knew herself to be no match for the impenetrable Knight of Tor, and time was growing ever shorter. 'Twere better to leave the worrisome matter for another day, she wisely decided. They had yet to reach the Grove, where even now Crane and the young squire might be lying wounded, mayhap even dying.

Suddenly she was filled with a terrible urgency to be off, to reach Crane and the Sacred Grove without further delay. She could not bear it if she had lost him as well as Elwindolf. How would she ever be able to face Vandrel again?

"Nay, not infallible," she said darkly. "And neither is Crane. If they have harmed him, not even your precious Sorceress will be able to shield them from the retribution due them."

"No doubt," he commented drily. "And yet it seems to me that you tend to sell the young shape-changer short. I think you need have no fear for him. There is more to that bantling than even he surmises."

Without a further word the knight stalked away, leaving the Enchantress staring after him in openmouthed astonishment.

The malevolent wind shrieked through the groaning tamaracks with a fiendish vengeance. As if all the shades of Somn had been unbound and set free to ravage the Virgin's sacred ground, Aurora thought, as at last they came to the center of the grove. Overhead the angry swirl of black clouds formed a nimbus of Dred's concentrated evil, and the Enchantress shuddered as she envisioned the despair of a world ruled by Thromgilad. And yet within *The Tome of Prophecy* was written the victory of Throm, led by the Thromholan. Could such a one in truth be mightier than Harmon—mightier, indeed, than the sustaining power of the One? It could not be, and yet how could one gainsay the revelations of Throm, which had been envisioned by the First Generation of Immortals when still they were of lordly stature, the nearly perfect creations of the One's perfect psyche? For it was said that the Lords of Throm had had the power to glimpse the subtle workings of the Creator's profundity. Yet while they had had their lofty visions, their comprehension of the sublime mysteries had been imperfect. Wherefore had Dred and his deluded race committed the error of presumption, thus precipitating their fall from grace.

Such had been the lessons taught her by Garwin the Wise and Thegne the Elder of Hawthorn Glade when she was Anduan, Elf-Foundling. And as Aurora, the Enchantress with the Blade of Power, she, too, had been visited with strange, haunting visions of past and future. From whence had they come? she wondered not for the first time, and suddenly she was filled with fear that mayhap she had fallen victim to the same self-deluding labyrinth of false-pride that had proven

Dred's bane. For suddenly nothing seemed so clear as it had before, when she had first left Truewood, the dryad's father-oak, to seek her true-name. Then destiny had seemed a simple matter, and, filled with the ignorance of youth, she had been certain that in time all would be revealed to her. She need only persevere and the gods would grant her the truth. And, as if as a sign sent from the One, Frayne had appeared, emerging from the shimmering waters of Grendylmere, and nothing had since been either simple or the same. For though he had awakened her to the power of the god, he had also plunged her into a world in which what was real and what was illusion was most difficult to discern, as was a truth that seemed ever-changing with time. She could be sure of nothing, not of the god who had chosen her as his vassal and then had abandoned her to Elwindolf's savage madness, not even of Frayne, whose heart remained hidden from her behind a black veil of secrecy. How much less, then, could she be certain of herself?

Or so it seemed as the storm waxed ever more virulent the nearer she came to the heart of the grove. She was deluding herself that anything could subdue Dred's wrath, much less herself, nagged the persistent whisperings of her own uncertainties. He was a god and she naught but a nameless mortal, a foundling, an insignificant creature with illusions of grandeur. Oh, gods! In truth, she was an abomination, for in her arrogance she had slain Elwindolf, her friend, and no doubt Crane, as well. Crane, dear loyal Crane, who had only wished to serve her in some small way and who once in bitterness had accused her of needing no one, nothing, for had she not mastered Andruvien and was she not become a law unto herself? And she had thought to judge *him* for succumbing to Dred's madness, even going so far as to threaten to send him back to Vandrel till he was master of his powers; she, Aurora, who had stalked Ommat with bloodlust in her heart. Shades of Somn! She was unworthy of Crane's loyalty and Vandrel's sustaining faith. She had been blind. Blind to the truth. Nothing could prevail against the might of Throm. Nothing!

Thus the Enchantress of the Glade, who had dared to penetrate the mysteries of Krim's Keep and had challenged Dred in the Land of Somn, she who had sustained the judgment of Gesh and mastered Andruvien, knew at last the agony of bitter doubt, and all around her was darkness.

"Aurora!" shouted a voice out of the dark, and strong hands lifted her to a hard chest. Bewilderedly she wondered how long she had been lying prostrate on the ground. And when had the storm suddenly calmed? A preternatural stillness lay over the Sacred Grove. Then she shivered convulsively. Gods! She was soaked to the skin and covered with mud. Yet she hardly cared, for a paralyzing languor pervaded her limbs, and she felt impervious to the cold. And somewhere in the back of her mind was yet an awareness that something she had no wish to face awaited her awakening.

"Aurora," the voice persisted, "where is the crystal? The Virgin's Tear. Somn's strength approaches the apex. You must return the crystal to the Shrine. Now, before the dawning of the new day. Else Dred will have won."

"Nay," she muttered and rolled her head heavily

257

from side to side. " 'Tis no use. Let me sleep."

A low curse rent the air. Then merciless hands gripped her shoulders and roughly shook her.

"Wake up, damn you. You can't sleep now. It's in sleep that Dred works his will on you so that you dream the dreams of Somn."

An oddly painful spasm of laughter burst suddenly from her, to leave her weak and gasping for air when it had passed. Fool! she thought. Did he not know that they *lived* the nightmare of Somn? Indeed, was not Dred's the true reality, and all that she had ever known or thought she had known the empty illusion?

"And what of the One?" returned the voice implacably. "And the elves and your dryad mother-pair. What of Vandrel and Crane? Are they the figments of Dred's twisted mind?"

"Nay," she murmured, confused, for she did not recall having spoken her thought aloud. "For they know the joy of song and laughter." And suddenly her eyes fluttered open to behold, hovering over her, Frayne's face, taut with anger or worry or some other emotion she could not define. "But I have forgotten it," she whispered. "For I have seen the emptiness within myself. I am the illusion."

For a moment bitter pain dimmed the silvery sheen of the knight's falcon eyes glowing eerily in the murk and gloom of the dreadful night, even as a shudder shook his powerful frame.

"Curse my father for all eternity!" he uttered in a voice of awful doom. "Was it not enough for Dred to defile the Valdoran's pristine virtue? Must he also have the rape of this child's precious innocence? And what other evil shall he wreak ere his jaded, twisted

258

soul is finally appeased? Gods! Is there no one or nothing that can stop him?"

Aurora gasped, pierced by a rending pain like a sword thrust through her heart. Even as she reeled and struggled against an enveloping curtain of darkness, she felt the hand of the god upon her, and suddenly the world seemed to right itself. For it was Frayne's torment that had pierced her weary and battered soul, his need that was the touchstone of her love. And suddenly she was inundated by a terrible, sweet joy. Dred's malice might indeed have revealed to her the truth of her woefully apparent shortcomings, might even have shattered her faith in herself. But one thing he had not been able to sully—her selfless love for the Knight of Tor. For that lay in the province of the heart and soul, rather than in the mind, where Dred played his wicked games.

And suddenly she was overwhelmed by a fierce tenderness.

"Frayne," she whispered thrillingly, and her arms stole up to grasp him, almost with desperation, to her. "Frayne, I am awake at last!"

She felt him grow rigid in her embrace and exulted in the glorious sweep of the god's power through her as his heart quickened against her heaving breast. The long, powerful arms like bands of steel wrapped around her slender body even as his lips pressed convulsively against her hair.

"Aurora," he breathed on a long, shuddering sigh. "Blessed be the One."

Then he had pulled away from her to look long into her eyes gleaming darkly in the white blur of her face, and it seemed to her that their minds briefly touched and that the gloom of Dred's invidious night was suddenly less black, so that she could clearly see the beloved countenance, the harsh lines of despair slowly giving way to dawning gladness. And as, at last, he bent to explore the mystery of her sweet passion, she felt stronger than she had ever felt before, for truly they were one and she was not alone.

When at last he released her to once again drink in the mystery of her woman's soul shining forth from her eyes, a fleeting smile touched the austere planes of his face with a godlike beauty.

"You astound me, Enchantress," he said, a hint of laughter in his deep voice. "You dare once again to challenge Dred, and, further, have the audacity to win. Think you we might put an end to his bluster anon? Or have you developed a fondness for wallowing in the mud?"

She stared up at him in wide-eyed astonishment. Then suddenly her golden laughter bubbled forth as she realized she was covered with muck from head to foot.

"Egad! What a sight I must be," she gurgled. Then her brow furrowed with a wry grimace. "My clothes! They are utterly ruined. They are the ones Vandrel gave to me ere we left her hidden valley. Oh, I shall never forgive Dred for this. It is not enough that I am forced by reason of my human condition to cover myself with the cumbersome things, but now I must needs resemble a homeless waif as well."

Then did the knight's rare laugh rumble in the deep chest as he beheld the Enchantress's purely feminine indignation. She was priceless, was this indomitable child-woman who could laugh in the face of Somn.

Then suddenly he had sobered, and, rising, he held out a lean, powerful hand to Aurora.

"Come," he said, a beautiful light in his eyes for the girl who had captivated his soul. "It is time to put Dred's malice to rest."

They made their way through the sodden ooze of mud toward the place where the Shrine had stood, and their hearts were made lighter by the laughter they had shared. No longer were they troubled by the insidious whisperings of Somn, for at last they were as one, their strength joined. All about them the storm of Dred's frustrated ill-will raged anew, a shrieking wail of pure invective, which buffeted and battered their mortal bodies, yet for all its virulence could neither touch their melded souls nor break their spirits. And at last Aurora and the Knight of Tor stood before the threshold of Dred's defeat.

"But it is there! I know it!" Aurora shouted to be heard above the tempest. "Crane has made of it some sort of shelter and woven about it a binding spell. If they are still here, they must be within the thicket. But I cannot find the way in without knowing the spell he used. Blast the muddlehead! Why did he not leave some clue as to the password! It could take hours to discover the correct one."

The knight seemed to consider their dilemma as he calmly studied the mass of thorny limbs heaped about the Shrine.

"If they are alive and well, then perhaps they can hear us. Call out to them," he suggested reasonably.

But no matter how they shouted and beat about the impenetrable barrier the shape-changer had wrought all too well, they could arouse no response from the interior of the woody bower.

"It's no use," Aurora panted after a time. "Either they cannot hear us above the storm, or—"

She left the sobering thought unspoken. Yet she was nigh to overcome by fear for the young mage-lord and the poor lad whom he had been left behind to protect. Blast! They must find a way inside. Dawn could not be long in the offing. But how?

Feverishly she reviewed the spells and counterspells that had comprised a sizable portion of her lessons with Vandrel. Yet nothing seemed to work, and it was growing harder and harder to concentrate amidst the incessant din of wind and storm. Almost she was tempted to call on the power of Andruvien to blast her way through the spellbound thicket. Yet she knew she dared not. Even if the Crystal's flames did penetrate what appeared an uncommonly potent binding spell, anyone within would indubitably be irreparably harmed. Nay. She must find another way.

"Have you tried every spell you and Crane learned from Vandrel?" Frayne queried after a time. "Could Crane have used something he picked up on his own that you wouldn't know about?"

"Nay! We always worked together. And 'twas more likely that I should have come up with a spell *he* would not know. For he was never much of a scholar, the truth be known. Whereas I was always poking through Vandrel's books. Why, I remember one incident in particular . . . !"

Her voice faltered abruptly as suddenly it came to her the one spell she had not tried.

"Oh, gods help us if he has used *that* one," she

exclaimed with such vehemence that Frayne's arrogant eyebrow shot upward. "Vandrel was most insistent that nothing but trouble could ever come from it."

"Then undoubtedly that is the very one our enterprising young mage has employed," observed the Knight of Tor with a sapience born of familiarity with Krim's venturesome grandson. "Do you know the counterspell?"

"That's just it," she retorted peevishly. "There apparently is no counterspell. At least not in the way we usually think of one. You must simply solve the riddle in which the spell is couched."

"I see," Frayne mused, one hand tugging thoughtfully at his bearded chin. "And I don't suppose offhand that you know the solution to the riddle?"

"Actually I was never very good with riddles," she hedged.

"Well, then I suggest you tell it to me, that perhaps together we can come up with a solution."

"Aye. That would seem the thing," she agreed with a wry grimace, and frowned slightly as she sought to recall the lines of the rhyme. "It goes like this:

I invoke the spell which hides and binds,
Conceals, reveals, and sometimes finds,
The stricture which releases souls,
The yawning rift which yet mends holes,
That which is both in and out
And whispers, groans, but cannot shout.
'Tis an end and a beginning,
A farewell and a welcoming,
A haven of a kind,
Or a prison of the mind,

For indeed the name
Remains the same—
A spell that ye revoke
With that which ye invoke.

"Does it make any sense to you?" she queried
doubtfully as she gazed worriedly up at the knight's
shadowed face.

"Not much," he admitted. "But then riddles are
most often simple truths obscured by tortuous reason-
ing. Most likely the answer is staring us in the face."

"Well, 'twere better if it shouted in the ear, for even
now I feel the dawning nigh upon us."

"Then it behooves us to put our minds to the task,"
observed the knight coolly. "What hides and binds,
conceals, reveals, and finds? Come now. This is not
the time to panic."

"I am not about to panic," she retorted irritably
and with an effort sought to gather her scattered
thoughts. Blast the man! Did nothing ever rattle his
steely nerves?

"A blindfold conceals and when removed reveals,"
he postulated imperturbably. "But it hardly fits the
succeeding lines. Nor does a box, a cave, or a cell."

"Think you it might be a treasure map?" Aurora
offered hopefully. "It conceals, reveals and can be a
beginning and an end."

"But can it whisper or groan?" Frayne mused
doubtfully.

They fell silent for a time as they sought to puzzle
through each paradox of the rhyme. Aurora swiftly
discarded darkness and light, a path, a road, a book,
and half a dozen other possibilities, none of which

fitted all the strictures of the riddle. Then suddenly she brightened.

"Think you it might be air?" she queried eagerly. "It cannot be seen and thus might be considered a rift. And it fills holes, so might be thought to mend them. Air is both in and out. As wind it whispers and groans. 'Tis the first breath, which is a beginning, and the last, which is an end. And thus it is both a welcoming and a farewell."

"Yet does it reveal and conceal? Can it be both a haven and a prison of the mind?" the Knight questioned critically.

"Nay," Aurora groaned, her shoulders slumping wearily once again. Gods! Wherein lay the answer to the plaguy riddle? Was this to be the ignoble end to all their travails? To stand upon the threshold of Dred's defeat only to be denied the door through which they might enter?

Suddenly she was filled with unreasoning anger and terrible despair. Was Elwindolf's death to have been for naught? Where was the god? What use was the power he had granted her if she could not use it to gain entrance to the Shrine?

"Blast the shape-changer and his cursed spell!" she cried ringingly and drew forth Andruvien. The Blade of Light flared in the darkness, a pulsating flame of pure power. "If the door will not reveal itself, then I shall just have to make one." And she raised high the scintillating sword.

"Aurora! Wait!" Frayne shouted and grasped her sword-filled hand in a steely grip.

"Nay!" she choked, her heart leaden in her breast as she struggled to free herself from the knight's unyielding hold. "The dawn is but a breath away. We cannot tarry longer even for Crane and the boy."

"We need not tarry, little spitfire," grinned the knight. "You have solved the riddle!"

"But I did nothing!" she cried. "I have failed in everything. But I cannot fail in the final task. The crystal must be returned to Ariana. Let me go, Frayne, I beg you!"

"I'll let you go when you'll listen to reason. We needed only to demand the door. Look. There is the entrance to the bower."

As his words sank in at last, she turned to stare at the narrow rift that had magically appeared among the thick, leafy branches. Gradually Andruvien's brilliance dimmed as the Enchantress slowly lowered it, her anger quenched.

"But how . . . ?" she mumbled distractedly.

"It revealed itself when you uttered the word *door*. Obviously that was the answer to the riddle."

"Crane!" Aurora shouted and tore free from Frayne's loosened grip. "Oh, gods. Let him be alive and I shall ask nothing further."

Then she was through the rift and groping in the darkness for the figure of the Valdoran, the crystal tear grasped tightly in her hand. And at last she had reached it. With frantic fingers, she found the shallow depression in the otherwise smooth cheek from which Groul had gouged the crystal free. With bated breath, she set the Arlana once more in its rightful place and drew back.

Suddenly the tempest stilled and the clouds vanished, as the first fingers of dawn sprawled across the sky. The lovely face of Ariana glowed in the soft iridescence of the crystal tear, and the interior of the rude shelter sprang into view. Fearfully Aurora turned from the Holy Maiden's Shrine, a painful lump in her throat.

"Crane! Where are you?"

A low mumble reached her ears, and she crossed quickly to a pile of furry pelts heaped in a shadowy corner. Oh, Gods! From the sound of it the young mage-lord was sore beset. In dread, the Enchantress knelt beside the bed, and with a trembling hand, reached out to pull the topmost covering back.

For a moment she stared in horrified disbelief. Then a low hiss escaped her bloodless lips.

"Crane!" she cried piercingly. "In the name of the One, I shall have your head for this!"

Chapter Ten

"A-Aurora. Frayne. You're back," Crane mumbled, rubbing his eyes, and yawned. A little dazedly he raised himself to one elbow. Then, as he felt Janine stir next to him, he came suddenly and irrevocably awake. "Egad," he groaned and bolted upright. Feeling as though a hand were at his throat slowly choking the life from him, he glanced from Aurora's livid fury to the knight's chilling stare. Then he was scrambling hastily to his lanky height, his face beet-red.

"Er—Did everything go all right? D-did you find the crystal?" he stammered, acutely aware of the tall knight observing the emergence of the sleepy-eyed girl from the snug cocoon of furry pelts.

"Aye. We found it. But coming back, we ran into a little surprise," Aurora said in an ominously quiet voice. "Did you by any chance have visitors in the grove during the night?"

"Visitors?" Crane echoed, his voice unnaturally high. Whereupon a look of enlightenment flashed across the freckled face. "Oh, you must mean Baldrac

269

and the Imposter," he acknowledged in a rush and giggled inanely. The One be praised! he thought fleetingly and nearly sagged with unutterable relief as he realized he was not to be immediately drawn and quartered for having been discovered abed with the girl entrusted to his care. Furthermore, a slave-girl who belonged to the Knight of Tor!

"You bet they were here!" the boy acknowledged in an almost frantic eagerness to get everything out in the open. The dread uncertainty of his immediate future was like to be the death of him. "And they weren't sightseeing, either. But I changed into a hedge and just kind of blended into the scenery, if you know what I mean. They never had a notion they were anywhere near the Shrine. And that was when I overheard them talking and found out that *he* was a *she*," he said and waved a hand at the girl huddled amidst the pile of furs, her eyes enormous in the small oval of her face. Hopefully he shot a covert glance at Aurora. Surely she would know that he could not misuse an innocent like Janine and would stand by him should the stern knight be less understanding. But the Enchantress only stared fixedly at him as if he were possessed of two heads or something, so that once again he began to feel distinctly uncomfortable. "I mean, that Jan was Janine," he offered in the way of further explanation, beads of sweat beginning to break out on his forehead. And still Aurora's expression had not altered a whit. Cripes! What did she want from him? he fretted and began to tug at the neck of his tunic, which had suddenly become unaccountably snug. "That—oh, what's the use," he finished miserably and shot a piteous glance of appeal over Aurora's head at Frayne.

But the knight only shrugged his broad shoulders, as if to say that Crane needn't look to him for help and leaned indolently against the carved figure of the hart the more comfortably to observe the unfolding of the farce.

"How *could* you, Crane?" Aurora suddenly exploded, accenting each word with an accusing finger.

"B-but nothing happened," the boy yelped and backed a hurried step, his hands raised in front of him as if he thought she might bodily assault him. "I swear it! We just fell asleep. That's all."

"Oh, indeed," Aurora commented witheringly. "You fell asleep. After invoking Lil's spell of binding and concealment. Have you any notion of the trouble you caused? Do you know that if I hadn't accidentally said the password that we most assuredly would not have gotten in in time to put Dred's malice to rest?"

"You—you solved the riddle?" Crane gulped, the ludicrous grin twitching across his lips incongruous against the sickly pallor of his face. So that was what had sent her up in the boughs, he thought incredulously. It had not been the girl at all. And with the facility of the young, who are both cursed to pass with bewildering rapidity through ever-threatening states of impending doom to unnerving heights of rapture and likewise blessed with the amnesiac faculty of total and instant dismissal of previously nerve-shattering eternities of crisis, Crane blithely turned to matters of more immediate interest.

"What *is* the password?" he asked with characteristic, boyish enthusiasm. "You know I was worried that I might not be able to figure it out for myself. But I knew you could do it. And there didn't seem a chance in Somn that Cranith would know the riddle, let alone the solution. Which is exactly why I decided to use it. After all, I was worn to the nub what with roaming about in the rain for two nights so that Janine could sleep in the shelter. I mean, once I'd discovered she was a girl, I couldn't very well sleep with her, you know. And with Dred's madness getting stronger, I was afraid to change into something better suited for the rain. I might not have been able to change back, you see."

"For two days! You mean you knew before the evil ones came that I-I . . ." faltered the slave-girl, blanching as white as the desert sands.

Crane shifted his weight awkwardly from one foot to the other as he belatedly realized where his bumbling tongue had got him to.

"Er-Well, yes. I did find you out. But then I didn't know how to let you know," he answered, spreading wide his hands as if that explained everything.

"But how?" whispered the girl, her eyes huge in her small face.

"Yes, lad," drawled the Knight of Tor, a gleam of unholy amusement in his silvery eyes. "How did you discover the girl's true gender?"

Helplessly the foundering youth looked from one to the other of his potential future executioners. Oh, gods. What had he done to deserve this? After all, he had only kissed the girl!

"Well, Crane? How did you find it out?" queried the Enchantress with puzzled interest. Whatever was wrong with the boy? He was behaving decidedly oddly. Could Dred's infernal madness have perma-

272

nently addled his brains? she wondered anxiously. Yet even in the midst of madness she would not have expected the shape-changer's next explosive utterance.

"I opened her shirt!" he blurted, then slammed a hand to his forehead and groaned. Gods, he had done it now. But there was no backing out, he decided after one sweeping glance at the various expressions around him, which were all in one way or another decidedly extreme. Desperately he plunged headlong into a tortured explanation. "Egad. The girl had swooned. And her blasted tunic was laced so tightly about her throat that I thought she couldn't breathe. So I tried to loosen it. O-only the knot was so tight that when I finally got it undone, I simply jerked it open, and-and . . . well, it was an accident. I never meant to-to—I didn't know. I mean, how could I? Oh, curses of Throm, forget it. Forget everything. You wouldn't believe me anyway!" he ended miserably and turned his back on a befuddled Enchantress and the grinning Knight of Tor.

There was a moment of uncomfortable silence. Then suddenly the slave-girl's timorous voice trembled in the uncertain quiet.

"You suffered the discomfort of the storm to safeguard *my* honor, *sayyid*?" she queried. And something in her voice brought the young shape-changer about-face to stare dazedly into her enormous blue eyes shimmering like twin stars in the dim light seeping through the leafy walls of the bower. He swallowed hard before managing a deprecating shrug.

"Well, that and because I had to keep an eye out for possible intruders. After all, there was no way of knowing whether the wolf pack might not track us

273

down again or something. And as it turned out, I was right to be on guard. There's no telling what those bloody fiends might have done if they'd found us."

"But to invoke the forbidden spell!" Aurora interjected, reminded at last of the reason she had been so put out with the plaguy boy upon discovering him unhurt and peacefully asleep in the arms of a girl whom she had been led to believe to be something quite different. And a beautiful girl at that, who, furthermore, was mysteriously traveling about with Frayne. It really was too much to expect her to accept the whole thing without even a satisfactory explanation of what was going on, which, on the face of things, appeared to be Frayne's unspeakable strategy. Well, she would not rest until things were made patently clear to her. And if the Knight of Tor could not be made to clear things up, then it would just have to be someone else, she vowed, her glittering gaze hard upon the squirming young mage-lord.

"Good gods, Crane! I thought you had been grievously wounded by the blackguards. I pictured you torn and bleeding to death the whole time I was wracking my brains for the solution to that blasted riddle. Have you any notion the agony I suffered? And all because you could not resist the temptation to try out Lil's absurd spell!"

"Aw, it wasn't like that at all, Aurora," the youth disavowed, much aggrieved.

"Are you not being a trifle hard on the boy?" Frayne broke in at last, his deep voice vibrant with hardly suppressed laughter. "After all, he did in all likelihood save the child's life."

"Oh, indeed. Let us hear from *you*, my lord," said

the Enchantress witheringly and turned to impale the knight with eyes fulminating golden fire. "Just what are you doing roaming about the countryside with this—this *bogus* squire? A girl, moreover, who would be better off at her mother's knee than playing the Sorceress's deadly games. It is hardly in the usual style of the Knight of Tor, after all, to be willingly burdened with a female. You were adamant enough in your refusal to allow *me* to ride with you. Indeed, as I remember, I was forced to resort to blackmail and worse to win your grudging assent."

"Worse?" queried the knight imperturbably, one arrogant eyebrow rising quizzically.

"Aye, worse! For did I not sustain a beating at your hands? Tell, me, Knight of Tor. Do you raise your hand to this poor child as well?"

"I am *not* a child. And my Lord Frayne has never treated me unkindly," Janine interjected indignantly. She could not bear to hear the golden-eyed termagant so malign her much adored *sayyid*.

"Aye. No doubt he has been the soul of generosity," Aurora agreed scathingly.

"You say it, but you believe otherwise," the slave-girl persisted, having forgotten in her unwonted sense of outrage to be humble, as befitted one who was *mamluk*. It was clear the beautiful Enchantress had no heart. She did not deserve the love of *Sayyid* Frayne or the young *Mogush*. "Oh, you are not at all like the lovely Almira, though you possess her eyes of golden fire. She was noble and just and a great warrior who fought valiantly against Amaur in the Great Wars. She was Al-Murabit *muwallad*, a true daughter of the House of Doane. But you. You are like *al-zambur*, the hornet."

Aurora's face had gone a deathly white beneath the streaks of mud as she stared in astonishment at the indignant slave-girl.

"What are you saying?" she whispered hoarsely. "What do you know of a warrior-woman with eyes like mine?"

Janine, suddenly conscious of her blatant misconduct, rose trembling to her knees, one dainty hand going to her forehead in the sign of obeisance.

"Oh, my lord Frayne," she murmured with bowed head. "I beg you will forgive my unseemliness. I am deserving of *al-chaugan*, to be taught the humility of the stick."

"Never mind that," Aurora interrupted with an impatient wave of the hand. "Who are you? And what of this warrior-woman?"

The girl glanced beseechingly at the lordly knight, who nodded slightly in encouragement. It was most odd, Janine thought to herself. The *sayyid* did not seem at all put out with her, though she had spoken as no slave had ought. Rather had he seemed to derive pleasure from her brief show of spirit, as if, indeed, he looked with fatherly pride upon a child who had displayed a previously unsuspected precociousness.

Taking heart from the growing conviction that she had not displeased her master, Janine met the golden flash of the Enchantress's eyes with greater self-confidence.

"I am Janine, daughter of Ahbin-ben-ami, the Khan of the desert tribes," she said clearly, her small head lifted in unconscious pride. "And I was sold into slavery by my father, who wagered me on the losing toss of *al-zahr*, the dice."

Thus did Janine, the desert slave-girl, tell her story yet again, while Aurora with the golden eyes listened in growing excitement to the strange tale of Almira and Leilah, the daughters of Al-Murabit, and the Knight of Tor looked on, a strange glitter in the falcon eyes.

So, he thought fleetingly, the stern lips curving in a cold, sardonic smile. The little Wendaren was not so insignificant in the scheme of things as he had imagined. No doubt the hand of the god could be discerned in all that had led up to his accepting Baldrac's wager, as well as in the subsequent turn of events. He watched the kaleidoscope of shifting emotions sweep across Aurora's heart-shaped face, lovely despite the smudges of mud and the faint shadows of weariness beneath the marvelous eyes. All along the slave-girl had possessed the secret to the young Enchantress's past. Had the Sorceress known? Had she sent her two lapdogs to steal the child away ere she could reveal what she knew? Indeed, had she sought to slay her Knight out of fear that he had already learned the truth of Almira and her dark sister Leilah?

Perchance, he darkly mused, and yet it was not like the Sorceress to make so strategic an error. For it would seem she had little enough to lose in having her doubtful past made known to the knight, who was nevertheless bound to serve her, and a great deal to be gained by allowing him to complete his mission for her. No. He was not by any means convinced that his devious mistress had been behind the attempt to assassinate him and to abduct the slave-girl, Janine.

Indeed, 'twas much more likely Baldrac had plotted on his own to retrieve his lost property along with his vengeance against the gamester who had had the temerity to win her. Then, too, Dred, Frayne's loving father, might very well have prompted, for his own obscure reasons, the murder of his son and heir. But why? Had the Prince of Throm discovered the deep and deadly game Frayne played?

The knight's private musings were interrupted by Aurora's sudden exclamation.

"But you shall take me to Seraisharaqa!" she uttered in tones that precluded any possibility of denial. "Almira has to be the warrior-woman who perished in Hawthorn Glade, and thus it stands to reason that she was my mother and that I, too, am a daughter of the House of Doane," she ended in a hushed voice, and wondered that *Al-Murabit* had chosen to adopt the elfin name of Doane, which meant "dweller of the dunes." Had he, too, known the language of the Old Ones? Indeed, had he possessed the gift that enabled him to commune with birds and beasts, as she did?

"I cannot take you there, *mem-sayyid*," returned the slave-girl, her dusky lashes lowered before the flash of eyes glittering with *zarcun-nar*, the golden fire. "For I am *mamluk* to Sayyid Frayne. I can do only as he commands."

"Then he shall command it," the young Enchantress stated flatly. "Shall he not, *sayyid*?"

The Knight of Tor smiled stonily as Aurora pierced him with her glance.

"I am sorry. But I fear I have other plans for Janine," he drawled at his most maddeningly aloof.

"As you have already pointed out, the child is unsuited for the perils of a knight on a quest. I had thought to leave her with the first suitable family I could find who would accept her."

"Oh, no, *sayyid*! I beg you. I cannot wish for such a separation!" the girl cried and flung herself at her master's feet.

The knight's brow turned thunderous as the child reached up to cling to his legs, her face uplifted in fearful supplication.

"Enough, Janine!" he ground out harshly. "You forget yourself."

Crane, who had judiciously kept his peace throughout the lengthy interchange preceding the girl's outburst, uttered an explosive oath and started toward the girl, only to be halted by the Enchantress's slim hand about his wrist. Gritting his teeth to keep from interfering unwisely in what was really none of his business, he grudgingly settled back on his heels to await further developments. Yet puzzled resentment, plain to read on his boyish, freckled face, seethed within him. Blast the man, anyway! Couldn't he see the girl worshiped him? If she were to ever look at *him* that way, *he'd* not be so bloody cold.

Frayne might have appeared to be indifferent to the child's poignant gaze, which pleaded for him to keep her with him, but not so Aurora. The golden eyes had narrowed in glittering speculation on the tender scene of the lovely child prostrated before the godlike knight. Nor had she missed the fleeting warmth that had shone briefly in the steely eyes when earlier the noisome child had leapt magnificently to his defense. There was more here than would seem to meet the eye, she thought, and grew suddenly cold inside.

But immediately the slave-girl had shrunk back as though she had indeed received a blow from *al-chaugan*, the slave-master's instrument of punishment. With obvious effort, she subdued the tumult within her breast and resumed the slave's impassive facade of humility. But her enormous eyes were yet aglimmer with unshed tears, and the small hands were gripped tightly before her to conceal their trembling.

"I-I beg you will forgive me, *sayyid*," she managed in a hushed voice, which yet tugged at Crane's heartstrings and struck a spark of unreasoning dislike from Aurora. Egad! Surely Frayne's impregnable heart had not truly been won by the girl. She was only a child. And yet the normally unshakable knight appeared to vibrate to the softly spoken words, which only imperfectly masked the girl's fear and sorrow at the threat of *al-hajr*, the dreaded separation from her master. A fleeting shadow, like pain, flickered briefly in the silvery eyes, then vanished so that Aurora wondered if she had truly seen it.

"And where do you propose to find such a family?" she said curiously and wondered if it were truly wise to seek to thwart the knight's plan to rid them of the girl's troubling presence. Yet only this daughter of the desert clans could lead them to the Palace of the Rising Sun, and thus Aurora had no choice but to do all she could to win Frayne's consent to have Janine take them there. Shades of Somn! Surely the gods did not mean for her to discover her true-name only to lose her love? With a helpless feeling of doom, she heard the knight's ironic chuckle rumble forth.

"I had hoped to place her in Sedgewick," he admitted ruefully. "But obviously that is impossible now."

"Then you are not so pressed with time as you would have had me to believe," she deduced, watching him out of the corner of her eye. "You plan to further delay your mission, whatever it may be this time, to seek a place of safety elsewhere for the girl?"

The knight's silvery glance gleamed with wry humor as he allowed himself to be maneuvered into a corner.

"On the contrary. It has occurred to me that there is one who would willingly oblige me. And it will be a matter of short order to conduct her there in safety, thanks to the special talents of our young shape-changer."

"Crane?" exclaimed the Enchantress, startled even though she had surmised the knight was up to something. A frown darkened her brow. "But he can only materialize where he has been before. Or where I have been. And I warn you, I will not show him the way."

"I did not imagine you would, little spitfire. But your help will not be necessary. Crane already knows the way."

"Vandrel!" Aurora uttered explosively. "I might have known."

Then Crane shivered in his boots, as suddenly he found himself the cynosure of three pairs of eyes. May the gods have pity, he inwardly groaned, and wished he dared to vanish in a trail of mist. The Enchantress was like to curse him with all eleven hundred of the Droonish Curses if he did as Frayne demanded. And the knight? A single rapierlike thrust of the chilling eyes was more than he wanted from the awesome Knight of Tor should he choose to refuse him. Oh, gods! What was he to do? Even Krim would have been easier to live with than either the Enchantress or the knight, should he find himself in their disfavor. The sorely beset young mage-lord squirmed on the horns of a fiendish dilemma and was unable either to choose one or defy the other. Then, as if compelled, he looked into the enormous blue orbs that had the power to bedazzle and bewitch, and suddenly there was no question as to what he would do.

Deliberately straightening to his full height, he faced them all, a stubborn jut to his bony jaw.

"I beg your pardon, but no one's thought to ask me my opinion of the matter," he said with all the puffed-up dignity of a foreign potentate. "But nonetheless, I'm going to speak my mind. Janine may be a slave, but she's still a human being, and it just doesn't seem meet that a knight of Tor should deny her the right to make up her own mind about where she goes or what she does. I know you mean it for the best to send her to Vandrel where she'll be safe. I myself told her that was the place for her. But she doesn't want to go. And I wouldn't feel right taking her there against her wishes. So unless *she* asks me to do it, I've got to say no. No matter how much I may be made to regret it later on," he added under his breath and braced himself to withstand the full force of the knight's displeasure.

But the expected furor did not materialize, as Frayne merely shrugged and shoved himself away from his languid position against the statue of the hart.

"So be it," he drawled indifferently, though a discerning eye might have perceived the pale glint of sardonic humor beneath the drooping eyelids. "I'm afraid you've tied my hands where the slave-girl is concerned. And since you have seen fit to take exception to the manner in which I treat my slave, shape-changer, I give her to you to do with as you will. Henceforth, Crane shall be your master, girl. And may you both learn a lesson from it."

"B-but I never meant . . ." began the boy who had sought to lecture the Knight of Tor on moral turpitude, his bubble of self-importance deflated at a single, masterful thrust from the older man. "I-I cannot accept. . . ."

"But you have no choice, I'm afraid. You see, I cannot in all conscience take her with me. Nor have I the time to find another place for her, if you cannot bring yourself to send her to Vandrel, with whom she would be safe. Hence, I see nothing for it but that she must go with you. And, indeed, I wish you all the best."

And with that he turned and stalked without another word from the shelter into the glade.

For a moment the three stared wordlessly at the opening flooded with sunshine through which the Knight of Tor had so precipitously vanished. Then Janine burst into heartbroken sobs, and Aurora was on her feet and through the door.

"Frayne!" she cried ringingly as she beheld the Knight striding easily across the clearing, his saddle slung over one broad shoulder. "Where do you think you're going?"

Indolently he came to a halt a scant pace from the

shelter of the trees and turned, his face unreadable in the golden shafts of sunlight streaming through the leafy boughs.

"In search of my horse," he replied and glanced casually at the sky. "The morning quickly wanes, and it is time I was on my way."

"You mean to go without us?" she queried aghast. "Without me?"

"But how not?" he countered. As if it had never occurred to him that they should not again be parted, Aurora fumed, and suddenly she was filled with a terrible hollowness that she had thought never again to know. "I have enjoyed your company, but nothing has changed. You have your path, and I mine. It has ever been thus, has it not?"

"But must they be separate paths? Can we not find our way more surely together?"

"I think not," he answered, his gaze distant. And Aurora bit her lip to keep from crying out at him in vexation. She well knew that stony look. The man was as unmovable as Ice Mountain when he was determined on a certain course of action. It behooved her to tread carefully.

"I see," she temporized, frantically searching for a way to break through the seemingly impenetrable wall he had erected between them. If only Minta and Valesia were there to advise her. She had need of their gentle wisdom now. Yet she doubted if even the dryads, who had lived untold ages in Endrith's Forest, had ever encountered anyone of Frayne's ilk. He was a law unto himself and answered to no one. Except the dratted Sorceress of Tor, she amended with a growing sense of fury. But she herself was not one to be so lightly dismissed, she reminded herself, and turned the full force of her golden eyes upon the man.

Assuming a nonchalance she was far from feeling, the Enchantress strolled deliberately toward the tall, caped figure, till she stood before him, her breast heaving. She sensed that he had grown suddenly taut, though his aquiline features were as unreadable as ever, and she lowered her head to hide the slight curve of her lips. He was not as immune to her as he would have her believe, she exulted, and felt the first stirrings of the god's power within her.

Slowly she raised her eyes to his.

"You would leave without a farewell?" she murmured, and her trembling lips seemed to accuse him. "Is your task so demanding that you cannot spare the time for one last embrace?"

He uttered a short bark of laughter, and she stared at him, uncertain whether it was directed at her or himself.

"I thought I had shown you the error of using woman's wiles to try to win your way with me," he said at last, and his smile was not pleasant. "But I see I was mistaken. Yet I have not forgotten the subtle power of your slightest touch. As much as it pains me, I fear I shall have to forgo the pleasure of a farewell embrace."

"Do you then fear the power that you yourself awakened in me?" she countered swiftly, and though her heart seemed filled with desperate yearning, yet was her glance contemptuous upon the knight.

"With all my heart, Enchantress," he answered, an odd glitter in the silvery eyes.

Then swiftly he bent his head to brush her lips with

285

a feather-light kiss.

"Farewell, Enchantress," he murmured, straightening as quickly to his full height.

"Frayne . . . ?" Aurora uttered in a strangled voice, but he silenced her with his fingertips pressed lightly to her lips.

A shadow flickered across the falcon eyes as he gazed for an endless moment into her upturned face. Then he drew away and turned to leave her.

"You may keep whatever you need from my pack," he called over his shoulder. "And I shall try to send the mare to you. The slave-girl will need to ride, no doubt."

Then he was gone. Vanished like a shadow into the thickness of the wood.

For a moment the stricken girl stared after him. Was this, then, how it was all to end? she wondered dully, and she thought she must perish from the wound he had delivered to her heart. He could leave her without a thought, *her*, Aurora, who had vowed they should never again be parted. Her love had meant nothing to him, and everything they had shared had been a lie. Indeed, the gods themselves seemed to mock her.

She reeled beneath the awful weight of disillusionment and the god's betrayal, her head clutched between her hands as she struggled against a descending curtain of darkness.

"Nay," she groaned, sinking to her knees. "Nay. It is but the lingering madness of Somn. A nightmare from which surely I must awaken."

Yet in her heart she knew that Frayne was truly gone and would never of his own volition return to her.

Then it seemed that all that she had undergone—the loneliness, the endless hours of study, the terror of Dred's madness, and the horror of Elwindolf's death—all had been for naught. For in the end the Prince of Somn had won. And abruptly she laughed, a harsh and ugly sound that seemed to dim the glory of the morning sun; and, indeed, the Enchantress of the Glade seemed lost in darkness.

Whereupon a silvery note pierced the vacuum of her despair. A sweet and glorious song, which trembled on the breeze like a faint memory of a lovelier, gentler time when innocence had been a dream of flowers drinking in the sunlight and butterflies flitting through the air, a time of unicorns and magic and elves singing the old songs, a time of awakening power and the first yearnings of new love. Slowly she lifted her head.

Above her, perched on a low branch of a tamarack, was a yellow warbler, the feathered breast bared to the sunlight as he emitted the high, clear notes of the mating song. Aurora's breath caught painfully in her throat as, miraculously, an answering call chortled out of the shadowy depths of the trees. Then the woods seemed filled with birdsong and the wondrous flash of brightly colored wings. Silver-winged moths and great monarch butterflies danced among fragile blossoms awakening to the new day. A timid cottontail peeked out at her from beneath a burgeoning rose hedge, then, apparently judging her harmless, hopped into the clearing and nibbled contentedly at the tender shoots of grass growing in the glade. All around her she could feel the forest quickening with returning life, and suddenly it was as if she, too, were emerging from a dream of death.

Like a flower reaching for the sun, she rose to her feet and spread her arms wide in silent celebration of the wonder of life. Once she had been Auduan and tree-child and one with the forest, her spirit nourished and sustained by its enduring strength. Yet when she had returned from the knight's quest as Aurora and Andruvien, she had been a part of and yet separate from that which she had always known, for she had gone beyond the boundaries of the forest into the world and had learned what it was to be utterly alone—as once Frayne had said that everyone was alone and solitary—for the Knight of Tor had won her heart and then left her. Nor had she known the blessedness of a whole spirit through all the long months of waiting for the time when she should be judged ready to brave the world of men in search of her true-name and her love. Yet even as she had healed the forest of its malaise by returning the Arlana to its rightful place, so had the Forest healed her. And suddenly she knew that even as she was one with Frayne, her power tied in some mysterious way to him, yet was she also irrevocably bound to the forest. Her strength, her knowledge of self, like the strength of the Glinden Tree, whose roots tapped the wellsprings of the Anglaron, derived from the earth itself.

Once more she looked to the place where the Knight of Tor had vanished into the trees, and suddenly her golden laughter rang through the glade, for her mind was crystal clear again and working with a keen intensity, and at last she knew exactly what she intended to do. Indeed, had not the secretive knight himself revealed to her his destination? And was she not intent upon reaching the same illusive castle as he, though for far different reasons?

Abruptly she turned, a dangerous sparkle in her eye, and called out.

"Crane! Janine! Hurry! We have work to do."

Frayne's tall form made swiftly through the dense woods, his long swinging stride unfaltering. The signs of the bolting horses were clear to one of his keen senses, despite the havoc wreaked by the storm, and he had little difficulty in following the trail of broken branches and occasional hoofprints in the soggy earth. At least Boltar and the mare had fled west, which was the direction in which his own chosen trail led, the direction of the sandy wastelands inhabited by the Wendaren. He would have to travel swiftly to reach the Castle of the Rising Sun ahead of the Enchantress and her small band, for he had no wish to run into them again. He might not be able to walk away from Aurora's tantalizing sweetness another time, he mused grimly.

He had not known when he walked into Crane's cozy little bower that he should discover the means of relieving himself of the worrisome burden of the slave-girl and at the same time deliver into Aurora's hands a clue to the riddle of her obscure past. It had struck him as ironic in the extreme that, as Janine had revealed the history of Al-Murabit and the golden-eyed warrior-woman, he had seen how he could fulfill his part of the bargain made long ago beside the silvery waters of Grendylmere to help the Enchantress discover her true-name in exchange for her aid in completing his own quest for the horn of the unicorn.

Moreover, he had known scant moments after Crane shot from the bed of furs, a study in abashed innocence caught in the midst of damning circumstances, that the boy was in love with the little slave-girl, though he doubted that Crane knew as yet what ailed him. Nor had he for a moment believed the lad had taken advantage of the child. Frayne remembered all too well the shape-changer's mortification at suddenly beholding Aurora in all her unclad splendor beneath the elderberry tree in Vandrel's hidden valley so long ago. The boy was incapable of performing a base act. He was too inherently decent. Whether Crane's love was reciprocated by the girl was less certain, for he had long since learned the futility of trying to comprehend either the feminine psyche or a woman's heart. Yet he could not doubt that Janine would in time learn to appreciate Crane's intrinsic worthiness, and in the meantime she could have no more dedicated a protector than the love-stricken youth, nor none more formidable than the Enchantress.

Thus, all his obligations fulfilled in the single gesture of giving the slave-girl over to Crane, he had determined to walk away from three of the four people in the world for whom he would willingly have given his life had circumstances demanded it. And no doubt had he stayed longer with them, just such circumstances would have arisen sooner or later, for he was the mortal son of Dred, and the Sorceress's minion, and as such, death was his constant companion.

He had thought to feel a measure of satisfaction in having done what was necessary to protect the three innocents from the peril that his continued presence could only bring them. Had he not heard once that virtue was its own reward? And yet he was conscious of a growing irritability with the waxing beauty of the sun-filled morning, which was not usual with him. The ever-increasing evidence that the forest was quickening with renewed life wore oddly at his nerves. He had no wish to behold the wonder of wildflowers blooming in the wake of Dred's storm—pink flea-bane, snowy-white sweet cicely, purplish periwinkle bearing the glory of a white star at its center, green dragon and Jack-in-the-pulpit, yellow star grass and golden ragwort—or of hummingbirds and honeybees, giant moths and dragonflies stealing from blossom to blossom. They reminded him of Aurora and Gren-dylmere and the enchanted paradise, which had been as much a state of the mind, a serenity of the soul, as a place in time or space. The effulgence of health and beauty without the Enchantress at his side was noth-ing but a painful reminder of what might have been had circumstances been different, had he and the lovely Aurora not been bound by separate and oppos-ing legacies of an immortal world beyond their con-trol.

His lip curled sardonically at the thought that the feared Knight of Tor could entertain sentiments better suited to the lovesick Crane. His callow youth was far behind him, and he had had no wish to fall victim to love's enervating spell at this, or any, time in his life. He had always known his ultimate destiny, and love had not played a part in it. Yet he had never taken into account the possibility of a chance encounter with an Enchantress whose devastating power lay in an innocence so sweet and deadly that he had suc-cumbed like the veriest green and untried pubescent with his first full-fledged woman ripe for the plucking.

Or had it indeed been a chance encounter? he wondered, not for the first time. Nothing seemed left to happenstance where the Enchantress was concerned. The power of the god enveloped her like a shimmering aura, which even in the dark flux of Somn had shone undimmed by the lightless nightmare of Dred's malevolence. He had seen her as a child, a vision of untouched loveliness, a wood-sprite stealing forth from the verdant wood to bewitch and entrance him, as the Sorceress had never been able to do. He had beheld her a woman, with a woman's loving heart, and a warrior unafraid of death. He had sensed her battle with Andruvien, the sliver of the Vendrenin, and had felt the raw surge of power course through her as at last she came into her own, the Enchantress with the Blade of Power. And he had watched her die a hundred times, first in the swirling black mists of the Sorceress's Seeing Eye, then again and again in his tortured dreams. And through it all, even during the lost months in Tor, events had already been set into motion that would inevitably bring them together again. And before that, before even he had set eyes on the timid wild thing emerging from the thicket of waterwillow along the shores of Grendylmere, long before the warrior-woman had suckled a child in an elfin glade and then perished at the hands of her enemies, long before Dred had forced himself on a Valdoran virgin and fathered a half-god, half-mortal son and heir, the Lords of Throm had envisioned the coming of an unnamed Enchantress who would learn the meaning of the undeciphered symbols that command powers greater than those of the gods themselves, a child of earth and flame who would be the chosen one of her people. And they had foreseen as well the birth of the Thromholan, Dred's only son, who would lead the Thromgilad to ultimate victory.

If the prophecies were true, how then could chance play the smallest role in anything that touched the lives of those whose very existence had in ages past been foretold? And yet over this one thing, the seeming inevitability of his being the instrument of Aurora's defeat and destruction, if in nothing else, he must somehow prevail. He would die by his own hand ere he allowed himself to destroy this rare creature, this lovely child-woman, this Enchantress of his heart.

Suddenly the Knight of Tor was jolted from his musings by the distant sounds of fighting. He straightened to his full height then stilled, his head cocked slightly to one side as he strained to hear the commotion of shouting men and the clang of steel against steel. The clarion call of an enraged stallion carried clearly on the breeze.

"Boltar!" he uttered under his breath and flung the saddle to the ground. Thrimheld, Swift-Blade, flashed in his hand as he stole noiselessly forward through the trees.

He had gone perhaps a quarter of a mile when he burst suddenly upon a scene of utter chaos. A sleek grey mare bearing two riders wheeled wildly away from two mounted men straight for the knight. While beyond them three others warily circled a great, lunging warrior-steed. Boltar! And on his back, a silvery flame leaping from her hand, was the Enchantress, with the Blade of Light.

With the quick reflexes of an athlete, Frayne twisted out of the path of the fleeing horse. The mare thundered past, but not before the knight had glimpsed a white, freckled face turned back over a bony shoulder and the slender form of a raven-haired girl huddled low over the steed's outstretched neck.

"Crane! And Janine!" he rasped in startled accents. Then swiftly recovering, he turned to meet the pursuing brigands.

The first was nearly on him, a great-thewed brute of a man bristling with black hair and whiskers, his loutish face screwed in a permanent snarl by a scar running from thick lips deep into a fleshy jowl. He was rough-garbed and brandished a heavy wooden bludgeon wickedly spiked at one end. The lout let out a lusty shout as at last he spotted Frayne crouched and waiting.

Then the rangy bay was bearing down upon the knight, and Frayne was leaping lightly from beneath the pounding hooves. The rogue leaned heavily to one side and brought the club hurtling down toward the knight's bare head. Frayne ducked beneath the blow, then, with lightninglike swiftness, bounded up. His lean hand darting out to grasp the grisled wrist, the knight wrenched down on the arm and dug in his heels. The burly rogue bellowed as his legs shot up and the bay ran out from under him. Swiftly Frayne dispatched the lout, then swiveled to meet the second horseman coming at him with a lance aimed at his heart.

In a single swift move, the knight sidestepped the deadly shaft and leaped astride the horse behind the startled villain. Ere the rogue knew what had hit him, Frayne brought the haft of his sword down hard against the back of the fellow's head. The man grunted and slumped forward across the horse's neck. Then Frayne had flung the limp body to the ground and was vaulting forward into the empty saddle. Catching up the reins, Frayne pulled the animal to a plunging halt.

"Aurora!" he shouted and shot a swift glance over his shoulder, his heart hammering painfully in his chest.

He had feared to see her grievously wounded or worse. He had not thought to behold her riding toward him on Boltar at a trot, her eyes flashing golden sparks and her lovely lips curved in an excited grin.

"That was handily done, m'lord!" she cried as she reined Boltar in beside him. "I feel sure I could not have done better myself. But unfortunately the other three had no taste for the Knight of Tor. They turned craven and fled upon first sight of you, else we'd have taught them a thing or two."

"I am no doubt gratified that you think so," he uttered in acid tones. "And now what, may I ask, are you doing here!"

Chapter Eleven

The day was well advanced when at last the four wayfarers came to the edge of the forest and looked out over the Plain of Shintari. Aurora, astride the dainty little mare that the knight had bought off a horse trader in Tor for his squire's use, shifted stiffly in the saddle and hoped Frayne would call a halt for the night. She gazed longingly over her shoulder at the still pool of water fed by a bubbling spring at the center of the wooded dell at their backs. She had not yet had the opportunity to wash the filth from her body since braving Dred's storm the night before, and she already knew from her previous foray into the broad plain that waterholes there were few and far between. She little relished traveling perhaps several days in her present state, but she bit her tongue to keep from suggesting they make camp. The knight was little pleased with his three uninvited companions and had spoken hardly a word to any of them since leaving the scene of the morning's battle with the ragtag band of outlaws who had sought to steal Boltar and the little mare from the Enchantress and her two young friends. She thought it best not to press their luck, for she well knew the Knight of Tor could be pushed only so far ere he was like to wish them all to Somn and go his own way without them. Nay. 'Twere better to leave well enough alone till Frayne's black mood had worn itself out with time. And there was certainly no doubt that the man yet seethed within.

Recalling Frayne's thunderous expression at being informed that if he did not choose to travel with them, he would just have to follow behind them, Aurora grinned. She had caught him off guard with the revelation that she knew his mission for the sorceress took him to Seraisharaqa and that they had no intention of allowing him to reach the palace before them.

"You cannot escape us this time," she had informed him with a smugness that brought a steely glint to his eyes. "We can always find you the same way we did today. Through Boltar. All I have to do is see through his eyes and Crane through mine, and poof! We are there."

"I see," he drawled boredly, but the muscle had leaped along his jawline and she had known he was not so unconcerned as he would have them believe. "And if I choose to leave Boltar behind, shall you still find me, I wonder," he had added with a cold suggestion of a smile and turned away from her.

For a moment she had been rendered speechless. 'Twas true that she had never considered the possibility that he might choose such a means to thwart them.

Where there was Frayne, there was always Boltar, and she knew a bond lay between them that would not be easily broken. Yet once before he had informed her that he was a man of single-minded purpose who would allow nothing to stand in the way of his completing whatever he had set out to do. It would not be beyond him to go even to such lengths as to give up the warrior-steed he had raised from a colt.

"I do not believe you would choose to do without Boltar," she had ventured at last, her regal head lifted in proud defiance. "But if you did, I should still follow you, even to Tor if I must. For I am bound by destiny," and by love, she reflected to herself, "to pursue the trail to my past wheresoever it shall lead me. And I-I feel . . . Nay, I *know* that the truth of who and what I am is in some way linked to you. For why else would the god have brought us together time and again?" She paused, her hand lifting involuntarily toward him as if in supplication. But the knight had remained with his back to her, and she could sense the tense rigidity in the broad shoulders. Yet for once she had been determined to say what was in her heart no matter what it might cost.

"I find that I am no less single-minded than you. And like you, I shall ever find a way. So would it not be foolish for you to give up your horse for nothing? In the end we shall see the palace of my forebears together. And nothing you do or say will change that."

Thus had she stood firm in her resolution that she would not be parted from this difficult man who had won her heart. Nor had any of them relented in the face of his icy rage. Not even Janine, who had dared to inform her Lord Frayne that since she was no longer his property, she need not obey his commands. She belonged to Sayyid Crane now and would do as he desired for her to do.

The girl had spoken with the usual low-voiced humility, but Aurora had detected a glimmer of hurt resentment in the blue eyes before Janine had veiled them with thick black lashes. It would be some time ere the child forgave Frayne for what must seem to her the knight's betrayal. He had given her away just as her father had done, without a hint of regret. And, further, he had walked away without even a fare-thee-well.

How very like the Knight of Tor! Aurora thought with a wry smile. The man was as determined as ever to alienate anyone who threatened to come too close to his fiercely guarded heart. For the Enchantress little doubted that the knight was truly fond of the child and that he had deliberately estranged the little slave-girl for some obscure reason of his own. Just as he had ever sought to drive *her* away since first they had become lovers and together drunk of the elixir of the gods. And like Janine, Aurora had often felt wounded and bewildered by the knight's incomprehensible change of moods. One moment he would be the infinitely tender lover and the next a stern and forbidding stranger. Yet Aurora had long ago begun to suspect that whatever motivated Frayne was far more profound than he would have anyone believe, that the cynicism, the often perplexing indifference, indeed, the quality about him that frequently seemed sinister, all were deliberately contrived to camouflage his true purpose, which was to protect those for whom he had come to have an affection. But to protect them from what? she pondered. From himself? Or from the Sorceress whom he served? From the dread secret that he kept jealously to himself? Or from some presentiment of danger, which he alone perceived? She did not know. Not yet. But then the knight was speaking, interrupting her reverie.

"We'll camp here for the night," Frayne said, and there was a wry edge to his voice as if he mocked himself.

Startled, Aurora glanced quickly up to catch an odd expression in the silvery eyes that made her wonder if he had somehow known what she was thinking. But almost immediately he had turned away and dismounted, leaving her strangely discomfited.

They were all weary, except for the slave-girl, who had rested relatively well in the little bower amidst the tamarack grove, and they made a hasty camp. Much to Aurora's secret amusement, Crane took pains to contrive a crude tent for the slave-girl from a blanket slung between two stout sticks and anchored on either end with ropes tied to stakes wedged in the turf. And when, proudly, he conducted Janine to the entrance, she gazed shyly up into his homely face, but with such sweet adoration that he blushed to the roots of his flaming red hair and, turning awkwardly, fled into the woods as if pursued by the fiends of Somn.

The Enchantress did not linger in the camp after that, for Janine had assumed the tasks of preparing a meal and Frayne had remained taciturn and unapproachable, so that she was glad to be alone to tend to her own needs. Thus she retrieved her pack from the foot of an old oak tree in the boughs of which she was determined to spend her last night in the woods and stole away through the lengthening shadows to the still pool bordered by loosestrife and spicebush. The first green shoots of soapwort, too, had begun to push their way through the soil, and with a delighted smile, she knelt to dig up a few of the tender roots. Eagerly she shed her soiled clothing and waded through the green clusters of featherfoil growing in the shallows until she had reached water so clear that she could see the pebble-strewn bottom. Then, standing in water up to her waist, she ground the roots of the soapwort together until she had produced a rich lather and began to cleanse the filth from her body and the long raven tresses falling about her shoulders to her waist.

It was glorious to be clean again, and Aurora scrubbed until her skin was pink and glowing. And when she had finished at last, she slipped beneath the water's surface and swam along the bottom of the pool delighting in the feel of the cool water against her tingling skin. For a while she lost herself in the still beauty of the pool, as time and again she rose to the surface for a breath of air and then dove once more to the bottom to chase schools of small silvery moonfish and once a slithery green water snake. But at last she felt tired and was contented to float dreamily on the surface while she fashioned unicorns and dragons out of clouds and sang softly a song taught her by her dryad mother-pair long ago.

I would be the river
Forever flowing to the sea
Or the wind
Whispering secrets in the trees.
I would be a cloud

Drifting whimsically
Or a mountain,
Reaching for eternity.
Or I would be me—
A universe of endless possibility.

Though she was weary from the day's march and
from all that had happened to her since leaving
Vandrel's protected glen, she was yet suddenly filled
with a sort of restlessness. Her nerves tingled as they
did when she sensed danger or when she experienced
a presentiment of some untoward event. She could not
quite define what she felt, though she knew it was not
fear. Deliberately she lowered her feet to the pebbly
bottom and glanced about her.

The sun had dipped low in the sky so that the
woods seemed aglow with soft shafts of sunlight
filtering through the trees, and she looked up to see
Frayne watching her, the sunbeams dancing about his
still form like a glorious golden halo. Her breath
caught painfully in her throat as she stared back and
waited for she knew not what.

He had removed his boots and his shirt and now
deliberately unlaced the calf-length breeches and
stepped free of them. Then he was entering the water
his gaze yet intent upon her, and behind him the
drifting clouds blushed pink and golden with the last
rays of the setting sun. The Enchantress watched him
come with a feeling that somehow she had been
transported to another world, another time, and that
the man there with her was Frayne and yet not
Frayne, but something else—a god, perhaps. For he
was beautiful, with the aura of the setting sun creating

a nimbus about him, and the clouds edged in brilliant pastels were like some ethereal city floating in the sky, indeed, like Galesiad, the Eternal City of the Eilderood in the Land of the Silver Clouds.

Then he was before her, and the vision of the Eternal City had vanished with the sun as she gazed up into the strong face wreathed in shadows cast by the gloaming light of dusk, and she drew back, afraid. For she knew him and knew him not. He was Frayne, and he was the god veiled in darkness who had sought to take the Enchantress as his bride in the Land of Somn. Only then he had had hair as black as ravens' wings and the eyes had been glittering, lifeless things. Oh, gods! What was happening to her? Who was this man?

He held her with eyes gleaming like silvery points of fire with a light all their own, and she could feel the awesome power within him, the leashed puissance of a god. Her breasts heaved as she fought to breathe in the suddenly stultifying air. A buzzing filled her ears and her brain reeled so that she thought she must swoon, when at last she remembered the pouch still clung about her neck on a leather thong, and from somewhere she summoned the strength to grasp it in her hand.

Andruvien, the thing of power within the pouch, throbbed to her touch and she straightened, her mind suddenly clear again. Instantly she sent her thoughts outward, as she had done with Crane and finally Elwindolf. And suddenly the vision of a malevolent Immortal dispersed before a glorious burst of dazzling light. She felt pain and hopeless despair and a yearning that tore at her heart. And a passion so strong that she reeled before it.

Then, like a door slammed shut, the images vanished.

For a moment she stood stunned, staring into eyes that were suddenly closed to her.

"Why?" she whispered, her heart pounding within her breast, for at last she knew that he had deliberately clothed himself in the vision of Dred. Why had she never guessed that he could slip into her mind even as she could think the thoughts of others? And worse, how often had he done so in the past?

"It was time you knew the truth," he said and shrugged, his face hard in the first pale light of the rising moon.

"The truth?" she echoed incredulously. "That you can mold my fantasies as an artisan molds images out of clay? How often have you planted such illusions in my mind?"

"Any illusions in your mind are your own," he jeered and glanced away as if he could not stand to look at her. "The illusions of a child who thinks she is in love. The gods know I have done my best to *dis*illusion you of such absurdities."

His laugh chilled her soul, and suddenly she flung herself against him, her arms locked tightly about his neck as she clung to him with desperate need.

"Don't!" she whispered huskily. "That is the one thing which I know is real. For it has nothing to do with the mind. And can you not see that nothing else matters? I do love you. And even as a shepherdess once pledged her heart to you on the moonlit plains, so now does she do so again." She felt him stiffen and knew that he had not forgotten the magic-filled night

305

when she had pretended to be a simple shepherdess and he had lent her his heart till the sun should rise again.

"Frayne," she said, compelling him to look at her. And at last, as if against his will, the falcon eyes found hers.

For an eternity he stared into her face, which glowed with an inner radiance that was for him alone, and knew himself to be utterly lost. She was like some ethereal thing, a vision spun from moonlight, a nixie rising from the shimmering waters to bewitch him. And all around her the night was filled with glittering, magical things—faeries in the guise of fireflies flitting about the silvery pool of moonglow rippling gently in the perfumed breeze. In awe he beheld, leaping from the water like captured moonbeams reaching for the sky, the elusive gilden fish, pale gold and moon-spawned, creatures of legend fashioned by the Moon-Goddess Shin. The aroma of spicebush and enchanter's nightshade, mingling with the sweet, clean scent of Aurora's hair, teased his senses, even as her supernal loveliness seduced his will.

Forgotten was the vow he had made when the enchantment of her song had sought to weave its sweet spell about him—that he would make her see the truth. Forgotten was his terrible secret and the torment of a love that could never be. With a groan he clasped her to him.

As Shin the Moon Goddess sailed through the sea of night, Frayne lifted the Enchantress in his arms and bore her from the rippling waters to his bed beneath a spreading ash. And in wonder he bent to taste the sweetness of her lips, for no longer was she the untutored child who had enchanted him so long ago beside the still waters of Grendylmere, but a woman with a woman's love. And as such, she was a marvel to him.

She was supple beauty, responding to his every need with a desire that matched his own. She was silken loveliness whose touch was liquid sensuality flowing over him, bearing him upon rapturous waves of rising tension to frenzied crests of passion. He demanded more and more of her, and she never ceased to grant ever greater heights of ecstasy. Indeed, she was boundless in her love, an Enchantress who transmuted passion into magic and created a paradisaical plane of sensuosity beyond fantasy. And yet there was nothing of the practiced harlot in her ardor, but rather a sort of innocence that somehow humbled him, for he knew it was not the innocence of the untouched virgin, but the unaffected passion of a woman who was incapable of deceit. She gave wholly of herself, simply because she was Aurora and he was Frayne.

Never had he thought to know such delicious madness in the arms of a woman. And when at last she lay asleep within the circle of his embrace, her lips curved in a dream of contentment, he stared long into the endless sweep of stars and wondered what price the gods would exact for this night of forbidden love. Then suddenly he knew he would pay any price to know such enchantment again.

They were up with the sunrise and riding at a steady clip across the vast plain, the desert slave-girl and Crane leading the way astride the rangy bay they had taken as spoils of a battle from the outlaw band. They made their way south and west, toward the southern tip of the Confounded Lands, bordered by volcanos belching fire and smoke into a hazy sky, for there, Janine had told them as they stood at the edge of the forest looking out over the Plain of Shintari, the grass-covered prairie gave way to the drifting sands of the desert wastelands.

"It is near the time of *Mawsim*, the Season of the Rains," she had said in her quiet way. "But now the *simoom*, the sultry winds of Huri, the Virgin Goddess, sweep the earth. The waterholes will be *sifr*— empty. It is not a good time to come to the land of the Wendaren. We will go west to Al-Wadi-Hashiy, the Dry River. There we should seek *al-funduq*, the inn for the caravans seeking to cross the Land of *Erg*, which is called *fesh-fesh*, for it is treacherous with shifting sands."

"I have heard tales of these inns," Frayne said quietly. "Would it not be better to avoid settlements? The Bakhshidan desert raiders have eyes everywhere, and we lack the safety of numbers."

"Perhaps," the girl reflected. "And yet we have need of *merharim*, the camels for riding, which may be purchased there. For the horses are not suited to carry burdens long distances across the sand. It is four days to Al-Ouahe-Julab, the Oasis of the Sweet Water. And from there we follow Samt-ur-Ras, the Path of the Gods, south into the midst of the Valleys of Thunder, till we come at last to Aliy-Kadah-ur-Saqr, the Heights of the Hawk, all of which shall take us another three days. It is near here that we shall perhaps find what we seek. I would not advise that we try this journey without first preparing ourselves. The desert is not merciful even to those who know it well and whose hearts are *malaka*," she finished, her lovely eyes distant and shadowed, as though haunted by some private sorrow.

"*Malaka?*" Aurora questioned, mystified by this strange child of the desert.

The girl seemed to come to with a start. A blush tinged her cheeks as she met Aurora's glance.

"Possessed," she translated. Then, when the Enchantress continued to stare at her in perplexity, she spread wide her hands in the expressive manner of the Wendaren. "It is said among my people that to live in the Land of Erg, one must be *maskharat*, the fool, or *malaka*, possessed. And to be born Wendaren is to be both, for none who escape the desert can ever know peace till they return. It is Fatwa-ur-Mar, the judgment of God, who placed us in the barren wastes that we might learn patience, strength, and cunning. For the legends say that once we lived in the Land of Mamona, a land of riches, and were favored by the gods. But we grew complacent and ceased to practice the rites of *sajada*, adoration. And the Lord of All grew angry and sent us from Mamona to Erg, that henceforth we should know the lessons of *murr*, which is bitterness, and *salama*, which is resignation, till *Maran atha*, the Day when the Lord cometh in judgment."

Janine fell suddenly silent as she looked out over the vast plain, and it seemed to Aurora that she had forgotten them. But then she had turned once again to sweep them with an unfathomable glance, which seemed to linger on Crane's boyish face.

"And it is true," she uttered in accents of doom. "To be Wendaren is to be cursed. And there is no escaping it."

The girl had refused to say more after that, but had seemed to retreat behind an impenetrable barrier of silence from which even Crane could not woo her, and Aurora, covertly studying the taut young face, had felt the first stirrings of pity for the child. It occurred to the Enchantress that if Janine were indeed cursed to learn the lessons of bitterness and resignation that she had more than done so, for she had been sold into slavery by her own father and had been made to suffer the loss of all that she had ever known and possibly loved. Could this be the judgment of the One? If so, then truly there was little justice in the world, for the child was innocent and undeserving of so merciless a fate. Nay. 'Twas not the One, but the wickedness of the father who could condemn his own seed to a life of degradation and sorrow, she mused darkly. Such a man-beast should suffer the torments of Somn. Thanks be to the One that *she* was no daughter to the desert Khan!

Then suddenly she sobered, her brow furrowing into a pensive frown. For it had occurred to her that she knew nothing of her own father. Indeed, up to now, she had not really given much thought to the identity of her unknown sire. Oh, she had wondered, of course, who he was and whether or not he was alive. And she had created childish fantasies of a hero who must have loved the raven-haired woman with the golden eyes and who must surely have grieved to find her gone from him. But they had been daydreams, nothing more. The truth was that she had not actually thought beyond the tale of the warrior-woman, for she, at least, had seemed somehow real, while the one who had fathered her was less even than a phantom. Why had she never questioned that the warrior-woman should be apart from the father of her child? Indeed, might he not have been one of the men who had died at the hands of the black knights in Hawthorn Glade? Garwin had said there was a tall warrior whose death had sorely grieved the lady. Mayhap 'twas he.

The thought depressed her, for she had never really considered that she might not only be nameless but orphaned as well. And what if that was not the worst of it? What if he had not been the one to die in the elfin glade but instead had been one of the men from whom her mother had been fleeing in dread? After all, if a father could sell a child of his loins into slavery as Janine's had done, it was not inconceivable that a father would likewise seek to slay one of his own seed. But nay! She would not think such thoughts, she told herself in sudden anger, for they would buy her nothing but trouble, and firmly she turned her attention to contemplation of the terrain through which they passed.

Except for short spells to breathe the horses, Frayne did not call a halt till long after the sun had given over to night. Aurora had expected nothing less from him, for she knew him of old. He would drive them all to the limits of their endurance and demand even more of them ere they were through. But he would drive himself even harder. He was a knight on a quest, and he would not rest until he had reached his goal. That was Frayne, and in this he had not changed. But she had not been prepared, upon emerging from sleep that morning, to find him still beside her, his head propped on one elbow as he watched her slowly awaken to him.

He had appeared so young and handsome, with his fair hair tousled and the stern lines of his face softened with a smile, that for a moment she had thought she was beside Grendylmere once more and that Crane had transported them back in time. Then she remembered where she was and realized that the sweet passion they had shared had not been a dream. A smile had trembled on her lips as she gazed up into falcon eyes glowing with a silvery fire.

"I have been watching you, little Enchantress," he murmured softly and reached out to curl a raven lock about his slender finger. "Was it a dream of Endrith's Forest, I wonder, which made you smile so enchantingly in your sleep?"

"Nay," she whispered back, her eyes golden with the memory of her dream. "I dreamt that you held me beneath this very tree and swore your undying love for me."

His hand had stilled suddenly in her hair as for a long moment he gazed deeply into her eyes. And when he had spoken at last, she could not believe her ears.

"That was no dream, my sweet love," he had said and bent to kiss her.

Thus it was with keen-hearted joy and a sense of wonder that Aurora had ridden across the grassy plain beside the Knight of Tor all that day and the next and beheld the marvels of blue sky unfettered by cloud stretching into a distance so great that the mind was dazed by its vastness and must seek the tiny, insignificant thing on which to focus—the grey-green clumps of mesquite dotting the plain, silvery sage, delicate clusters of yellow, purple, and white wildflowers like bouquets ready to be gathered up, small, rounded cacti nestled amidst the prairie grass, and yellow, flowering yucca standing like flaming candles ensconced in a spray of bristling, razor-sharp spikes. Small, sleek lizards darted from beneath the horses' hooves, and long, rangy jackrabbits zigzagged before them, to bolt finally at a sharp angle away and freeze in a rigid pose till they knew themselves to be safe. Quail, soft grey doves, starlings and yellow-breasted meadowlarks, great black crows and swift prairie hawks, antelopes, ground squirrels, slow-moving tortoises, and the occasional bullsnake met her keen eye. Everywhere the prairie quickened with wildlife.

Twice they made camp on the broad plain, and each night Frayne held her near and made love to her with such sweet tenderness that she thought she must be in the grips of a new sort of madness. No longer did he seem cold and forbidding, but conversed easily with her about the world beyond her sheltered childhood as he had been used to do in the golden days beside Grendylmere. He had been everywhere, seen everything, she thought wistfully as he described the long sea voyages of his youth and the strange lands he had visited on those journeys—the floating isles of Kylandros, which drifted through the timeless flux, forward and backward through the ages, so that one who set foot on them might leave them in a far different time span from the one in which he had disembarked. She listened in awe to tales of Gorn, the Land of Mist, ruled by dragonlords, and of Shandel, the city of forgotten children. He had beheld the rich cities of the east in their own land and ridden into the Unknown Lands to the south where, it was said among the elves, one might converse with the gods. But he would tell her little of what he had seen and done beyond the Black Marble Cliffs, which separated the known regions from the unexplored territories. Indeed, the silvery eyes went suddenly opaque, as if with some dreadful memory, so that she was afraid to press him further, fearing that this blessed time of truce might come to an end. And thus had they come at last to the edge of the verdant plain and looked out upon a forbidding land of shale and rock worn smooth by the dry winds flowing out of the desert.

"It is Zamin-mat, the Dead Land," Janine said in a voice that sent a shiver down Aurora's back. "Here nothing can live, for there is no water. The rains, which come only rarely, run off the rock into great rivers, which flow until the heat sucks them dry again. Such a one is Al-Wadi-Hashiy."

The girl shaded her eyes with one hand and pointed westward across grey barren ridges rippling into the distance like the exposed ribs of some giant, fleshless corpse.

"There," she said. "Maybe half a day's journey."

But when Frayne wordlessly lifted his reins to ride on, the desert slave-girl reached out to grasp his sleeve.

"No, wait, sayyid!" she cried, then quickly dropped her hand, the dusky lashes sweeping down modestly to veil her eyes. "My people have a saying. 'He who would walk beneath the stars shall see the sun rise again.' It means . . ."

"I know what it means, Janine," Frayne interrupted with the hint of a smile. "Very well. We camp here till sundown. And henceforth, we travel only at night."

They found what shade they could in a shallow depression beneath a low overhang of rock and prepared to outwait the merciless sun. Aurora, huddled with her back against the stone and her chin propped on unbent knees, felt the energy drawn from her by the sweltering heat and no longer marveled at the slave-girl's insistence that they bring along the heavy bag of grain discovered tied to the saddle of the rangy bay. The girl had called it an omen sent by the gods, a sign that they smiled upon this journey, and Aurora, who had previously known only the bounty of forest and plain, had not understood, at least not until now. For as she had looked out upon the desolation of seemingly endless miles of rock shimmering with heat waves, she had not seen the smallest sign of life anywhere, nor even the withered remains of life. There was only the vast emptiness of desert, sun, and sky.

At least the horses would eat, she thought somberly and closed her eyes.

Aurora awakened to a persistent tickle along her cheek. Murmuring an incoherent protest, she swatted at the irritant and snuggled more comfortably against the secure warmth that pillowed her head and shoulders. Yet again the pest returned, and again, until at last she opened wide her eyes, an elfin oath on the tip

315

of her tongue remaining unspoken as she beheld Frayne's silvery eyes laughing down at her and realized she lay in the cradle of his arms.

"I regret having to call you from so tranquil a slumber," he smiled, and tugged gently at the raven curl with which he had teased her to wakefulness. "But dusk is upon us, and if ever you would see this palace of your ancestors, 'twere best that we were on our way."

"Has time passed so swiftly, then?" she sighed, more than contented to remain where she was. She could hear Crane and Janine saddling the horses, their voices a disembodied murmur on a welcome breeze that had sprung to life with the fading heat of day, and knew she could not prolong this moment of quiet bliss much longer.

"It has, little lazyboots. And we must make haste. Janine says the inn lies better than a night's journey before us, and we have little enough water to take us there."

She nodded reluctantly, but did not immediately rise.

For a long moment he studied her troubled expression before raising his hand to gently smooth her brow.

"What is it?" he queried softly. "Sorry so soon that you coerced me into bringing you along?"

Her startled gaze sought his.

"Nay! Never!" she uttered scornfully, then grinned a trifle ruefully as she saw that he was laughing at her. Immediately she sobered, her eyes twin agates in the gloaming light of dusk. Deliberately she ran her fingertips along the strong line of his jaw. "I would go anywhere with you. Dare anything. Surely you know that already."

"You've given me little reason to suppose otherwise," he agreed with a wry grimace. "Though such singularity of purpose proves only that you are an utter chucklehead. Now tell me what is bothering you so that we may be on our way."

"I was just thinking about something Janine said earlier. About being cursed never to know peace except in the desert. She had such an odd look about her. Do you think she was referring to herself?"

"No doubt," he said with a slight shrug and glanced away from her earnest gaze. "But then most people seem to yearn for the home of their childhood. Why should it trouble you?"

"I'm not sure. And yet there was something about the way she said it. As if it was the peace of death she was talking about. As if she knew something we did not. Frayne, I was suddenly afraid for her."

For a moment the knight was silent, his expression as serious as Aurora's as he appeared to consider the possible dangers before the desert slave-girl.

"There is peril for all of us in the desert," he said finally. "But perhaps Janine dares more than the rest of us. After all, her father is the Khan, and he did sell her into slavery. It is possible that her own people are now a greater danger to her than the desert itself."

Startled, Aurora bolted upright to face the knight in horrified astonishment.

"But why?"

"When the Khan sold her into slavery, he removed the mantle of his protection from her. He declared her dead to him. Dishonored. By Wendaren law it is a

317

father's right. Or a husband's or a brother's. To the people of the desert tribes, Janine is dead already."

"But she is one of them. Surely there must be some among them who love her still. Would stand her friend. What of her mother? Surely she would not stand by and do nothing."

"There would be little or nothing she could do," he answered, a peculiar twist to his lips. "She is just a woman, after all. And less than nothing to the Khan."

"And he is no better than the meanest grub beneath a rock! Is this then the way of the man-beasts? I am a woman. Am I less than nothing?" demanded the Enchantress with righteous indignation.

"You, little Enchantress, are an innocent," returned the knight, his smile enigmatic. "With much to learn. Do you account yourself as less than a man?"

"I am not less than anyone—man or woman," she said proudly, and her back was straight, her head held high.

"Quite so," he agreed with a gleam in his eye. "But you are more elf and dryad than man. Nor are you Wendaren. Janine and her mother are. Therein lies the difference. They are women trained from infancy to serve and obey men. Consequently, you must not expect too much from the girl. You will only bewilder and confuse her."

"Pooh!" Aurora scoffed. "The girl has no spirit. She will learn that no man need be her master. Just as no man or woman should be a slave. Henceforth she shall be free and then you will see," she declared. Then, bounding to her feet, she stalked away from the grinning knight to inform the slave-girl of her newly

318

gained freedom.

But Janine was to prove more difficult than Aurora ever dreamed possible.

"No. I beg you," she cried, falling to her knees before the startled young shape-changer. "Do not listen to her. Do not send me away. I will serve you well all my days. If I have displeased you, beat me. But do not banish me into exile."

"Don't be silly, Janine," Crane said, patting the girl awkwardly on the head. "No one's going to send you away."

"B-but the golden-eyed one said I was no longer your slave. She said I was free to go whither I would," sobbed the girl and gazed up at the youth through tear-blurred eyes.

"She did?" croaked the young mage-lord in no little consternation, then frowned when the girl nodded emphatically. "Well, never you mind. You're my slave, and only I can send you away. And don't worry about Aurora. I'll deal with her."

"Oh, will you?" interposed the Enchantress, who, aware that Janine had misunderstood her, had followed after the child to explain.

Crane gulped and swung around to find Aurora standing with legs braced and hands on hips, one exquisite eyebrow imperiously arched. And beyond her, Frayne observed them all with amused interest. Egad! the boy groaned, acutely aware that he found himself poised between twin forces of doom, for both girls awaited his response to the Enchantress's challenge with keen expectancy.

"Er—yes. Well, you see, I was just explaining to Janine that no one wants to send her away," he began judiciously, his voice pitched unnaturally high. Then he faltered to a halt as he heard the slave-girl's muffled sob and realized she thought he was about to recant on his promise to her. His face flushed red, then paled to a ghostly white as he girded himself to prove to the drooping girl that he was no coward. Resolutely he drew a deep breath.

"No one does want her to go, do they?" he queried belligerently. "Because if they do, they'll have to go through me. Janine belongs to me and that's the way it's going to stay."

"That's just it, you noddy," Aurora stated flatly. "She doesn't belong to anyone but herself. She's a human being. Surely you of all people would wish to see her free as she was meant to be. After all, you were little better than a slave to your grandfather."

"I beg to differ. I was never a slave," Crane began with cold hauteur.

"Well, he treated you like one. Making you creep around that horrid old castle like live bait for his pet Asgeroth. Admit it. You were glad at least to be free of that. And if you're honest, you'll admit you're glad to be free of him, too."

"We'll never agree on that," the boy said stiffly, and Aurora bit her tongue in dismay at where its waywardness had led her. Her lips parted to tell him she was sorry, that she hadn't meant any of it, but he had puffed up like a toad before a snake.

"You're just jealous because she belonged to Frayne and mad because he gave her to me," he accused her a trifle wildly. "You don't want her around in case Frayne changes his mind about her. Well, you don't have to worry. Because it wouldn't do him any good if

320

he did decide he wanted her back. She's mine now. And I'll look after her from now on. Come on, Janine. Let's get out of here."

In speechless astonishment, Aurora watched the young gudgeon pull the slave-girl to her feet and saunter off with an air of a cock who had won the right to rule the henhouse.

"Oh!" gasped the Enchantress with hardly suppressed fury. "The arrogant little popinjay! How dare he speak to me like that! Jealous indeed!" she fumed and turned to impale the Knight of Tor with a fulminating glance.

"Don't look at me," shrugged the knight with an air of profound innocence belied by the gleam of unholy amusement in his eyes. "I tried to warn you what would happen."

"And so you did," she agreed dangerously. "But don't think this is the end of it. I haven't finished with Crane yet."

"No, I don't suppose you have," he murmured, his sympathies with the condemned lad. "But as one who has had greater experience with the nature of the man-beast, I should tell you that it might be wiser to leave well enough alone. Things have a way of working themselves out all by themselves given enough time."

She eyed him dubiously for a time, her anger slowly giving way to her ever lively sense of the ridiculous, and suddenly her laughter rang golden in the quiet of the evening.

"I did not handle that at all well, did I," she gurgled, and a bemused Frayne thought that at that instant she little resembled the Enchantress who moments before had scintillated with wrath, but rather a delightful little imp with twin devils of laughter in her eyes.

"No," he agreed affably. "You showed a marked lack of diplomacy. But never mind. No doubt it did them both a world of good to have gotten the better of you. A little boost in self-confidence never hurt anyone."

But Frayne was to think better of his words as the night's journey wore on, for the young shape-changer seemed to have metamorphosed all in an instant from a gawky youngster, unsure of himself but appealing nonetheless, to a veritable cock of the walk, puffed up with self-importance and possessed of a suddenly discovered profundity of wisdom and experience far beyond his years. And Janine, who exhibited all the symptoms of an advanced case of hero worship, hung on his every word with an abject devotion that only encouraged him in his excess of newfound maturity.

"He's become a conceited little prig," growled the Knight of Tor sotto voce as he dropped back to ride beside Aurora after having attempted to speak with the slave-girl about what they might expect to encounter at the *funduq.* "Informed me as polite as you please that anything I had to say to her I could say through him. And damned if the impudent little piece of baggage didn't go along with him! She would not say a word till her precious young lord and master had relayed to me my exact words. And then he had the gall to repeat everything she said back to me. If he weren't so funny, I'd wring his scrawny neck."

"Well, you did say a little boost in self-confidence might do him a world of good," Aurora reminded the

322

knight with a demure smile. "Apparently we shall just have to learn to put up with it till the boost wears off."

"If he lives so long," Frayne grimly reflected, then uttered a short bark of laughter. "But on the other hand, it should prove interesting to see just how long he can live up to the heroic image Janine has imposed upon him. It shall either be the making or the breaking of him. After all," he added pointedly, "it is not an easy thing to forever be a woman's fancied knight in shining armor."

"Is it not?" queried the Enchantress innocently. "But how could you possibly know? You have ever sought to make it quite clear to me that you are no such thing. But then I shall just have to take your word for it, shall I not. You are, after all, so much more experienced in worldly matters than I."

"You, my dear," drawled the knight forbiddingly, "are certain to become vastly more experienced than you would wish if you persist in throwing my ill-conceived words back in my face. Two young jackanapes are enough of an aggravation without having you to follow their example as well."

Thus they rode through the night silvery with moonglow until at last they came upon a broad, winding gulley, shadow-haunted and vaguely sinister in the pale light of the waning moon.

"Al-Wadi-Hashiy," pronounced the slave-girl in a hushed voice, and she looked pensively to the south. "We follow the rim to the *funduq*. But for no reason must you ride into the riverbed. To do so is to court death."

"What do you mean?" queried Aurora, a little irritated at what seemed a penchant for the dramatic

323

in the child. Egad, she seemed obsessed with death and determined to frighten them all with her cryptic remarks.

But Janine merely shrugged.

"The *wadi* is dry now and may remain so. But I have seen men die who trusted to its treacherous path. For without warning it can be inundated with flood waters from the north, though the sky overhead may be clear for as far as the eye can see. The wise man does not set foot in the great *wadi* if he can avoid it."

She said no more, but headed her mount south, letting the animal pick its own way over the perilously smooth rock. The ring of iron-shod hooves echoed eerily off the sheer cliffs that lined the dry wash, the only sounds of life in all the vastness of Zamin-Mat, the Dead Lands encased in stone, and Aurora, hugging her elfin cape more snugly about her, shivered with more than the chill of the desert night.

With silent longing, she conjured up a mental image of Endrith's Forest, the comfort of greenery and the beauty of Grendylmere, the father-oak and Hawthorn Glade, laughing brooks of sparkling water, and trees soughing in a dew-kissed breeze. There one felt nurtured by the goodness of the gods. One felt alive! Here they were like lost souls in the country of the dead, and like as not, not even the gods could find their way out of it, she mused fatalistically, and could not keep from glancing over her shoulder at Frayne silhouetted against the backdrop of the moonlit sky. The tall, shadowy figure riding easily in her wake reassured her, as she had known that it would, and with a lighter heart she turned once more to the dreary task of staying awake and in the saddle. Even so, she caught herself swaying drunkenly atop the little mare, when suddenly Janine called out softly and pointed dead ahead.

"Al-funduq!" she cried. "And to the west, Zamin-Erg. The Desert of Sand and land of the Wendaren."

Chapter Twelve

"Remember, please, that always the men of the Turaq tribe cover their faces with the *litham* and their heads with the *dulband*," Janine instructed the Enchantress as they readied themselves to enter the gates of the *funduq*. "And you must take care, *mem-sayyid*," she added softly to Aurora, "to keep the golden eyes hidden. The tales of Al-Murabit are well known throughout the desert-tribes. Any who behold the eyes of golden fire will instantly suspect who you are and where we go. It would perhaps be better to keep such information to ourselves, for it is rumored that a great treasure is hidden within the walls of the Palace of the Rising Sun. There are many who would not hesitate to attack us for the secrets of the House of Doane."

"Nor are they likely to be merciful to females

masquerading as men," Frayne added by way of warning as he inspected the makeshift disguises Janine had contrived from an old cloak discovered among the possessions of the slain outlaw. The girl had torn the fabric into long strips, which she wound about their heads to form the *dulband,* or turban. With their faces covered below the eyes by the square of fabric Janine called the *litham,* and their forms draped in their own cloaks, they hoped to be able to pass as a couple of slender boys of the Turaq tribe to the south.

Frayne had donned the spurs, silver mail, and other accoutrements of his calling as a Knight of Tor, while Crane appeared as he ever did, in the raiment Vandrel had given him. It had been decided that Janine would present herself and Aurora as the servants of a knight and his squire on a pilgrimage to the ancient ruins of But-Kadah, the Temple of Gawr, the Fire-God, who inspires warriors to greatness in battle. As the knight's hired guide, Janine would do all the talking necessary to purchase camels and the supplies required for their trek.

The morning was already well advanced when at last they passed through the gates of the inn. The *funduq,* constructed of sandstone and arranged in a square to afford an enclosure, or *zaribat,* for the camels, goats, and other livestock of the great caravans, was a turmoil of dust and milling animals. Squawking chickens scattered from beneath the horses' hooves, and the shouts of camel drivers vied with the bleating of thirsty animals being driven to the watering holes fed by sweet water wells at the center of the *zaribat.* Aurora's mount snorted and sidled nervously as a pair of snarling dogs nipped at its heels. Aurora guessed they were the guard dogs that Janine had told them traveled with every caravan to sound the warning of approaching intruders, and they appeared as vicious as the girl had warned they would be. But at last the small band dismounted before a roofed portico supported by carved arches, which Janine informed them in a low voice was called *al-kushk*. Here the men of the caravans sat on woven mats spread on the flagstone floor to feast and gossip or to haggle over matters of trade.

"I beg you will sit and eat," Janine said, bowing her head respectfully. "The men of the *karwan* talk business. If there are camels to be purchased, we shall learn of it here."

Then she left them with a single low-voiced warning to take care not to speak too freely among themselves, for there were ears everywhere.

Frayne hesitated only a moment before sauntering easily toward an unoccupied corner somewhat away from the other patrons. His tall, caped figure and fair hair and skin drew many covert looks from among the swarthy men of the desert as he seated himself cross-legged on one of the mats and signaled for Crane and Aurora to join him.

It was not long ere the slave-girl returned followed by a dusky-eyed wench bearing a heavy tray laden with food. Murmuring something in the musical tongue of the desert-tribes, she knelt gracefully, and leaning forward to set before them a sumptuous repast, revealed an enticing glimpse of plump breasts beneath a sleeveless spangled garment laced tightly across the voluptuous bosom. Curiously, Aurora thought, Crane suddenly choked and averted his gaze, his face having assumed a particularly brilliant red. Now what was wrong with the boy? she wondered and sensed Janine grow suddenly rigid beside her.

"*Shukran*." Frayne thanked the wench in her own tongue, and favoring her with an appreciative glance, tossed a coin in her direction. Briefly a glitter lit the black eyes at the sight of the gold. Then the fingers of one plump hand retrieved the coin and furtively tucked it amidst the tantalizing bulge of her ample charms beneath the spangled bodice.

"I am pleased to serve the *sayyid*," she murmured, raising her hand to her forehead in the sign of humility. Yet something in her manner set Aurora on edge. She glanced up to find the wench regarding Frayne with a most peculiar smile on lips that seemed unnaturally red. It appeared to Aurora that she leered at the handsome knight out of the corners of her eyes, which were heavily outlined in something like black paint to give them a slanted cast. And, furthermore, the drooping lids were a bizarre blue. Likewise, her cheeks had been tinted a dusky red, and a small black dot had been painted at one corner of the provocatively pursed lips. Never had the Enchantress seen anything like this female, yet suddenly she understood why Crane had blushed and why Janine stood with her small hands clenched into tight little fists. Indeed, her own fingers had curled like the talons of Agrypha, Sky-Dancer, when the falcon reaches out to clutch his prey in the death grip. For Frayne was returning the wench's smile in a manner in which he had never smiled at Aurora, and the silvery glitter of his falcon eyes, as they roamed freely over the plump hips and

330

generous thighs beneath the girl's loose-fitting and nearly transparent trousers which were gathered about the small waist and shapely ankles, infused the Enchantress's veins with a slow heat. Gladly would she have plunged Glaiveling into the wretched female's heart. Then she realized the creature had glanced up to catch Aurora staring at her. Instantly the Enchantress looked down to conceal the golden glitter of her eyes. But not before she had seen a fleeting frown flicker across the wench's brow.

"Ah, you speak the tongue of my people, little rose blossom," Frayne was saying. "I am pleasantly surprised. And curious how that may be."

The wench tittered and lowered her thick lashes coyly.

"There was a man who stayed long at my father's inn. He once was *munshi*, the language master, for the young prince of Khalifar. But, alas! He was not—how do you say—*safiy*, pure in his thoughts? His teachings displeased the boy's father and he was forced to flee for his life. It was nearly two turnings of the seasons before the assassins of the *khsatra-pava*, the Guardian of the province of Khalifar, found him here. I was very young, but he taught me many things ere he paid the forfeiture of the Guardian's judgment."

"No doubt," drawled the knight ironically and began to toy absently with a second gold piece. "You are obviously a bright girl. Perhaps you can tell me why those men seated near the far wall seem to interested in my servants. They have not taken their eyes off them since we sat down."

Aurora glanced up in surprise at the steely edge to

331

Frayne's softly spoken query and surreptitiously sought out the men in question. Though all the score or more patrons of the inn looked bewilderingly alike in the white robes and *dulbands* of the desert clans, their faces swarthy and adorned with coal-black moustaches and short beards neatly trimmed to a point beneath strong chins, she picked them out instantly. One was of powerful physique, broad-shouldered and barrel-chested, and handsome in a bold sort of way. There was something about him of Arkon, Rogue-Wolf, a ruthlessness in the insolent curl of the lips coupled with an arrogance that was evident in his every sinuous move. He would use people and animals with insensate cruelty, she thought, and unconsciously gripped the hilt of the elfin dagger at her belt till her knuckles shone white. With an effort she tore her gaze from the wolf and quickly assessed his two companions as Shaggel, the Weasel, and Gulo, the Wolverine, for they were smaller and furtive-seeming, appearing to skulk in the shadow of the big one, and yet vicious, too, with wicked-looking curved sabers thrust through the roped belts tied about their waists, and curiously sharp features, which seemed never still. Perhaps twenty feet and a dozen people separated the two parties, and yet even at that distance she could sense something sinister in the cold glitter of black eyes watching her and her companions, and suddenly she shivered.

The serving wench appeared to pale slightly beneath her paint. But her gaze never wavered from the glitter of gold between the knight's slender fingers, and her black eyes were suddenly calculating.

"They are bad men, those three." she said slyly. "If

332

you have won them for enemies, you shall have need of many prayers to avoid a fate like the *munshi*. And even then," she shrugged, "who can say the gods will choose to listen?"

"They will listen, little pigeon," smiled the Knight of Tor, and the woman appeared suddenly fascinated by the cold gleam in the silvery eyes. "These, then, are assassins like the ones who dispatched your friend?" he asked carelessly and flipped the gold coin into the air with a flick of a thumb, then deftly caught it again.

The wench ran a pink tongue along her upper lip as she watched another coin appear between the knight's fingers, apparently from thin air.

"The big one is called Yataghan-Girmizi, for it is said his saber is stained crimson with the blood of those he has killed. He is *al-sardar*. A dangerous man to cross. The other two are *yarbu*, desert rats," she said contemptuously. "They kill for the pleasure it brings. You do not wish to be found in your beds by those two."

"*Al-sardar?*" queried the knight.

"Chief of the *sipahi*," pronounced Janine in a hard voice. "An army of desert cutthroats. No caravan is safe from them unless they agree to pay the *bakhshish*, the gratuity for protection."

"The boy speaks truly, *sayyid*," the woman said, her black eyes curious on Janine's veiled face. But Frayne paid her no heed.

"Why, I wonder, is the chief of the Bakhshidan desert raiders interested in us?" he murmured softly. But the wench had snatched up the gold coins and vanished into the shadowy interior of the inn.

After arranging for the safekeeping of their horses with the proprietor of the *funduq*, a man who had impressed them as one who would keep his word in exchange for the promise of a hefty bag of gold upon their return, the small band stole from the inn at the end of a great caravan heading west across the desert. Janine had managed to purchase only one of the highly prized *merharim*, the riding camels noted for their easy swinging gait, but with the intelligence, Janine informed them with a wry grin, of a beetle. And, indeed, the cud-chewing dromedary, blatantly misnomered Mush, or Mouse, by her previous, fond owner, seemed possessed of a mulish disposition, an irascible temperament, and a decidedly foul odor. She resisted with a daunting persistence all attempts to coax, cajole, or terrorize her into rising from her knees as one after the other of the four climbed aboard the *hawdaj*, the litter secured to her back, and tried his or her luck at mastering the recalcitrant camel. Not even Aurora, who could tame Grimhard, Grizzly Bear, with a thought, and who once had charmed Sheelar, mightiest of the Seventy-seven Serpent Lords of Somn, with a song, could move this single, wretched beast of burden.

"Come, Mush," she urged, trying to keep the impatience from her thoughts. "Is it indeed so much to ask that you carry us across the desert sands? After all, 'tis only what you were bred to do. You, who are *merharim*, the most prized of all the desert dromedaries. You cannot, I know, begrudge us this simple service. We shall in turn see that you are well fed and that you are the first to drink whenever we come to water. Nor shall you be unduly burdened, for, as you see, we travel lightly."

"Lightly?" scoffed the insufferable beast and raised her snout into the air so that she looked down upon the Enchantress for all the world like one of the haughty dames of noble birth whom Frayne had once described to her. "Why, there are three of you and but one of me. No doubt I shall be asked to carry all of you and heavy bags of feed and water and all your paltry possessions, as well. If you think that is so insignificant a burden, then you yourself can carry it, for I will not."

"Oh, nay!" Aurora hastened to reply. "Not insignificant to us. But to one of your wondrous size and strength, 'tis surely not too great a task."

"Oh, it's easy enough for you to say," sniffed the beast, nearly swallowing her cud in apparent indignation at what she certainly must have viewed as Aurora's impertinence. "But you have not been forced to go for days on end without water to places you had never the slightest wish to visit. You have not been made to kneel while all sorts of things are hung upon your back, then forced to rise and walk for endless miles while the master and all his brood ride. You, my dear, have not felt the humiliation of the stick against your hide. Pooh! You man-beasts are all the same. Never giving even the tiniest thought as to how we feel about being forever forced to cater to your every whim. I'd just like to know what makes you think you are any better than the rest of us. Moreover, you are fools, the lot of you. For only a fool would wish to venture forth into that miserable wasteland when there is food and drink right here for the asking. Well, I for one see no reason to accompany you on another feckless venture, which shall offer me nothing either along the way or at the end but the prospect of the thankless journey back again."

"Oh, indeed," the Enchantress retorted, amazed that Janine had thought these strange creatures to be dull-witted. This one might belong to the breed of sophists about whom Frayne had spoken disparagingly as being irrational masters of rationality. "And yet 'tis man's wit and ingenuity that has made available that very food and water. The least you can do is honorably earn your share of it."

"Harumph!" the camel snorted. "You need not speak to me of honor. I am, after all, nothing but a poor, dumb beast. What have I to do with such silly notions? Nay, my dear. You shall have to do better than that to convince me to abandon all reason. Otherwise, I shall not set foot beyond the security of these walls. Of that you may be certain."

"Oh! I give up!" exclaimed the Enchantress, flinging up her hands in utter exasperation, for it was obvious the creature was determined to be unreasonable.

"Very wise, I am sure, my dear," observed the camel imperturbably and returned to chewing her cud with the equanimity afforded by a total indifference to the man-beasts' plight.

"It is hopeless," Aurora reported to the others. "She insists nothing could lure her away from the comfort of these walls, for she has nothing to gain by it and much to lose. And truly, I can think of no rebuttal to such an argument. She seems very well acquainted with the regrettably self-centered nature of the man-beast. I'm afraid there is nothing more that I can do."

But Crane was equally determined not to be bested by a shaggy, misbegotten spawn of a fleabag.

"I'd sooner eat the beast as try to ride her anyway," he declared, regarding Mush with a baleful glare. "Stand back. I'll show her a thing or two about the man-beast that she'll never forget."

What the shape-changer had intended in his brash declaration, the others were never quite sure. The fact of the matter is that suddenly, where a tall, gawky, red-headed boy had stood a split-second earlier, there had appeared a particularly disreputable-looking dromedary with knobby knees, scrawny neck, and a startling top-knot of flaming red hair. Moreover, the unexpected alteration of boy into camel wrought a startling effect upon the hitherto unimpressionable Mush. Uttering an eager grunt, the creature heaved suddenly to her feet, a wild gleam in her eye, and lumbered toward the rather dazed and most definitely spindle-shanked bogus bull with an alacrity astonishing in one who had previously displayed all the advanced signs of chronic torpitude.

"It was obviously love at first sight," Frayne remarked later to Aurora as they swayed to the smooth rhythm of Mush's walk, and, indeed, the creature seemed to hang on Crane's heels with silent adoration. Nor did the fact that the young shape-changer appeared neither to return the sentiment nor to welcome it deter the sorely stricken camel. Mush apparently had at last discovered a reason for accompanying the man-beasts on their feckless venture into the desert, for never once did she balk again so long as she could see Crane going steadily on before her.

Thus they passed an uneventful hour in the company of the caravan before veering off alone and unnoticed to the south. Aurora, feeling more than a little intimidated by the immensity of the pale drifts of sand, which seemed to stretch endlessly in all directions, gazed for a long time over her shoulder at the long train receding at a sedate but steady pace into the moonlit vastness. They marched to the endless rhythm of the desert, slaves to a whimsical fate, she mused somberly as she recalled Janine's repeated warnings that they must ever remain alert for the dust storms, which could suffocate in moments a whole caravan, poisonous snakes, which lay buried just beneath the surface of the sand, the perils of falling asleep and wandering for miles out of the way when they had only enough water to carry them the shortest, most direct route from oasis to oasis, and, of course, the never-ending threat of *ghawl*, the sudden, swift attack of the feared desert raiders. And yet she could not help but be drawn almost as greatly as she was repelled by the sinister mystique of the desert. Almost she understood the feeling of *malaka*, of being possessed by a dread fascination for the sheer magnitude of desert and sky, against which one seemed as insignificant as the single grain of sand, and which yet paradoxically constantly reaffirmed what was meaningful and unique to the human spirit—the daring to accept the challenge and the will to survive against impossible odds. Then, resolutely, she turned her face forward. It would not do to allow herself to grow too fanciful, for she sensed that the terrible reality of the desert was too great, and there would be too little of sanity to which to cling amidst the vast emptiness.

Janine did not call a halt till the morning sun forced them to seek what shelter they could find in the shadows cast by the camels nestled on the desert sands, their legs folded contentedly beneath them as they ate from feedbags containing the day's allotment of grain. The Enchantress slept fitfully through the heat of the day and was grateful when at last Frayne roused her for the night's endless trek. She accepted with alacrity the wedge of sweet melon the slave-girl offered her and savored the soothing relief of its liquid, which was like salve to her painfully dry mouth and throat, but she could manage only a few mouthfuls of the raisins and dried figs and dates. She found herself standing as if transfixed and realized she had been lost in a daydream of Endrith's Forest and the cold, clear waters of Grendylmere, and afterward, she could not bring herself to eat anything. She felt no hunger, only a terrible longing for the sight of a green, living thing.

That night and the next assumed the proportions of a strange dream of silence, moonlight, and the endless sway of the camels' walk; and the days, the anguish of sun and wind and the desert sand shimmering in heat waves. Daily the three grew more aloof and silent, instinctively drawing into themselves in order to conserve strength steadily sapped from them by the blistering sun and the dry wind of the *simoom*. Aurora cleaved to Frayne's stolid presence, sustained by his quiet strength and uplifted by the still, grey eyes that never ceased to shine upon her with an enduring tenderness she had thought never to behold in their depths. Never had she loved him more. Yet even so, the desert took its toll on her, slowly draining her inner reserves and filling her with a sense of desolation, until she began to wonder if they were doomed to wander the sandy wastes forever. But at last, near the dawning of the fourth day Mush abruptly lifted her head and set out at a long, loping run, Crane lumbering along in her wake.

"What is it?" Aurora squealed, clutching at Frayne to keep from falling off her suddenly precarious perch on the lurching *hawdaj*.

"The oasis!" the knight shouted back. "She must smell water."

Eagerly the Enchantress peered ahead, her pulse suddenly racing. For a time she could make out little in the moonless dark that precedes daybreak. Then, just as the sun peeped over the eastern horizon to send pale streaks of pink and gold across the sky, they topped a low rise, and Aurora beheld below them trees such as she had never seen before and the pale shimmer of water, more lovely at that moment even than her memories of Grendylmere.

"Al-Ouahe-Julab!" Janine uttered, a small flutter of laughter easing the subtle lines of strain and fatigue from her face, and for the first time Aurora realized the uncertainty that had lain beneath the girl's outwardly calm demeanor. They had all been depending upon her, this offspring of the wastelands, to bring them to safety, and yet she was actually little more than a child. With shame, Aurora recalled her earlier, unfavorable impressions of the girl. She had thought her a milksop unworthy of the knight's esteem. A wry smile touched the Enchantress's lips. Never again would she underestimate the little slave-girl, for

Janine was a true daughter of the desert clans, and she had forever earned if not the Enchantress's affection, then certainly her respect.

They rested all that day beneath palm and date trees, which were a marvel to the tree-child reared by dryads. She lay in Frayne's arms staring dreamily through half-opened eyes at the gentle sway of palm leaves against the cloudless sky and was utterly content. Indeed, only Mush appeared less than happy with her lot, for Crane, after having been relieved of the *hawdaj* balanced on his humped back, had suddenly, before her very nose, abandoned his role as dromedary and resumed his true form.

"Back, you knobby-kneed, flea-bitten varmint!" he snapped peevishly at a sorely bewildered Mush and waved his arms at her in an attempt to drive her from him. The camel grunted, her head lifting on her long neck as she eyed the lanky shape-changer with something of panic in the blinking eyes.

"But, Crane, how can you be so cruel?" Aurora exclaimed, her lips trembling with hardly suppressed laughter. "Can you not see the poor thing has been cruelly disillusioned? She has sustained her first disappointment in love and no doubt shall now pine away. For shame on you for using her so."

Unamused, Crane made a face at the grinning Enchantress and rudely thwacked the lovelorn camel on the nose as she lowered her head to sniff at the shape-changer.

"Shoo, you hairy bag of bones! Be off with you," he yelled abrasively.

"No, Sayyid Crane!" Janine shrieked too late, for even as Crane turned his head in startled alarm, the much offended Mush drew back thick lips and shot a yellow stream of spittle straight at the unfortunate youth.

For a moment Crane stood in horrified silence as the full impact of the camel's offensive gesture sank in. The shape-changer's mouth opened and closed in voiceless indignation. His hands spread wide, and his gaze rose skyward as though questioning the whimsy of an unjust fate. Whereupon Janine glided to his side and reached up on tiptoe to gently mop his befouled person with a clean cloth.

"Forgive me, *sayyid*," she said, shamefaced and wretched at having failed her lord and master. "I should have warned you against angering the *merhara*. It is seldom wise to incur their displeasure, as sadly you have just been made to learn."

Slowly his eyes rolled down to regard the girl's bowed head in wordless disbelief. Then, as if her softly spoken words had freed his tongue, Crane erupted into vociferous indignation.

"B-by the gods," he sputtered in impotent rage and revulsion, his freckled face paling to an alarming shade of white as he swiped a sleeve across it. "I-I'll change myself into a dragon and consume the misbegotten spawn of a dung heap with flames. I'll reduce her to a pile of ashes. But no," he vacillated, his gaze lighting as though he had just been struck with a marvelous new thought. "That would be too merciful. Instead I'll become a stone in her hoof. Or even better, a plague of cactus needles imbedded in her nose. Or a stinging fly always in her ear. Or a green, luscious tuft of grass always receding beyond her reach."

342

"Yes, *sayyid*," murmured Janine in a soothing voice as she led him, still plotting his terrible vengeance, away from the others. "Indeed, my lord . . . Even so, Lord Crane . . . As you wish. . . ."

Reluctantly Aurora awakened from a deep, dreamless slumber. The lovely sound of a low breeze sighing through the trees and the gentle plash of water against a sandy shore greeted her. Languorously she noted that the sun was already low on the horizon and realized she must have slept through the morning and most of the afternoon. No wonder she felt so deliciously sluggish, like Sheeva, Garter Snake, basking in the sun.

Yet something else had disturbed her rest, something not quite right. Slowly she turned her head to discover Frayne stretched out on the ground beside her, his head pillowed in the crook of one arm and his breathing deep and regular with the rhythm of sleep. Briefly a tender smile touched her lips. In the white robes and *dulband* Janine had procured for him at the caravan inn, he seemed quite different—less stern and somehow more intriguing, she thought whimsically. His beard, already bleached by the desert sun, shimmered a pale gold against the deep, golden tan of his cheeks, and her heart constricted painfully in her chest. He was so beautiful, a man of whom all others must take instant notice, a man to be loved or feared, but never taken for granted.

A sudden whisper of movement impinged upon her thoughts, and she stiffened, instantly alert. Cautiously her hand stole to the dagger at her belt.

Careful not to move her head, she searched the oasis from beneath partially closed lids, her muscles tensed and ready.

There it was again! The soft susurrus of cloth against sand. And out of the corner of her eye she glimpsed an elusive flicker of movement and the brief flash of the sun's slanting rays glinting off steel.

"Frayne!" she whispered harshly and pulled the dagger.

The pounding of hooves thundered across the oasis as the knight bounded to his feet, Thrimheld flashing in his hand. Two robed desert-raiders dropped to the deadly blade even as a heavy body flung itself at the Enchantress. Instinctively Aurora bent her knees to her chest, letting the soles of her boots catch her assailant in the midriff. Then, rolling backward, she used the villain's momentum to sling him over her head. Instantly she was up, her hand reaching for the pouch slung on a thong about her neck, reaching for Andruvien.

A startled cry escaped her lips. The pouch was gone! Instantly she guessed that it must have been torn from her in the brief struggle with the brigand. Futilely she cast a darting glance over the sand at her feet, but the pouch was nowhere in sight. Some inner sense must have warned her of the rogue's renewed attack, for suddenly she looked up to see cruel lips stretched in a leering grin—Golu, the Wolverine, she thought fleetingly, who killed for the pleasure of it. And in his left hand, the pouch and Andruvien! Bitterly she grasped the elfin dagger more firmly in her hand and braced herself to meet the vicious attack of the desert raider.

He rushed her with a bloodcurdling yell, his black eyes glittering in the feral mask of his face. Crouched and ready, she let him come. Then he was upon her, and with the swiftness of Teelar, the Panther, she sidestepped, lashing out with the elfin blade. The blow jarred her wrist as the blade plunged to the hilt in living flesh. Golu screamed and twisted, tearing the knife from her hand. The Enchantress swallowed the bile in her throat as the man fell at her feet and she saw the hate-filled eyes darken with sudden, terrible realization ere they grew blank and fixed with the sightless stare of death. However, the Enchantress was not to be allowed time to experience the full sweep of revulsion at having been forced to take another's life, as suddenly she found herself pinioned from behind, a lean, sinewy arm locked about her throat and a knife held with deadly intent before her eyes.

Reacting with the sure instinct of Anduan, Tree-Child, who had been reared by elves and dryads and taught the lessons of survival by the forest itself, Aurora immediately sank her teeth into the limb clamped about her neck. The villain let out a startled oath and jerked his tortured forearm free, whereupon the Enchantress, swift to take the advantage, caught his knife wrist in both her hands. Holding tightly to it, she slipped down and out of the slackened strangle-hold, then, bringing the captured arm up, twisted sharply under it. With a yelp the villain flipped neatly head over heels to come down hard on his back, the air knocked from him. Momentarily rendered help-less, he writhed upon the ground gasping for breath, while Aurora wheeled and started for the villain's knife, lying where he had dropped it in the sand.

Snatching it up, she turned to find him already shoving himself up, a murderous gleam in the beady eyes. With only a slight start she recognized the sharp, weasellike features of Golu's companion from the inn. A cold smile touched her lips as she brought the butt end of the knife down hard against Shaggel's head. The little weasel stiffened and toppled backward, a sickly grin on his thin lips.

Without pausing to view her handiwork, the Enchantress bounded to Golu and knelt to prise open the hand still clutched tightly about the pouch. Then, sternly fighting down the nausea that threatened, she dragged Glaiveling from the lifeless body and quickly turned to look for the others.

Immediately she froze, her heart in her mouth, as she beheld the Knight of Tor surrounded by desert raiders.

Frayne, dauntless and magnificent, a dagger in one hand and Thrimheld, Swift-Blade, in the other, held at bay four circling swordsmen who, even as she watched, closed in for the kill ere she could spring to his aid. In awe Aurora saw the knight's teeth flash in a chilling grin and the falcon eyes glittering silvery in the stern mask of his face as he dared them to come, and she thought fleetingly that she would not for the world wish to be in the raiders' boots. Indeed, Frayne fought with the cold fury of an avenging god. Deftly turning upon the hilt of his dagger the swordthrust of the first poor devil to reach him, he neatly ran him through with Thrimheld and pulled the blade free, swinging the sword backhanded over one powerful shoulder to parry a swiping thrust at his back, then forward again to meet the frontal attack of the other two. He moved with swift agility, like one of the silver-haired men of the Shintari, who dance in honor of Shin, the sleeping Moon Goddess. Then one, a great brute of a man, frustrated and bewildered by the knight's dazzling quickness, shoved aside the other two, and growling like an enraged grizzly, charged the knight, his curved scimitar slicing a deadly arc before him as he sought to disembowel the Knight of Tor. Frayne ducked lithely under the slashing blade, then, thrusting up beneath the larger man's guard, let the brute impale himself to the hilt with the momentum of his own ponderous attack. Aurora gasped as she watched the giant topple, dragging the hilt of the sword from the slayer's hands, for the others were coming at Frayne, one from the front, his sword grasped in both hands and brandished high over his head with murderous intent, and the other from behind, his cruel features distorted in a wild, triumphant grin as he lunged at the knight's unprotected back. Aurora almost closed her eyes, unwilling to behold her beloved knight so cruelly cut down. Yet ere he could be either skewered or his head cloven, the intrepid Knight of Tor had leaped lightly from between them, leaving the back-thruster to spit his comrade on the sword-thrust meant for Frayne. Hardly had their swarthy faces assumed expressions of startled disbelief ere Frayne had ended the misbegotten life of the remaining knave with a single blow of the dagger.

For a moment the knight stood, his chest heaving from his exertions and his terrible eyes like pale daggers sweeping the oasis for further assailants. Then, deliberately, he straightened, and striding to

347

the body of the felled giant, set his boot against the gory chest. With cold contempt he yanked Thrimheld free and wiped the blade clean with the dead man's robe ere turning to see the Enchantress watching him, the fear she had felt for him only just beginning to recede from her pallid face.

Aurora stared at him in unutterable relief, and in astonishment as well, for the entire battle from start to finish had lasted scant moments. Suddenly a piercing scream cut across the uncanny stillness of the after-battle. Aurora, the hair rising on the nape of her neck, swiveled to see Janine struggling in the arms of a tall, powerful man mounted on a lunging stallion, a group of close-packed horsemen rallying about them, and, nearly beneath the animal's feet, a crumpled body facedown in the sand. It took only a single glance for Aurora to recognize the bold, arrogant features of Yataghan-Girmizi, *al-sardar* of the Bakhshidan desert raiders, and Crane lying in a lifeless heap on the ground.

With a cry, the Enchantress bounded after them, but ere she had gone half the distance, Frayne had intercepted her. One steely hand clutching her arm in a painful grip, he swung her hard about and caught her to his chest.

"Aurora!" he shouted harshly in her face as she struggled furiously to free herself. "It's too late!"

As his words finally sank in, she slowly stilled, her golden gaze lifting in dazed disbelief to meet Frayne's gimlet eyes. Immediately his look softened.

"They are gone," he said gently. "You never had a chance of reaching them in time. And it would not have done for you to fall into their hands in a brash rescue attempt."

After a moment she let go a shuddering breath.

"Nay, I suppose not," she murmured, only half convinced. Then abruptly she stiffened. "Oh, gods, Crane!" she uttered in anguished tones and pulled free of the knight.

Aurora's heart lurched painfully beneath her breast as she knelt beside the shape-changer's lank form and beheld the wicked gash over his temple welling blood. Carefully Frayne eased the lad over on his back and felt for a pulse at the base of his throat. In an agony of suspense, Aurora waited for the knight's pronouncement, and when at last it came, she nearly swooned.

"He lives," Frayne said. "But he shall have a deucedly painful head when he comes around."

By the time Aurora had gently bathed the nasty cut and Frayne had bound it with the skill of one all too familiar with battle wounds, the youth had, with a low groan, begun to stir. Tenderly Aurora brushed an unruly lock of red hair from the boy's forehead as at last his eyelids fluttered open, then squinted painfully, one hand lifting to his bandaged head, as he sought to focus his blurred vision on the Enchantress's face.

"O-o-oh, my head," he mumbled thickly and closed his eyes against a world gone suddenly topsy-turvy. "Wha-at happened?"

"It would appear you attempted to stop the butt end of a sword with your skull," Frayne observed with the hint of a smile. "Just lie easy for a spell till the dizziness passes."

For a while the lad did as he was bidden, but the deep furrow in his brow was mute evidence that he was using the time to try to clear the cobwebs from his brain. Instinctively Aurora braced herself. Soon he would remember everything.

It came with a rending cry.

"Janine! Oh, god, he took Janine!" he shrieked and bolted upright, only to go deathly white and sink weakly back again.

"Softly, lad," Frayne cautioned. "If we're to have any hope of catching up with the rogues, you must be fit to travel."

Immediately the boy opened his eyes to look upon the knight with deadly intensity.

"I won't rest until I've got her back again," he vowed. "And we needn't waste time trying to trail them afoot across this blasted wasteland." He paused to let his words sink in. Then with a mirthless grin he added, "Ignorant of our Enchantress's singular gifts, they made the mistake of taking Mush with them. Never would I have dreamt it possible I could be grateful for that, miserable old fleabag. But wherever she goes, we can instantly follow."

However, it was well past midnight of the third night after Janine's abduction ere Aurora and her two companions finally materialized nearly on top of a camel too weary even to do much more than flinch at their unexpected arrival, for Crane had been taken with a fever as a result of his head wound, which had kept them at the oasis until he had regained his faculties and a measure of his strength. The fever had lasted a night and a day, but the Enchantress, despite Crane's vociferous protestations that he had fully recovered, had refused yet another day to send her thoughts outward to locate their stolen camel. It would hardly help Janine were they to arrive at the scene of rescue only to have Crane suffer a relapse and collapse at the girl's feet amidst her enemies. But at last, only scant moments earlier, she had allowed herself to be persuaded.

Obviously, Mush had been pushed hard and with absolutely no regard for her probable preference not to have accompanied the desert raiders at all, let alone at such an unseemly and fatiguing pace. She eyed them dully, as if to say she could no longer be surprised at anything the man-beasts might choose to do. Clearly they were beyond her comprehension. Upon which she determined pointedly to ignore their presence, closing her eyes to them in pursuance of the comforting rumination of her cud.

"Poor Mush," Aurora murmured, rubbing a sympathetic hand along the camel's neck. "The beasts have used you badly, I fear."

But Crane silenced her with a low hiss, and gesturing significantly towards a high-peaked tent lit from within by the steady glow of oil lamps, dropped soundlessly to the ground, dragging Aurora down with him.

"A guard," he whispered in her ear as he sensed the indignant protest in her rigid form. "I don't think he spotted us."

The Enchantress nodded and settled more comfortably on her belly as she cautiously raised herself on her elbows to better scan their surroundings.

They appeared to be in the midst of a nomadic camp, comprised of some twenty or so tents pitched at the base of an immense pinnacle of solid rock that jutted perhaps two hundred feet or more into the air. Whether this lone and eerily incongruous sentinel had

351

been fashioned by gods or by men ages earlier when the land had yet been a lush and fertile plain, or whether it was a natural phenomenon created out of the gods-only-knew-what cataclysmic forces, Aurora could not begin to guess. No doubt it would remain a mystery till the end of time.

At any rate she had no time for lengthy speculation, for already Frayne had risen to his knees, and after indicating with a short gesture of the hand that they should remain where they were, stole silently away through the shadows in the general direction of the nearest tent.

In wordless protest the two young mage-lords watched him go. But after a while they turned to lock glances for a pregnant moment, and a slow grin, mirrored on Crane's youthful face, curved Aurora's lips as together they rose and went in pursuit of the Knight of Tor.

There was a great deal of activity about the camp. The low murmur of voices and an occasional shout mingled with the sounds of animals moving restlessly in the darkness. Aurora was surprised at the number of horses, most of them small, sleek mares tethered on ropes near each tent. Even in the dim light cast from the lamplit tents she could see they were carefully groomed, their manes combed and braided with colorful beads and ribbons woven into the strands of hair. They were like dainty ladies dressed for a gala event, she thought and remembered that Janine had said that the Banatim-ur-Rih, the Daughters of the Wind, were treated like honored members of the family. For they were quick and agile in battle and possessed of great-hearted stamina, traits that were highly prized among the desert clans.

All the tents looked very much alike. Made from tightly woven goat or camel hair and dyed brown or black, they were roughly cubicle, with peaked roofs draped over a single tall post in the center. But one was larger than the rest and boasted half a dozen of the graceful mares tethered about its outskirts. And off to the side, a tall stallion, shining a pale, ghostlike silver in the waning moonlight. Aurora's breath whistled in her throat as she recognized the fiery mount that *al-sardar* of the Bakhshidan desert raiders had ridden the day of the raid. Her hand stole out to grasp Crane's sleeve.

"There," she whispered and pointed toward the tent. She saw the boy's jaw harden and the eyes narrow to glittering slits as he deliberately nodded his head once in understanding. Then they were slipping like silent shadows around to the back of the tent.

The low rumble of a man's laughter came clearly to their ears as the two young mages dropped to a crouch beside the tent. Unconsciously Aurora's teeth clenched at something sinister in the sound.

"Come, little desert flower," the man said. "We are of the same blood, you and I. And you must know the anger I bear for my brother, the Khan. When I heard that he had given you to the slavers, I swore I would get you back again. He is a fool to relinquish so fair a jewel to the infidels. You, who were promised at birth to my youngest son."

Aurora watched Crane's fist open and close as the velvet voice briefly paused, then after a moment continued, this time with a biting edge of steel beneath its deceptive softness.

"Why do you not speak, little one? Have you no tongue?"

At first it seemed that whomever the desert chieftain addressed would not answer, but then a girl's voice rang out, the low-pitched tones bitter and without hope. Aurora's hand clutched the shape-changer's arm as he uttered a low gasp. It was Janine speaking, and Aurora marveled at the cold defiance in the usually placid voice.

"Of what use are words, Uncle? Especially from one already *fatwa*—doomed. What is it you want from me? Surely you do not expect me to believe you have brought me here to wed your son. I am not such a fool. No man of the desert tribes would have me now. When you have finished with me, you will take me to the Well of *Gharafa* and throw me in. It is the law of the tribe, and not even you can defy it."

"Perhaps. And yet it might be that your fate need not be so unpleasant. I might, for example, allow you to rejoin your infidel friends."

"In exchange for what?" rejoined the girl.

"Unlike my brother, the Khan, I have seen something of the world beyond the land of our fathers. I was, after all, educated in Tor. There I learned many things besides the language of the infidels. I learned that to be Khan of a few scattered desert tribes is nothing. I learned what it was to be a man of vision. I am such a man, for I have seen the desert reclaimed. I have seen rivers and lakes and fertile fields where now there is only sand. And I have seen our tribes joined and molded into one great people with me as their king. Oh, you believe I am mad. I see it in your eyes. But it is the madness of revelation. The vision of

354

truth. As surely as I stand here before you, all of these things shall come about. I shall see that they do."

"And what have I to do with it?" the girl queried in guarded tones.

"When the priest of Gawr was found wandering in the desert, blind and babbling about Seraisharaqa, he was brought to my brother, was he not?"

"You know that he was. Sakhira was of our tribe before he went to join the Brotherhood of Gawr."

"And you, my niece, nursed him until his death. You listened to him talk of the secrets of Doane. To you he revealed how to find the palace in the Valleys of Thunder and how to gain entrance into the Kingdom of Crystals, which lies beneath. That is the knowledge I require to realize all that I have dreamt. You will tell me these things, Janine, my little flower. And then you shall go free. I give you the word of Yataghan-Girmizi."

It was Aurora's turn to gasp. No wonder Girmizi had gone to such lengths to abduct the little slave-girl. But what lay beneath the enchanted Palace of the Rising Sun that could possibly enable the Bakhshidan chief to realize his fantastic ambitions?

She was not given time to speculate further on the desert chieftain's startling revelations, for a furtive step at her back sounded a warning in her stunned brain. She sprang to her feet and turned, her hand reaching for the dagger at her belt. But even as she pulled it from the sheath, two men loomed out of the darkness and with a shout imprisoned her between them. Rendered helpless in their cruel grip, she was

355

quickly bound and dragged unresisting to the entrance of Girmizi's tent. Even as they flung her sprawling at the sandaled feet of the desert chieftain, it suddenly came to her to wonder about Crane, for as she had turned to meet her captors, the shape-changer had simply vanished.

Chapter Thirteen

"So, Janine," purred Yataghan-Girmizi, *al-sardar* to the Bakhshidan desert raiders. "Your friends have come in search of you, after all."

Aurora lay where she had fallen facedown on a lovely woven rug of brilliant colors as Girmizi turned away, apparently to question her two captors. Vainly she tugged against the bonds about her wrists, then eased her head around to get some idea of her surroundings. She could gain little of an impression of the chieftain's tent from her vantage point on the floor, save that his quarters were surprisingly roomy and luxurious, with fine rugs spread over the sand. In front of her, at the center of several large cushions heaped in a half-circle, was one of the strange pipes Janine had called a *huqqat*, around which the men at the *funduq* had sat smoking. The unfamiliar scent of incense cloyed in the air along with the aroma of *qahwah*, the heavily spiced coffee she had sampled ages ago at the inn, and *khoshaf*, the mixture of raisins and dried figs steeped in honey and the juice of the lemon. Evidently she had disturbed Girmizi as he partook of the customary midnight supper, she noted with a wry twist of the lips, when a shadow fell over her and she winced at the touch of cold steel against her wrists. Then the ropes gave way before the razor-sharp blade, and she was hauled unceremoniously to her feet. She stood with her head carefully lowered to conceal the eyes of *zarcun-nar* from Girmizi, the Desert Wolf, and tried to assume the humble aspect of a *fellah* of the Turaq tribe.

Briefly she glimpsed out of the corner of her eye the slave-girl standing a little to one side of her uncle, the young face pinched and white with fear, and behind her, the grinning countenance of Shaggel, the Weasel, a soiled bandage tied about his head. Then she groaned inwardly, as she became aware that Girmizi must have spoken to her in the language of the desert tribes and was now apparently awaiting some response. Egad! What was she to do now? she wondered. But Janine's voice filled the taut silence that had fallen.

"The boy is simple. He does not understand you," she said, and the Enchantress marveled at the child's quick wit and desperate courage. "My master purchased him along with the *merhara* that you stole from him at Al-Ouahe-Julab. He tends the camel. Nothing more."

"Ah. A pity," Girmizi crooned with reptilian warmth, his hand rising to stroke his beard as his glance flickered consideringly over the ragged creature hunched in abject humility before him, then to the girl, wooden-faced and calm, and back again.

The Enchantress could sense his eyes on her like a knife poised between her shoulder blades, and she struggled against the impulse to meet him stare for stare. What was the fiend up to? she fretted and felt the sweat begin to trickle down her sides beneath her shirt.

He struck with the quickness of the adder, snatching the *litham* from Aurora's face with brutal deliberation.

"Yet if he is so simple, how did he find his way to Aliy-Kadah alone and on foot?" he said, in a voice that cut like the lash of the whip.

The Enchantress saw the child wince, then one large hand closed cruelly on Aurora's chin and she gasped as Girmizi forced her head back.

For a moment Aurora stared into the boldly handsome features of the Wolf. She saw the black eyebrows snap together in dawning enlightenment and heard the sudden, sharp intake of his breath, and knew with an odd relief that the charade was at an end. His eyes were glittering embers of greed that held her in helpless fascination as he unwound the *dulband* from about her head, allowing the mass of raven hair to cascade down about her shoulders. Then, abruptly, he released her, and the tent reverberated with the rumble of his laughter.

"Ah, my deceitful little Janine," he gloated when at last his laughter had died away. "You have brought me a prize beyond my wildest imaginings. A golden-eyed spawn of Doane."

Aurora stiffened, her head held high in tight-lipped defiance, as Girmizi's heated glance roamed appreciatively over her. Egad! It was as if he could see right through her clothes to her nakedness beneath. She shuddered, and wondered in confusion why Girmizi's look should cause her skin to crawl and the blood to rush to her face, for she had never before felt the need to hide her body from another's eyes. But suddenly she recalled the woman in the cottage in Endrith's Forest who had killed her daughter and then herself rather than be "touched" by the butchers who had invaded her home. And, too, there had been Frayne's warning long ago in Vandrel's hidden glen that if ever she were to enter the world of men, she would have to learn to keep herself covered so as not to rouse the passion of every man she met. Then she had not understood what he meant, but now she felt the heated gaze of the Bakhshidan chieftain like an assault upon her womanhood. She would kill him if he touched her, she decided, and returned his gaze with one of open contempt.

"Beware, Bakhshidan," she said. "I am not a helpless child. You will release the girl to me now, that we may be on our way."

She saw the slave-girl flinch and shake her head ever so slightly in taut warning. Then Girmizi swiveled with an agility surprising in one of his stature.

"Silence, woman!" he rasped.

The back of his hand struck her brutally across the mouth, snapping her head back. She staggered with the blow and nearly fell. Seething with barely constrained fury, the Enchantress slowly straightened to

360

her full heighth and favored the desert bandit with the full force of her loathing.

"You will learn soon enough not to tempt the sharp edge of my anger," he said, smiling affably, but it was the smile of the wolf, and she could see in the cold glitter of his eyes that he meant to break her, for only thus could he be sure of his own strength, the strength of the master over the slave.

Deliberately she touched her fingers to her battered lip, her eyes never leaving the man-beast's, and felt the moist warmth of her own blood. She thought she detected a sudden flicker of doubt in him, like a shadow passing across his face, as she let her mouth curve slowly upward in a smile that left her eyes singularly cold.

"I am Aurora and Andruvien," she said evenly. "I have fought the Asgeroth and faced Dred in the dark land of Somn and lived to tell of it. I fear no man or beast."

Girmizi laughed shortly, as if merely amused by her show of proud disdain, but she felt the hairs rise at the nape of her neck and watched him warily. Even so, she was unprepared for the suddenness of his next attack or for his abrupt shift in tactics as he barked a sharp command at his weasel-faced lieutenant.

Janine uttered a low cry as Shaggel imprisoned her in a stranglehold, and Aurora froze in helpless fear at the sight of the slave-girl's throat bared to the point of the weasel's knife. Silently the Enchantress cursed Girmizi's cunning and herself for a witless fool. But then the desert chieftain was once more before her, and it was all she could do to contain her rage at his bold-faced insolence as, deliberately, he ran his hand over the silky smoothness of her skin.

"You see. There are many kinds of fear," he observed, and with his thumb caressed her throat where the pulse visibly throbbed. "In the end, you will learn to submit to me. One way or another. You are, after all, only a woman. No doubt the gods have delivered you into my hands that I may teach you humility and obedience."

The roving hand wandered to the back of her slender neck and without warning closed like a vise to drag her to him. She clenched her teeth to keep from crying out and kept her gaze steady on his, knowing that to show fear or weakness before the wolf would be only to feed his lust. And all the while her mind was working, waiting for the right moment to teach him that she was indeed a woman, a woman to be reckoned with.

For a moment he stared into the eyes of golden fire as if fascinated by something he alone could see. Then, "Perhaps it would be well to begin the lessons now," he uttered thickly, and forced her mouth to his.

It was like the kiss of the serpent, she thought in revulsion as she forced herself to remain impassive when her whole being cried out to strike him down with the fury of Andruvien. She must be strong, for it would be Janine who paid the price if she gave in to weakness. In disgust she felt his hands roving over her and for the first time knew shame at a man's touch. She tried to remove herself from what was happening to her, tried to think of Minta and Valesia and Endrith's Forest as he tugged at the lacings that bound her shirt together, and, pulling the garment down off her shoulders, bared her to the waist, his breath whistling harshly in his throat as he beheld the perfection of her body.

She stood rigid with defiance, knowing what must come next and knowing she would not let it happen. She was somehow detached and yet acutely aware of everything around her—of Girmizi's hands upon her and Janine weeping softly nearby, and of Andruvien pulsating against her, strengthening with every pulse beat of her growing rage against this man-beast of the desert who saw her only as something to be mastered and used. But she was the Enchantress, the vassal of a god, and she would not be so used by a spawn of the serpent. She could feel the power of the god stirring within her, awakening to her need, quickening to her rage.

Girmizi, who had in his insolence thought to teach her humility, indeed, who had wished to shame her and break her to his will, felt the arousal of the god within her and was suddenly afraid. He pulled away to sear her with eyes glittering with desire and something else—a sort of fearful awe; indeed, an awakening awareness of that which set her apart from all other women.

"No," he muttered and shook his head as though trying to clear it. In wonder she saw beads of sweat form on his forehead and his tongue flick nervously over dry lips.

"Cease!" he uttered wildly and took a step back from her. "Or the girl will die." He was breathing hard, and the veins in his neck stood out like cords.

"It is true, what the Sorceress said about you. A single kiss, a touch of the hand, a glance from the eyes of golden flame, and you would make me a captive to desire. Desire that is like a hunger, which can never be satisfied by any other."

He stared at her as if she were some monstrous creature who both fascinated and repelled him. Then, abruptly, he tore his eyes away and wheeled with such violence that his robes billowed out around him.

"But I am Yataghan-Girmizi, *al-sardar* to the Bakhshidan desert warriors!" he cried ringingly. "I am no man to be ruled by a woman. I shall not be made to submit!" And yet Aurora heard the edge of uncertainty to his voice and knew he needed to remind himself of who and what he was. Abruptly he ceased his wild pacing to stand with his back to the Enchantress, the muscles at the base of his neck tense and bulging and his huge fists clenched at his sides with such force that the knuckles shone white. Then, in horrid fascination, she saw the hands unclench and the shoulders go suddenly lax. Slowly he turned to stare over her head, his eyes shuttered and his face set.

"You see," he smiled mirthlessly, "Girmizi is stronger than your magic. If you are wise, Sorceress, you will not try your spells on me." Nevertheless, he would only look at her obliquely, out of the corners of his eyes, and Aurora could sense the wariness within him, the wariness of the rogue wolf who has beheld the hidden fangs of his quarry and is yet compelled to offer challenge.

"I am no sorceress, nor did I invoke the magic of a spell," Aurora retorted coolly. "But if I chose to have

364

done, you would even now be pig fodder. As you will be yet, if ever you put a hand on me again."

Briefly his eyes touched on her, a flicker of something like admiration for her in their glittering depths. Then the look was gone and she could read nothing in the cruel mask of his face.

"I intend to enter the Kingdom of Crystals," he said, almost in a conversational tone. As if he were merely indulging in polite pleasantries with a little-known guest, Aurora thought, and shuddered despite herself. "And so, I fear, I must insist that you reveal to me the Secrets of Doane. Else I will order my men to slit the girl's throat here and now."

Egad! Aurora groaned inwardly. This was a fine coil in which she had got herself. The man was as soulless as a serpent. And where had Crane and the Knight of Tor gotten themselves off to? she wondered, beginning to feel more than a little desperate, for she did not doubt for a moment that Girmizi would do exactly as he had threatened unless she could somehow give him what he wanted. And since she could make nothing of his persistent gibberish about the blasted secrets of Doane and his precious Kingdom of Crystals, there seemed little chance of that. Clearly it behooved her to keep the cursed man talking till help should arrive.

"I know nothing of this kingdom of crystals," Aurora said at last, and with cool disdain pulled her shirt back into place and laced it. "Or any secrets of Doane."

"Do not play the fool with me, woman!" Girmizi rasped and began to move nervously about again, as if the very thought of whatever it was he sought gave him no peace. "Would you have me believe you did not come to this cursed land seeking your birthright? The mantle bearing the secrets of a power granted by the gods themselves—*al-mandil-baraka-ur-Murabit*?"

"My reasons for being here are none of your concern," Aurora countered swiftly. "And I know naught of this thing of which you speak. I accompany a Knight of Tor on a pilgrimage into the lands of Gawr and must return to his service as soon as I have won the release of the girl."

"You lie," uttered Girmizi coldly. "But it will avail you nothing. You know as well as I that the mantle is more precious than gold. This is why you have come. You want it, just as I do. And the Sorceress. But it is not a thing to be possessed by women. The power it commands is meant for a soldier, a man who commands men. Rightfully, it should be mine. It was to me the vision was granted."

Egads, Aurora thought. The man was a conceited ass. And yet it was better so, for the longer he talked about his grand ambition, the greater the chance that Frayne would discover them in time. Nor was she loath to hear more of this mantle and the Sorceress's part in the plot surrounding it. She had ever a ready ear for anything involving Frayne's devious mistress.

"Then tell me about this vision that I may judge for myself whether it is a true one," Aurora suggested and was amazed that her voice could sound so calm when her pulse had suddenly begun to race and her nerves to tingle as they always did when she felt herself on the brink of something momentous.

"Oh, it is a true one," Girmizi said and turned so that Aurora beheld the man's eyes glowing strangely in the swarthy face. "A vision sent by the gods. I, Yataghan-Girmizi, looked into the dark soul of the world through the Seeing Eye of the Sorceress, and I beheld Mamona where before there was Erg; a land of abundance where before there was nothing but sand. And in the vision, the mantle came to me out of the darkness and I reached out to take it in my hands. But then it vanished before yet another image. The image of a palace rising out of the dunes. And at last I knew what I must do."

Aurora stifled a small gasp.

"You have been to the Sorceress's castle atop the pinnacle of Tor?" she questioned in disbelief.

"That surprises you?" the man rejoined, his lips twisting cynically. "Yet how could you know that the Khan, fearing the ambition of his younger brother, plotted the boy's death. Or that, warned in a dream of the assassins' approach, the youth fled in the night to the country of Kafir, the land of the infidels. The Sorceress herself granted him safe asylum and the vision of the Seeing Eye. And when he had reached the age of manhood, she sent him back into the desert to rally the malcontents into a single, unified army to crush the Khan's puny forces."

He swung around to face Aurora squarely.

"I was that youth. And I have already been made to wait too long for what was promised me. Vengeance and *shah mat*, the death of the Khan, my brother. It will come to pass when the mantle is mine. I have seen the vision and dreamed the dream. When *al-mandil-baraka-ur-Murabit* passes once more into the light, a new rule will begin. My rule. The rule of Yataghan-Girmizi. I will be king."

But you are a bigger fool than I thought!" Aurora exclaimed more astonished than ever at the man's seemingly boundless arrogance. "It certainly will not be Girmizi who rules with the mantle of the Infidel, but the Sorceress. Who doubtless views it as *her* birthright. the birthright of Leilah, the elder daughter of Al-Murabit and the dark sister to Almira of the golden eyes. Can you not see that she is using you to obtain the mantle for herself? Do you honestly believe she will let you keep what she considers hers by right?"

If Aurora had thought to throw Girmizi off balance, she was doomed to be disappointed. The man was utterly convinced of his own masculine insuperability.

"Of course she means to take it from me," he agreed without a flicker of an eyelid. "But she is only a woman. And I will have the mantle. No one, not even the Sorceress of Tor can stand against the man who possesses the secrets of the Crimson Cloak. In the end the Sorceress will bow to me."

"Wha-at did you say?" Aurora gasped and felt the blood drain from her face, for suddenly she knew the mantle of power did not lie hidden within the kingdom of crystals at all. Nor was it the birthright of Leilah, the Sorceress, but her own. For had it not been bequeathed to her upon her mother's death at the hands of assassins in the glade of the elves? And did it not even now reside in her own pack still

368

securely lashed to the litter atop Mush's weary back?

But the desert chieftain had apparently grown impatient with small talk.

"Enough!" he growled with a fierce gesture of his hand. "Do you give me what I ask? Or does the girl die?"

"Nay! I shall give you nothing!" Aurora uttered in a chill voice and yanked the pouch from her neck. The crystal leaped in her hand, calling forth the power wrought by the gods. "It would be obvious to a nodcock that you have never intended to let us go. Even so, I might be brought to spare *your* life if you release the child now."

Slowly, as if compelled, Girmizi turned to look again upon Aurora's slender figure, and at last he saw her as she truly was—an Enchantress scintillating golden flames of leashed power.

"Release the girl, Girmizi," she said in a dangerously quiet voice. "Or I swear by the gods you will feel the fury of Andruvien."

His glance flicked away from hers and for a moment she thought that she had won. Then the swarthy face grew crafty with the sharp-toothed grin of the wolf as he spoke to Shaggel in the language of the Wendaren.

She heard the girl's sharp gasp and saw her face go deathly white.

"Tell me what you said to him!" she commanded harshly. "And beware, Girmizi. Your life hangs by a thread."

"I do not think so. You see, I have ordered Hasid to cut the girl's face if you so much as make a move," he said and laughed as he saw Aurora's horrified glance fly to Janine. "Come. I know you are only a woman, but you must try to be reasonable. Submit, Daughter of the House of Doane, and her death will be quick and painless. Or watch her die slowly, inch by inch, till she herself begs you to end her life."

Janine's eyes were dark with fear, yet she summoned the courage to shake her head in defiance of her father's brother.

"Do not listen to him, I beg you!" she cried. "He is *jinniy*, a demon. You must kill him, *mem-sayyid*! You must!"

"Silence!" Girmizi rasped and lifted his hand in a gesture whose meaning was grotesquely significant.

Janine's captor grinned in malicious anticipation and raised the knife. The girl screamed.

"Nay!" Aurora shouted, and knowing she would be too late, nevertheless leaped frantically across the tent toward Janine. Oh, gods! Where were Crane and the Knight of Tor when one needed them? she thought in despair. Then the knife rising to forever disfigure the girl was suddenly not a knife at all, but the brilliant feather of a peacock. The Enchantress faltered, a helpless gurgle of laughter startled from her as she saw Hasid's weasel face sag in comical disbelief.

"Crane!" she chortled, and quickly recovering her wits, kicked Hasid with great satisfaction and bone-crunching force squarely on the shin.

"Aiee!" he wailed, releasing the girl and dropping the useless feather as he clutched at his sorely assaulted leg.

In a flash Aurora yanked the stunned slave-girl

safely beyond his reach and shoved her toward the entrance to the tent. Girmizi, red-faced and bellowing something in Wendaren, drew the scimitar from his sash and came after them. Aurora shouted at Janine to flee and wheeled to ward off the enraged assault of *al-sardar* of the Bakhshidan desert raiders. But even as she turned, Aurora groaned, for out of the corner of her eye she saw the girl falter in terror before the threat of three armed men who had rushed the entrance in answer to their chieftain's call.

There was the sound of a blade slashing through fabric, and suddenly the Knight of Tor was in their midst, silencing Girmizi with a hard fist to the jaw. Then utter chaos broke loose.

Aurora was not given time to wonder how it had come about that the interior of the tent was suddenly filled with the hulking form of a frantic camel complete with *hawdaj*, for Frayne had reached her side and was yelling at her to mount the beast.

"Nay!" she protested. "I cannot leave Janine!" But wordlessly the knight dropped to one knee, and grasping her about the legs, heaved her bodily across the camel's back. There was nothing for it but to scramble awkwardly aboard and hang on for dear life as the dromedary suddenly lunged at the press of bodies surrounding the desert girl.

The Bakhshidan raiders fled before the camel's onslaught, leaving the girl to fend for herself as they fought each other to win through the narrow opening to the outside. A scream rose to Aurora's throat as she saw the girl stagger and fall in the path of the dromedary, but the beast instantly stilled, and with a grunt, dropped to its knees to nuzzle the girl with all the solicitude of an anxious lover. As indeed he was, mused the Enchantress with a lopsided grin.

In fascination, Aurora watched the girl stir. The incredibly blue eyes fluttered open, and for a breathless moment she blinked in bewilderment at the disconcerting sight of ponderous camel lips poised scant inches from her face. Then, abruptly, she let out a glad cry and threw her arms about the beast's scrawny neck.

"Sayyid Crane," she choked and immediately burst into tears.

"No doubt I should find this all very touching," observed the Knight of Tor in ominously pleasant tones as he obtruded himself upon the rather curious scene of the lovely slave-girl sobbing endearments to the less than asthetically pleasing dromedary, "were it not for two score or more Bakhshidan cutthroats just aching to run us through. Would it be asking too much, I wonder, if we were to get the blue blazes out of here?"

Instantly the girl appeared to return to awareness of their peril. With a small cry, she scrambled hastily to her feet and stood with hands folded humbly before her as she met the knight's daunting aspect with a hesitant bow.

"I beg forgiveness," she began uncertainly, but the knight, apparently in no mood for the amenities, cut her short with a muttered oath. His hand shot out to grasp her by the scruff of the neck.

"Get aboard," he growled, "lest you find yourself begging for a lot more than forgiveness from those beggers waiting out there."

They burst into the open as if all the shades of Somn were hot on their heels, and the fearless Bakhshidan desert warriors fell back before the awesome sight of a wild-eyed dromedary tearing through the center of the camp, dragging in its wake the tent of Yataghan-Girmizi, their own feared leader. The night was shattered with the confusion of fear-maddened horses buck-jumping and pulling up their tethers to scatter madly into the darkness. Dogs howled and men shouted, and at last the three atop the lumbering apparition managed to free the dromedary of Girmizi's cursed tent. But only one hulking creature heaved to its feet to set off in eager pursuit.

Frayne let Crane run till the sounds of chaos had receded far behind them. Then, fearful lest the shapechanger, even in the body of a dromedary, might become overtaxed, he pulled their gallant steed to a lumbering halt.

"We must go back!" were Aurora's first words as the knight turned to ascertain that everyone had gotten through the ordeal without injury.

"No doubt Girmizi would be delighted should we attempt anything so patently foolhardy," Frayne observed mildly, but even in the dim light of the stars she could see the arrogant lift of one imperious eyebrow.

"You don't understand. My pack is back there. And in it, the Crimson Cloak of Power!"

"Sh-h-h!" Janine hissed and strained to see through the thick curtain of darkness behind them. "Someone is coming."

And, indeed, the muffled pounding of hooves carried clearly to them all across the eerie stillness of the desert.

" 'Tis only one!" Aurora murmured. "And a brave fool to come alone."

"There!" Janine whispered thrillingly and pointed to a faint shadow lumbering toward them at break-neck speed.

The waiting stretched into an eternity of suspense as the three watched the unwavering approach of the hard-driven camel. Then suddenly Crane heaved and emitted something resembling a groan.

"It's Mush!" Aurora cried, unable to believe her own eyes. Truly the god was with her yet, she marveled as she beheld the *hawdaj* and all their gear still securely lashed to the camel's back.

"It would perhaps have been better had you slain him when he was at your mercy," Janine pointed out to Frayne with the humility proper to a woman of the desert tribes, but her blue eyes—ere she hid them beneath the luxurious veil of dusky eyelashes—were faintly accusing. "With Girmizi dead, the others would have fallen to bickering in the manner of *shah mat*, the confusion engendered by the death of a leader. Now he will have them on our trail with the falling of night."

The knight's silvery glance rested speculatively on the girl's downcast face. The child looked worn to the nub, he thought, and no wonder. For three days she had been Girmizi's captive and no doubt had entertained little hope that rescue was forthcoming. And then to be made to suffer further the agony of the nearly fatal rescue was enough to tax the strongest heart. Of what use would it be now to try to explain to her that with Crane thrashing about in the guise of an enraged camel, he had not dared to risk the sword lest he wound the young mage-lord, or even Aurora?

"It hardly serves to dwell on what is already past changing," Aurora interjected irritably and flung a handful of sand into the desert wind. "Mayhap 'twere better to contemplate more immediate matters. We are lost, are we not?"

The slave-girl winced and seemed to contract within herself.

"Yes," she murmured, then lifted her head to stare out across the shimmering dunes heaped like huge ocean waves frozen at their crests, some as high as four hundred feet or more. In despair, she tried to shut her mind to the din of the restless drifts of sand, as boom after pulsating boom, like the reverberations of a legion of drums, rumbled over and around her, the sounds of billions of particles of sand slipping down the faces of the dunes echoing and re-echoing within the multiplicity of dune valleys, till they reached the amplitude of a thunderstorm.

She had led them into the Valleys of Thunder even as she had promised, but only the gods knew where the Palace of Doane lay. In his delirium, Sakhira, the priest of Gawl, had said over and over that the way to Seraisharaqa followed the moon-shadow of the hawk as it fled towards *sharq*, the rising sun, and so she had thought to discover the palace to the east of Aliy-kadar-ur-saqr, the Heights of the Hawk—for what other meaning could the poor man's ramblings have had? And yet they had found nothing but the brooding emptiness of the dunes amidst the endless rumble of *fesh-fesh*, the slowly shifting sand. The palace could be anywhere, buried beneath any one of the massive drifts, and they would never know which one, unless Huri, the Virgin Goddess, should choose to send Simoom, her wind-servant, to free it once more from its mountain of sand.

"The palace is here," she said slowly, her eyes bleak with the knowledge that even should the palace appear magically before them at that very moment, it would little matter. For their water, which if not for the presence of the Bakhshidan raiders they would have replenished from the wells at Aliy-kadah was gone. "But the gods have chosen not to reveal it. It is *fatwa*, the judgment of doom."

"Fiddlesticks!" Aurora countered impatiently. "It is only a temporary setback. We shall come about directly."

"But you do not understand," persisted the slave-girl. "Without water we shall surely perish."

"We shall do no such thing. Have you forgotten that we have Crane with us?" Aurora said a trifle impatiently. "If worse comes to worse, he can simply think us back to the oasis. Or anywhere else we choose to go."

"Uh—I'm afraid it may not be all that simple," Crane interjected uneasily and sighed heavily as Mush nibbled playfully at his ear. The youth, having assumed his true form at the end of the night's exhausting march, hunkered in the sand with his back

376

against the camel and his chin propped on bony knees drawn to his chest. He had been strangely withdrawn all that day, his brow creased in a faint frown as he stared morosely out over the empty waste of sand and sky.

Immediately Aurora turned to regard him with narrowed eyes.

"What do you mean by that?" she said, perhaps more sharply than she had intended. "Surely you cannot doubt your ability now, after all you have done. You were marvelous last night. And you undoubtedly saved us all."

The boy ducked his head, his face assuming a slow flush that nearly blotted out the multitude of freckles.

"It's not that exactly. Chances are I could get us out all right. It's getting back that would be a problem. Well, just look around. Don't you see that once we made it back to the oasis, it'd be damned near impossible to find this place again?"

With a suddenly sinking heart Aurora gazed out across wave after wave of slowly drifting dunes, all of which appeared alarmingly alike and none of which would remain the same for longer than it took the restless winds to reshape them.

"Of course, we could materialize in Girmizi's blasted camp and do the whole thing over again, I suppose," Crane suggested despondently. "But actually, I'd rather not." The young mage lifted troubled brown eyes to the Enchantress's face. "I don't know, Aurora. I've been thinking maybe we should just call the whole thing off. After all, I've got Janine to think of now. Maybe I was wrong not to take her to Vandrel from the very first. And I'm not so sure I shouldn't just go ahead and do it now before something else happens to her. Egad, that buzzard Girmizi nearly slit her throat back there! And it was pure accident that I happened to be in a position to stop him. One moment I was there outside the tent with you and the next I was a dagger in Hasid's empty scabbard. It just seemed to happen all by itself, and the next time I might not be so lucky."

"Luck had nothing to do with it," Aurora insisted and glanced helplessly at the knight, who stood gazing into the distance, his back turned to them. Obviously he had no intentions of interfering. "Crane, you have got to have more faith in yourself than that," she ended in exasperation.

But the freckled face had assumed a set expression that warned that the youth had irrevocably made up his mind. And who could blame him? Aurora thought wearily, recalling Janine's staunch courage and her own feeling of helplessness as Hasid had raised the knife to the girl's face. They had already asked a great deal more of the child than they had any right to have done.

"Very well, then," she said, her expression softening as she looked down at Crane's earnest young face. Somehow the boy seemed to have grown up overnight, and there was no mistaking the cause of his sudden newfound sense of responsibility. Crane was in love, and she had no right to stand in the way of his happiness. She felt an unexpected pang at the thought that henceforth the shape-changer would not be at her side. "Go back to Vandrel and take Janine with you.

378

No doubt you are right to take her out of harm's way. Certainly I shan't blame you."

She watched the boy's throat work convulsively and turned away.

"You had best be on your way now," she added, her voice sounding oddly muffled, "ere I change my mind."

"But you and Frayne are coming with us?" the youth blurted and started to his feet. "Aurora. Not even you can survive without water. And the gods know you cannot find your way back without Janine."

"She's going with you, right enough," Frayne interjected harshly and turned to favor Crane with a stony glance. "You make sure of that, lad, or you'll answer to me."

Deliberately he crossed to the camel and began tugging at the rope that held the packs in place, his powerful hands going still for the space of a heartbeat as Aurora's voice rang out.

"What do you think you are doing?"

"I expect you will want your pack," he said without looking at her.

"The pack be damned! I'm staying here with you!"

"You, my dear, are getting out of here whilst you can. You have what you came for. I doubt that you would learn little more from your ancestral home even if you were to find it. Which has become exceedingly unlikely and is at any rate academic now. Look there to the west. And when you are done feasting your eyes on Girmizi's band of cutthroats, behold what lies in store for us to the east. While you and your young

379

friends have been involved in your little debate, it would seem the gods have managed to tip the odds against us. In short, we find ourselves in a damnable coil from which I am left no choice but to see to it that you are extricated. And Crane appears to offer the only sure means of seeing you out of here."

"Wha-at!" cried Aurora and turned to discover that Frayne had only spoken the simple truth, for etched against the crimson and gold of the sun sinking gloriously in the west were the silhouettes of the *sipahi*, the horsemen of Bakhshidan, and, perhaps two leagues to the east, the awesome sight of a whirling brown cloud sweeping with the speed of the dragons of Gorn across the desert. It was like a ravenous beast that devoured both the sky and the great dunes as it passed, a monstrous creature of death and destruction.

"The *simoom*!" Janine cried in despair. "Sent by the Virgin Goddess! We are indeed lost."

"That cinches it," Crane said grimly. "I'm getting us all out of here right now."

"Nay! I will not leave ere I have seen my mother's palace. 'Tis why I came," Aurora shouted above the rising thunder of the *fesh-fesh*.

"Don't be a fool, Aurora! What chance do you have against Girmizi or the storm?"

"What chance shall I have against Dred or the Sorceress if I do not know the truth of who and what I am? Nay, Crane. I will not go."

The young mage-lord met the golden blaze of the Enchantress's eyes and knew he was wasting his breath. In helpless entreaty, he turned to the tall knight.

"Frayne! You tell her." But Frayne was staring at the Enchantress, an odd light in the silvery eyes, as she turned to lock glances with him.

"I will not go without you," she said softly, as if there were only she and Frayne in the whole world. "Of what use would be my life if you were no longer a part of it?"

For an eternity they stood, the beautiful young Enchantress shimmering golden in the last rays of the setting sun and the Knight of Tor, tall and fearless with a subdued aura like a god's. It seemed to the awed Crane that they exchanged some unvoiced message, whereupon the glimmer of a smile touched the knight's stern lips, and, without taking his eyes from Aurora, he spoke in a quiet voice to the young shape-changer.

"Take Janine and go, Crane. The Enchantress and I have unfinished business here."

For a moment Aurora's whole being felt infused with a marvelous light. Then, with a joyous cry, she flew to Frayne's waiting arms.

"I love you!" she laughed as he lifted her high and swung her around and around in his arms, till at last he grew still, his loving gaze on her rapt and glowing face, and let her slide slowly to the ground.

Crane threw up his hands in defeat as Frayne bent to kiss the Enchantress lingeringly on the lips.

"They're mad. Both of them," he uttered in accents of doom and turned to look despairingly at the slave-girl, who stood silently observing them all.

"It is the madness of *sajada*," she said and brushed

a hand fleetingly over her eyes. "The adoring heart. It is a rare and beautiful thing."

Crane was silent for a moment. Then he shook his head, his expression grim.

"Maybe," he said, unconvinced. "But the fools will be no less dead."

Then a fierce cry brought his head around. The vanguard of Girmizi's men had reached the foot of the dune.

"Aurora! Frayne!" he called out and ran toward the slave-girl.

"I can't leave them to face this alone!" he shouted down at her. "I'm going to send you on ahead to Vandrel's glen. Wait for me. I'll be there when I can."

"No! You will not send me away," she cried, clutching at him with her small hands. "I have earned the right to remain here with you."

"Janine, I can't let you stay. I'm responsible for you. Don't you see? I couldn't stand it if anything happened to you."

"No, it is true what the Enchantress has said. I must learn to be responsible for myself. I have the right to decide for myself."

Desperately the boy dragged her hands down and held her from him. Cripes! This was a fine time for the girl to declare her independence. He could hear the *sipahi* even now at his back.

"Enough, Janine!" he said, brutal out of necessity. "You're my slave, d'you hear? You belong to me, and you'll do as you're told."

"No. I won't. I have seen what it is to be free. I have seen the Enchantress. She belongs only to herself. It is the way I would be, for I see truly now that no one has the right to own another. I will not be sent away!"

The young mage-lord opened his mouth to tell her she was becoming a pig-headed brat who would earn the flat of his hand across her rump if she did not cease to be so absurd, but suddenly the raiders were upon him, and there was nothing he could do but throw himself in front of the girl to shield her as best he could with his body, a seemingly futile gesture, since he was unarmed. In helpless terror he watched them come, half a dozen fiercely yelling raiders riding straight for him, and he too paralyzed with fear to do aught but stand and wait as they loosed their lances at him. Then he uttered a despairing cry.

"No! Not now!" But he was changing, solidifying, becoming ponderous with immovable weight and density, and there was nothing he could do to stop it. The deadly shafts flew unerringly to the mark. From somewhere Crane heard Aurora's piercing scream. Then the lances struck and careened harmlessly off the solid wall of granite that stood protectively about the slave-girl, Janine.

They swarmed the dune, twenty of Girmizi's fiercest warriors, and *al-sardar* himself at their head. Aurora had only time enough to free Andruvien from the pouch ere they were upon her. She heard Frayne yell at her to stay close to him, saw him fell his first man with a single, swiping blow and turn to meet another. Then she lost sight of him as she lifted the pulsing blade of silver flame and unleashed the fury of Andruvien.

It seemed that the world had become a nightmare of dying men and screaming horses, and at the center of it all the Enchantress wielded the awesome might of the god-thing, the sliver of Vendrenin wrought by Dragus for a god's vengeance on a god. The power surged within and through her, pulsing crystal flames of destruction, and Aurora, who once was Anduan and tree-child, knew only the consuming fire of Andruvien.

Then there was silence and the fierce beating of her heart, and she stood alone amidst the dead and dying and did not know who she was.

"Aurora! 'Tis done. Sheathe the Blade of Power."

She wheeled, the sword uplifted to strike again.

"Aurora! They're gone. Look at me! It's Frayne!"

With a shuddering sob, the Enchantress lowered the blade and sank slowly to her knees.

"Oh, gods," she moaned. "I were better off dead than to have lived this day."

But Frayne was beside her, lifting her roughly to her feet.

"Not now!" he rasped and shook her till her teeth rattled and the horrid clamp of death loosened its hold on her. "We shall all be dead if you give in to despair now. The blasted storm is nearly upon us!"

He dragged her to the granite wall, which was Crane.

"Call him out of the spell, Aurora! The shape-changer is our only hope."

Somehow she managed to still the silent screams that ripped through her mind and reached out with her thoughts to the shape-changer.

"Crane. Return to us. Think my thoughts and be molded by my image of you. Now, Crane! We have need of you."

The first fierce breath of simoom, wind-servant of the Virgin Goddess, swooped over them, staggering them with the malevolence of a thousand demons, a swirling pall of sand that battered and suffocated them, deafened them with its roar. Then all was eerie silence, and the first light of dawn was slowly spreading pink and golden streamers across the wasted land.

Aurora smothered a painful sob as she lifted her head from Frayne's shoulder and looked out upon a palace shimmering golden in the sunlight.

"Seraisharaqa," she murmured, her voice hardly more than a whisper of sound. "The Palace of the Rising Sun."

Chapter Fourteen

"But how—?" Janine exclaimed in stunned bewilderment.

"I merely thought us ahead in time," Crane answered with a lopsided grin, and waved one hand toward the rising sun. "To dawn of the next day, as a matter of fact. And only just in the nick of time, too, or I miss my guess."

"Dearest Crane," smiled Aurora somewhat shakily. "Whatever would we do without you?"

The Knight of Tor clapped a hand to the youth's shoulder.

"You pulled us out of a tight coil, lad, and without a doubt saved us from a damned uncomfortable end," he said, yet the falcon eyes were grim as he turned to gaze at the walled palace already shimmering in heat waves. "But we've a ways to go before we may count ourselves out of the meshes. We are still without water, and we have yet to gain entrance to the palace, which is, if I am not mistaken, guarded in some manner from intruders."

"Oh, gods!" Aurora groaned. "The Crimson Cloak! It was still tied to the litter on Mush's back when the raiders attacked."

"And still is, so far as I can tell," offered Crane a little sheepishly, then shrugged as three pairs of eyes turned to regard him in some astonishment. "Well, I couldn't just leave her to suffocate in the storm, now could I? She's over there sleeping it off. I'm afraid all this has been a bit too much for the old girl."

"That was very kind of you, sayyid," Janine said softly as Frayne and the Enchantress left them to see to the camel. She awarded the blushing young mage a glowing look from her dazzling blue eyes. "Poor Mush. It is sad to love hopelessly, I think. Even for a camel."

"Fiddlesticks! She's nothing but a cantankerous old fleabag, and I'll probably be sorry I didn't get rid of her when I had the chance. But she's stuck with us in spite of everything. And I guess I owed her one. So let's just forget it, okay?"

"As you wish, my lord," murmured the girl, touching her forehead with the tips of her fingers in the customary gesture of respect and obedience. But the youth glimpsed a mischievous sparkle in her eyes before she veiled them with her lashes, and his heart gave an uncertain leap.

"Hey, it's 'Crane.' Remember? And I thought you'd decided you weren't my slave anymore," he observed suspiciously. "Don't tell me you've changed your mind about wanting to be on your own. You were damned sure about it not so very long ago."

"Oh, I have not changed my mind, *sayyid*. But the habits of a lifetime are difficult to forsake, are they not? Doubtless I will learn in time the ways of your people. Perchance it would be well to pattern myself after the golden-eyed daughter of Doane, think you?" she ended guilelessly. Then she lifted her small head in startled bewilderment as the young mage groaned, one hand rising to his forehead in unmistakable horror.

"Egads! I don't think any such thing. In fact, that's the last thing I think you should do. Gods, it would be the ruination of us both."

"But I do not understand," she said, her lovely eyes dubious on the young mage-lord's face. "You have said you admire very much the *mem-sayyid*. Is this not the truth?"

"Of course it's the truth. I think the world of Aurora. Egads, who wouldn't. She's one of a kind," he hurried to assure her. "But, well, she's Aurora, and you're you. And even if you are pig-headed at times and a troublesome brat, I sort of just like you the way you are, you see?"

But it was obvious she did not see at all, as she continued to regard him out of grave blue eyes, her bottom lip childishly pursed in a frown.

Had Crane been older and more experienced, perhaps he would have realized that the girl was bewildered and a little daunted by the strange ways of *kafir*, the infidel. For they and their world were far different from anything she had even known. Indeed, nothing was as it had been. She was no longer Wendaren. She had been banned from her home and disowned by her people. She belonged nowhere and to no one. And she had fallen hopelessly in love with the young Mogush who not only refused to see her as a woman, but whose heart had been captivated by a golden-eyed Enchantress against whom she could not hope to compete. For, after all and despite everything she had been made to suffer, she was yet a young girl hovering on the brink of womanhood and was thus prey to all the torments of endless yearning and accompanying self-doubt that are an unavoidable part of growth and self-discovery. In her youthful fantasy it was inevitable that she must see herself as insignificant, plain, and inept when viewed next to the marvelous, captivating Enchantress, as it was perhaps equally unavoidable that she should be blind to Aurora's similar plight, for the Enchantress was no more than three mortal years her senior and, further, had been reared among elves and dryads, far from humankind. She was ignorant of her parentage and her truename and was struggling to understand both herself and the unfamiliar world of the man-beasts. In many ways Janine was older and wiser than Aurora, for she had, at least, been always among her own kind and had learned early the treachery and deceit of which men and women are capable.

As it was, Janine had come to admire Aurora very much, for the Enchantress was not only beautiful, but selfless and courageous as well. After all, had not the golden-eyed daughter of Doane risked her life to save a slave from worse than death? she asked herself. Janine recognized that Aurora was a woman who would always stand out among other women, a figure who must ever inspire awe and respect. And she knew as well that the Enchantress attracted men without even trying; indeed, without being aware of the devastating effect she had on them. But despite her awe-

390

some aura of leashed power, there was yet a certain simplicity about her, an innate kindness and generosity, an innocence that charmed and captivated all who came to know her. Moreover, Janine envied the Enchantress the fierce independence, which, in a woman, was so foreign to the world of the Wendaren, and her dauntless spirit, which doubtless could never be broken or tamed, and in this, yearned to be like her. Yet she was jealous, too, and resentful, though she knew that had circumstances been different, she would have liked above everything to be Aurora's true friend. But there was Crane, and, yes, the Knight of Tor as well, between them. For so long as the Enchantress possessed their hearts, Janine told herself, she would always rank second place in the affections of the only two men she had ever loved.

Thus tormented by a sense of ambivalence and guilt generated by her feelings for the Enchantress, the little Wendaren responded to the young mage's clumsy expression of affection with helpless resentment.

"I see that you think of me still as a slave," she rejoined in low, injured tones. "Or as a child not to be taken seriously."

"Well, and so you are," the youth blurted unwisely. "A child, that is. And even though you may not be my slave anymore, I'm still responsible for you. Because Frayne gave you to me. And because you're too young to be off on your own."

"Oh, but you are *al-maskharat*, the fool!" she cried suddenly and turned away from him to hide the glimmer of tears that had sprung to her yes. "You look but you do not see."

"Huh? Don't see what?" he queried, considerably

391

taken aback by her vehemence, but Janine had fled without another word, and the young shape-changer glared at her straight-backed retreat with a vague feeling of foreboding. Good grief! There simply was no understanding females, he decided in no little exasperation and wondered what he had done to set up her tailfeathers this time. But Aurora was calling to him to come on, so with a helpless shrug, he shoved the matter to the back of his mind and hurried to catch up with the three striking out for the beckoning palace, the camel in tow behind them.

Seraisharaqa sprawled amidst the quickening glory of the new day, a granite monument to the vanished mage-lord who had erected it long ages past. Silent and dreaming now within a spell of enchantment, it glimmered in the morning sun, an impenetrable fortress of sheer rock walls resting upon a raised platform of stone blocks. A gradually ascending ramp on the east side led to a blank wall, in which the figures of two magnificently sculptured gods supported either end of a carved arch set into the stone wall.

"Gawr," Janine murmured, her blue eyes awed as she tilted her small head back to look up into the strong face of the fire-god. "And Amaur, the god of darkness."

There was a compelling sadness about the stern-lipped god of fire, a suggestion of compassion in the wide-set eyes gazing out over the broad expanse of desert. The chin was strong, the brow noble, yet the artist had captured a subtle expression of sensitivity in the whole, which Aurora would not have expected in the rendering of a warrior-god. The Enchantress stared entranced at the marvelous countenance, captivated by the sculptor's vision of godly beauty. On one powerful arm he held an oval shield, upon which was emblazoned a hawk rising from a field of flames, and at his hip was a great sword appropriate to the patron god of warriors. Yet in his hand he held a harp. She felt drawn to the enigmatic figure, haunted by a feeling that even so would one who had loved deeply portray the one who was beloved. Only reluctantly did she turn her eyes to the other sculpture.

The figure of Amaur was furtive, with the head turned pointedly away from the sun. Moreover, the god was enshrouded in a shapeless cloak, the symbolic cloak of darkness, and the face was indistinct beneath a concealing hood. A hooded raven perched on one arm, and upon the other was a black shield bearing a half-closed eye. It was the Seeing Eye of Somn, Aurora realized in surprise, and though this might be Amaur, he was also Dred, the fallen prince of Throm. But if he was Dred, then was not the other Harmon, the Warrior-God of the Eilderood? Still, why should the two arch-enemies guard the mage's palace? she wondered. And why should the one have been rendered with such loving detail? It made no sense, and yet she felt that the answer to the conundrum was in some way vital to her.

Still puzzling over her discovery, she turned away to find Frayne watching her strangely. For an instant their eyes locked, and Aurora's heart beat heavily within. Then Crane spoke up, and the moment was gone.

"This must have been the way in," the shapechanger said, bracing one hand experimentally against the solid stone blocks that sealed the portal.

With an effort Aurora tore her eyes away from Frayne and struggled to regain her equilibrium as the knight, too, tested the wall.

"No doubt you are right," he agreed presently. "And perhaps it is still the way in."

"For an army with a battering ram, y'mean," Crane rejoined skeptically. "Or maybe a shadow-phantom of Somn. They can go right through solid stone."

But Aurora had not failed to catch Frayne's trend of thought.

"You mean the wall might be an illusion," she said. "A binding spell like the one Crane used in the Sacred Grove."

"It would seem a likely possibility," Frayne nodded. "But as one who is not versed in the arts of gramarye, I cannot be certain."

"Wouldn't it be funny if it turned out the old mage had used Lil's spell?" Crane speculated and eyed the closed portal as though tempted to immediately put the riddle to the test.

"Don't you dare!" warned the Enchantress. "When Lil invoked the spell, she freed the Gandorf from the betwixt and the between. We were just lucky not to have ended up with a like creature on our hands when you so foolhardedly used it before. And I, for one, have no wish to tempt fate. Nor do I think, somehow, that Al-Murabit would make use of a spell with such uncertain side-effects. Nay. I think we must try something else."

"If you will permit me," Janine interjected quietly, "I would tell you what the priest of Gawr revealed in his delirium. Perhaps it would be of some small help."

Aurora turned to regard the girl with suddenly

glittering eyes.

"Of course. I remember now," she said quickly. "I overheard Girmizi say that you had nursed this Sakhira after he was found wandering around in the desert. That was doubtless why Girmizi was so keen to carry you off. Just what did the priest have to say?"

A tinge of color touched the slave-girl's cheeks as she found herself suddenly the center of attention. Self-consciously she lowered her eyes as she sought for the words in the language of the Kafir.

"He talked very much, but the threads of his thoughts were often *taftah*, twisted one upon the other like the coils of the serpent, so that I could not make sense of them. Even so, I listened. And when you let it be known that you wished for me to lead you to Seraisharaqa, I remembered his words. That is how I knew the palace was in the Valleys of Thunder in the path followed by the shadow of the hawk seeking the sunrise. For so did he say it would be."

"But what else did he say? Did he tell you how he got in the palace?" Aurora prodded when the girl paused, apparently to reflect.

"Yes," Janine uttered shortly and clasped her hands nervously before her. "Please to be patient. I am trying to recall his exact words. It is difficult, you understand. For they made no sense to me."

"Sure, sure. Just take your time," Crane said, patting the girl on the shoulder and sending a quelling glance at the Enchantress. "We've got all the time in the world."

The slave-girl flashed the youth a grateful look, then swallowed and began again in a stronger voice to tell the story of Sakhira, the priest of Gawr.

"Sakhira was of our clan and so was brought to my father's tent when the men from the caravan returned him to us. As the eldest unwed daughter, it fell upon me to care for him in his sickness. I think he did not know where he was or who tended to his needs. For his mind had been sorely stricken and his eyes made blind because he ridiculed *al-nar-baraka*, the flames of power, and because he used the secrets of the priesthood to open the sealed door. Yet he seemed possessed by the need to tell what he had seen and done."

One small hand fluttered with an air of uncertainty.

"He revealed to me the words of secret knowledge, which only one initiated into the priesthood of Gawr may know. To repeat them is to invite death," she said, almost in a whisper.

For a long moment no one spoke. Then Frayne gently placed a hand on each of her shoulders and bade her look at him.

"Child, I do not believe Gawr will cause you to be harmed for repeating those words to us. It is his likeness that guards the door. And it is a spawn of the House of Doane who seeks admission to the palace of her ancestors. I believe the gods have brought us here together for that very purpose. Janine, Aurora has in her possession the mantle of Al-Murabit."

"This is the truth?" the girl uttered in astonished accents and turned to look upon the Enchantress with awe.

"Show her, Aurora," Crane suggested eagerly.

"It is true, Janine," Aurora said then, and swiftly removed from her back the small pack that she had retrieved earlier from Mush's litter. "The cloak is right here."

A small gasp escaped Janine's lips as at last the Enchantress stood before her utterly transformed. The crimson cloak draped over the slender form shimmered in the sunlight, the undeciphered symbols of power flashing brilliant golden sparks. But neither the cloak nor the symbols wrought in gold were more dazzling than Aurora's marvelous eyes of golden fire.

"I will tell you the words of the priest," Janine said in a hushed voice, "for truly you are a daughter of the House of Doane."

Aurora took one last look at the carved figure of the Eilderood warrior-god and breathed a small prayer to the One ere she prostrated herself before the sealed portal, her forehead pressed to the ground in the posture of humility and obedience upon which Janine had insisted. The words of summoning did not come easily to her, despite the fact that the slave-girl had made her repeat them over and over till the meaningless sounds were committed to memory. She felt the sweat tickling her sides as she forced herself to remember the priest's prayer to Gawr, the Lord of Fire.

Gazihakim, salama fatwa.
Maralmah, sajada.
Muwallad walad ur safiynar
Bakhshid' al-mann ur gabr-al-shestdar.
Tahar' al-bab ur al-batn-samt.
Mar ur narharam,
Sajada.
Salama.

There, it was done, and suddenly a sound as of beating wings filled her ears. Aurora raised her head and beheld the stone hawk of Gawr transmuted to living flesh and ascending into the heavens. Flinging one arm over her eyes against the sun, she watched the flight of the hawk till the creature was a tiny speck in the pale sky. Whereupon it seemed to hover, before folding its wings to plummet earthward with blinding speed. Larger and larger it loomed in her vision as it plunged, till it had blurred in her sight, its bird form consumed within a streaking ball of fire falling unerringly for the slim figure clothed in the crimson cloak of power.

"Aurora!" someone shouted, but the Enchantress paid no heed. She seemed frozen in time, rooted to the earth, her head flung back and her arms upraised as though she would embrace the plummeting god's fire. She felt herself to be detached and yet an inseparable part of what was happening. Though her heart thundered within her breast and her breath came painfully as though there was not air enough to fill her lungs, she knew no fear. This was the minion of Gawr, who was Harmon and Immortal Eilderood, the master of Vendrenin and servant of the One, and she was Aurora and Andruvien—and something more, something she sensed but could not define. She felt the awakening fire of the living god, whose hand was upon her, and the power of Andruvien throbbing with the leap of the flames within her veins, and knew somehow that they and the flames of Gawr were all one. And suddenly the words of the god's priest sounded within her awakened soul, and she knew them.

O, Wise Judge, I am resigned to thy judgment.
All-knowing Lord, I prostrate myself before thee.
Begotten son of the pure fire,
Grant this favor to thy priest who possesses the
    sacred girdle.
Throw down the gates which bar the way within.
O, Lord of the Sacred Fire,
I prostrate myself.
I am resigned.

Then suddenly she was deafened by the roar of the god's fire and felt the chill of the sacred flames against her face, and her heart throbbed with the ecstasy of the consuming god as she prepared herself to embrace the flames of Gawr.

The impact of a hurtling weight flung her to the ground beyond the path of the descending flames. She lay stunned and gasping for breath, held to the ground beneath the lean, hard body shielding her from the jarring concussion that shattered the air. The ground trembled beneath her even as the world erupted into blinding brilliance. Then all was as still as death.

"I could not move. I was one with the fire. I wanted to be one with the god," Aurora said dully as she stared at the ruin that had been the outer wall of the palace.

The god's fire had obliterated the closed portal, leaving nothing of the arch or the sculptured figures of the gods but a charred pile of rubble. And beyond the gaping hole lay a forest of fluted columns topped by stone lintels and a great slabbed roof.

"Well, it's a good thing Frayne was able to get to you in time," Crane rejoined, the freckles standing out against the pallor of his face. "I couldn't tear myself loose."

"Be that as it may," remarked the knight quellingly, "we've other business at hand. The sooner we find the Kingdom of Crystals buried beneath this pile, the sooner we can get out of here."

Aurora glanced uncertainly up into the knight's closed countenance and suppressed a sigh. She could sense the driving urgency in him that had ever seemed a part of him and yet that had been in abeyance since the night he had carried her from the waters of the pool nestled in the hollow along the fringes of the forest and surrendered his heart to her. A heaviness bowed her slender frame, for she knew without words that the truce between them was at an end. His thoughts were on the Sorceress and the quest that had brought him to the palace of her ancestors, and when he had what he had come after, he would return to Tor and the deadly game he played with the forces that molded the earth's destiny.

But this time she would be with him, she vowed and felt a sudden chill course down her spine, as if she had been touched by a faint echo of the god's vanished presence.

"Aye," she said, straightening her shoulders in an effort to conceal her sudden weariness of spirit. "I would talk within the halls of Al-Murabit."

Yet ere they descended into the palace grounds, it was decided that one at least of their number should be immediately returned to a kinder place.

"Mush," said Aurora, sending her thoughts outward. "May your next master be content to remain at home."

But the dromedary, too weary and too utterly bewildered at being whisked without notice from one place to another, merely grunted sourly and ignored her. No doubt ultimately she was grateful to find herself suddenly returned to the funduq along the banks of Al-wadi-hashiy, and in time, as is the way with beasts and the fortunate among mankind, eventually got over her unfortunate first love affair as well.

The wide, sculptured stairway leading down from the outer wall was miraculously untouched by the devastation wrought on the portal. Aurora took a deep breath as she stepped out of the sunlight into the shadowed walks beneath the stone portico. The shaded interior seemed almost cool after the searing heat of the sun, and for the first time she became aware of her parched lips and throat. Once there must have been water in abundance here—wells or springs or perhaps the *ganat*, the tunnels excavated beneath the ground for transporting water from a nearby oasis, in this case, the oasis at Aliy-Kadah. Perhaps, if the gods were smiling upon them, they would discover that whatever had supplied the palace with the life-giving liquid was not yet dry.

They passed through a great corbeled portal into an interior maze of marble halls lined with graceful pilasters made to resemble trees with thick, leafy branches. In wonder, the four wandered through a white marble forest of beautifully sculpted oaks, maples, elms, and hawthorns. Clerestory windows supplied muted light, which danced off brightly tinted frescoes portraying another time, another place. With slightly trembling fingers, Aurora traced the glazed figure of a young woman reclining amidst forest wildflowers, a dark-haired infant suckling at her breast and a small girl-child at her feet weaving flower garlands. In the background a waterfall wreathed in rainbow-riven clouds of vapor toppled from the craggy heights of a sheer cliff. Pine forests inhabited with deer brought an ache to the Enchantress's heart, and somehow she knew that the suckling infant was Almira and the girl-child Leilah, Almira's dark-eyed sister.

The palace was laid out in a regular pattern of small, empty chambers, each of which faced onto an open courtyard. They discovered five of these clusters ranged about an even larger courtyard, which might at one time have housed camels or horses. At its center, surrounding a sunken pool paved in stone, were the skeletal remains of date, palm, and fig trees. Aurora averted her eyes from Crane's bleak expression as he stared at the sand trapped in the bottom of the dry pool, and hardly aware that the others turned to follow, made her way determinedly down a branching hall graced with fluted columns, until at last she came to a great dome-roofed chamber.

While the other cells had been singularly lacking in furnishings, this fabulous hall, bathed in golden shafts of light seeping through vertical clerestory windows beneath the vaulted dome, boasted a marble dais on which rested a massive carved throne overlaid with gold and inset with lapis luzuli. In front of it, at the center of the chamber, rested a mammoth stone disk bearing the carved symbols of the planets and stars all of them inexplicably interconnected by etched lines forming definite, if meaningless, patterns.

"What is this place?" Crane said, the whisper of his voice echoing eerily through the hall.

"The Throne Room of the God," Aurora answered without thinking, then blinked as though emerging from the depths of a dream.

She flushed slightly as she looked around to find the others staring at her oddly.

"Well, it is," she added defensively. "I don't know how I know, but I do."

"The *mem-sayyid* has spoken truly," Janine said. "It is even as Sakhira described it to be from the sacred scrolls of Haramalama. The priest was able to come no further than the *aliy-bab*, the high gate of the outer walls, for it was there the gods blinded him with the sacred fire. Yet he spoke endlessly of the Throne Room in which resides the Drum of the Heavens, Al-tabl-ur-ras. Sakhira believed the passageway to the secret kingdom lay beneath the stone drum."

"Oh, great," Crane muttered, one sapient eye cocked at Aurora's rapt face. "That thing must weigh a ton. I don't suppose the old loon told you how he was going to move it."

"I am not sure," said the girl regretfully. "The rest was *gebir*, the tongue of *baraka*—magic. Perhaps they were the words that command the drum. But they meant nothing to me. Indeed, they are fled from my mind."

Only imperfectly concealing her disappointment,

the Enchantress turned away from the grave-faced girl and stared at the massive stone disk.

"There must be a way to move it," she said doubtfully and glanced at Frayne. The knight lounged against the stone, watching her from beneath hooded lids, his thoughts unreadable behind the aloof mask of his face. Blast the man! Why should he suddenly choose to hold her at arm's length? Now, when she was so close to uncovering the secrets of her origins? She had always suspected that he knew more about her past than he was willing to let on, and now she was sure of it. But what was there in that knowledge he so bullheadedly guarded that could turn him from her? What had he seen in the sculptured faces of the gods? Was she an enemy that he could not tell her what was in his heart? Then, with a feeling of despair, she watched the thin lips curl and nearly winced at the silvery opacity of the falcon eyes fixed so intently upon her.

"I suggest that you look more closely at the stone, Enchantress," he murmured. "It would seem you have overlooked the obvious."

For a moment longer she stared into the knight's impassive features, her own questioning and tinged with the hurt his coldness had inflicted. But at last she turned and with an effort forced herself to concentrate on the symbols carved into the surface of the stone.

At first she could see nothing in the jumble of meaningless scratchings to justify the knight's odd remark. Then suddenly something about the planetary spheres and interconnected stars began to assume a familiarity that nagged at her. She had seen them somewhere before, but where? In rising excitement, she combed her memory for a clue, feverishly called to mind the innumerable drawings sprawled across the pages of Vandrel's tomes of gramarye, the books of Lil, Kern, Ghef, Brynn, and Stehl, and all the other works of the mages over which she had pored with such eagerness. But while many had contained maps of the stars, none resembled the bizarre patterns carved into the surface of the great stone. In mounting frustration she realized she had not encountered the etchings in any of Vandrel's numerous books. Yet where else could she have seen them? She had never even beheld a book before Vandrel had inducted her into the marvelous world of the written word. In perplexity she studied the intricate web of spheres and lines and suddenly it occurred to her that she was looking at the written symbols of some obscure language; indeed, undeciphered symbols, the very symbols fashioned in golden thread upon the fabric of the Crimson Cloak of Power!

"Indeed, they are the same," she said, smiling up at the expectant knight, and spread wide her arms so that the symbols on the cloak shimmered golden in the filtered sunlight. But immediately she sobered, for knowing they were the same brought them no nearer to knowing either their use or their meaning. "But how does this help us?" she added and let her arms fall limply to her sides. "Not knowing how to read their message, I can hardly make use of them."

"Perhaps not. Yet it occurs to me that you possess two keys to the puzzle. The cloak; and the song with which you freed Gleb from the nightmare of Somn and charmed Sheelar, the Serpent-Lord. Either one or both might be enough for the rightful heir of Doane to move the stone."

Aurora visibly blanched as Frayne's meaning became clear to her. He knows! she thought and felt the icy touch of fear upon her as all the old doubts returned to haunt her. He knows that I will fail. And how not? For does he not belong heart and soul to the Sorceress, Leilah, who sees everything in Sheelar's Seeing Eye? She thought she must die if she learned that in truth such was the dark secret of his soul, and yet she could not stop herself from pursuing the shadowy phantom of her deepest, deadliest fear.

"And if I am not the rightful heir?" she said tonelessly. "If it is Leilah, as the mage's elder daughter, who is the legitimate heir, or if, indeed, I am not even truly of the House of Doane, and Almira is not my mother? What then?"

The knight's broad shoulders lifted in a shrug that tore at her already sore heart.

"Then, no doubt, we shall have to come up with a different solution," he answered, as if it hardly mattered. "But perhaps we shall have learned something in the bargain."

Aurora averted her telltale eyes that he might not behold the agony of her soul. Oh, gods! He mocked her! Had everything been a lie? The sweetness of his love, the rapture of the god's power melding their spirits into one? And if she had not his love, did she dare to put to the test all her cherished hopes and dreams? For if the cloak failed her, if she could not summon the song, then would it not prove that she had no claims on the golden-eyed Almira? Would she not be left once more groping in the dark, without even the assurance of Frayne's love to sustain her? Oh, gods! Was this then the end of the quest begun an eternity ago?

Unbidden, an image came to her mind of Minta and Valesia, her dryad mother-pair, as they told her she was to embark upon a quest for her true-name. Then it had seemed a glorious game, and she had set out with the lighthearted optimism of youth, never doubting that she would succeed. That very day Garwin and Gleb, her elfin foster-fathers, had revealed to her the story of the battle in Hawthorn Glade in which the golden-eyed warrior-woman had perished, and they had given her the crimson cloak in which they had found her wrapped, a squalling infant without a name or a past. Anduan they had called her, elf-foundling, for that was what she was. Then Frayne had come, like a vision granted by the gods, to change her life and to give her a new name—Aurora, the Enchantress of the Glade. And she had sworn that it would be hers till she should discover her true-name, and, knowing that she would one day come into her own, she had been content. Until now. But now she knew she could not bear it if it had been all a lie, a creation of her own yearning, her childish fantasies, which demanded that she belong somewhere, to someone, to some past. Without Frayne's love, the dream was all she had, and if she was to lose Frayne, she could not bear to lose the dream as well.

Helplessly she raised shadowed eyes to Frayne's unyielding face, needing him, his strength, to help her overcome the doubts, the fears, which he himself had roused in her. Without conscious thought she extended a quivering hand in mute appeal and prayed that the god might banish this granite-visaged stranger who stood before her and return to her her beloved.

"Frayne?" she whispered, bearing her soul to him in that single, lingering glance. "I am afraid."

She sensed the shudder that swept the length of his powerful body and glimpsed the flicker of pain in the silvery eyes. Did she ask so much of him, then? she wondered. Was his love indeed so fragile?

Then she marveled to see his features soften with the glimmering of a smile.

"Afraid? You?" he said, his voice vibrant in the haunting stillness of the great room. "What can you fear? The answer to a question you were born to answer? The end of a quest that has taken you into the plasmic flux of Somn, to the depths of the Black Mountain and the Crystal Room, and even to the heart of Dred's infectious madness? If you are not the daughter of the golden-eyed Almira, you are still Aurora and Andruvien, and the vassal of a powerful god. You have forged your own name. Is that not enough even for you?"

"Nay, it is not enough," she answered, her eyes shimmering golden through her tears. "For I would forsake all of those things and whatever secrets are buried beneath this wretched stone to be forever a simple shepherdess in the arms of her beloved."

The silence stretched into an eternity as she waited for him to say what was in his heart. She saw the muscle leap along the firm line of his jaw and the grey eyes flicker with a shadow—of what? Uncertainty? Pain? She could not tell. Yet she sensed the battle that waged within him and wondered, her heart like a stricken, dying thing thumping heavily within her breast. Then he was shaking his head as though she were a mystery beyond his understanding.

"You, my love, could never be a simple shepherdess," he said, and his eyes gleamed silvery in the muted sunlight. "Nor can I promise that you shall forever be in the arms of your beloved. But though you should look at me one day across your raised sword and name me your enemy, know that even then you possess my heart. Then and always. Nothing can ever alter that."

For a moment she thought she must swoon with joy. Then she was in his arms, the tears flowing freely at last.

"You are not my enemy," she whispered, cleaving to him with all her young strength. "The gods could not be so treacherous."

"The gods are capable of anything," he said gravely, and placing a hand beneath her chin, turned her face up to his. "As are you."

His kiss breathed fire into her veins, scourging her, body and soul, of the last remnants of doubt and weariness. By all the gods, they were one. She rejoiced and felt the hand of her god upon her.

She could never distinctly recall what happened after that. It was as if she moved through a dream fashioned by the god, a dream in which she saw clearly the symbols inscribed upon the stone and the heavenly bodies suspended in the universe like the words of a song, a song that sprang easily to her lips and vibrated within her very soul. Then it was as if somewhere a door to another plane of existence opened up to her, and energy such as she had never known before, the energy of pure power, of magic, of the universal soul—she could never afterward quite describe it—flowed in and through her, and in truth she felt she could do anything. So this is what it means to be a god, she exulted, and with a word commanded the stone to rise.

She emerged slowly from the dark dregs of the vanished dream, her head pounding and her mouth cottony dry, as if she had partaken too freely of Vandrel's potent elderberry wine and must now pay the price of her intemperance.

"She's coming out of it," absurdly observed a familiar voice. Well, of course she was. Nobody perished from an occasional overindulgence, she thought giddily, though perhaps they might wish to have done.

Experimentally, she opened her eyes, then with a groan closed them again. Oh, gods. Was it too much to ask that she be allowed to sink back into the comfort of healing slumber? But no. Someone was lifting her, forcing a flask between her lips so that she needs must either drink or strangle. She sat up, sputtering and choking, her throat aflame from the fiery liquid that had been brutally poured down her throat. Her eyes watered as she struggled to catch a breath.

"Whose idea was it to poison me?" she wheezed when the paroxysm of coughing had passed and she was able to focus her eyes on the three who hovered anxiously over her.

"Frayne's," Crane offered, a lopsided grin cracking the taut planes of his face. "Gods, Aurora. We thought you had left us for good."

"And when you discovered I hadn't, you decided to make sure of it?" she retorted wryly and grasped her head between her hands. "O-oh," she moaned. "What happened?"

"I suspect you are suffering the aftermath of divine ecstasy," the knight said, straight-faced, and mercilessly pulled her to her feet so that she stood swaying drunkenly as the world spun crazily about her. "Softly, child. You shall come about directly," he added, reaching out to steady her as she jerked her head up to stare searchingly into his face.

"It was not a dream?" she whispered hoarsely. "I caused the stone to be moved?"

"See for yourself," he suggested, and stepped aside so that she beheld clearly the stone lying next to a gaping hole, through which the uppermost reaches of a carved staircase could be glimpsed descending into darkness. Aurora stared for a long while into the murky depths, trying to stop the sickening whirl of her brain and make sense of everything that had happened. The undeciphered symbols on the cloak, the vision of the symbols written among the heavenly bodies, the song of power, the harp held by the Immortal Harmon—somehow they were all connected, all parts of a riddle she must somehow resolve. And then there was the mystery, too, of the sculpted gods, Harmon so lovingly portrayed, ranged beside the dark lord of Somn. Who were Al-Murabit, Leilah, and Almira really? Where and how had they come to possess the secrets of so awesome a power?

"You were magnificent," Crane said suddenly behind her. "I-It was like the whole palace was suddenly

411

alive with music. It was so beautiful. It vibrated right through me, so that I think I was vibrating, too. And the stones, the air, everything was all vibrating together. For the first time I think I understand what Vandrel meant when she used to say we should try to be in harmony with each other and with the world in general. You know, when we were bickering with each other and nothing seemed to work right?" He chuckled softly, recalling the peaceful days in Vandrel's hidden glen when they had been so anxious to be turned loose and about their business in the world. "Like your wart-preventative spell that sprouted warts all over the floor. Remember?"

The Enchantress nodded, smiling a little.

"I remember. There's so much that Vandrel tried to tell us, and I was too impatient to listen. I wonder if she knew what the cloak really is. The symbols are a written record of the song of power. And the cloak—I don't know. 'Tis as though the cloak intensifies the song or channels the energy through the wearer. Those other times when the song came to me, when I did not have the cloak on, it was like a whisper of the song. It stilled the beasts and even the breeze, but there was not this feeling of boundless energy so powerful that it frightens me."

She turned suddenly to look the young mage-lord straight in the eye.

"Crane, no mortal was ever meant to wield such power. It is a thing meant for the gods. I believe it is the heart and soul of the Vendrenin. Oh, gods, Crane! What am I going to do?"

Suddenly at a loss for words, the youth stared in open-mouthed perplexity upon the lovely face turned so beseechingly up at him. The haunted eyes tore at his soul. What could he say to her? She was the Enchantress, and he was naught but the bumbling grandson of a mage who would always be remembered as one who had been tricked by Dred.

"You are going to do as you have always done," said a deep voice at the youth's shoulder, and with a hardly suppressed sigh of relief, the boy yielded his place to the Knight of Tor.

The beautiful child-woman smiled gravely at the knight, one delicate eyebrow arching quizzingly.

"Am I?" she murmured and glanced away to hide her suddenly troubled expression. "And what is that?"

"You shall do as your heart tells you to do. And right now it is telling you to seek the kingdom of your past. And that lies below."

She made no answer for a time as she mulled over his words, her gaze distant. Thus she did not see the look of tender yearning that fleetingly softened the austere planes of his face or the telltale quiver of his hand reaching out to her, only to be snatched immediately back again.

"Aye," she said, drawing a deep breath and letting it slowly out again ere she lifted her head once more to search the depths of her beloved's eyes. "And the gods only know where in the end my heart shall lead me."

Chapter Fifteen

"I suppose I might become a bat and find my way in the dark," Crane said doubtfully as he stared morosely into the beckoning well of darkness. For they had been able to find nothing that might have served as a torch to light their way down the staircase into the mage's Kingdom of Crystals. And though Crane had suggested that the radiance of Andruvien might serve to light their way, Aurora had been reluctant to call upon the Crystal, for she was still weak and a little wobbly, not quite yet herself again, after having been granted even so fleeting a vision of the soul-shattering ecstasy of an empyrean power. She was shaken far more than she was willing to admit even to herself, and instinctively she shied away from putting her mastery of Andruvien to the test.

Even so, the Enchantress shuddered at the shape-changer's newest suggestion.

"Must it be a bat?" she groaned. "I cannot like to have a bat as my guide. Nor do I relish the thought of groping blindingly about in a black pit that might be infested with poisonous snakes, spiders, or the gods only know what."

She stiffened at Frayne's sudden, sardonic rumble of amusement and flushed slightly in embarrassment tinged with pique. After all, she had been through a great deal of late and was, furthermore, tired, thirsty, and half-starved. Was it any wonder that she might be just a little irritable?

"I see nothing funny in what I have just said," she observed petulantly, and favoring him with a small moue of displeasure and a purely feminine toss of her raven curls, indicated quite clearly that she thought him relegated neatly to his proper place. She was, however, quite mistaken, for, seldom at a loss, the tall knight rose immediately to the occasion, startling her with an elegant bow that lost nothing in gallantry for its total lack of sincerity.

"I do beg your forgiveness if I have in any way offended," he drawled in the courtly manner of exaggerated ennui, and Aurora could not quite suppress a small burble of laughter as she glimpsed a devilish gleam beneath the drooping eyelids. "Yet surely you must admit it a trifle odd that one who has just commanded the mystical force of the heavenly bodies should quail at the very thought of a small, furry, winged mouse."

"I am not quailing," she objected, turning disdainfully away that he might not glimpse the grin that tugged at the corners of her mouth. How good it was to play again! she thought whimsically. To make light of the cares pressing so heavily upon her young shoulders, for ere she was ever Aurora, she had been Anduan, a creature made for joy and laughter.

"No. Perhaps *quail* is too strong a term," he agreed, all affability, and folding his powerful arms across his chest, stroked his bearded chin with an air of one giving the matter serious consideration. "*Boggle* might be more apt," he dutifully amended after a suitable pause. "And yet, be that as it may, I should never have thought *you* could be squeamish. Alas! No doubt Girmizi had the right of it, and in the final analysis you are indeed only a female, after all." Then, ignoring her small gasp of indignation, the knight magnanimously added, "However, you may take heart. Crane will not have to become anything so noxious as a bat, since I shall undertake to serve as your guide."

"Better a loathsome bat than a conceited ass!" she retorted irrepressibly and giggled at his expression of pained indignation. "And just how do you propose to find your way through the lightless depths?"

"Contrary to your poor opinion of me," he mused, striking a whimsical pose, "I do have my occasional uses. Talents, as it were, which have at various times in my past stood me in good stead. I possess, you see, the peculiar faculty of being able to see in the dark. Bequeathed to me, no doubt," he added with an oddly mocking twist of the lips, "by the author of my darker self."

The jarring note of cynicism in his last remark, uttered rather as an aside, momentarily marred the mood of lightheartedness that had prevailed earlier. Aurora regarded the enigmatic, slightly bored features with a suddenly sober aspect. There had been the ring of truth in what he'd said, but for the life of her she could make nothing of it. But then he was again the smiling, charming courtier who was used to move with ease among the exalted beings of kings' courts and ladies' sitting rooms.

"But I see that you require proof of the pudding," he said disarmingly, and placing her hand in the crook of his arm in the manner of one who proposes nothing more alarming than an afternoon stroll about the countryside, led her to the mouth of the forbidding stairwell.

"Now, let us discover what wonders lie in the old mage's Kingdom of Crystals," he quipped, "that we may be quit once and for all of this plaguy mystery surrounding your admittedly intriguing past."

The darkness enfolded them like the suffocating fabric of a cloak as they made their way down the seemingly endless staircase, their hands clasped to from a human chain. The knight led them unerringly, his voice a murmur in the velvet silence as he directed their faltering steps. The darkness was total and complete, and the three who walked blindly into the depths, their senses strained and their nerves taut, tingled to the reverberations of their own footsteps rebounding hollowly off walls they could not see. The air was heavy and stagnant, musty with the scent of antiquity, chill with the dankness of a tomb. With an effort, Aurora quelled the rising waves of panic as she clung to the knight's hand as if to a lifeline.

"We are near the bottom now," he said softly, and the calm assurance of his tone was like balm to Aurora's raw nerves. "Careful, the step here is cracked and may give way. Easy. Yes. We have reached the end of the stairs."

"Blast! I can't see a thing," Crane grumbled, his voice ringing through the screaming, dark-enshrouded silence.

"His-st!" Frayne whispered sharply. "I thought I heard something."

"Like the clink of bones together!" Aurora whispered back, the hair at the nape of her neck rising.

"Listen!" he answered, giving her hand clutched in his a painful squeeze. She could hear nothing above the thumping of her own heart as the seconds of taut waiting stretched into an eternity. Then—

"There it is again. Like something being dragged over the floor. There is someone or something down here."

"Yes, I heard it, too," came Janine's frightened whisper.

"Wait here. I'll be back."

"Nay!" Aurora protested on an explosive breath, but Frayne was already gone.

"Blast the man!" she muttered under her breath and strained to pierce the darkness with squinted eyes.

"Sayyid Crane! Where have you gone?" Janine wailed somewhere behind her, and Aurora uttered a low oath as she felt the brush of bat's wings against her cheek.

"Janine. Stay where you are," she cautioned softly. "I'll try to work my way to you."

"As you wish, *mem-sayyid*," the girl responded in a voice that quavered only the tiniest bit. "I am at the foot of the stairs."

Then Aurora's hand touched the warmth of living

419

flesh, and the slave-girl uttered a small, stifled cry.

"Softly, child," the Enchantress whispered. " 'Tis only I."

Hardly daring to draw a breath, the two girls clung to each other and waited for some sound of the vanished heroes.

"Egads! What was that!" Aurora breathed as suddenly the stillness was shattered by a blood-chilling shriek.

"Fiend! Sneak-thief! Villain! Be gone, I say. Else I shall be forced to scourge you with dragon's breath."

"Dragon's breath?" Aurora echoed, startled less by the threat than by the language in which it had been couched, for it had been uttered in the words of elves and beasts, the Old Tongue of the Beginnings.

"Back, I say. I shouldn't like to hurt you, but I shall, do you not take yourself immediately away."

This was passing strange, thought the Enchantress, for a creature who claimed to be a dragon, for it had not the sound of the fearsome, fire-breathing beasts of dragon lore. Indeed, it sounded rather more plaintive than menacing, more frightened than bilious. The creature's next wail brought her to her feet, her heart unaccountably in her throat.

"Oh, no-o! Put up your sword, I beg you! 'Twas all a hoax! I swear it. In sooth, I meant you no harm!"

"Frayne, nay!" Aurora cried, knowing that the knight could not have understood the beast, for none there but she and it spoke the language of the Old Ones.

Without conscious thought she raised her hand to snatch from her neck the pouch wherein resided Andruvien. The crystal flared with painful brilliance.

The Enchantress gasped and flung her arm across her eyes as the darkness scintillated blinding shafts of light, which shattered against a thousand thousand-faceted planes.

How long she crouched, the Blade of Light clutched in her hand and her eyes clenched tightly shut, she could not tell. But at last she hazarded a cautious peak from between slitted lids. A sigh breathed through her lips and she opened wide her eyes to behold the marvel of a crystal world suffused with glorious iridescent light. And more marvelous still, a towering dragon, intricately wrought from glass, cowered before Thrimheld, Frayne's drawn sword, like a giant before the deadly horn of a unicorn.

"By the gods!" she exclaimed in sudden sympathy. " 'Tis little wonder you care naught for swords and such. One blow from even so small a blade must surely precipitate a shattering end."

The hyaline creature visibly shuddered, causing the layers of vitric scales covering its back to tinkle with the pure, bell-like quality of crystal glass.

" 'Tis too horrible to contemplate," it quavered. "Yet 'twould hardly be an end, since I was wrought by the mage's magic. Rather say my troubles should be multiplied, for from each sliver of glass would grow a duplication of myself, till every space should be filled with such as I. Whereupon 'tis inescapable that some should be dashed one against the other or pressed against the cutting edge of the crystals ubiquitous within the kingdom of the mage, thus proliferating myself again and again in an endless cycle of destruction and reproduction. Oh! I beg you. Tell the knight to sheathe his weapon ere we are all overborne with a preponderance of draconic disasters."

"At once, my frangible friend," giggled Aurora, caught up in the spirit of the thing. "After all, a prodigy fractionated and hyperbolized so prodigiously would be prodigality carried to absurdity."

"Egads!" groaned the dragon. "Singularized and single for an infinitude of ages, and who but a wagwit must obtrude upon my insularity. I am indubitably cursed."

"Be that as it may, I advise you to make no untoward moves. My companion has felled far less fragile adversaries." And on that sober note, the Enchantress turned to relate in the man's tongue all that had passed between herself and the dragon.

"I cannot say how or why the flames of Andruvien should have had such an effect on the crystals," Frayne said as the four companions gazed about them in undiminished awe. "It is as if the light of the sword has been absorbed into the heart of the gems, igniting within them an inner fire, which in turn is refracted and dispersed outward again. Hence, the rainbow effect."

"I have never beheld anything so beautiful," breathed Janine, reaching out to touch the delicate perfection of a crystalline wildflower radiating an opalescent glow.

They strolled amidst a marvelous garden of flowers wrought from the purest crystal—rubies, sapphires, and emeralds set amidst the lesser splendor of opals, moonstone, and garnet. Turquoise beetles perched on leaves and stems of purest jade, while amethyst butterflies and citrine honeybees poised within the crystal petals of blooming hyacinth.

The garden itself was contained within a many-faceted crystal cave shimmering with a soft, steady, translucent light, light that had been sparked to life by the power of Andruvien. The cave itself sprawled in broad, stepped terraces, each one seemingly more magnificent than the last; indeed, more wondrous and fantastical, with creations spun all from crystals or, occasionally, from glass. A sparkling hyaline river, so artfully wrought as to appear liquid despite its frozen state, flowed endlessly from one terrace to the next, creating the illusion of cascading falls, through which the inner light, refracting outward into the air, shimmered opalescent rainbows. Ethereal clouds of finely spun glass fibers, through which a topaz sun shone with muted splendor, graced the high, vaulted roof of the foremost terrace, while yet another was a wonderland of forest trees captured in the attitude of autumn nigh unto dusk. And so it went, each terrace a separate and distinct creation of its own and yet somehow harmonious with the whole, so that the four who wandered through tier after tier of the mage's marvelous creation wondered at his mystic vision.

It seemed to be a panorama of the cycles of being, set into motion at the Beginnings by the One, and yet particularized within the boundaries of the mage's own unique existence. It was as if the essence of the mage's own being had been forever captured in crystal, so that Aurora thought she could actually feel his presence lingering there, his soul, his intellect, his spirit; and it was a powerful, loving presence, graced with gentleness, beauty, and enduring strength. She seemed to experience his boundless joy in the miracle of life, joy that was somehow tempered with an underlying sorrow, for even as death is a definition of life, so is sorrow the touchstone of joy.

"I-I wish I might have known him," she murmured a trifle unsteadily.

The knight glanced down at her, his silvery eyes softening at the sight of the wistfulness in her lovely face. Deliberately he pulled her near, wrapping her in a gentle hug meant to comfort.

"But you do know him," he said softly, his gaze embracing the crystal kingdom wrought by the mage. "There is more of him revealed here than you will learn of people you have known all your life. His legacy to you is himself."

"To me?" Aurora questioned, raising her eyes to his. "Or am I merely an intruder? An interloper? How can I know if I am indeed Almira's daughter?"

"How not, little peagoose?" Frayne teased, flicking the tip of her nose with his forefinger. "You unlocked the secrets of the stone. You wear the crimson cloak. The mage's kingdom of crystals awakened to you."

"To Andruvien," she interjected in troubled tones.

"And are you not Aurora and Andruvien?" he countered in amusement tinged with impatience. "Aurora, you are prodigiously hard to satisfy. What more do you need?"

"I need to know who my father is, or was," she answered steadily. "I need to know why Almira died in Hawthorn Glade. Who was she fleeing, and why?"

With an explosive sigh, she pulled away from the knight and turned to gaze across the crystal terrace to where Crane appeared to hover about the slight figure of the slave-girl like some ungainly butterfly about an exquisite perfumed flower.

"There are so many things I still do not know," she murmured. And behind her, the knight's powerful frame appeared to vibrate to the yearning in her voice. For a moment he seemed to waver, then the lean, hard jaw clenched, and when Aurora swiveled to search his face with beseeching eyes, he was himself again, the Knight of Tor, his thoughts hidden behind a cool, collected smile.

"I thought that here, within Al-Murabit's crystal kingdom, I should come at last to the end of my quest for self. And instead I am met with a host of still unanswered questions," she said. Then she smiled wryly and shrugged her slim shoulders. "So my quest continues. And what of your quest for the perfect crystal rose? Aye. I overheard that much outside Groul's foul den. And like you, I thought you would find the rose here. Yet I have seen nothing the least bit suggestive of a rose. Have you?"

"No. Not yet," he answered, suddenly wary, for he sensed a change in her. She was studying him obliquely, out of the corners of her bewildering eyes, and suddenly she was too cool, too beguiling.

"Have you thought to question the dragon?" she asked innocently, running the tips of her fingers carelessly over the smooth surface of a jade lizard perched in an emerald bush.

"The thought had crossed my mind," he admitted, with only a hint of dryness in his tone. "However, I find myself somewhat at a loss as to how to go about it. I am hampered, you see, by the language difference

425

between us."

"But there can be no difficulty there, surely. I can be your go-between. You only have to ask and it is done."

"And what shall you ask of me in return? I wonder," he said as guilelessly as she.

"Why, what can you mean? Why should I demand anything of you?"

"Why, indeed?"

He caught his breath as her golden eyes, more exquisite than any of Al-Murabit's priceless crystals, flashed dangerously up at him. For an instant their glances locked, then suddenly Aurora's entrancing laughter bubbled forth.

"You beast!" she gurgled, her lovely voice still vibrant with mirth. "You refuse to play by anyone's rules but your own." Then just as suddenly she was deadly serious and more dangerous to him than when she had sought to beguile him with her innocence. "You know what I would have from you," she said softly, and 'twas all he could do to meet the entreaty in her eyes.

"I cannot promise to take you to Tor," he answered evenly. "You may be of the Sorceress's blood, but that does not make her any less your enemy."

"I am not afraid of her!" Aurora insisted, compelling him with her whole being to relent, and briefly she thought she had succeeded as his silvery gaze embraced and held her for the space of a single heartbeat. Then suddenly he was bent over her, his eyes piercing on her upturned face.

"A plague take you, Aurora!" he said, and she winced beneath the lash of his voice, though he had spoken softly. "You fear bats and snakes, but you would walk into the spider's lair with no more knowledge of what you face than a witless gnat. You are no match for her, my ignorant little Enchantress. Perhaps one day, but not yet."

"If you will not take me, yet still will I go, Knight of Tor," she warned in chilling tones. "With or without you."

"Then be forewarned, for on the day you face the Sorceress in her citadel, you will stand alone. In her domain I can do naught to help you. In Tor I am the Sorceress's minion and hers alone."

For an eternity their glances locked in a silent clash of wills, the slender child-woman wearing the mantle of a mage-lord and the tall knight with the bearing of an unbending god.

"So be it," Aurora said at last, weariness dragging at her voice. "Shall we question the mage's dragon now that that is settled? I would be done with the business and away from here at last."

"But why should you want to go there?" quailed Kev, the mage's gargantuan glass dragon, his scales tinkling musically as he tried to suppress a shudder. " 'Tis utter folly even to contemplate so disastrous an undertaking. The Winter Garden was the master's final creation. 'Twas there he consigned himself at last to the crystal coffin and there where he lies even now, though none could see him, amidst the restless blades of crystal grass where none dare to tread."

"But why not?" Aurora pursued, impatient with the cowardly dragon.

"Did I not tell you? Were you not listening?" he shrieked with a rattle of his breastplates. "The crystal blades, wrought from the most perfect of all crystals—the white diamond. They are vicious slashing things and never still. They would cut you instantly to ribbons were you want-witted enough to walk among them."

"But the roses are there. You are quite sure."

"Sure? Of course, I am sure! Though little good it shall do you. Even if you were to come close enough to one, you could never pluck it. 'Twould shatter in your hands. Nor will *his* wretched sword be of any use," predicted Kev with utter conviction, and cocked a still-resentful glass eye tinted blood red at the knight lounging easily to one side. "Nay. Only another crystal with a heart as pure and perfect as the crystal of the rose can cut it. And 'tisn't likely there shall be one like that lying close to hand, methinks."

"Then your head is as empty as your transparent glass belly!" Aurora retorted and rapped him playfully with one small fist where the rounded paunch of his undersides shone with a smoky green luster, through which could be seen the purple splendor of a cluster of amethyst grapes drooping on an emerald vine behind him.

To Aurora's astonishment, the resultant tiny, bell-like "ping" set the glass dragon instantly all atwitter.

"Nay. Don't strike me!" he squealed piteously and attempted with such frenzied haste to wheel away from the Enchantress that his entire frangible, vitreous bulk began perilously to totter. "O-o-oh, n-o-o!" he wailed in helpless despair, his wings of fibrous spun glass flailing wildly in a frantic attempt to regain his

428

balance.

"Oh, gods! Frayne!" Aurora shouted and threw her proportionately insignificant weight against the immensity of the teetering dragon.

Instantly the knight was at her side, bracing the lurching glass hulk with a powerful shoulder. Together they strained, desperate with the horrifying expectation of being inundated by a proliferating multitude of draconian glass frangibles. Miraculously, they halted the dragon's precipitous fall, managing to hold the poor creature at a precarious tilt. But even the knight's matchless strength was not enough to tip Kev's glass bulk firmly back on both feet again. It soon became apparent that, far from averting the threatened tragedy, they had succeeded in placing themselves in an exceedingly tenuous position. In short, they had reached a dangerous impasse, with little hope of a happy resolution.

"Run, Aurora!" Frayne panted, his muscles bulging with the strain of his efforts to offset the inevitable disaster.

"I can't—leave—him—to just fall!" gasped the Enchantress. "CRANE! For pity's sake—where are you?"

"Good heavens!" ejaculated that worthy, Aurora's frantic scream having jarred him from a daydream at the far side of the garden. For a fleeting second he stood paralyzed with the certainty that he was about to witness the shattering destruction of both his friends.

"You must help them, *sayyid*," Janine said, tugging frantically at his arm.

Helplessly he glanced down at the girl's frightened

429

face. Cripes! What could he do? It would take a behemoth to avert the almost certain disaster.

"Hurry, *sayyid*!" the girl cried, and the young mage, seeing the innocent trust in her eyes, groaned.

"Well, here goes nothing," he muttered, and squeezing his eyes shut, tried to think himself into the shape of a giant.

Immediately his tall gangly form began to waver and blur. However, it was not a giant that emerged from the plasticity of the shape-changer's art, but a seven-inch-long swift, streaking on sure wings straight for the roof of the crystal cave. There, affixed by the magician's artistry to the ceiling some twenty feet or more above the dragon's tilted head, were the fiber-spun clouds that Aurora had earlier admired.

In a flurry of speed the little bird grasped the fibrous stuff in his beak, and trailing it behind him, streaked to the precariously unbalanced Kev. Back and forth from dragon to roof, Crane flew feverishly, till he had created a thin but substantial truss of fibrous glass cloud strung from the ceiling to the dragon's extended head and neck.

Tentatively, Frayne eased his shoulder from the dragon's side, letting the glass-fiber rope take the full strain. Kev, rigid with fear, moaned feebly as the makeshift halter stretched, then held.

"Thank the gods!" Aurora breathed, standing back to view the shape-changer's handiwork with grateful amazement. "And Crane."

Whereupon the shape-changer fluttered on weary wings to the ground beside her and with a brief shimmer instantly returned unto himself.

"Of what use, I ask you," Crane exploded, red-faced and panting from his heroic exertions, "is a glass dragon? One, moreover, incapable of flight?"

"Flight?" queried the dragon, surprising them all with unexpected use of the man-beast's tongue. Cocking its serpentlike head to one side against the restrictive confines of its fetters, Kev fastened one unwinking eye on the fuming young mage. "Do dragons—real dragons—fly?" he queried incredulously.

"Well, of course they do. Why else should they have wings?" Crane blustered.

"Wings?"

"Those things on your back. They're for flying. You move them like this," the boy instructed, working his skinny arms up and down in a vague imitation of a featherless bird seeking improbable flight.

"Crane," Aurora began cautiously, "I don't think—"

However, she was too late, for Kev, a studied look of concentration on his unlovely dragonish face, was already flapping his ungainly wings with such fervor that her words were swept away in a resulting gust of wind.

"Push off with your feet!" Crane shouted, then, clutching at his unwinding turban, gaped as the gigantic glass creature tore loose from its bonds and unbelievably lifted ceilingward. "Watch out for the roof!" he warned, gesturing frantically. But the creature had already discovered the rudderlike propensities of his posterior extremity. Lifting his tail and dipping his head, Kev soared, suddenly graceful, just beneath the high-vaulted ceiling.

'Twas a glorious sight, the transpicuous green hyaline dragon swooping and soaring just as he had always been designed to do.

"But why had you never tried it before?" Crane asked later, his freckled face expressive of incredulity.

"Well, 'tis obvious, is it not?" returned the dragon rather shamefacedly. "I am an oddity, the master's prodigy, as it were. The only one of his creations he ever granted life. You see, soon after creating me, he lost interest in experiments in animated glassware. Nevertheless, he gifted me with seven languages and kept me around just to have someone to talk with. Everyone else had gone by then, you understand, and I suspect he might have been lonely. At any rate, he never saw fit to inform me what real dragons do. Mostly I just stood in a corner too afraid to move."

"Poor Kev," Aurora uttered sympathetically. "It is difficult being one of a kind. And I hope you can forgive me for nearly startling you to death." She paused then, as if gathering herself to hurtle some private obstacle.

"Kev," she continued after a moment. "You have told us your master crated all of this." She appeared to embrace the magnitude of the crystal kingdom with a sweeping gesture of the arm. "Obviously, he must have been someone very special."

"Oh, indeed," agreed the dragon, tilting his head curiously at the girl. For she had spoken with compelling gravity. "He was the Master Magician of Sib, you know. Before, at length, he found his way here."

The Enchantress caught her breath, then let it out very slowly.

"Nay. I did not know," she said as evenly as she could, for her pulse had leaped at this unexpected revelation.

The Master Magician of Sib! she marveled, trying to recall to mind all that she had heard of the fabled college of magicians. The school had been housed in the City of Figenigm, which was located in the Country of Myrialoc on the plane of Hylmut, which meant that only those gifted with the natural talent of gramarye could hope to find their way there. They were drawn to Sib by their compelling need to know more of the magician's art, but need or desire was not enough to get them there. To do that, it was necessary to solve the conundrum of Hylmut, which was comprised of matter forever changing in substance and form, and of Myrialoc, which might be anyplace or in several different places at any given time. Only a true magician could perceive the unordered pattern of flux and change to discover the uncharted landmarks that guided the adept to the gates of Figenigm, wherein riddles were fashioned to be resolved and resolved to provide the clues to the greater enigmas of the broader universe of unresolved worlds. And the creator of the crystal kingdom had been the master of all those master magicians.

"But what was his name?" she asked. "Which of the line of masters was he?"

"His name?" Kev echoed in apparent puzzlement. "But do you not know?"

"Nay. How should I?" countered the Enchantress in equal perplexity.

"How not, when you are obviously Almira of the golden eyes?"

"Oh, but I am not!" she cried after the first shock of surprise had worn off.

It seemed that they should never succeed in convincing the mage's dragon that she was indeed not Almira returned to claim her father's kingdom, but Aurora and Anduan, the Enchantress in search only of a name. But at last Kev was made to accept that Almira had perished in Hawthorn Glade and that Aurora was very likely her heir.

"You are prodigiously like her," he said, peering at her with glass-eyed intensity. "Indeed, I should say the very image. But then, I never really knew her, except from the crystal likeness the master made. She had left to fight in the last great uprising shortly before the mage brought me into being."

"Tell me about the mage, Kev," Aurora urged. "Tell me his name."

"He was Rab of Zelig," the dragon answered simply. "And he was the greatest magician who ever lived."

Aurora had known the creator of the crystal kingdom had to be a mage of some renown, but never in her wildest imaginings had she guessed it could be Rab, the hero of a hundred tales of wondrous happenings. It had been Rab, a young student of gramarye, who with his feline familiar, Hess, had stolen from Dred the staff of Mum, which could silence a wagging tongue or inspire speech where before there had been none. And Rab, too, who had tricked Lothe, the Dragon-king of Gorn, into giving him to wed the fair and lovely Princess Chandra, his only daughter and a gifted singer of enchantments. And it had been Rab, the Master Magician, who, near the end of the First Great Uprising, had closed the doors to Sib, sending the students and the schoolmasters away to safety while he stayed behind alone to defend Myrialoc against Dred's advancing armies.

That had been the end of Sib, and the last word, save for a rumor here and there, of Rab. Some said he had perished in the fall of Myrialoc, which had simply vanished, or that Dred had imprisoned him in Somn, but while no one had known for sure what became of the Master Magician, the much-disputed tale persisted that he had fled with Chandra to the Mountains of Thunder far to the north, and there had settled into a tame existence of fathering and rearing a family.

But he had come here with his family, or at least with two young daughters. But why? And why not with Chandra? What had become of the legendary beauty whose voice reputedly had possessed the power to entrance and charm? Kev knew the answers to none of these.

"And Almira?" Aurora urged the dragon. "What do you know of her?"

"Not much," Kev admitted regretfully. " 'Twas she who in the end broke Rab's heart. She left him against his will to fight the forces of Somn in the Second Uprising. And when the fighting was done, she still did not return, but wed a commander in the allied forces of Eilderood and mortal men."

"Who, Kev?" Aurora broke in, unable to hide her eagerness. "Who did Almira wed?"

Kev blinked and drew back a little, startled by her sudden outburst.

"Er—Alain, I think the master called him," stammered the dragon, a trifle disconcerted. "Aye. Alain, the Bard of Naefredeyan."

435

"Naefredeyan? I have never heard of it. What place is that? Where is it to be found?" Aurora queried, her whole being concentrated on the riddle of her father's identity. Thus she did not see Frayne's eyebrows snap together or the falcon eyes flare with sudden comprehension as they darted to Aurora's eager young countenance.

"Where? I-I know nothing of the outside world. I—"

"Frayne, do you know of it?" Aurora interrupted, turning impatiently to the knight.

Did he hesitate just the briefest moment? Did a shadow flit across his eyes? She could not be sure as she watched him briefly shrug his shoulder and deliberately shake his head.

"In truth, I have never before heard that name," he said evenly and watched her youthful fervor dimmed with disappointment.

Kev saw it, too, and was sorry for it.

"Is there nothing more you can tell of him or of Almira?" Aurora queried of the dragon.

Kev hesitated, seeming to ponder the question.

"Once, some years ago, I fancied Almira had returned," he offered hopefully after a time. "I thought I heard footsteps on the stairs and the sounds of weeping in the slumbering darkness. And later, the feeling of power being wielded, like the master's when he was about his work of crystal-crafting. And the thunder of rocks or heavy boulders being moved about, as if someone was building something in the old palace up there. But I was held within the bonds of the master's dream-enchantment, so that I could not open my eyes to see what was going on. And ere

436

long the noise stopped and I was left to sleep in peace. Till you and your friends disturbed the spell and awakened me."

Kev fell silent then, and Aurora looked up to find the others watching her, Frayne still-faced and unreadable, Crane with boyish awe, and Janine reserved and perhaps a little frightened by all that she had seen and heard. They were thinking that she was the granddaughter of the greatest magician of the ages, no doubt, and wondering about it and about her. Had she the master's gifts? Was hers the legacy of the illustrious name and audacity that had challenged Dred? She was a little shaken at the thought, for it seemed a great load to carry, and she was not at all sure she was the one meant to shoulder it. There was still too much uncertainty, too many questions left unanswered, so much that she had to know, and suddenly she was filled with a compelling urgency to be about the task of resolving all the riddles surrounding Rab, Almira, the mysterious Sorceress of Tor, and an infant rendered nameless and motherless in an elfin glade long ago.

"Thank you, Kev," she said at last. "You have been very helpful. But now 'tis time we were in pursuit of the crystal rose. I'm afraid we shall have to say good-bye."

"Oh, dear. Must you?" queried Kev, bending his vitreous neck so low that his ruby-red eyes were on a level with Aurora's.

"Indeed, we must," Aurora firmly nodded.

"I shan't ever forget you," he said and sniffed sadly. "I was just getting used to having humans around again, you know. I don't suppose you would take me along? Now that I can fly like a dragon, I shouldn't be frightened quite so easily."

"I am sorry, Kev. But you must see how impossible it would be. A frangible glass dragon wouldn't last very long in the real world, I fear."

Having reluctantly agreed that on second thought it would not be at all practicable for him to leave the kingdom of crystals, Kev bade them a sorrowful farewell and watched them strike out for the Winter Garden, which lay far into the interior of the terraced system of caverns. Following the hyaline stream, the four were soon lost to sight. Yet hours later the lonely dragon, muttering to himself, still sat staring in the direction in which his new friends had gone.

"Oh, but it is a terrible place," he shuddered. "Dark and dreary. And the blades shivering and slashing like dry grass in the wind. But there isn't any wind, and they still keep moving. Like as not it's the master's restless spirit that keeps them at it."

For a long time after that he was still. But then suddenly he rose to his full, dragonish height, his whole glassy bulk suggestive of unusual resolve.

"But they are my friends," he said clearly. "And they taught me to fly."

And with that he spread wide his wings and took flight after the four vanished humans.

The four had passed through a seeming multitude of marvels as they followed the hyaline river deeper into the crystal kingdom. They were surrounded by crystal creatures of legend, which never more were seen in the world of men and elves—ghorns and norns, grizzels and lilliads, the toeless tree-burrower, and the flowering minstrel bird. They had seemed the wonders of a miniature walled city constructed all of moonstone and set atop an emerald hill. Whereupon the kingdom wrought of crystal and the vision of the mage had seen to grow progressively colder and darker, as though they journeyed into dusk of a wintry day, until at last they had come to Almira of the golden eyes, frozen in crystal splendor as she must have appeared the day ages past when she bade farewell to her father to go to the wars. Young and beautiful, with her chin set in youthful determination, her eyes the color of gold coins and shadowed with the hint of sorrow, she could have been Aurora. The Enchantress swallowed a lump in her throat and reluctantly followed the others past the crystal figure of the warrior-woman into a kingdom of moonless night glittering with the illusion of an infinitude of stars.

"Do you hear that?" Crane whispered hoarsely, as, squinting in the unaccustomed near-darkness, they halted at the edge of a steep cliff.

"Like a multitude of wind-chimes or icicles knocking one against the other in the wind," Aurora answered, and she shivered in the chill dampness of the cave.

"The crystal blades, no doubt," observed the Knight of Tor, kneeling on one knee to peer intently over the edge of the precipice. "There's no way to climb down here," he added, straightening. "It seems we find ourselves at something of an impasse."

"Why does it look so white? Like snow or frost?" Aurora asked.

"Maybe that's what it is," offered Crane with a shrug. "Ice is a kind of crystal."

"If only we could see better," Aurora fretted. "There must be a way to get down there."

But short of flying, there seemed no immediate solution to the problem. One after another they discarded impractical ideas, till there was nothing for it but to turn to Crane, who had known all along that eventually they would.

"Sure I want to help," he said, scuffing the toe of one boot against the ground. "It's just that I'm not sure I can. Maybe if I had something to eat. Or if I could just sleep for a while. When was the last time we had a decent meal or a night's rest? I can't remember anymore. And, well, my mind is all kind of hazy. I just have the feeling nothing's going to work for me, if you know what I mean."

And indeed Aurora did, for the shape-changer was like to change into anything or nothing at all, or worse, lose the shape without an instant's notice just when it was most inconvenient. Yet she saw nothing for it but that they must take the chance.

"I know you are tired and hungry," Aurora said, feeling on the edge of collapse herself. "We all are. But you must try. What other choice do we have?"

"None, I suppose," Crane muttered on a sigh.

"Then what are you waiting for?"

"Oh, all right," he relented grudgingly. "Here goes. I just hope you won't be sorry."

With a vague feeling of foreboding, the Enchantress watched the reluctant shape-changer clench his eyes closed with such intensity of concentration that his whole face seemed scrunched together in a puckering frown. Unconsciously gnawing on the knuckle of her fist, Aurora saw the youth's scrawny shape begin to shimmer and blur. Then the fist dropped and her mouth gaped at the sight of the great lump of a boulder that had taken form at her feet.

"Mayhap he means for us to toss him over the edge," Aurora suggested dourly as she perched wearily on the stone, chin in hand, her elbow propped on one knee. Then she bit her lip at Janine's horrified gasp and grimaced apologetically.

"Never mind," she said, a gleam of wry humor in her eye. "I did not mean it. And besides, we should only have to figure a way to get him out again after all."

The first hint they had of impending catastrophe was a faint whirr crescendoing to a sibilating whish, like the wind passing over the open mouth of a glass bottle or a stone falling through the air from a tremendous height.

Aurora, too lost in her own weary dejection, did not see Frayne suddenly start and stare intently back the way they had come. Nor did she hear Janine utter a small strangulated cry, the back of a hand lifted to her mouth.

"There *must* be a way down this cursed cliff," the Enchantress muttered to herself. "I wish I could find it right now—instantly!"

Whereupon her wish was granted, for one moment she was sitting hunched on the boulder at the very brink of the precipice, and the next she was hurtling over the edge, her scream of despair trailing woefully after her.

"AURORA-a-a-a!"

Frayne's cry of utter horror sounded vaguely in her ears, then she was deafened by a thundering flap of wings. She had the brief impression of a monstrous, swooping thing of transpicuous green, then she was snatched, breathless and gagging from her pitched descent.

"Kev!" she choked when she had got her breath back again. "Thank the gods."

" 'Twas all my fault," moaned the dragon, circling gracefully about the glittering crystal roof, the Enchantress securely clutched in his great glass talons. "I was in such a hurry, you see, to catch up to you. I never thought to come upon you in such a manner. And I-I . . . well, I just *couldn't* stop."

The Enchantress giggled feebly despite herself.

"Well, I suppose all's well that ends well." Then, as Kev banked sharply in a steep turn and made for the cliff again, it came to her that in truth her wish had been answered.

"Nay, Kev!" she called. "Take me to where the crystal roses grow."

"Oh, I couldn't!" shivered the dragon. "The blades would slash you to ribbons."

"You must, Kev. I must have the crystal rose. For Frayne," she added, almost as an afterthought. And suddenly it struck her most oddly that at some time she had ceased to think of the rose as the object of Frayne's quest for the Sorceress. Nay. Somehow it had become her own. Inexplicably it had become vital that *she* find the perfect crystal rose.

"Just fly low enough so that we can spot it," she urged. "Then mayhap we shall see how it may be retrieved."

It seemed that Kev, circling endlessly round and round, would not only fail to find the courage to do what must be done, but would in the end have succeeded in nothing more momentous than making Aurora quite thoroughly ill. In fact, she had nearly reached the point of ordering him to land anywhere just as quickly as it might be safely done, when the dragon appeared suddenly to have reached a firm resolve.

Tucking his tail, he seemed momentarily to pause, then with hair-raising suddenness they were swooping at a distinctly nerve-shattering angle straight for the crystal-covered floor.

"Oh, gods!" Aurora screamed silently, and in horrified fascination watched the crystal-simulated frozen landscape approaching with terrifying speed. In a sort of paralysis, she had accepted the inescapable end, when, just as abruptly as he had begun the death-defying dive, Kev spread wide his wings, thrust upward with his head, and giving a sickening lurch to her stomach, swerved from the inevitableness of instant death. Unbelievably, they skimmed safely scant feet above the slashing, deadly blades of crystal.

It was some time before Aurora had recovered sufficiently to realize that the wild throb against her breast was not the thunder of her own heart but Andruvien pulsating with awakening power. With a trembling hand she retrieved the crystal from its pouch, and in awe saw it leap as if in answer to a silent summons. Then she saw them, the crystal roses shining with dazzling beauty, and in their midst, a flushing glow of ruby fire.

"The rose, Kev!" she cried. "I see it!"

With painstaking care, Kev hovered just above the small clearing in which the roses stood.

"Now, Kev!" Aurora shouted, and immediately the dragon released her.

The Enchantress landed in a crouch, and waving the dragon away, watched him for a moment as he soared in perfect dragon flight straight for the safety of the cliff.

"May the One keep the others safe from his uncertain landing," she murmured with a wry smile, then instantly forgot everything else as she turned to behold the dazzling perfection of the roses perched on slender crystal stems.

She saw that they were of intricately worked white diamonds possessed of an inner fire that rivaled even the brilliance of Andruvien, but it was the other one that attracted and compelled the golden-eyed Enchantress, a ruby so perfect that it filled her with breathless awe. She seemed to feel it like a heartbeat within her, a part of her, a living, vital thing. Indeed, as at last she knelt reverently before its ruby-red perfection, she had the odd notion that she alone had been born to hold it in her hands.

Aurora reached a trembling hand out to the crystal rose, then with a gasp snatched it back again. For it was if she had touched warm, yielding, living flesh rather than a lifeless crystal thing.

Stunned by something she sensed, something she could not resist, she stared into the blood-red heart of the rose until it seemed that she must lose herself, for there was a mystery here, a presence or an essence of

444

something beyond her understanding. And yet it called to her and compelled her and filled her with a yearning that was like love or fire or the need to be free, and suddenly she knew what it was and what she must do.

She grasped the rose tenderly and raised the crystal sword with a steady hand. Then she let the blade drop, and the deed was done.

Lovingly, the Enchantress raised the red rose to inhale its perfumed sweetness, for it had not been a crystal that fell from the stem but a delicate, living flower. Nor was it a crystal kingdom through which she strolled when at last she turned and wended her way among the wonders preserved by Rab's loving heart. The slashing blades parted at her passing, gentle blades of grass, and behind her the roses shimmered with dewdrops rather than the blazing brittleness of dazzling diamonds. With a glad heart, the enchantress looked upon the living loveliness of Myrialoc and rejoiced at having freed Rab's essence that the magical land might live again.

Chapter Sixteen

The boulder lumped at the edge of the steep precipice stirred and blurred until at last Crane appeared curled in a ball on his side, one long arm clutched between his knees and the other tucked beneath his head. Slowly he straightened and stretched, one spindly hand rising to rub the sleep from his eyes as he partook of a huge, contented yawn. The sound and scent of rushing water impinged oddly on his consciousness, and suddenly he was made aware of the parched condition of his lips, mouth, and throat. A long, cool drink seemed very much in order, he thought hazily, then looked up to encounter the golden eyes of the Enchantress observing him in some amusement.

"I do hope you are quite rested," Aurora said sweetly, as the young shape-changer blinked and appeared to make some attempt to bring his thoughts into order.

Immediately a look of dawning comprehension swept the homely face with chagrin. Crane bolted upright, groaning as the blood rushed from his head with the suddenness of his move.

"By the gods, Aurora. I couldn't help myself. I tried to imagine myself a dragon, but all I could think of was how stone weary I was. And . . . well, I guess you know the rest," he ended morosely. "I'm sorry I let you down, but my head is clearer, and maybe I can work the spell properly now."

"Never mind, nodcock," said the Enchantress fondly. "The thing is done, thanks to Kev. And after all that you have done, you well deserved the rest."

"Kev?" pondered Crane, scratching his head. "What does Kev have to do with it?"

But the Enchantress only smiled enigmatically and leaned over the puzzled youth to call down to someone below the cliff.

"He's awake! And 'tis time we were on our way."

Almost immediately the shape-changer was startled by the distant thunder, as of great wings beating against the wind at his back, and the realization that where before a river of solid glass had been, real, sparkling water now flowed. Furthermore, he was no longer within the dark crystalline confines of a cave, but beneath a glorious blue sky across which soft white clouds drifted lazily with the promise of an early evening shower.

Awkwardly he twisted round to see behind him, and having forgotten that he had fallen into slumber atop a precipice, nearly flung himself unwittingly over the side.

"Whoops, not that way!" Aurora cried, dragging him hastily back. "It is the quick way down, but I cannot honestly recommend it."

But Crane was paying little heed to the Enchantress. His eyes were fixed and staring at the marvelous sight of a great-winged, soaring serpent that had risen from the depths and was even then embarked on glorious flight straight for the gawking young magelord.

"Duck, Aurora!" he shouted, and dragging her down beside him, buried his face in the dirt, one long arm thrust protectively over his head.

The wind of the creature's passing buffeted them both, and then all was dreadful silence. Cautiously Crane peaked out from beneath his arm to find Aurora, her face smudged with dirt, regarding him in rueful disgust. And beyond her, a magnificent, real-life dragon.

"So when Rab's essence was freed from the heart of the ruby, the binding spell was broken. Myrialoc was returned to its natural, living state, along with all the creatures within its bounds. All, that is," Aurora added a trifle sadly, "with the exception of Almira, whose crystal likeness was never more than that. It was the one thing of manufactured art that the mage left behind him."

"But what about the rose?" Crane asked, turning to look at the knight, who stood gazing out over the magnificent panorama of Myrialoc's flower gardens. Frayne glanced back over his shoulder and shrugged slightly.

"It is a rose and nothing more," he said, a bemused expression in the still, grey eyes. "No doubt the

Sorceress will be unamused at this unexpected alteration in her plans. But what's done is done."

" 'Tis ironic," Aurora said musingly, "that the crystal rose she had thought to use in her potion was of far greater importance than she could have imagined. The heart of her own father's magic, which at her touch should have become her legacy from him. Do you think she knew?"

Frayne, remembering the Sorceress's peculiar slip of the tongue regarding the fragmentary nature of the visions obtained from the looking glass, could not be sure. But somehow he felt she had not known that the castle she had imperfectly beheld in the Seeing Eye had been her father's. Rab had guarded his secret all too well. And doubtless, it was only the fact that it had been his own daughter, Leilah, who had sought the vision that had enabled her to perceive even so hazy an image of it.

But that was neither here nor there. The crystal rose was naught but a wilting flower now, and he had still to face her anger. If she learned the truth, that her younger sister's daughter, Aurora, had been the one to receive the gift of the magician's power, she would be incensed beyond all rationality. And Aurora would be the one made to suffer for it. Somehow he must discourage the Enchantress from pursuing her madcap scheme to come face-to-face with the Sorceress. And suddenly, as he looked at the lovely child-woman conversing quietly with the shape-changer, he was afraid.

"But I am a real dragon now," Kev said plaintively.

"I don't see why I can't go with you."

"You may be real, dearest Kev," Aurora answered reasonably, "but you should be no less an oddity where we are going. It is a city. Like the restored Figenigm. There would be no place, indeed, no space great enough to hold you within its walls. You will do much better here. But one day, when I have done what must be done in Tor, I shall send for you. You will hear my thoughts and know where I am. Then you will come to me, I promise."

"Oh, I suppose you are right," grumbled the downcast dragon. "But I don't like it. This Sorceress sounds a nasty customer. I shouldn't trust her too far if I were you. And if you do get into trouble, I hold you to your word to call on me."

Thus, Kev's sorrowful farewell seeming to echo yet in their ears, the four companions materialized within the leafy bounds of the Tamarack Grove, there to be met by Boltar's clarion challenge and the soft-eyed grey mare, both of whom the shape-changer had fetched there before them. The Knight of Tor strode forward to meet the gallant steed and to stand for a long moment in silent, glad-hearted welcome.

"I think maybe I'm beginning to get the hang of this," Crane said with satisfaction as he realized everyone had arrived in one piece and without any undesired alterations.

"You were magnificent, *sayyid*," murmured Janine. Whereupon the shape-changer blushed and thrust his hands deep into his pockets.

"Now, what in the world," he mumbled as his fingers came in contact with a small, hard object with sharp edges. Withdrawing his hand, he stared in perplexity at the beautiful, many-faceted tear-shaped crystal resting in his palm. "How did this get in there?"

"What is it?" queried the Enchantress, coming to stand beside her young friend, and taking the exquisite thing in her hand, held it up to the fading sunlight to examine it.

"By the One, it looks just like the Arlana, but it could not be. Could it?" she said in wonder and carried it to the shrine to make certain the Virgin's Tear was yet safely where she had left it a seeming eternity earlier. But the crystal that had been stolen by Anders Groul, the lapidary, and returned with so much heartache and difficulty, was still safe upon the smooth carved cheek of the figure of Ariana. Yet the other appeared almost an exact duplicate.

"But if not the Arlana," she said, turning mystified eyes upon Crane and Janine. "then what, indeed, is it?"

"Something from the crystal kingdom?" Crane suggested.

"Mayhap, but somehow I doubt it," Aurora answered ponderingly and made as if to return it to the shape-changer.

"Unh-unh. You keep it," Crane said, shaking his head. "I've had enough of crystals to last me a lifetime. Besides, something like that's bound to cause trouble sooner or later." And, taking Janine's arm in his, he led the girl away to discuss pressing matters of another kind.

The Enchantress watched them go, a small, wistful

smile on her lips, for they had the air of lovers who wished to be alone. Then, sighing a little, she placed the mysterious crystal in the pouch that had previously contained Andruvien, and checked to make sure the sliver of the Vendrenin still resided in the golden setting of a bracelet Kev had given her. Dear, sweet Kev, she thought, fondly recalling the great dragon's self-consciousness as he led her away from the others to the secret place in which, at Kev's direction, she had discovered a small casket that once had been Almira's.

"The thing of power should be more conveniently placed about your person," he had suggested shyly. "I thought perhaps the bracelet once worn by your mother might suit. As you see, the original stone has been lost."

And, indeed, it had suited, accepting the crystal almost as if it had been made for it.

Still thinking of the kindhearted dragon, the Enchantress wandered absently from the shrine, only to be nearly run over by Janine, tearful and obviously in a high dudgeon.

"I-I hate him!" stammered the girl, her enormous eyes ablaze with hurt and rage. Rendered momentarily speechless by the unexpectedness of Janine's pronouncement, Aurora was unable to do aught but stare witlessly back at the outraged girl. Whereupon Janine, stifling a heartrending sob with the back of her hand, spun about and fled precipitously, leaving the Enchantress to gape in open-mouthed astonishment after her.

"Well!" she exclaimed softly under her breath. "I

wonder what that was all about." But no sooner had she recovered from that startling encounter than she was set upon by an equally incensed young mage-lord.

"Where'd she go?" Crane demanded biliously. "I know she came this way. You needn't deny it."

"I've no intention of denying it," retorted the Enchantress dangerously. "Why in the world should I?"

"You're a female, aren't you?" the youth snapped, as if that were sufficient grounds to doubt her word.

"I should have thought that was obvious," Aurora rejoined, not sparing the sarcasm. "Now, why don't you get down off your high horse and tell me what's going on?"

One look at the ominous glitter in Aurora's eyes was enough to dampen the youth's bellicosity.

"Aw, I was only thinking of her own good," he said, subsiding into a hangdog retreat. "But would she listen? No, not her. Accused me of being a pig-headed, self-centered something-or-other with the brains of a camel. A camel!" he repeated in no little disgust. "Said as far as she was concerned even Mush was too good for me. Then she ran off. And all I'd said was that she was too much of a kid to tag along with us to Tor and that I was going to send her to Vandrel. I'll never understand females."

"You poor dunderhead," Aurora offered in the way of comfort. "You are, indeed, blessed with the wits of a camel." Whereupon she proceeded to enlighten the misguided youth as to the desirability of employing a measure of tact when dealing with sensitive young girls.

* * *

Overcome with embarrassment at having encountered the Enchantress in a state of discomposure and still seething with hurt resentment at Crane for declaring that on a dangerous mission he could not be saddled with a kid of a girl, Janine fled blindly into the forest. She had no thought except to escape, and consequently paid no heed to where she went. She ran until her breath came in painful gasps and her side ached abominably, and at last she stumbled and fell sobbing on a bed of cushiony grass. There she cried herself into an exhausted sleep.

The raucous cry of a raven jarred her at last from her dreamless slumber. The girl stirred fitfully, then froze at the muffled sound of footsteps and a deep voice that she could not fail to recognize.

"So you have found me, Carrion-Crow," Frayne said in a voice edged with steel. "Recite the Sorceress's message and begone."

"Speak not so to Kreekow, knight. Lest I tell *her* how you fondle the changeling. To me she will listen. She will listen to me."

"Tell her what you will, miserable spawn of Somn," uttered the knight coldly. "But waste not my time. What does your mistress want of me now?"

"Naught but the changeling and her pretty bauble," shrieked the crow in a shrill imitation of a cackle. "The bauble for the shriveled rose, the bauble and the changeling. Bring them to Tor, knight. To Tor you must bring them. Know, as well, that she sends the shapeless one and his hirelings. Of you she would be sure. Sure of you she shall be."

Janine shuddered at the crow's venomous chortle,

455

which trailed after the receding flutter of wings.

The knight cursed.

"And so the game begins in earnest," the girl heard him mutter, and then there was naught but the sound of retreating footsteps.

For a long time Janine was too frightened to move from her hiding place. But at last her fear for Crane's safety became greater than her fear for herself. Cautiously she climbed to her feet, and after searching the thick shadows of falling dusk for signs of the man or the crow, she stole swiftly in the direction the knight had taken.

Terror was like a beast tracking her through the murky depths of the forest. She ran, heedless of the clutching branches of bushes and low-hanging trees that tore at her clothing and raked her tender skin. In her panic she stumbled over a hidden root and sprawled, gasping, to her knees. For a moment she remained on all fours, too weary to rise. Then she was up again, the breath rasping in her throat and her heart pounding furiously as she realized night was closing in on her. The certainty that she would be utterly lost if she did not find Crane ere darkness fell sent her into panic-stricken flight. Thus she did not hear the fierce sounds of fighting till she was nearly upon the clearing.

Clutching one hand to her mouth to stop the scream that had risen to her lips, the slave-girl crouched amidst the concealing foliage of a thick hedge and watched helplessly as Aurora struggled in the grasp of two brawny men. Frantically Janine searched the glade for the lanky form of the shape-changer, then shrank, nearly swooning as she recognized the hideously scarred face of Baldrac, her former master, and the indistinct shadow-form of the Imposter, black-caped and sinister. Yet she had discovered no sign of Crane, and she nearly sagged in relief, so sure had she been that she would behold him grievously wounded or already dead. Then she saw Frayne stride boldly forward to confront the Enchantress and in horror heard him taunt his raven-haired love with a callousness Janine had never dreamed possible in the Knight of Tor.

"I must beg your forgiveness, my dear," he drawled in a voice the slave-girl hardly recognized, "for the manner in which you shall at last enter Tor. Such a pity really that you shall not be able to enjoy the more pleasurable and interesting sights of the city. But, alas! That's the way of it. Perhaps I shall be able to persuade the sorceress to at least allow you the pleasure of my bed at night," he ended on a jeering note.

"By the One, you are vile!" uttered the Enchantress in a voice of utter loathing.

"And how not?" quipped the Knight of Tor lightly. "I am, after all, Dred's only spawn."

The Enchantress recoiled as if she had been struck.

"YOU!" she rasped and could not go on.

Yet it was as if the knight had read her mind.

"At last you understand, Enchantress," he said and uttered a hard, mirthless laugh. "The shining knight you welcomed so eagerly to your bed was none other than the Thromholan of prophecy."

Then it was as if his soulless admission freed the

Enchantress from the bounds of paralysis and brought the punishing vengeance of the gods swooping from the sky, as Aurora suddenly twisted out of her captors' grasp even as a great-horned owl appeared to fling itself screeching at the traitorous knight. Frayne ducked, flinging up his arms to ward off the deadly talons. The owl lifted into the air, then swooped again. The knight cursed, blood streaming from a jagged cut on one forearm, and still he made no move for his sword.

Janine watched in helpless terror then, as the Enchantress, dodging and slashing at the villains with her elfin blade, turned the glade into a scene of utter chaos. She saw her reach for the bracelet that she had worn on her wrist since Myrialoc and saw as well that it was gone, pulled from her arm when she broke away from the men who had held her.

"Crane! The bracelet!" she cried piercingly and somersaulted from beneath the grasping arms of one of the villains. Instantly the owl ceased its assault on Frayne and dove toward something gleaming golden in the half-light of dusk. The great talons reached and closed about the thing. Then the owl was beating powerful wings, lifting into flight again. But a hawk had appeared from nowhere to strike at the owl from above. Crane faltered, began to plummet earthward. The hawk clinging to his back with vicious talons released its hold at last to save itself from Crane's plunge toward certain death. Oh, gods, Janine breathed. Do not let him die. And suddenly 'twas not an owl but an eagle, lifting, soaring into the sky. Then he was gone, and the hawk, having descended to earth, assumed its true form—Cranith, the Imposter, his evil, fleshless face distorted with hatred terrible to behold, as he watched the eagle vanish into the falling night.

Janine drew a deep breath and sent a prayer after Crane. Then she heard Aurora's lilting cry and looked up to see the Enchantress scintillating a godly wrath as she fearlessly fought Cranith's black-garbed hirelings. Never had she appeared so dangerous to the girl watching in breathless terror from the thicket. The dagger flashed in a slashing arc, and a brawny rogue fell back, blood streaming from a gash across his face. Yet another felt Glaiveling's sharp-edged steel ere suddenly the Enchantress turned and dropped into a wary crouch as Baldrac shoved his fellows aside and boldly stepped to the fore.

"The witch is mine," he warned the others. The brutish lips curled hideously as he raised the stump of his mangled arm and leered at Aurora. From the security of her hiding place the slave-girl stared in horrid fascination at the cruel, gleaming point of the hook slashing with deadly significance through the air. "She owes me," Baldrac snarled, and lunged.

The Enchantress bounded effortlessly to one side. Then, as Baldrac lumbered past, she lashed out with the elfin blade. The brute bellowed and swung ponderously around, the twisted fingers of his single hand rising to the gaping cut along his jawbone. But Aurora was already bounding toward him. Hurtling herself feet first through the air, she struck him full on his massive chest, toppling him. Instantly she had rolled head over heels to her feet and come around, Glaiveling glinting silvery in her hand.

Then Frayne's iron fist struck out of nowhere, landing the Enchantress a stunning blow flush against the side of her jaw. Aurora dropped to the ground to lie as still as death.

For a stunned moment no one moved. Then Frayne dropped to one knee beside the unconscious Enchantress and with an odd gentleness brushed a lock of hair from her face. Almost Janine thought the lean hand trembled as he lightly touched his fingers to her jaw where the mark of his fist shone dark and swollen against the marble whiteness of her skin. Then, deliberately, he slipped his arms beneath the slight body, and rising easily to his feet, lifted her from the ground.

"Hold it," Baldrac growled, and catching the knight's arm in the curve of the deadly hook, halted Frayne. "I'll take the wench," he leered, "Unless, of course, you have some objection?"

For a moment the knight stood quietly, his back to the grinning lout. Then slowly he turned his head, and suddenly Baldrac's expression paled to a queasy caricature of a smile. The hook lifted harmlessly from Frayne's arm, and Baldrac backed up an unsteady step.

"Sure, you take her," he rasped, his tongue flicking like a serpent's over brutish lips. For a moment he watched the tall knight's slowly retreating back. Then one hand rose to the angry wound oozing crimson gore, and briefly he let slip his mask. "But you'll not keep her long," he added venomously beneath his breath. "The Sorceress has her own plans for the bitch."

Janine watched the Knight of Tor ride from the glade, the Enchantress held before him and the others following more slowly in their wake. Then she waited to see no more, but slipped silently into the abandoned camp, and, snatching up Aurora's discarded pack, fled back into the safety of the thick woods. Working her way in a wide half-circle around the now silent clearing, she came at last to a faint path leading away into the forest. For a moment she paused uncertainly, her glance straying back over her shoulder the way Frayne had gone. Then, drawing a deep breath, she turned and set out firmly along the trail— north and west toward the mountains, and, the gods willing, to Vandrel.

Aurora awakened to the dread of a new day and vainly sought to resubmerge herself in the black pit of forgetfulness. One day he would come to her again, as he had that first night after Leilah, the Sorceress, had condemned her to eternal damnation. For the cunning Sorceress had chosen the ultimate in revenge for herself, the cruellest torture for Aurora—to give her as slave to Frayne, the false knight, the soulless Knight of Tor.

Oh, gods! Frayne! she screamed silently, and bit her lip until it bled, to somehow contain her anguish. He was the Thromholan. And traitor to his god, and to her. Like phantoms in a nightmare, the events of his ultimate treachery returned to haunt her, his eyes, cold and grey as winter on a cloudy day, freezing her to the soul as he made a mockery of their love and

461

ripped her heart in twain. 'Twere better had he let her die at Baldrac's hands than to slay her slowly piece by piece. Already he had killed all her faith in him and in herself as well. Oh, how could she have been so deceived in him? Should she not have sensed his evil? Could one so utterly depraved possess the semblance of a noble heart, a facsimile constructed perhaps of the plasmic stuff of Somn? Somehow it had fooled even the god who had molded their spirits into one. Or was it her god who was the empty illusion? Had this artful fiend, the only spawn of the Prince of Throm, created the illusion of the god within her mind, just as he had fashioned the image of Dred that time so long ago, indeed, the very night he had sworn his love to her?

His love! What a cruel mockery was that. And yet, had he not told her all along that he had no heart to give? Nay, not that he had no heart, but that his heart was not his to give. Clearly the first was nearer to the truth, and he had been merely twisting the meaning to suit his evil purpose. The real, inescapable truth was that he had deliberately betrayed her. Then, indeed, did her heart cry out, for it was even as he had said it would be. All of it, like some black prophecy come inevitably to pass, and the words of his warning uttered on the shores of Grendylmere a lost eternity ago seemed now cruelly to jeer at her.

"I will always do what I must to achieve my ends. That is the one thing on which you can rely. One day I will destroy your faith in me. Remember that I have warned you."

"And so, my love, shall I do what needs must be

done," Aurora whispered to the empty room. "For though it means my own end, even so shall the Thromholan perish by my hand. By the gods, I swear it!"

Whereupon she fell to brooding over the plan that had come to her as she had lain beside the knight and watched him sleep, her heart bitter with the knowledge that in spite of everything she had responded to his touch with a passion undiminished by pain and disillusionment. That had been the only time he had used his slave in passion, but he would do so again. She would make sure of it. And then, his bestial lust sated, he would sleep. And she would plunge the dagger through his heart and kill him. But for this she must somehow procure a knife and secret it away till he came to her again; and there was only one place within Leilah's dark and dreary domain where she was certain she could find a blade—the Sorceress's Chamber of Visions, where Glaiveling lay, contemptuously discarded by the Sorceress herself, as she dismissed Frayne and his newest slave.

Aurora's eyes glittered coldly with resolve as she flung back the fur pelt and left the bed. Shivering in the chill dampness that not even the fire crackling in the carved black marble fireplace could dispel, she hurried into the lovely rich robe lined with ermine that Frayne had given her to wear. Nor was this his only gift. He had showered her with exquisite gowns and even jewels. Her hands clenched suddenly at her sides. How could one man be such a paradox of conflicting personalities? she agonized and closed her eyes against the haunting image of Frayne standing close to her, his fingers toying with a lock of her hair, and his eyes—oh, gods!—his eyes, silvery in the candlelight, seeming to drink in her loveliness, and his lips, the lips that had betrayed her, brushing against her hair with all the old illusion of tenderness.

"Nay! I will not think of it!" she whispered in the stillness of the room. "I will clasp to my heart instead the vision of my triumph over the cursed Thromholan when at last he lies dead."

So saying, she stole quickly from her room, and gliding on silent feet, made her way along the empty corridor toward a narrow door beyond which she knew she would find the winding stone staircase that would take her to Leilah's lofty tower. Fearful lest someone discover her ere she had finished what she had come to do, the Enchantress fairly flew up the steps, never once pausing even for breath. Endlessly up, till her heart pounded and her limbs were like lead, and at last she came to the closed door that led to the Sorceress's forbidden chamber and leaned her forehead weakly against the carved wood till her breath had ceased to come in great, gasping sobs and her heart to pound like a drum announcing her presence there. Then cautiously, ever so slowly, she eased the latch and pushed against the door.

The Chamber of Visions brooded in the velvet silence, dark and lavish and scintillating with the Sorceress's lingering presence. A draught played among the tapestries hanging on the walls so that they rippled and billowed as if the chamber itself were alive and breathing. Frayne had called it the spider's lair, and, indeed, Aurora tingled with the feeling that somewhere within the brooding, shadow-draped chamber, the Sorceress waited for her to entangle herself in some invisible web. The Enchantress shuddered and firmly quelled such paralyzing fancies. Quickly! She must find the knife and be gone ere Leilah did indeed find her there.

She made her way across the chamber, around chairs and thick cushions strewn seductively about the floor, until at last she came to a small marble-inlaid table on which, when last she had seen it, Glaiveling had lain. She reached out a trembling hand to search the tabletop, and at last her heart leaped at the cold touch of steel. Her fingers closed familiarly about the handle and then she turned, more than ready to flee the Sorceress's dreadful chamber.

In her haste she came up hard against a raised stone dais and gasped as an inky well of darkness stirred and seemed suddenly to emit a muted nimbus of pale, purplish light. For a moment she stood indecisively, wanting with all her heart to flee and yet held there, mute and trembling, and drawn by a terrible, nagging curiosity that compelled her to look ever more deeply into the heart of the black, gleaming oval eye. In helpless fascination, she leaned out over the edge and reached down with fingers that quivered, closer and closer to the still, murky surface, wanting to pull them back, wanting to scream, until at last, in a single swift movement, she plunged her hand down into the icy depths and out again.

Aurora stared at the ripples spreading outward from the point of disturbance and lost herself in a memory of herself submerged in a crystal-clear stream and looking up through the flowing surface of the water at Frayne as he had stood above her on a grassy river-bank. His form distorted with the rippling effect of the water, he had seemed unreal, a figment of fancy, and somehow she had been afraid to surface lest in shattering the image she might somehow shatter him. The image was as fresh in her mind as the day that she had lived it, every detail—Frayne's bare torso, his hair wet and clinging to his forehead after his recent ablutions, the stillness of his face—everything about him stood out clearly in her memory. Whereupon she gasped, realizing that the image was reflected not within her mind but upon the rippling surface of the Seeing Eye! Then, even as she looked more closely, the vision changed, and he was a younger Frayne, unscarred and strangely vulnerable, and he was not alone, for with him was Ariana, the same lovely face filled with serenity and an enduring faith that had graced the carved figure in the Grove of the Holy Maiden.

In her mind, the Enchantress heard him call the Holy Maiden "Mother," and suddenly she understood. Ariana had offered herself as the sacrifice, the bait to lure Dred from hiding, and he had come, ravaging her as he once had ravaged the innocent loveliness of Throm. And out of the foul deed Frayne had been conceived, the son of Ariana and the Prince of Somn, the Thromholan of prophecy, half-mortal and half-god.

In wonder, she saw the boy grow to manhood, a strong and able warrior who one day knelt solemnly before the Menhir of Tor as he dedicated his sword and himself to the One. She did not know how long she stood staring into the looking glass as Frayne's life passed before her in image after rippling image, till at last she beheld him, little more than a youth yet already a tried and proven veteran of many a battle, bent and weeping with grief. In impotent rage she watched the Sorceress lead him to the looking glass, and gloating with some secret knowledge, bid him look therein at the image of his mother, Ariana, imprisoned by the Sorceress's magic within the flux of timelessness. She had no need of the looking glass to visualize the succeeding years of his servitude to Leilah, his father's concubine, for she had read the record of the havoc they had wrought, the disillusion and cynicism, the secret torment of his soul, in the lines etched about his mouth and in the hard glint of his falcon eyes. Then, as she saw him ride one day into Endrith's Forest in search of a unicorn, she beheld herself, a tree-child and Anduan, stealing through the treetops towards Grendylmere and the first fateful encounter with the man-beast from Tor. She could bear to look no more.

Stifling a bitter sob, she turned and fled the Chamber of Visions and the looking glass therein. Thus she did not see the vision of herself and Frayne clasped in a long embrace or their flight upon the back of a soaring dragon from the battlemented heights of the Sorceress's castle. Unseen by human eye, the visions of future possibilities slowly blurred and faded, till the fleeting glimpse of Aurora bent over a sleeping Frayne, Glaiveling poised and deadly above his bare chest, shimmered briefly on the darkening surface of the looking glass, then vanished as the ripples smoothed and stilled to a visionless inky blackness, and the Seeing Eye slept again.

Aurora, magnificent in an ebony gown that shimmered with a lovely silken sheen, paced restlessly about the confines of her room. The chamber had neither lock nor key and was furnished luxuriously. Still, it was a prison. For none could leave the castle perched atop the craggy tor, save by way of a single door made impregnable by the sorceress's own secret binding spell. Yet 'twas neither the door nor the spell that held her there, but Frayne, and the occasional gleam of hope that had ignited in her heart, a fragile flame that yet flickered within the turmoil of uncertainty. Even though she knew what hold the Sorceress had on the Knight of Tor and had begun to suspect that his soul might not be quite so black as he had painted it, he was still Dred's only spawn and undeniably the Thromholan. Thus she wavered between a slowly burgeoning rebirth of faith and the stultifying reality of his prophesied destiny. It was foretold that in the Third Uprising he would lead Thromgilad ultimately to victory. Was she not honorbound to avert the fulfillment of so portentiously disastrous a prediction? Had she not sworn by the gods that the Thromholan must die?

The sudden click of the latch brought her spinning around, the gown swirling about her legs as she froze almost in an attitude of flight. Her golden eyes wary, she watched the door swing open and saw him framed in the doorway. Her breath caught painfully in her throat as she looked up into the still, hard planes of his face, the familiar face of a stranger.

"Am I intruding upon your privacy, Aurora?" he said, his deep voice piercing her heart with its unexpected gentleness. Indeed, his whole manner seemed somehow softened, less cold and distant. For since the dreadful day of his betrayal, he had been an utter stranger, using her as a master uses a slave.

She flushed in anger remembering how he had flung her contemptuously at the Sorceress's feet, commanding her to kneel before her betters. Kneel! She would kneel to no one, let alone to the woman with the coal-black hair and eyes like hard, glittering diamonds—her mother's sister, who bore Almira's likeness and her own. And so had Aurora informed him as she rose to her feet to stand defiantly with legs braced and her fists clenched and resting on her hips. Whereupon his hand had closed about her wrist in a grip of steel. And though she had resisted, in the end the pain had forced her to her knees. She could still hear Leilah's laughter, like the triumph of the jackal, and see her press her full, woman's body against the knight, her arms slithering like serpents up and about his neck, while he had stood quiescent, his lip curled in shared mockery of Aurora. But she, Aurora, had had the last laugh, she thought with a secret smile, for the treacherous fools believed Andruvien had yet resided in the pouch about her neck. But 'twas not Andruvien that would feed the potion Leilah brewed to enslave the power of Vendrenin. Nay. But Crane's mysterious crystal, the twin to the Arlana.

"And now that I have the Andruvien," the sorceress had purred, holding the crystal up to admire its inner fire, "what would you have me do with this pathetic little upstart?"

"You might fling her from the battlements," Frayne had drawled, chilling Aurora with his cold indifference and causing Leilah's soulless gaze to narrow on his patently bored features with what seemed oddly like suspicion.

"You would see your little Enchantress dead?" she had demanded curiously.

Whereupon the knight had shrugged.

"How not?" he said. "She means nothing to me."

Leilah's answering laughter had rung falsely in the Sorceress's chamber. Indeed, there had been an element of uncertainty in the way she wheeled and paced shortly for a time, the long, curving nail of her forefinger tapping against her chin as she seemed to consider Aurora's fate. And, inexplicably, it had come to Aurora that the Sorceress was afraid to slay her. Nay, more than that. She had felt that Leilah dared not do it! At any rate, she had seemed more than glad to accept Frayne's suggestion, uttered with sardonic amusement, that he should take Aurora as his slave, in exchange for the one he had most regrettably lost in Endrith's Forest.

Thus had she been made slave to Frayne, and though she had been prepared to be beaten and humiliated, made to submit to his slightest whim, he had instead, for the most part, ignored her. Ignored her, that is, save on the first night, when in burning hate and rage she had thrown herself bodily at him, wanting to slay him with her bare hands. And though she had fought him with all the fury of her wounded heart, his greater strength had in the end overborne her. She had lain imprisoned beneath him, her wrists pinned to the floor above her head, and suddenly she had seen the glint of passion come to his eyes and known that he would take her then and there, despite her loathing of him. Even so, she had sworn he would have only her body and nothing of herself. Yet he had taken all.

From that time on he had been generous, showering her with gifts, and even kind in an odd sort of way—yet cold, too, as if his heart, his very being, had, like Myrialoc, been turned to crystal. And now this unexpected glimmering of humanity. Why? she wondered. What was he about? If indeed it was a ploy, it was not a new one. For there was about him the Frayne who had borne her from the waters in his arms and made love to her with such sweet tenderness that she had foolishly believed him when he had said his heart was forever hers. Aye. She had believed him then, but she would not be so fooled again.

Deliberately, she folded her hands in the attitude of humility that became a slave in the presence of her master and bowed her head as she had seen Janine do countless times in his presence.

"Can the master be said ever to intrude upon his slave?" she countered in the cool, emotionless tones that were a slave's sole refuge. "Indeed, can a slave possess so wondrous a thing as privacy?"

She could almost feel his sudden, swift anger, like the leaping flare of dry tinder abruptly touched with

471

flame. Then, just as swiftly, he was cool again, his manner calm; indeed, he sauntered into the room with the careless ease of one who owned it and everything within.

"Quite so, my dear," he drawled, and her traitorous heart quivered as he drew near her and paused, one hand trailing insinuatingly along her bare arm just as Girmizi's had done an eternity ago. But her blood had not leaped like fire within her veins at *his* touch, nor had her limbs trembled and grown suddenly weak so that she thought she must swoon did he not cease to tantalize her so. "You are trembling," observed her tormentor with an air of one who has viewed a curiosity with only the faintest of interest. Then he moved away, and she could breathe again.

"You should not go about so inadequately clothed," he remarked, settling into a tapestry-covered chair near the fireplace. "I should find it inconvenient should my slave become suddenly indisposed. Cover yourself and then fetch a cup of wine, if you please."

She moved to do as she was bid, but she was careful to keep her head lowered that he would not see the sudden blaze of anger in her eyes. Cover herself indeed! And had she not dressed just this way to please him? And, worse, done so despite her vow never to don a single garment that came from him. He had been displeased with her refusal of his gifts. Yet now that she had relented, he had not even noticed!

Whereupon the cursed man abruptly reminded her that she must guard her thoughts from the mind-reading Thromholan.

"The gown suits you," he said, and for a moment

472

her pulse quickened as she thought she detected a glimmer of warmth in the sleepy eyes. But then he ruined all with a single, infuriatingly pompous utterance. "I am relieved. A slave, after all, who seeks to please her master is become a treasure worth the keeping."

"Indeed?" Aurora queried sweetly. Egads, but the man was contemptible! "And had my master intended parting with this, his humble slave?"

"I must confess that the thought had crossed my mind of late," he admitted without a flicker of an eyelash. "For when it seemed I could not win your submission by simple bribery, I was faced with the rather more unpleasant alternative. Something I did not like to contemplate. So fatiguing, you know, wielding the whip. And utterly distasteful, too. All that blood. The very idea is enough to spoil one's digestion."

"OH!" Aurora blurted ere she could stop herself, then bit her tongue in consternation and quickly lowered her head.

Thus she did not see the sudden twitch at the corners of his lips.

"I beg your pardon?" he queried innocently. "Did you say something?"

"Nay, my lord," she managed, with only the slightest quiver.

"No doubt it was only the wind."

"No doubt, my lord."

"Yes, well then, where was I? Ah, yes. The matter of instilling obedience in a slave . . ."

"*Perhaps*, my lord," Aurora interjected a trifle too

473

quickly. But immediately upon having gained his undivided attention, she continued in a manner calculated to keep it. "We might pass the time more pleasurably with less conversation?"

"Indeed? Had you something specific in mind?" he rejoined, one noble eyebrow climbing toward his hairline.

Egads! Aurora thought in rising perturbation. Must she say it baldly?

"I had thought, my lord, that we might retire." Whereupon she was astounded to see him yawn!

"I am rather tired," he admitted. "And the thought of bed is not distasteful. How thoughtful of you to notice," he added, rising to his feet. "I'm sure you will forgive me then, if I bid you an early good-eve?"

"Oh, *no*, my lord!" she cried dumbfounded as she saw him heading for the door. "I meant that *we* might retire. Here. Together, you and I."

Unbelievably he seemed to pause as if he needs must consider the matter!

"That would be rather more convenient. It is a deuced long way back to my lodgings. 'Tis settled then. I shall take the bed, and you may have a pallet on the floor. Goodnight, my dear. And thank you for a pleasant evening."

"A-a pallet!" she cried, utterly abandoning the charade in a helpless blaze of anger. "Oh, I *shall* kill you! You are utterly contemptible. A-and vile! And to think I would have given myself to you. Gladly. I thought my love had died. And then I saw you and Ariana in the Seeing Eye, and I knew that, Thromholan or not, you could not be evil. For were you not a part of *her* and a part of me? But I was wrong. You have no heart. And if I cannot kill my love for you, I should rather kill myself than to go on loving you."

She was sobbing almost hysterically, beating him with her fists against his chest.

"Aurora. No!" he uttered in an agony of remorse and grasped her wrists in his lean, powerful hands. "Forgive me, my love. I never meant to let it go so far."

When she said nothing, but only looked at him out of soul-stricken, disbelieving eyes, he groaned and dragged her to his chest.

"The gods help me, I had to strike you and treat you as a slave, be the brutish churl. Else she would have cast you into the flux, or worse. It was the only way to convince her that you meant nothing to me. To get her to give you into my keeping. I never thought to take advantage of your vulnerability, but when you lay beneath me, all fire and beauty, I-I could not stop myself. I vowed upon my honor as a Knight of Tor never to use you so brutally again. But then, tonight, you flailed me with my guilt. It seemed that in the end your spirit had indeed been broken. I could never have stood to see you truly an obedient, humble slave. And so I set out to awaken the Enchantress who had sworn to call no man her master. The fiercely proud and independent Aurora whom I love."

"Nay. You are lying. You have no heart. You want the Andruvien for your cunning Sorceress. You have somehow discovered the one you have is false."

"Foolish little innocent," he murmured with a tenderness which tore at her resolve. "Did you think I should not know the forgotten tear of Ariana when first I saw it?"

"The forgotten tear?" Aurora cried in sudden enlightenment. "But of course, it had to be. The second one left lying in the glade. But how did it get into Crane's pocket?" Then she was suddenly overcome with remorse. "Oh, gods, in all my selfish obsession with my own problems, I forgot about Crane. He was wounded grievously by the hawk. I saw him. And Janine, lost somewhere in the forest. I must be away from here! I must find them. And the Andruvien and the Crimson Cloak of Power. Leilah must not be allowed to have them. Nor must Dred!"

"Softly, child," Frayne murmured, tightening his arms around lest she flee from him. "We will escape Tor. Soon."

"We?" she whispered, her golden eyes wide upon the godlike countenance.

"How not?" He briefly smiled. But then he was sober again, the silver eyes gleaming with a hard sheen. "The Sorceress has no more use for her Knight of Tor. The potion is complete. Nor will she feel it necessary to keep Ariana alive within the flux. It is time I moved to set her free. And you, my marvelous love, have at last provided the key to her release."

"I?" echoed the Enchantress in astonishment. "But how . . . ?"

"Never mind that for now. All soon shall be made clear to you," he said, lifting her suddenly into his arms and bearing her with smiling deliberation to the bed. "First, there is unfinished business between us, which can no longer wait. Come, my little slave. 'Tis time you saw to your master's pleasure."

"OH! You—!" But he stilled her unfinished protest with a deep, lingering kiss.

"My sweet indestructible love," he murmured as he laid her down amidst the thick fur pelts and gazed upon her with wonder in his eyes. "If indeed I have no heart, 'tis only because I lost it to you long ago when first you gave yourself to me with such loving innocence. Then you were a child. But you are a child no more. You are a woman, with a woman's loving heart. And an Enchantress. The Enchantress of my heart."

"And you are life to me," she whispered. "But I cannot be your slave. For I am Aurora, and I have a destiny. And a quest, which has yet to be fulfilled. Oh, my love! I am afraid! for you are the Thromholan, and I am a vassal of the One. Shall we yet live to see the day when we are enemies sworn? Our weapons drawn one against the other? And our love, our sweet enchanted love, naught but a hated memory?"

"Hush," he said and bent to kiss a tear from her cheek. "What the gods have written shall be, and nothing we do can change it. It may be that the time we have is short. But it is our time. Our love. Let us live it now while we may, and let the gods worry about tomorrow."

She said no more, but even as she lost herself in the wonder of his arms, she knew that somewhere Andruvien and the Crimson Cloak of Power yet waited to reclaim her. And as did the unfinished quest for her true-name and for Alain, the Bard of Naefredeyan—the phantom of her father . . .

CONTEMPORARY FICTION
From Zebra Books

ASK FOR NOTHING MORE   (1643, $3.95)
by James Elward

Mary Conroy never intended to become the Other Woman, but suddenly she belonged to a world of exotic hideaways ecstasy filled nights. . . . and lonely Sunday mornings. A world where desire and desperation, love and betrayal, were separated only by a plain band of gold.

JADE   (1744, $3.95)
by Nancie MacCullough-Weir

Inside the all-white interior of Ivan and Igor's Spa, Manhattan's very rich and pampered women worked their already beautiful bodies into perfect shape. Jade Green was one of these women. She had everything except the love she craved.

SOMEBODY PLEASE LOVE ME   (1604, $3.95)
by Aviva Hellman

Beautiful high-fashion model Cat Willingham became a vulnerable, sensuous woman in Clay Whitfield's arms. But she wondered if her independence was too great a price to pay for passion.

WHAT THE HEART KEEPS   (1810, $3.95)
by Rosalind Laker

When Lisa met Peter she instantly knew he was the man she had been waiting for. But before she surrendered to the fires of desire, Lisa had to choose between saving herself for a distant wedding night or having one night of unforgettable sensuality to cherish for the rest of her days.

WINTER JASMINE   (1658, $3.50)
by Pamela Townley

From the instant they met in the crowded park that steamy morning, Beth knew that Danny Galloway was the man she wanted. Tired of life in the fast lane, Danny was ready for someone like Beth. Nothing would stop him from making her his own!

Available wherever paperbacks are sold, or order direct from the Publisher. Send cover price plus 50¢ per copy for mailing and handling to Zebra Books, Dept. 1894, 475 Park Avenue South, New York, N.Y. 10016. Residents of New York, New Jersey and Pennsylvania must include sales tax. DO NOT SEND CASH.